SEVEN FOR A SECRET

Seven for a Secret

VICTORIA HOLT

DOUBLEDAY

New York • London • Toronto • Sydney • Auckland

PUBLISHED BY DOUBLEDAY

A division of Bantam Doubleday Dell Publishing Group, Inc.
666 Fifth Avenue, New York, New York 10103

DOUBLEDAY and the portrayal of an anchor with a dolphin
are trademarks of Doubleday, a division of
Bantam Doubleday Dell Publishing Group, Inc.

Library of Congress Cataloging-in-Publication Data

Holt, Victoria, 1906–
Seven for a secret / Victoria Holt.
p.   cm.
I. Title.
PR6015.I3S48   1992
823′.914—dc20   91-35802
CIP

ISBN 0-385-46800-8 (large print)
42406-X

**This Large Print Book carries the
Seal of Approval of N.A.V.H.**

Printed in the United States of America
September 1992
3   5   7   9   10   8   6   4   2

Contents

SEVEN FOR A SECRET

EASTER FLOWERS

Very soon after I went to live with my Aunt Sophie, I became acquainted with the strange sisters, Lucy and Flora Lane, and because of what I discovered, forever after I called their cottage the House of the Seven Magpies.

I often marvel that I might never have known the place but for the trouble over the decoration of the church that long-ago Easter. But perhaps that is not exactly true and it was not entirely due to the flowers—they just brought it to a head.

Aunt Sophie had been a rare visitor to our house till then, and there was never a mention of the rift between her and my mother. She lived in Wiltshire, which was a longish journey by train from London and then she would have to get from the capital to Middlemore in Surrey. I imagined she did not feel it worth the effort to come and see us, and my mother certainly thought the journey to Wiltshire too arduous for her, particularly when the result would be a none-too-felicitous encounter with Aunt Sophie.

Aunt Sophie was almost a stranger to me in those early days.

My mother and Aunt Sophie, though sisters, were as unlike each other as any two people could be.

My mother was tall and slim, beautiful too; her features looked as though they had been cut out of marble; her eyes were light blue and could be quite icy at times; her eyelashes were long and fair, her eyebrows perfectly marked and her fine hair was always neatly coiled about her head. She was constantly letting everyone know—even those in the household who were very well aware of it —that she had not been brought up to live as she did, and it was only due to "circumstances" that we were obliged to do so now.

Aunt Sophie was my mother's elder sister. I think it was two years which separated them. She was of medium height, but plump which made her look shorter; she had a round rosy face and little sharp brown eyes which looked rather like currants, and when she laughed they almost disappeared: it was a rather loud laugh which my mother said "grated" on her nerves.

It was small wonder that they kept apart. On the rare occasions when my mother spoke of her, she invariably said that it was amazing that they had been brought up together.

We lived in what is known as "genteel poverty"—my mother, myself and two maids: Meg, a relic from those "better days," and Amy, who was in her early teens, a Middlemore girl, from one of the cottages on the other side of the Common.

My mother was much occupied with keeping up appearances. She had been brought up at Cedar Hall and I always thought it was unfortunate that this mansion was close enough to be perpetually in view.

There it stood, in all its grandeur, which seemed the greater when compared with Lavender House, our humble abode. Cedar Hall was *the* house in Middlemore. Church fêtes were held on its lawn and one of its rooms was always made available for ecclesiastical meetings when necessary; and the carol singers assembled in the courtyard every Christmas Eve for mulled wine and mince pies when they gave their performance. There were many servants and it dominated the village.

My mother had two tragedies to suffer. Not only had she lost her old home, which had had to be sold when her father died and the extent of his debts had been revealed, but it had been bought by the Carters, who had amassed a fortune from selling sweets and tobacco in every town in England. They were undesirable on two counts—they were vulgar and they were rich.

Every time she looked in the direction of Cedar Hall, my mother's face would harden and her lips tighten, and the deep anger she felt was obvious; and of course that happened when she looked out of her bedroom window. We were all accustomed to the daily lament. It dominated our lives as well as hers.

Meg said: "It would have been better if we's got right away. Looking at the old place all day don't help much."

One day I said to my mother: "Why don't we move away? Somewhere where you don't have to look at it all the time."

I saw the horror in her face and, young as I was, I thought: she wants to be here. She couldn't bear not to be. I could not understand then—but I did later—that she enjoyed her misery and resentment.

She wanted to continue as she had in the old days in Cedar Hall. She liked to participate in church matters—taking a leading part in organising bazaars and that sort of thing. It irritated her that the summer fête could not be held on *our* lawn.

Meg laughed at that and commented to Amy: "What! On six feet of grass! Don't make me laugh!"

There was a governess for me. In our position it was essential, said my mother. She could not afford to send me away to school and the idea of my attending the one in the village was quite out of the question. There was only one alternative, so the governesses came. They did not stay long. References to past grandeur were no substitute for the lack of it in Lavender House. It had been Cottage when we came, Meg told me. "Yes, for years it was Lavender Cottage, and painting 'House' over 'Cottage' did nothing more than that."

My mother was not a very communicative person and although I heard a great deal about the glories of the past, she said very little about the subject which interested me most: that of my father.

When I asked her about him her lips tightened and she seemed more like a statue than ever—just as I saw her look when she spoke of the Carters of Cedar Hall.

She said: "You have no father . . . now."

There was something significant about the
"now" and the pause before it, so I pro-
tested: "But I had once."

"Don't be absurd, Frederica. Of course
everyone had a father once."

I had been called Frederica because there
had been many Fredericks in the family of
Cedar Hall. My mother had told me that
there were six of them in the picture gallery
there. I had heard of Sir Frederick, knighted
on Bosworth Field; one who had distin-
guished himself at Waterloo; and another
who had shone in the Royalist cause during
the Civil War. Had I been a boy, I should
have been Frederick. As it was, I must be
Frederica, which I found inconvenient and
inclined to be shortened to Freddie or even
Fred, which had on more than one occasion
led to obvious confusion.

"Did he die?" I asked.

"I have told you. You have no father now.
That is an end of the matter."

After that I knew there was some secret
about him.

I did not remember ever seeing him. In
fact, I could not remember living anywhere
but in this house. The Common, the cottages, the church, all in the shadow of Cedar
Hall, were part of my life till then.

I spent a great deal of time in the kitchen

with Meg and Amy. They were more friendly than anyone else.

I was not allowed to make friends with the village people and as far as the Carters up at the hall were concerned, my mother was distantly polite with them.

I soon learned that my mother was a very unhappy woman.

Now that I was getting older, Meg used to talk to me a good deal.

"This life," she said on one occasion, "is no life at all. Lavender House, my foot. Everyone knows it was Lavender Cottage. You can't make a house grand by changing its name. I'll tell you what, Miss Fred . . ." Although I was Miss Frederica in my mother's hearing, when we were alone—Meg and I—I was plain Miss Fred or sometimes Miss Freddie. Frederica being one of those "outlandish" names which Meg did not think much of, she could not be expected to use it more than was necessary.

"I'll tell you this, Miss Fred. A spade's a spade, no matter what fancy name you give it, and I reckon we'd be better off in a nice little house in Clapham . . . being just what we was and not what we're pretending to be. There'd have been a little bit of life up there, too."

Meg's eyes were misty with longing. She

had been brought up in the East End of London and was proud of it. "A bit of life there was up there, Saturday night in the markets with all them flares on the stalls. Cockles and mussels, winkles and whelks and jellied eels. What a treat, eh? And what is there here? Tell me that."

"There's the fête and the choral society."

"Don't make me laugh! A lot of stuck-ups trying to pretend they're what they're not. Give me London."

Meg liked to talk of the great city. The horse buses that could take you right up to the West End. She'd been up there at Jubilee time. That was something. Only a nipper she was then, before she'd been such an idiot and settled for a job in the country . . . that was before she'd worked at Cedar Hall. Seen the Queen in her carriage, she had. Not all that to look at, but a Queen she was . . . and she'd let you know it. "Yes, we could have lived up there instead of being down here. A nice little place . . . Bromley by Bow, perhaps. Stepney. You could have got something dirt cheap there. But we had to come here. Lavender House. Why, even the lavender's no better than that we used to grow in our garden in Stepney."

When Meg yearned for London life she would enlighten me considerably.

"You've been with my mother a long time, Meg," I said.

"All of fifteen years."

"And you would have known my father."

She was looking back to the London markets and jellied eels on a Saturday night. She drew herself away from that delectable scene with reluctance.

"He was a one," she said, and started to laugh.

"What sort of a one, Meg?" I said.

"Well, never you mind!" Her lips turned up at the corners and I could see that she was amused. It must have been due to memories of my father.

"I could have told her, I could."

"What could you have told?"

"It couldn't have lasted. I said to the cook . . . we had a cook in those days, a bit of a tarter she was . . . and I was nothing much . . . kitchen maid, that was me. I said to her, 'It won't last. He's not the sort to settle and she's not the sort to put up with much.'"

"What did she have to put up with?"

"Him, of course. And he had to put up with her. I said to Cook, 'That won't work,' and was I right!"

"I don't remember him."

"You wouldn't have been much more than a year old when he went."

"Where did he go?"

"With her, I suppose . . . the other one."

"Don't you think it's time I knew?"

"I reckon you'll know when it is."

I knew that that morning there had been a coolness between Meg and my mother, who had said the beef was tough. Meg had retorted, if we didn't have the best beef it was likely to be tough, to which my mother had replied that it should have been cooked a little longer. Meg was on the point of giving notice, which was her strongest weapon in these conflicts. Where would we get another Meg? It was good to have someone who had been in the family for years. As for Meg, I guessed she did not want the bother of moving. It was a threat to be used in moments of crisis: and neither of them could be sure that, if driven to extremity, the other might take action, and either one could find herself in a position from which it would be undignified to retreat.

The trouble had been smoothed over, but Meg was still resentful; and at such times it was easier to extract information from her.

"Do you know, I'm nearly thirteen years old, Meg," I said.

"Of course I know it."

"I reckon I'm old enough."

"You've got a sharp head on your shoulders, Miss Fred. I will say that for you. And you don't take after her."

I knew Meg had a certain tenderness for me. I had heard her refer to me when talking to Amy as "that poor mite."

"I think I ought to know about my father," I went on.

"Fathers," she said, lapsing into her own past, which was a habit with her. "They can be funny things. You get the doting sort and there's some who are ready with the strap at the flicker of an eyelid. I had one of them. Say a word he thought out of place and he'd be unstrapping his belt and you'd be in for it. Saturday nights . . . well, he was fond of the liquor, he was, and when he was rolling drunk you kept out of his way. There's fathers for you."

"That must have been awful, Meg. Tell me about mine."

"He was very good-looking. I will say that for him. They was a handsome pair. They used to go to these regimental balls. They'd look a picture . . . the two of them together. Your mother hadn't got that sour look then—well, not all the time. We used to go to the window and watch them get into the carriage, him in his uniform . . ." Her eyes glistened and she shook her head.

"Regimental balls?" I prompted.

"Well, he was a soldier, wasn't he? Cook used to say he was high up in the Army . . . an officer . . . major or something. Oh, but he was a handsome fellow. He had what you call the roving eye."

"What's that?"

"Oh, he liked looking round."

"What at?"

She gave me a little push and I could see that she was not going to pursue that line of the conversation, so I said hastily: "What happened to him? Did he go to war?"

"Not that I know of. There wasn't a war, was there? So he couldn't go to it. We moved about a bit. They do in the Army. You settle in and then you're up and off. There's marching and bands and things like that. It was quite a life."

"And you went with them?"

"Oh yes. I was with her before she married. A grand wedding, it was . . . from Cedar Hall. I can see her coming out of the church. It wasn't the Reverend Mathers then. Now who was it?"

"Never mind. What happened?"

"They went off on their honeymoon . . . and then we were in quarters wherever the regiment was. Hadn't been married more than three months when your grandfather died. And there was all that fuss about Cedar Hall being sold up and the Carters coming. Well, I could see it wasn't going to last. He wasn't the sort for married life. There was someone . . ."

"You mean after he married my mother?"

"That don't make no difference to some. They can't help it like."

It was getting very interesting and I was afraid something would happen to stop the flow, that she would suddenly remember my age and that she was talking too much.

"Well, you were on the way and that made a difference too. She couldn't go dancing around, could she?"

"And then?" I said.

"It went on. You were born but still it wasn't right. There were rumours. She didn't want to do anything about it. She was always the one for keeping up appearances."

"What do you mean, Meg?"

"Well, she knew about this other one. She was jolly, she was. A bit of a flirt. Well, that suited him, didn't it? She had a husband though. He caught them . . . in the act, you might say. There was a regular scandal. There was a divorce and I think in time he married her. And they lived happy ever after

. . . perhaps. Your mother never got over it. If Cedars hadn't been sold she could have gone back there and it might not have been so bad. But there wasn't much left after the sale and debts had been paid. It was shared between her and Miss Sophie. Miss Sophie bought that house of hers and your mother got this. She had something from your father, of course . . . but you see how things are."

"He's still alive?"

"Alive and kicking, I reckon. Your mother never got over it. She don't talk about it. If only she could have gone back to Cedar Hall, I reckon it wouldn't have been so bad. Now, don't you whisper a word of this. But you asked about your father and everyone has a right to know who they are."

"I wonder if I shall ever see him."

She shook her head. "He wouldn't come here, dear. But I can tell you this. A nicer gentleman you couldn't wish to meet. It was just that . . . well, you know how it is with some people. They just don't fit. Then comes the parting of the ways. And here we were, in Lavender Cottage . . . I beg its pardon —Lavender House."

Having told me so much, Meg found it difficult to stop, and whenever I could escape from the governess of the moment, I would seek her out.

She was not averse really. She enjoyed gossiping. I learned that she would like to be in a house with many servants. Her sister was in such a place, down in Somerset.

"There's a butler, housekeeper, kitchen maids, parlour maids . . . the lot. And they keep their carriage so there's stables and what not. There's a lot going on in a place like that. And this . . . well, it's neither one thing or the other."

"I wonder why you stay here, Meg."

"Well, you can jump out of the frying pan into the fire."

"So this is the frying pan!"

"You might call it that."

"Tell me about my father."

"I've told you, haven't I? Don't you go letting on to your ma what I've told you. But I reckon it was right you should know . . . something. One day she'll tell you . . . her side, of course. But I reckon he had something to put up with, and there's always two sides to a question. He was one for a bit of fun. All the servants liked him. He was always jolly with them."

"You seem to be on his side."

"You couldn't help it really. That other woman and all that. I reckon he was provoked in a way . . . your mother being what she is . . . and him being what he is . . .”

While I was talking to Meg on one occasion my mother came into the kitchen. She looked startled to see me there.

“Meg,” she said, “I want to discuss tonight’s menu with you.”

Meg raised her eyes to the ceiling and I escaped. There had been a small sirloin of beef yesterday, so there must be cold beef today, but my mother always came to the kitchen to discuss the menu with Meg. She would have liked to send for her but there was no one to send but Amy and that would mean taking Amy away from whatever her duty was and she was rather slow in any case. There were no bells in Lavender House and installing them would have been expensive. As for fixing a regular time for the meetings, that would not have been convenient for, as Meg said, she was rushed off her feet and couldn’t be tied down to times for this or that. So there was now no recourse but for my mother to go to the kitchen.

I wondered afresh whether it would be possible to explain to my mother that it was rather ludicrous to behave like the lady of a large establishment when ours was far from that. I thought of the words of Robert Burns:

O wad some Pow'r the giftie gie us
To see ourselves as others see us.

What a gift that would be—and particularly to my mother. If she had had it, perhaps her husband would not have left her and I would know my father. I saw him as a merry man with twinkling eyes which aroused an answering response in people like Meg.

On another occasion I had seen Meg preen herself in a certain way, as she did when she mentioned my father. This was for Mr. Burr in the butcher's shop, shouting "Buy, buy, buy" while he chopped up meat on his chopping board. He was jaunty; he wore a blue and white striped apron and a straw hat cocked at a rakish angle. His eyes danced as he joked with his customers; they were mostly women.

Meg said his remarks were "near the bone" but they made you laugh for all that.

On one occasion she said to him: "You get along with you. And mind your p's and q's, young man."

He winked and said: "On your high horse

today, Missus? You come along with me into my back parlour and we'll change all that."

"Saucy young devil," retorted Meg, twinkling.

And my father was the sort of man who could make her look as she did when in the company of Mr. Burr, the butcher.

That was significant and gave me something to think about.

. . .

I WAS ON the way to the vicarage to take a note to the Reverend John Mathers. My mother often communicated in this way when she was displeased.

This was due to some misunderstanding about the flower arrangements for the church. Last year, she complained, they were a great disappointment. Mrs. Carter and Miss Allder really had no idea. What could you expect from a jumped-up shopkeeper who had made a fortune by selling sweets and tobacco? Her display had been positively vulgar. As for Miss Allder, she was a poor simpering creature with a fixation on the curate and quite clearly Mrs. Carter's puppet. It was absurd, when my mother had had a vast experience in decorating the church in the days when she lived in Cedar

Hall and when the gentry had had some influence on church matters.

I knew my mother would suffer acutely over this, which was of no importance whatever, because she saw it as an affront to her dignity and that was of the utmost importance to her. She had written several versions of the note to the Reverend Mathers, torn them up and worked herself into a rage. It was the kind of occasion which created in her a state of tension out of all proportion to the matter concerned.

It was a lovely spring day. I crossed the Common past the seat by the pond on which sat two old men whom I knew by sight because they were there most days. They were two farm labourers, or had been, for they were too old to work now and spent their days sitting talking. I called a "good morning" to them as I passed.

I turned into the lane which led to the vicarage. The country was very beautiful at this time of the year when the horse-chestnut trees were in flower and the wild violets and wood sorrel were growing under the hedges. What a contrast to Meg's jellied eels in the markets!

I laughed to myself. I supposed it was rather amusing in a way—my mother, yearning for grandeur, and Meg longing for the streets of London. Perhaps people were inclined to want what they did not have.

And there was the vicarage—a long grey stone house with a pleasant garden in front of it and the graveyard stretching out beyond it.

The vicar received me in an untidy sitting-room with mullion windows looking out on the graveyard. He was at a desk littered with papers.

"Ah, Miss Hammond," he said, pushing up his glasses until they rested on his forehead. He was a mild man and I immediately noticed a look of apprehension in his rather watery grey eyes. He was a man of peace and he guessed that there might be some threat to that happy state which often happened after a communication from my mother. When I told him I had a note from her, his fears were confirmed.

I handed it to him. "I think there is a reply to come," I said gently.

"Oh yes . . . yes." He pulled his spectacles down to his nose and turned slightly so that I should not see his reaction to my mother's words.

"Dear, dear," he said, and his eyes were full of consternation. "It is regarding the Easter flowers. Mrs. Carter has provided them and naturally . . ."

"Of course," I said.

"And she . . . er . . . has asked Miss Allder to help her arrange them, and I believe Miss Allder has agreed to do so. So you see . . ."

"Yes, I see. I understand perfectly."

He smiled at me gratefully.

"And so . . . if you will convey my apologies to your mother and . . . er . . . explain that . . . the matter is out of my hands, I think there is no need to write."

Knowing my mother as I did, I felt sorry for him.

"I will explain," I said.

"Thank you, Miss Hammond. Please do convey my regrets."

"I will," I promised him.

I came out of the vicarage but did not hurry home. I knew there would be a storm. I felt impatient. What could it matter who did the flowers? Why did she care so much? It was not the flowers. It was that eternal bogey. In the days of influence *she* would have provided the flowers. *She* would have decided whether they should adorn the pulpit or the altar. It all seemed so trivial. I felt both angry with and sorry for her.

So I loitered, turning over in my mind how I would break the news.

She was waiting for me.

"You've been a long time. Well . . . have you got his reply?"

"There wasn't any need to write," I said.

Then I told her. "Mrs. Carter had already provided the flowers and Miss Allder is helping her arrange them because she has already asked her."

She stared at me as though I were announcing some great disaster.

"No!" she cried.

"I am afraid that is what he said. He is very unhappy about it and really seems sorry that you are upset."

"Oh, how dare he! How dare he!"

"Well, you see, he explained that he couldn't do anything else since Mrs. Carter provided the flowers."

"That vulgar woman!"

"It is not the vicar's fault."

"Not his fault!"

Her usually pale face was suffused with a purple colour. She was shaking and her lips were quivering.

"Really, Mama," I said. "It is only the Easter flowers. What does it matter?"

She had closed her eyes. I could see a pulse beating rapidly in her forehead. She gasped and swayed. I ran to her and caught her just before she would have fallen. I noticed there was froth on her lips.

I wanted to shout, this is absurd. This is ridiculous. But I was suddenly frightened. This was something more than rage.

Fortunately there was a big easychair nearby. I eased her into it and called for Meg.

. . .

MEG AND I, with Amy's help, got my mother to bed.

The doctor arrived and Meg took him into my mother while I stood on the stairs listening.

Miss Glover, my governess, came out and saw me.

"What is it?"

"My mother has been taken ill."

Miss Glover tried to look sympathetic, but not very successfully. She was another of those who were only staying until she found something better.

She went with me into the sitting-room to await the doctor's departure.

I heard him come down with Meg and say: "I'll look in this afternoon. Then we'll see."

Meg thanked him and then she came into the sitting-room where we were waiting.

She looked at me, her eyes full of anxiety. I knew that it was for me rather than for my mother.

"What has happened?" asked Miss Glover.

"He says it's a seizure . . . a stroke."

"What's that?" I asked.

"It's bad. But we don't know yet. We'll have to wait and see."

"How dreadful," said Miss Glover. "Is she . . . er . . . ?"

"He doesn't seem to be sure. He's coming back. She's . . . pretty bad."

"Is she all right by herself?" I asked.

"He's given her something. He said she won't know anything about it . . . yet. He's going to come back and bring young Dr. Egham with him."

"It sounds terrible," I said. "She must be really ill."

Meg looked at me mournfully and said: "I think she must be."

Miss Glover said: "Well, if there's nothing I can do . . ."

She left us. She was not really interested. There had been a letter for her in the post that morning. I guessed it was an offer of a new post more suited to her expectations than teaching a girl in a cottage—even though it called itself a house—employed by someone who had the airs of a great lady without the means to substantiate her claim. I was beginning to read people's thoughts.

I was glad when she went. Meg really cared.

"What does it all mean?" I asked.

"Your guess is as good as mine, love. She's pretty ill, I reckon. My Aunt Jane had one of them strokes. Couldn't move all down one side. Couldn't talk either . . . only mumble. She went on for a year like that. Just like a baby, she was."

"Oh no . . . no."

"Well, sometimes they don't recover. It can happen to any one of us at any time. You might be going about your business and the Lord will see fit to strike you down."

I kept thinking of my mother, so dignified, so proud of her breeding, so angry and bitter about the turn of her fortunes; and I was filled with pity for her. I understood then more than I ever had and I wanted to be able to tell her that I did.

A terrible fear had come to me that I should never now be able to and anger surged over me. It was all due to those stupid Easter flowers. It was her anger which had done this to her. Oh no! It was more than the flowers. It had been growing within her—all that anger, the bitterness, the resentment. The flowers had just brought her to that climax of the years of envy and pent-up rage against fate.

. . .

WHEN THE DOCTOR came back he had brought
Dr. Egham with him. They were with my
mother for a long time. Meg was in atten-
dance and afterwards they all came down to
the sitting-room and sent for me.

Dr. Canton looked at me in a kindly way
which made me fear the worst.

"Your mother is very ill," he said. "There
is a possibility that she may recover. If she
does, I am afraid she will be severely handi-
capped. She will need attention." He looked
at me dubiously and then he turned more
hopefully to Meg. "We will wait a few days.
Much could be revealed then. Is there any
relative?"

"I have an aunt," I told him. "My
mother's sister."

His face brightened. "Is she far away?"

"She is in Wiltshire."

"I think you should let her know the circumstances immediately."

I nodded.

"Well then," he went on. "We'll wait and
see . . . say till the end of the week. The
situation should be clarified by then."

Dr. Egham smiled at me encouragingly
and Dr. Canton laid a hand on my shoulder,

patting me soothingly. I felt too bewildered for tears but they were near.

"We'll hope for the best," said Dr. Canton. "And in the meantime, let your aunt know what has happened."

He turned his gaze on Meg.

"There is nothing much you can do. If there should be any change, let me know. I'll look in tomorrow."

When they had gone, Meg and I looked at each other in silence.

We were both wondering what was going to happen to us.

· · ·

AT THE END of the week Aunt Sophie arrived. My delight at seeing her was so great that I flung myself into her arms.

She returned my embrace; her currant eyes, creased up with emotion, were slightly moist.

"My dear child," she said. "What a to-do this is. Your poor mother. We'll have to see what can be done about all this."

I said: "Here's Meg."

"Hello, Meg. This has been a great blow to you all, I know. Never mind. We'll sort something out."

"Would you like to go to your room first, Miss Cardingham?" asked Meg.

"Perhaps. Just dump this bag. What a journey!"

"Then I expect you will want to see Mrs. Hammond."

"That seems a good idea. How is she now?"

"She doesn't seem to know much about anything. She might not recognise you, Miss Cardingham."

"Well, I'll go and wash my hands. Dirty things, trains. Then we'll get to work. You come with me, Frederica."

We went to the room which had been prepared for her and Meg left us together.

"She's a good woman, that one," said Aunt Sophie, nodding at the door through which Meg had just departed.

"Oh yes."

"Must be a worry for her. We'll have to see what's got to be done. What does the doctor say?"

"He doesn't think there is much hope of her recovering completely. They think there may have to be someone to look after her."

She nodded. "Well, I'm here now." She smiled at me ruefully. "Poor dear . . . such young shoulders. You must be . . . how old?"

"Thirteen," I said.

"Hm," she murmured.

Amy brought up hot water and Aunt Sophie washed while I sat on the bed and watched her. As she dried her hands, she looked out of the window and grimaced.

"The old homestead," she said. "And she had that in view all the time!"

I nodded. "It used to upset her."

"I know. Pity she couldn't get right away from it."

"She didn't want to."

"I know my sister. Oh well, too late now." She had turned to me with a tender smile. "Thirteen. It's too young for such burdens. You ought to be enjoying yourself. Only young once." It was a feature of hers to speak in jerks, I discovered, and her thoughts often went off at a tangent.

"Never mind," she continued. "What's done is done. Got to go on. Don't you fret. Old Aunt Sophie will find a way. Meg's been with you a long time."

"Always," I told her.

She nodded towards the window.

"She was with us over there. Good woman. Not so many of them about."

I took her to see my mother, who, I was sure, would not recognise her. I found it almost unbearable to look at my mother. Her eyes stared vacantly before her; her lips moved. I fancied she was trying to say something but neither of us could understand the mumbling which came from her lips.

We did not stay with her long. There was no point.

"Poor Caroline," said Aunt Sophie. "To think she has come to that. I hope she doesn't know it. It would distress her so much."

Then she turned to me and put an arm round me.

"Don't worry, dear child. We'll do something."

I felt a great deal better since the arrival of Aunt Sophie.

When Dr. Canton called he was obviously delighted to see Aunt Sophie there, and after he had examined my mother he had a long talk with her.

When he left, Aunt Sophie took me to her room and there she explained the position to me.

"I know you are very young," she said, "but sometimes these things are thrust upon us . . . no matter how old we are, they just happen. Now I am going to be frank. Your mother is very ill indeed. She needs expert attention. Meg's a good woman and a strong one, but she couldn't manage it on her own. I've been thinking a lot about this. Now, we could have a nurse to live in. That would not be easy. She would have to be fed and looked after. There is another alternative. Your mother could go into a nursing home where she would have expert care. There is one not far from where I live. We could get her in there."

"Would it cost a great deal?"

"Ah, there is a shrewd head on those shoulders, I see." Aunt Sophie laughed—the laugh which had grated on my mother's nerves but which was soothing music to me. It was the first time I had heard it since she had arrived.

"Yes, my dear, it would cost. Indeed it would. I do not live in such straitened circumstances as your mother. I have a small house and one servant—my good and faithful Lily. I do not have to keep up appearances. I am content in my little house. We have a big garden and grow our own vegetables. Compared with your mother—though on a similar income, for we shared what was left of our poor father's estate—I live in comparative comfort. Not rich enough to support your mother in a nursing home, I fear, but I have a plan."

She looked at me with great tenderness.

"I have always had a soft spot for you, Frederica. What a dignified name that is.

Just what your mother would give you, of course. I always call you Freddie to myself."

I said: "It sounds . . . friendly." And I was thinking, I hope she won't go away. I wanted to cling to her, to beg her to stay. She brought hope that everything was not as bad as it had seemed.

"All right," she went on. "Freddie it is. Now listen. You're thirteen. You can't live here on your own, that's clear. I'm going to suggest . . . if you like the idea . . . that you come back with me. I'm the only one you've got. Isn't much choice, I fear."

I smiled at her wanly.

"Well, I'm not so bad and I've got a notion that we'd get on."

I said: "What about . . . ?"

"I'm coming to that. It's a bit of an up- heaval. Meg and the young girl. They'll have to look for other places. The house could be sold. The proceeds would pay for your mother's care . . . and with that and the lit- tle income she has, we might get by. You come with me. Frankly, Freddie, I can't see any other way. I've talked to the doctor. He thinks it's a good idea. Well . . . not only a good idea, but the only one we've got that makes any sense."

I could not speak. I felt that my life was breaking up about me.

She was watching me intently. She said: "I've an idea you wouldn't find it too bad. Lily can be a bit shrill sometimes, but she means well. She's one of the best and I'm not such a bad old thing. I've always liked young people."

I found myself clinging to her.

"There, there," she soothed.

. . .

MEG SAID: "IT'LL be hard after all these years, but she's right. It's the only thing. I couldn't manage the other and I couldn't abide having nurses in the house. They can be fussy— wanting this, that and the other, not only for the patient but for themselves as well. The worst thing will be parting with you, Miss Fred."

"You will have to find another post, Meg."

"I've already written to my sister in Somerset. There's that big house there and she did say they was always wanting people. Didn't know what it might be . . . but anything will do for a start. I've always wanted to be in that sort of house. Well, I started off at Cedars, didn't I? I've mentioned to Amy, there might be something for her."

"Oh, Meg, I shall miss you so!"

"I'll miss you, love. But life's like that. Changing all the time. And I reckon you'll

be all right with Miss Sophie. I remember
her from the old days. A bit of a caution, she
was. Hoyden sometimes, but her heart's in
the right place, and that's what counts. It'll
be more lively with her than it was with your
ma."

"I do hope everything is going to be all
right."

"It will be. As soon as she come here, she
seemed to throw a light on a dark subject, as
they say. We've got to face the truth. Your
ma is not going to get any better. She's got
to have proper care and she'll get it in this
place. You'll be able to go and see her often.
It couldn't be better. Trust Miss Sophie. She
was always the one to get things done."

It was true. The house was up for sale. It
was a pleasant place and there were prospective buyers. Aunt Sophie was practical in
the extreme. She said the servants must stay
there until they found posts. They could not
be turned out.

There was good luck in that direction.
Meg's sister wrote that there was a place for
Meg. It was only housemaid, but it was
something and there was a chance to "work
her way up." There was nothing as yet for
Amy but there were many big houses in
the neighbourhood and the servants were
friendly with each other and she had heard

that a tweeny was wanted in one of them. She would speak for her and a recommendation went a long way.

We were very optimistic and our hopes were not disappointed.

It was as though Aunt Sophie had come like a fairy godmother and waved her magic wand.

I said to her one day: "What of my father?"

Her expression changed slightly. It became what I could only call watchful.

"What of him?" she asked, rather sharply for her.

"Should he be told?"

She was thoughtful for a while then she shook her head.

"After all," I pointed out, "he is her husband . . . and my father."

"Well, all that was finished, you know. They divorced."

"Yes, but he is still that, isn't he . . . he is at least my father."

"It is all a long time ago."

"It must be about twelve years."

"He will have a new life now."

"With a new family."

"Perhaps."

"So you think he wouldn't be interested in me?"

She was smiling and her face was tender.

I said: "You liked him, didn't you?"

"Most people did. Of course, he was not very serious . . . ever."

I waited for her to go on, and as she did not, I said: "Do you think he ought to be told? Or do you think he wouldn't want to be reminded of us."

"It could be . . . uncomfortable. When people divorce they sometimes become enemies. He was the sort who didn't like trouble . . . who turned away from it. No, dear, let's forget all that. You're coming back with me."

I was thoughtful, wondering about him. She laid her hand over mine. "They say, 'Let sleeping dogs lie,' " she said.

"I have heard that."

"Well, if you wake them up, there can be a lot of barking and perhaps unpleasantness. Let's go back to Wiltshire. See how you like it there. You'll have to go to school or something. There is your education, isn't there? These things are important. You and I have a lot of decisions to come to. We don't want to burden ourselves with what has gone before. We have to go marching on. That was your mother's trouble. Looking back all the time. It's no good, Freddie. I've a notion you and I will do very well together."

"Oh yes, Aunt Sophie. I don't know what to say to you. You came here after all those years and you've made it all seem so much easier."

"That's the ticket. I must say, I feel pleased about acquiring a niece, all to myself."

"Dearest Aunt Sophie, I feel very happy to have my aunt."

Then we kissed and clung together, and I felt a wonderful sense of security creeping over me.

．　．　．

A GREAT DEAL happened in the next few weeks. There was an auction of the furniture which raised more than we had hoped for, for among it were some treasures which my mother had brought with her from Cedar Hall.

Meg and Amy left for Somerset and the house was up for sale.

My mother was taken to the nursing home in Devizes, which was not very far from Aunt Sophie's house, so that we could visit her at least once a week. Aunt Sophie told me she had what was tantamount to her own carriage.

"No more than a dogcart really, and it belongs to old Joe Jobbings who does an hour or so a week in our garden, and he'll take us wherever we want to go."

Lavender House was up for sale. I took my last look at Cedar Hall with no regrets, as I blamed its proximity, with its continual reminders of lost grandeur and "better days," for my mother's condition; and I left with Aunt Sophie for my new home in Wiltshire.

St. Aubyn's

I was very fortunate after such a tragic upheaval, not only to have Aunt Sophie as my guardian but to be taken by her to what must be one of the most fascinating counties in England.

There is a strange ambiance about that part of the country of which I was immediately aware. When I mentioned it to Aunt Sophie she said: "It's the ancient relics. You can't help thinking of those people who lived here years and years ago, before history was recorded, and they've left their mark."

Chiefly there were the stones which nobody could explain, though they guessed they had been put there long before the birth of Christ to make some place of worship.

The village of Harper's Green itself was

very similar to many other English villages. There were the old Norman church, which was constantly in need of restoration, the green, the duckpond, the row of Tudor cottages facing it, and the manorhouse—in this case St. Aubyn's Park, which had been erected round about the sixteenth century.

Aunt Sophie's house was by no means large, but extremely comfortable. There were always fires in the rooms during the cold weather. Lily, who came from Cornwall, told me she could not "abide the cold." She and Aunt Sophie collected as much wood as they could throughout the year and there was always a store in the woodshed.

Lily had been at Cedar Hall. She had left her native Cornwall to go there, just as Meg had left London; she was, of course, well acquainted with Meg and it was a pleasure to talk of her to someone who knew my old friend.

"She went with Miss Caroline," said Lily. "I was the lucky one. I stayed with Miss Sophie."

I had written to Meg but her efforts with the pen were somewhat laborious and so far I had heard little from her except that she hoped I was well as it found her at present and the house in Somerset was a bit of all right. That was comforting and I was glad I was able to write to her glowingly of my new circumstances; and if she found difficulty in reading it herself, I was sure there would be someone who could do it for her.

There were two houses of distinction in the neighbourhood. One was St. Aubyn's Park and the other the red brick and gracious Bell House.

"It's called that," said Aunt Sophie, "because there's a bell over the porch. It's high up, nearly in the roof, and it has always been there. Must have been a meeting house at some time. The Dorians live there. There's a girl about your age . . . orphan. Lost both parents. She's Mrs. Dorian's sister's girl, I believe. Then, of course, there's the family at St. Aubyn's."

"What are they like?"

"Oh, they're the St. Aubyns . . . same name as the house. Been there ever since it was built. You can work it out. The house was built at the end of the sixteenth century and the Bell House was just over a hundred years later."

"What about the St. Aubyn family?"

"There are two children . . . well, children! Master Crispin wouldn't like to be called that! He'll be twenty at least. Very haughty gentleman. Then there's the girl, Tamarisk. Unusual name. It's a tree. Pretty feathery sort. Tamarisk is about your age. So you might get asked to tea."

"We never had tea with the people who bought Cedar Hall."

"That might have been due to your mother, dear."

"She despised them because they had shops."

"Poor Caroline. She'd always made a rod for her own back. Nobody cared that she hadn't got what she once had . . . except herself. Well, the St. Aubyns are the important family. I suppose the Bell House people come next. Never worried me that I was brought up in Cedar Hall and now live in the Rowans."

The Rowans was the name of our house, so-called because it had two rowan trees in the front—one on either side of the porch.

I loved to hear Aunt Sophie talk about the village. There was the Reverend Hetherington who was "past it," and whose sermons rambled on interminably, and Miss Maud Hetherington, who kept the household in order, and the rest of us as well.

"Very forceful lady," commented Aunt Sophie, "and essential to the poor Rev."

I was fascinated by the group of stones which were a few miles from the Rowans. I first saw them when I rode by in Joe Jobbings's dogcart with Aunt Sophie on the way to Salisbury to do some shopping which was unavailable in Harper's Green.

"Could we stop here for a moment, Joe?" asked Aunt Sophie, and Joe obligingly did so.

When I stood among those ancient boulders I felt the past close in about me. I was excited and exhilarated, yet I was aware of a sense of dread.

Aunt Sophie told me a little about them.

"Nobody's quite sure," she told me. "Some think they were put there by the Druids about seventeen hundred years before Christ lived. I don't know much else, except that it was a sort of temple. They worshipped the heavens in those days. The stones are laid out to catch the rising and the setting of the sun, they say."

I took her arm and held it tightly. I was glad to be there with her, and I was very thoughtful as we got back into the dogcart and Joe Jobbings drove us home.

I was so happy to be in this place, particularly when I looked back to the Middlemore days in the shadow of Cedar Hall.

We went regularly to see my mother. She seemed comfortable but not quite sure what had happened to her or where she was.

I felt sad when I left her; and, watching

Aunt Sophie, I could not help feeling that, if my mother had been like her, how much happier we might have been.

And Aunt Sophie was becoming dearer to me every day.

. . .

THERE WERE MANY practical details to be arranged—my education foremost among them.

Aunt Sophie took a prominent part in the affairs of Harper's Green. She had unbounded energy, and liked to direct. She kept the church choir together, organised the annual fête and bazaar and, although she and Miss Hetherington were not always in agreement, they were both too wise not to recognise the talents of the other.

True, Aunt Sophie lived in a small house which could not be compared with St. Aubyn's or the Bell House, but she had been brought up in a great house and knew the obligations of such and was well versed in the management of village life. I quickly realised that, though less affluent, we were in the same bracket as the gentry.

Before I met the people who were to play an important part in my life, I learned something of them through Aunt Sophie's descriptions. I knew that old Thomas, who spent his days on the seat looking over the duckpond, had been a gardener up at St. Aubyn's until the rheumatics "got to his legs" and put an end to that. He still had his little cottage on the St. Aubyn estate which he used to tell anyone who was sitting beside him he had "for the term of his natural life," which made it sound more like a prison sentence than the boon of which he was so proud. I was warned that I must say a quick "good day" to Thomas when passing if I did not want to be drawn into reminiscences of the old days.

Then there was poor old Charlie, who had long ago said goodbye to any wits he might have had; and Major Cummings, who had served in India at the time of the Mutiny and spent his days recalling that important event.

Aunt Sophie referred to them as the "Old Men of the Green." They assembled there each day when the weather permitted it and, said Aunt Sophie, their conversation was a mixed grill of Thomas's cottage and rheumatism and the Indian Mutiny while poor Charlie sat there, nodding and listening with rapt attention as if it were all new to him.

They were the background figures—the chorus, as it were. The people who interested me were those of my own age—in particular the two girls from St. Aubyn's Park and the Bell House.

Aunt Sophie explained: "Tamarisk St. Aubyn is a bit of a wild one. No wonder. The St. Aubyn's *mère* and *père* were wrapped up in themselves. Never much time for the youngsters. Of course, there were nurses and nannies . . . but a child needs special care from the right quarter."

She looked at me almost wistfully. She knew that my mother would have been too obsessed by those lost "better days" to have had time to try to give me some good ones.

"Merry pair, they were," she went on. "Parties . . . dancing. They had a riotous time. Up to London. Off to the Continent. You might say, what of it? They always had the nursemaids and governesses. Lily says it was unnatural. They had their son and I don't think they wanted any more—although as soon as the little mites appeared they could be handed over to someone to be looked after. But there would be that period before they arrived. Very restricting. Very inconvenient for the sort of life Mrs. St. Aubyn liked to live . . . For a long time it seemed there would only be Crispin. He did not interfere with the merry life at St. Aubyn's. I think they hardly knew him. You can imagine the sort of thing . . . brought down to be inspected now and then. He had a nurse who thought the world of him. He's always looked after her . . . her and her sister. They've always been together. Poor Flora, she's the one who went a bit wild. Never married . . . either of them. They've got a little cottage on the estate. Crispin sees they're all right. He remembers his nanny. But you want to know about the young ones. Well, the father died. Too much riotous living, people say. But, they do say things like that, don't they? Late nights, too much gadding up to Town and abroad . . . too much alcohol. In any case, it was all too much for Jonathan St. Aubyn. *She* went to pieces after that. They say she's still too fond of the bottle . . . but people will say anything. It was a mercy that Crispin was of a responsible age when his father died. He took over. I believe he's a great one for taking over."

"And he looks after the place very well, doesn't he?"

"Very much the squire 'and don't you forget it' kind. Most admit it is just what the old place needed, but there are some who haven't got a good word to say for him. He's got a fine opinion of himself to make up for that, though. That's the son of the house—now the lord of the manor."

"Is there a lady of the manor?"

"I suppose you'd say there was Mrs. St. Aubyn, the mother. But she's hardly ever out of the house. Gave up when her husband died and took to invalidism. They were devoted to each other. And she didn't care for anything but living the wild life with him. Crispin was married."

"Was?" I asked.

"She ran away and left him. People said they weren't surprised."

"So he still has a wife?"

"No. She went to London and soon after there was an accident on the railway. She was killed."

"How dreadful!"

"Some said it was just retribution for her sins. Pious old Josiah Dorian at the Bell House was sure of this. The more charitable said they could understand the poor girl wanted to get away from her husband."

"It sounds very dramatic."

"Well, dear, that depends on the way you look at it. We've got a mixed brew here, but you get that in any village. It all looks so peaceful and calm, but probe below the surface and you're bound to find something you didn't expect. It's like turning over a stone to see what's beneath. Ever done that? Try it one day and you'll see what I mean."

"So this Crispin, he's married . . . and yet not."

"It's called being a widower. He's rather young for that, but I suppose the poor girl couldn't stand living with him. Perhaps it will warn others not to attempt it. Although I must say that with a grand place like St. Aubyn's and he being master of it might be a temptation to some."

"Tell me about Tamarisk."

"She was what they call an afterthought. I don't think for a moment that merry couple wanted another child. Think of the jolly life Madam would have to give up for a few months. Well, Tamarisk arrived. It must have been about seven years after the birth of Crispin."

"They must have been very annoyed with her for being born."

"Oh, it was all right once she was born. Then she was handed over to nurses. She wouldn't be allowed to intrude. No wonder she's said to be willful and wayward. Like her brother. I expect the nurses gave in to them. It would be a nice easy job without interference from above. They wouldn't want to upset that. Poor little things. Their parents must have been almost strangers to them. But perhaps I should say poor Mrs. St. Aubyn. Her life had been with her husband

and she lost him. Maud Hetherington and I take it in turns to visit her. She doesn't want to see us and I am sure we don't want to see her. But Maud says it must be done, and there is no gainsaying Maud."

"Shall I know them?"

"That's what I'm coming to. But first the Dorians at the Bell House. Nice place . . . stands back from the road. Red brick. Mullioned windows. Pity."

"Why a pity?"

"Pity the Dorians are there. That could be a happy house. I'd like to live there. Rather large for me, I suppose, but we could use it. I think old Josiah Dorian can't forget it was once a meeting house. Quakers, most likely. It's not exactly a church, but as near as makes no difference. A meeting place for people . . . the sort, I imagine, who think to laugh means a ticket to hell. It's in that house still. Hangs on, I suppose, and Josiah Dorian is not the man to change it."

"There's a girl there, isn't there? You said a girl of about my age . . . like Tamarisk St. Aubyn."

"Yes, you'd be much of a muchness. Poor girl! Lost her parents some time ago. Pity for her she came to her uncle and aunt."

"*I* came to my aunt . . ."

She laughed. "Well, dear, I'm no Josiah Dorian."

"I think I was very lucky."

"Bless you, child. We both were. We'll bring luck to each other. I'm sorry for poor Rachel in a place like that. It's all very Sunday-go-to-meeting, if you know what I mean. They can't get servants to stay long. Mary Dorian weighs out the sugar and locks up the tea . . . at her husband's command, they say. Josiah Dorian is a mean man. Rachel's mother was Mary Dorian's sister. Well, what I'm getting at is this. I've taken my time getting round to it because I wanted you to know the people you'd be with. That's if I can fix it. It's your education I've got in mind. I want you to go to school . . . a good school."

"Wouldn't that be costly?"

"We'll manage when it's necessary. But not yet . . . in another year, say. In the meantime, Tamarisk has a governess up at the house . . . Miss Lloyd. Rachel shares the governess. She goes along each day to St. Aubyn's and has lessons with Tamarisk. You see what I'm driving at?"

"You think that I . . . ?"

Aunt Sophie nodded vigorously. "I haven't quite fixed it yet, but I'm going to. I can't see why you shouldn't join them. I don't think there'll be any difficulty. I'll have to get Mrs. Aubyn to agree, but she doesn't care much what goes on, and I don't expect opposition there. Then there is old Josiah Dorian. I suppose I'll have to get him to agree too. However, we'll see. It would certainly solve our problem for a time."

I felt excited by the prospect.

"It would mean your going to St. Aubyn's every morning. It will be nice to be with people of your own age."

While we were talking Lily put her head round the door.

"That Miss Hetherington's here," she said.

"Bring her in," cried Aunt Sophie. She turned to me.

"You're going to meet our vicar's daughter—his right hand and good counsellor in whose capable hands lies the fate of Harper's Green."

When she came into the room I saw that she was all Aunt Sophie had said she was. I recognised her power at once. Tall, large, hair drawn severely back from a face under a small hat which was perched on the top of her head and decorated with forget-me-nots, she wore a blouse, the neck of which was held almost up to her chin with supports and which gave her a look of severity; her eyes, behind her spectacles, were brown and alert; her teeth were slightly prominent; and about her was that unmistakable air of authority.

Her eyes immediately fell on me. I went forward.

"So this is the niece," she said.

"She is indeed," said Aunt Sophie, with a smile.

"Welcome, child," said Miss Hetherington. "You'll be one of us. You will be happy here." It was a command rather than a prophecy.

"Yes, I know," I said.

She looked satisfied and regarded me steadily for a few seconds. I think she was trying to assess what useful tasks could be assigned to me.

Aunt Sophie told her that she was hoping I might join the girls for lessons at St. Aubyn's.

"Of course," said Miss Hetherington. "It's only sensible. Miss Lloyd can teach three as easily as two."

"I shall have to get the agreement of Mrs. St. Aubyn and the Dorians."

"Of course they must agree."

I wondered what steps she would take if they did not, but I hardly thought they would dare to disobey her.

"Now, Sophie, there are matters to be dealt with . . ."

I slipped out of the room and left them together.

A few days later Aunt Sophie told me that the matter of the governess had been settled. I was to join Tamarisk and Rachel in the schoolroom at St. Aubyn's.

· · ·

EVER THOUGHTFUL, AND realising that it would be good for me to know something of my companions before joining them for lessons, Aunt Sophie invited both girls to tea at the Rowans.

I was very excited at the prospect of meeting them and went down to the sitting-room filled with curiosity and some apprehension.

Rachel Grey arrived first. She was a slight, dark-haired girl with big brown eyes. We regarded each other with some *hauteur* and shook hands gravely while Aunt Sophie looked on smiling.

"You and Rachel will get on well," she said. "My niece is new to Harper's Green, Rachel. You'll show her the ropes, dear, won't you?"

Rachel smiled rather wanly and replied: "As far as I am able, I will."

"Well, now you know each other, sit down and let's have a chat."

"You live in the Bell House," I began. "I think it looks charming."

"The house is nice," said Rachel, and then stopped.

"A real period piece," said Aunt Sophie. "Nearly as old as St. Aubyn's."

"Oh, not as grand as that," said Rachel.

"It has great charm," insisted Aunt Sophie. "Tamarisk is late."

"Tamarisk is always late," said Rachel.

"Hm," grunted Aunt Sophie.

"She's ever so keen to meet you," said Rachel to me. "She'll be here soon."

She was right.

"Oh, here you are, my dear," said Aunt Sophie. "Delayed, were you?"

"Oh yes," said the newcomer. She was quite attractive, with very fair curly hair, sparkling blue eyes, and a short *retroussé* nose which gave her a jaunty look. She looked at me with undisguised curiosity.

"So you're the niece."

"And you are Tamarisk St. Aubyn."

"From St. Aubyn's Park," she said, her eyes sweeping round Aunt Sophie's tastefully furnished but not very large drawing-room—and somehow belittling it.

"How do you do?" I asked coolly.

"Well, thank you, and you?"

"Well," I replied.

"You're going to have lessons with Rachel and me."

"Yes. I'm looking forward to it."

She screwed up her face and made a pouting expression with which I was to become familiar, implying that I might change my mind when I met the governess.

She said: "Old Lallie is a slave-driver, isn't she, Rachel?"

Rachel did not answer. She seemed timid and perhaps in awe of Tamarisk.

"Old Lallie?" I asked.

"Lallie Lloyd. Her name is Alice. I call her Lallie."

"Not to her face," put in Rachel quietly.

"I would," retorted Tamarisk.

"I am starting on Monday," I told them.

"You three can get to know each other," said Aunt Sophie. "I'll see about tea."

And I was alone with them.

"You've come to live here now, I suppose," said Tamarisk.

"My mother is ill. She's in a nursing home near here. That's why I'm here."

"Rachel's mother and father died. That's why she's here with her uncle and aunt."

"Yes, I know. She's at the Bell House."

"It's not as good as our place," Tamarisk

told me. "It's not bad, though." Again she gave Aunt Sophie's drawing-room that look of pity and contempt.

"We're going to school later on," Rachel told me. "Tamarisk and I shall go together."

"I think I probably shall too."

"Then there'll be three of us." Tamarisk giggled. "I shall be glad to go to school. It's a pity we're all so young."

"That will change, of course," I said, a little primly perhaps, and Tamarisk burst out laughing.

"You sound like old Lallie already," she said. "Tell us about your old home."

I told them and they listened intently and while they were talking Lily came in with the tea.

Aunt Sophie followed.

"You'll look after our guests, Freddie," she said. "I'll leave you to it. Then you can all get to know each other without the help of the grown-ups."

I felt important pouring out the tea and handing round the cakes.

"What a funny name," said Tamarisk. "Isn't it, Rachel? Freddie! It's like a boy."

"It's Frederica really."

"Frederica!" Her expression·was disdainful. "Mine's more unusual. Poor old Rachel, yours is ordinary. Didn't Rachel do something in the Bible?"

"Yes," said Rachel. "She did."

"I like Tamarisk best. I shouldn't like to be called by a boy's name."

"Nobody would mistake you for one," I replied, which sent Tamarisk into gusts of laughter.

Then we talked together freely and I felt they had accepted me. They told me about the vagaries of old Lallie, how easily she could be hoodwinked, though one had to take care when attempting this; how she had had a lover who had died when he was young of some mysterious illness and that was why she had remained unmarried and had to go on being a governess to people like Tamarisk, Rachel and me instead of having her own home, with a loving husband and a family.

By the time tea was over I had lost my apprehension and felt I could deal adequately with Tamarisk and had no fear of Rachel.

On the following Monday I set out for St. Aubyn's Park, full of cautious optimism to face Miss Alice Lloyd.

.   .   .

ST. AUBYN'S PARK was a large Tudor mansion with a winding drive bordered on each side by flowering shrubs. There was an impressive gate house under which Aunt Sophie and I passed and went into a cobbled courtyard. Aunt Sophie had come along with me, as she said, "to introduce you to the place."

"Don't let Tamarisk overawe you," she said. "She will if she has half a chance. Remember, you're as good as she is."

I promised I would not.

We were let in by a maid who said: "Miss Lloyd is waiting for the young lady, Miss Cardingham."

"Thank you. We'll go up, shall we?"

"If you would be so good," was the answer.

The hall was lofty. There was a long refectory table with several chairs round it and on the wall a full-length portrait of Queen Elizabeth looking severe in a ruff and a jewel-spattered gown.

"She stayed here once," whispered Aunt Sophie. "The family is very proud of it."

She led the way up a staircase; we came to a landing and, after more stairs, passed through a gallery in which were several sofas, chairs, a spinet and a harp. I wondered if Tamarisk could play them. Then there were more stairs.

"Schoolrooms always seem to be at the top of the house," commented Aunt Sophie. "They were at Cedars."

At last we arrived. Aunt Sophie knocked at a door and went in.

This was the schoolroom which was to become very familiar to me. It was large with a high ceiling. In the centre of the room was a long table at which Tamarisk and Rachel were sitting. I noticed the big cupboard, the door of which was half-open to show books and slates. At one end of the room was a blackboard. It was the typical schoolroom.

A woman came towards us. She was, of course, Miss Alice Lloyd. She was tall and thin and I imagined in her early forties. I noticed the faintly long-suffering expression in her face which must have come from trying to teach people like Tamarisk St. Aubyn. This was mingled with a wistfulness and reminded me that Tamarisk had said she looked back to a past which had held a lover and dreams of what might have been.

"This is my niece, Miss Lloyd, Freddie . . . that is, Frederica."

Miss Lloyd smiled at me and her smile transformed her. I liked her from that moment.

"Welcome, Frederica," she said. "You must tell me all about yourself. Then I shall know where you stand in relation to my two other pupils."

"I'm sure you'll get on well," said Aunt Sophie. "I'll see you later, dear."

She said goodbye to Miss Lloyd and left.

I was told to sit down and Miss Lloyd asked me a few questions. She seemed not dissatisfied with my achievements and the lessons began.

I had always been interested in acquiring knowledge; I had read a great deal and I soon realised that I by no means lagged behind my companions.

At eleven o'clock a maid came in with a tray on which were three glasses of milk and three plain biscuits.

"I've put yours in your room, Miss Lloyd," she said.

"Thank you," said Miss Lloyd. "Now, girls, fifteen minutes only."

Tamarisk grimaced at her back as she left.

The hot milk tasted delicious. We all took a biscuit.

"Free for a while," commented Tamarisk.

"Do you do this every day?" I asked.

Tamarisk nodded. "Milk at eleven. Eleven fifteen, lessons, and they go on till twelve. Then you and Rachel go home."

Rachel nodded in agreement.

"I expect you think this house is very grand," said Tamarisk to me.

"It isn't as grand as the house where my mother was brought up," I said, feeling a little exaggeration was not amiss. "It was Cedar Hall. You may have heard of it."

Tamarisk shook her head dismissively.

But I was not going to have that. I went into a description—imaginary, of course, for I had never been inside Cedar Hall. But I could describe its gracious interior on what I had seen at St. Aubyn's, making sure to make it more grand, more impressive.

Rachel sat back, listening intently, seeming to sink farther and farther into her chair.

"Of course," said Tamarisk, eyeing Rachel. "Rachel doesn't know what we are talking about."

"I do," said Rachel.

"Oh no you don't. You only live in the old Bell House, and before that, where did you come from? You couldn't know anything about houses like this, could she, Fred?"

I said: "You can know things. You don't necessarily have to live in them. Besides, Rachel's here, isn't she?"

Rachel looked grateful and from that moment I decided to protect her. She was small and pretty in a fragile way. I liked Rachel. I was not sure of Tamarisk.

We went on boasting about our houses until Miss Lloyd came in with the maid. The latter took away the tray and we settled down to the lesson.

On that first morning I remember we did geography and English grammar: and I became quite absorbed, to the pleasure of Miss Lloyd, which was apparent.

It was quite a satisfactory morning until we started to leave for home.

I was to walk back to the Rowans in the company of Rachel, for the Bell House and the Rowans were not very far from each other.

Miss Lloyd smiled benignly on me and said that she was pleased that I had joined them and she was sure I was going to be a satisfactory pupil.

Then she left us and went to the little room which she called her "sanctum" and which was next to the schoolroom.

Tamarisk came down the stairs with us.

"Huh!" she said, giving me a little push. "I can see you are going to be old Lallie's pet. Sucking up, that's what I call it, Fred Hammond. 'I am sure you are going to be a satisfactory pupil.'" She mimicked Miss Lloyd. "I don't like suckers-up," she added ominously.

"I was only being natural," I said. "I like

Miss Lloyd and I *shall* be a satisfactory pupil
if I want to. She needs at least one." Then I
looked at Rachel, whom I had promised myself to protect, and went on: ". . . or two of
us."

"Swot!" said Tamarisk. "I do hate swots."

"I've come here to learn and that is what
we are all supposed to do. What would be
the use of coming otherwise?"

"Just hark at her," said Tamarisk to Rachel.

Rachel lowered her eyes. No doubt she
was used to Tamarisk's bullying and felt she
had had to accept it as payment for being
able to share the lessons. But this sharing
was no business of Tamarisk's. It had been
arranged by the grown-ups, and I was not
going to pander to it.

Tamarisk decided to abandon the matter.
I was to learn that her moods were short-
lived. She could insult one moment and pro-
fess friendship the next. I knew in my heart
that she was rather pleased that I had come
to share the lessons; and the fact that I stood
up to her amused her. It broke the monotony of Rachel's meek acceptance.

As we came down the wide staircase a
man was at the bottom waiting to come up.

"Hello, Crispin," said Tamarisk.

Crispin! I thought. The brother! The lord

of the manor, who didn't want people to forget it.

He was just as I had expected from Aunt Sophie's description. Tall, lean, with dark hair and light greyish eyes . . . cool eyes . . . rather contemptuous of the world. He was in riding clothes and appeared just to have come in.

He nodded in acknowledgement of his sister's greeting and his eyes momentarily swept over Rachel and me. Then he ran past us up the stairs.

Tamarisk said: "That's my brother, Crispin."

"I know. You said his name."

"All this is his," she said proudly, throwing out her arms.

"He didn't take much notice of you!"

"That was because you were here."

Then I heard his voice. It was one of those clear voices which carry a long way.

He said: "Who is the plain child with the others?" He was talking to someone up there. "New, I imagine," he added.

Tamarisk was suppressing her laughter. I felt the blood rushing to my face. I knew I was not handsome like Tamarisk or pretty like Rachel, but "the plain child"! I felt bitterly hurt and humiliated.

"Well," said Tamarisk, who had little respect for the feelings of others, "he did want to know who you were. After all, it's his house, isn't it, and you are plain."

I said: "I don't care. Miss Lloyd likes me. My aunt likes me. I don't care what your rude brother thinks."

"That wasn't rude. It was just truth. 'Truth must stand when all is failing' . . . or something like that. You'd know that. You're clever. You're old Lallie's pet."

We walked to the door and Tamarisk said, without rancour: "Goodbye, see you tomorrow."

As I walked down the drive with Rachel, I was thinking: I'm plain.

I had never considered it before and now I was faced with the bald truth.

Rachel slipped her arm through mine. She had suffered humiliation herself and knew how I felt. She did not say anything, for which I was grateful, and I walked along in silence, thinking: I'm plain.

We reached the Bell House. It looked attractive in sunshine. As we approached it, a man came out of the gate. He was middle-aged with wiry ginger hair which was beginning to turn grey at the temples, and he had a short spiky beard.

He had his hand on the gate and I noticed it was covered with ginger hairs. His mouth was straight and tight and he had small light eyes.

"Good day to you," he said, and he was looking at me. "You'll be the newcomer from the Rowans. You have been having lessons at St. Aubyn's."

"This is my uncle," said Rachel quietly.

"Good afternoon, Mr. Dorian," I said.

He nodded, moistening his lips with his tongue. I had a sudden feeling of revulsion, which I could not quite understand, so definite was it.

Rachel had changed too. She seemed a little fearful. But then I supposed she always was.

"The Lord's blessing on you," said Mr. Dorian, and he continued to look at me.

I said goodbye and walked on to the Rowans.

Aunt Sophie was waiting there for me with Lily. Lunch was already on the table.

"Well," said Aunt Sophie, "how did it go?"

"Very well."

"That's good. I said it would, didn't I, Lily? I reckon you put the other two in the shade."

"I reckon you did and all," said Lily.

"Miss Lloyd seemed to think I was all

right. She said she was glad I was coming to her to be taught."

They exchanged glances. Then Lily said: "I haven't sweated over the fire all the morning cooking food that's let get cold."

We sat at the table and she served us. I could not eat very much.

"So," said Aunt Sophie, "it was an exciting morning."

I was glad when I could escape to my room. I looked in the mirror. Plain! I thought. Well, I was. My hair was dark and, although thick, straight. Tamarisk's was curly and a lovely colour, Rachel's waved prettily. My cheeks were smooth but palish, my eyes light brown with long, though pale, brown lashes; I had rather a large nose and a wide mouth.

I was looking at my face when Aunt Sophie came into the room. She sat on the bed.

"Better tell me," she said. "What happened? Didn't it go well?"

"You mean the lessons?"

"I mean everything. Has Tamarisk been getting at you in some way? It wouldn't surprise me."

"I can deal with her."

"I thought you would be able to. She's a puffed-up balloon. Let out the air and she's deflated. Poor Tamarisk. She can't have had the best possible of childhoods. Well, what was it?"

"It was . . . the brother."

"Tamarisk's brother Crispin! Where does he come into this?"

"He was there in the hall when we came out."

"What did he say to you?"

"He didn't say anything to me . . . but about me."

She was looking at me incredulously. I explained about the brief encounter and how I had heard him say, "Who is the plain child . . . ?"

"The cad!" she said. "You don't want to take any notice of him."

"But it's true. He said I was plain."

"You're not. You don't want to listen to such nonsense."

"It *is* true though. I'm not pretty like Tamarisk and Rachel."

"You've got something more than mere prettiness, my child. There is something special about you. You're interesting. That's what's important. I'm glad you are the one who's my niece. I shouldn't have wanted the others."

"Really?"

"Most certainly."

"My nose *is* big."

"I like a nose to *be* a nose . . . not like a bit of putty that's just been stuck on."

I couldn't help laughing and she went on: "Big noses have character. Give me a big nose any day!"

I said: "Yours isn't very big, Aunt Sophie."

"You take after your father. He had a good nose. He was one of the most handsome men I ever saw. You've got good eyes. Expressive . . . bright. They show your feelings. That's what eyes are for . . . and to see through, of course. Now, don't you fret. People say things like that when they're not thinking much. He was in a hurry, that was what it was, and he didn't look properly."

"He just glanced at me and that was all."

"There you are. He'd say that about anyone. If you're plain, then I'm Napoleon Bonaparte. So there!"

I could not help laughing. Dear Aunt Sophie! She had rescued me once more.

· · ·

So FROM MONDAY to Friday I went regularly to St. Aubyn's. I used to meet Rachel at the gate of the Bell House and we would walk to the house and go up the drive together. We formed an alliance against Tamarisk and I became a kind of champion to Rachel.

But I never forgot Crispin St. Aubyn's comment. It had made a difference to me. I was not plain. Aunt Sophie had made that clear to me. I had good hair, she insisted. It was fine but abundant. I brushed it until it shone. I often wore it loose about my shoulders instead of in the severe-looking plaits. I made sure my clothes were never crumpled. Tamarisk was aware of this. She did not comment, but she smiled secretively.

She was friendly towards me. Sometimes I think she tried to woo me from my alliance with Rachel. I was pleased and rather flattered.

I saw Crispin St. Aubyn only rarely and usually from a distance. He was clearly not interested in his young sister and her companions.

Aunt Sophie had said he was "a cad," and he was, I assured myself. He was trying to impress everybody with his importance. He was not going to impress Aunt Sophie or me.

One day when I went to meet Rachel, she was not there. I was a little early. The gate to the Bell House was open so I went into the front garden. There was a seat there and I sat down to wait for her.

I gazed at the house. It was indeed gracious, more charming, I decided, than St. Aubyn's Park. It ought to be a happy house, a cosy house, yet I was sure it was not. Tamarisk might be neglected by her family and have been brought up by nurses, but perhaps there could be something to be said for that after all. Rachel was not carefree as she was. Rachel was timid . . . afraid of something. I felt it might be something in that house.

Perhaps I was a romancer. Meg said I was a dreamer with my fancies, making up stories about people . . . and half of them without a trace of truth in them.

I heard a voice behind me.

"Good morning, my dear."

It was Mr. Dorian, Rachel's uncle, and I felt that urge to get up and run away from him as fast as I could. Why? His voice was very kind.

"So you are waiting for Rachel?"

"Yes," I said, getting up, for he was preparing to sit down beside me. He laid a hand on my arm and drew me back onto the seat.

He was looking at me intently. "You like your lessons with Miss Lloyd?"

"Yes, thank you."

"That is good . . . that is very good."

He was sitting very close to me.

"We shall have to go," I said. "We shall be late."

Then I saw, with relief, that Rachel was coming out of the house.

"I'm sorry I'm late," began Rachel. Then she saw her uncle.

"You have kept Frederica waiting," said her uncle with gentle reproach.

"Yes, I'm sorry."

"Come on then," I said, eager to get away.

"Be good girls," said Mr. Dorian. "The Lord bless you both."

As we went I saw him looking after us. I could not think why but he made me shiver.

Rachel did not say anything, but she was often quiet. Yet somehow I believed she knew how I was feeling.

The memory of Mr. Dorian lingered for a while. It was faintly unpleasant so I tried to forget it, but when I next called for Rachel I did not go into the garden but waited outside.

Miss Lloyd and I got on very well together and it was gratifying to be aware that I was her favourite pupil. She said I was responsive. We shared a love of poetry and often we analysed it together while Rachel looked bewildered and Tamarisk bored, as though what we discussed was beneath her notice.

Miss Lloyd said it would be pleasant if Rachel and I were asked to have tea with Tamarisk.

"Don't you agree, Tamarisk?" she asked.

"I don't mind," said Tamarisk ungra-
ciously.

"Very well. We'll have a little tea party."

Aunt Sophie was amused when I told her.

"You ought to see something more of the
house than that old schoolroom," she commented. "It's worth a bit of attention. I'm
glad you and Miss Lloyd are friends. Sensible woman. She realises how much cleverer
you are than the others."

"Perhaps I'm not so handsome but I learn
more quickly."

"Nonsense. I mean nonsense to the first
and true to the second. Hold your head high,
my dear. Think well of yourself and others
will too."

So I went to the tea party. There were
dainty sandwiches and delicious cherry cake;
and Miss Lloyd said that, as the hostess,
Tamarisk should entertain us.

Tamarisk made a familiar gesture of indifference and behaved just as usual.

Miss Lloyd had apparently asked Mrs. St.
Aubyn, whom, it transpired, Tamarisk visited
at four-thirty on those days when her mother
was well enough to see her, if she would like
to meet the girls who shared her daughter's
lessons. To Miss Lloyd's surprise, she had
agreed to do this, providing that, when the

time came, she felt well enough and they did not stay too long.

Thus it was that I met the lady of the house—the mother of Tamarisk and Crispin.

Miss Lloyd ushered us in and we hovered.

Mrs. St. Aubyn was clad in a *négligé* of transparent mauve chiffon with lace and ribbons decorating it. She was lying on a sofa with a table beside it on which was a box of fondants. She was rather plump but seemed very beautiful with her golden hair—the same colour as Tamarisk's—piled high on her head. There was a diamond pendant about her throat and the same gems glittered on her fingers.

She looked languidly at us and her eyes alighted on me.

"This is Frederica, Mrs. St. Aubyn," said Miss Lloyd. "Miss Cardingham's niece."

She signed for me to come closer.

"Your mother is an invalid, I heard," she said.

"Yes."

She nodded: "I understand . . . I understand full well. She is in a nursing home, I believe."

I said she was.

She sighed. "That is sad, poor child. You must tell me about it."

I was about to speak when she added: "One day . . . when I feel stronger."

Miss Lloyd laid her hand on my shoulder and drew me away, and I realised that Mrs. St. Aubyn's interest had been in my mother's illness rather than in me.

I wanted then to get out of the room and so it seemed did Miss Lloyd, for she said: "You must not tire yourself, Mrs. St. Aubyn."

And Mrs. St. Aubyn nodded with an air of resignation.

"This is Rachel," said Miss Lloyd, "and she and Frederica are very good friends."

"How nice."

"They are good girls. Tamarisk, say good-bye to your mother . . . and you girls . . ."

We all did so with some relief.

I thought what a strange family this was. Mrs. St. Aubyn was not in the least like her son or daughter. I remembered Aunt Sophie's saying that she had lived very merrily and had not really cared about anything except enjoying life. It must be very different for her now. But it occurred to me that she might enjoy being an invalid and lying on a couch dressed in chiffon and lace.

People were very strange.

Tamarisk and I were becoming quite friendly in a somewhat belligerent way. She was always trying to get the better of me, and to tell the truth I rather enjoyed it. She had more respect for me than she had for Rachel and when I contradicted her, which I did frequently, she enjoyed the verbal battles between us. She was faintly contemptuous of Rachel and pretended to be of me, but I think that in a way she admired me.

Sometimes in the afternoons we used to walk together on the St. Aubyn estate, which was very extensive. She liked to show her superior knowledge by pointing out the landmarks. It was in this way that I visited Flora and Lucy Lane.

They lived in a cottage not far from St. Aubyn's and had both been nurses to Crispin, she told me.

"People always love their old nannies," she went on, "particularly if their mothers and fathers don't take much notice of them. I like old Nanny Compton quite a bit, though she fusses and is always saying, 'Don't do that.' Crispin thinks a lot of Lucy Lane. What a funny name! Sounds like a street. I suppose he doesn't remember Flora. He had her first, you see, and she went all funny. Then Lucy took over. He looks after them both. Makes sure they're all right. You wouldn't expect Crispin to bother, would you?"

"I don't know," I said. "I've never really met him."

There was a cold note in my voice which was there whenever I said his name, which was not often, of course. I would recall his voice when I thought of him asking who was the plain child.

"Well, they live in this cottage. I might have had Lucy for my nurse, but she had left us when I was born to look after her sister because their mother had died. Flora had to be looked after. She does odd things."

"What sort of things?"

"She carries a doll round with her and thinks it's a baby. She sings to it. I've heard her. She sits in the garden at the back of the cottage near the old mulberry bush and talks to it. Lucy doesn't like people talking to her. She says it upsets her. We could call on them and you could see her."

"Would they want us to?"

"What does that matter? They're on the estate, aren't they?"

"It's their home and, as your brother nobly gave it to them, perhaps they should have their privacy respected."

"Ho, ho, ho," mocked Tamarisk. "I'm going anyway."

And I could not resist going with her.

The cottage stood alone. There was a

small garden in the front. Tamarisk opened the gate and went up the path. I followed.

"Anyone at home?" she shouted.

A woman came to the door. I knew at once that she was Miss Lucy Lane. Her hair was going grey and she had an anxious expression which looked as though it might be perpetual. She was neatly dressed in a grey blouse and skirt.

"I've brought Frederica Hammond to see you," said Tamarisk.

"Oh, that's nice," said Lucy Lane. "Come in."

We went into a small hall and through to a small, neat, highly polished sitting-room.

"So you're the new pupil up at the House," said Miss Lucy Lane to me. "Miss Cardingham's niece."

"Yes," I replied.

"And taking lessons with Miss Tamarisk. That's nice."

We sat down.

"And how is Flora today?" asked Tamarisk, who was disappointed because she wasn't there for me to see.

"She's in her room. I won't disturb her. And how are you liking Harper's Green, Miss?"

"It's very pleasant," I told her.

"And your poor mama . . . she's ill, I understand."

I said that was so and half-expected her to say "That's nice." But she said unexpectedly: "Oh . . . life can be hard."

Tamarisk was getting bored.

"I was wondering if we could say hello to Flora," she said.

Lucy Lane looked dismayed. I was sure she was preparing to say this was not possible when, to her dismay, and Tamarisk's delight, the door opened and a woman stood on the threshold of the room.

There was a faint resemblance to Lucy and I knew this must be Flora; but where Lucy had a look of extreme alertness, Flora's large bewildered eyes gave the impression she was trying to see something which was beyond her vision. In her arms she carried a doll. There was something very disturbing about a middle-aged woman carrying a doll in such a way.

"Hello, Flora," said Tamarisk. "I've come to see you and this is Fred Hammond. She's a girl, but with a name like that you might not think so." She giggled a little.

I said: "My name is Frederica. Frederica Hammond."

Flora nodded, looking from Tamarisk to me.

"Fred has lessons with us," went on Tamarisk.

"Would you like to go back to your room, Flora?" asked Lucy anxiously.

Flora shook her head. She looked down at the doll. "He's fretful today," she said. "Teething."

"It's a little boy, is it?" said Tamarisk.

Flora sat down, laying the doll on her lap. She gazed down at it tenderly.

"Isn't it time he had his nap?" asked Lucy. "Come. Let's go up. Excuse me," she said to us.

And laying her hand firmly on Flora's arm, she led her away.

Tamarisk looked at me and tapped the side of her head.

"I told you so," she whispered. "She's batty. Lucy tries to make out she's not so bad . . . but she really is off her head."

"Poor woman!" I said. "It must be sad for them both. I think we ought to go. They don't want us here. We shouldn't have come."

"All right," said Tamarisk. "I just wanted you to see Flora."

"We'll have to wait until Lucy comes back and then we'll leave."

Which was what we did.

As we walked away, Tamarisk said: "What did you think?"

"It's very sad. The elder sister—she is the elder, isn't she . . . Lucy, I mean?" Tamarisk nodded. "She is really worried about the mad one. How awful, really, to believe that doll is a baby."

"She thinks it is Crispin . . . only Crispin when he was a baby!"

"I wonder what made her go like that?"

"I never thought of that. It's years and years ago since Crispin was a baby, and after Flora went funny, Lucy took him over . . . he was still only a baby then. Then he went away to school when he was about nine. He always liked old Lucy. Her father used to be one of the gardeners and they had the cottage because of that. He died before Lucy came back here. First of all she was working somewhere in the North. Their mother stayed in the cottage when the father died and Lucy came back. Well, that's what I've heard and soon after that Flora went batty and Lucy became Crispin's nurse."

"It is good of Crispin to let them stay in the cottage now neither of them work for St. Aubyn's."

"He likes Lucy. I told you, she was his nanny, and most people are like that about their nannies."

As we walked back I could not stop thinking about the strange woman and her doll
which she thought was the baby Crispin.

It was hard to think of that arrogant man
as a baby.

In Barrow Wood

*M*y fellow pupils had been to tea at the Rowans and at St. Aubyn's. Then we were invited to the Bell House. Tamarisk found an excuse for being unable to go and consequently I was the only guest.

When I entered the front garden I felt a twinge of uneasiness. I passed the wooden seat where I had sat that day when I was waiting for Rachel, and her uncle had talked to me. I hoped he would not be there today.

I rang the bell and a maid opened the door.

"You're the young lady for Miss Rachel," she said. "Come in."

I was taken through the hall to a room with mullioned windows which looked out on a lawn. The curtains were thick and dark, shutting out much of the light. I immediately noticed the picture of the Crucifixion on the wall. It shocked me because it was so realistic. I could distinctly see the nails in the hands and feet and the red blood which dripped from them. It horrified me and I could not bear to look at it. There was another picture of a saint, I presumed, because there was a halo above his head: he was pierced with arrows. There was yet another of a man tied to a stake. He was standing in water and I realised that his fate would be to drown slowly as the tide rose. The cruelty of men seemed to be the theme of all these pictures. They made me shudder. It occurred to me that this room had been made dark and sombre by Mr. Dorian.

Rachel came in. Her face lit up at the sight of me.

"I'm glad Tamarisk didn't come," she said. "She makes fun of everything."

"You don't want to take any notice of her," I said.

"I don't want to but I do," replied Rachel. "We're going to have tea here. My aunt is coming to meet you."

Not the uncle, I hoped.

Rachel's Aunt Hilda came in then. She was tall and rather angular. Her hair was drawn back tightly from her face which ought to have made her look severe, but it did not. She looked apprehensive, vulnerable. She was very different from the uncle who looked so sure that he was always right and so good.

"Aunt Hilda," said Rachel, "this is Frederica."

"How are you?" said Aunt Hilda, taking my hand in her cold one. "Rachel tells me you and she have become good friends. It is good of you to come and visit us. We'll have tea now."

It was brought by the maid who had let me in. There were bread and butter, scones and seed cake.

"We always say grace before any meal in this house," Aunt Hilda told me. She spoke as though she were repeating a lesson.

The grace was long, expressing the gratitude of miserable sinners for benefits received.

When she had served tea, Aunt Hilda asked me questions about my mother and how I was fitting into life in Harper's Green.

It was rather dull compared with tea at St. Aubyn's. I wished that Tamarisk had been with us, for, although she could be quite rude at times, at least she was lively.

To my dismay, just as we were finishing tea, Mr. Dorian came in.

He surveyed us with interest and I was aware that his eyes rested on me.

"Ah," he said. "A tea party."

I thought Aunt Hilda looked a little guilty, as though she were caught indulging in some bacchanalian feast; but he was not angry. He stood rubbing his hands together. They must have been very dry because they made a faint rasping noise which I found repulsive. He continued to look at me.

"I suppose you are just about the same age as my niece," he said.

"I am thirteen."

"A child still. On the threshold of life. You will find that life is full of pitfalls, my dear. You will have to be on guard against the Devil and all his wiles."

We had left the table and I was seated on a sofa. He took a place beside me and moved close to me.

"Do you say your prayers every night, my dear?" he asked.

"Well . . . er . . ."

He wagged a finger at me and lightly touched my cheek. I shrank away from him, but he did not seem to be aware of this. His eyes were very bright.

He went on: "You kneel by your bed . . . in your nightgown." The tip of his tongue protruded slightly and touched his upper lip before it disappeared. "And you pray to God to forgive you for the sins you have committed during the day. You are young but the young can be sinful. Remember that you could be carried off to face your Maker at any moment. 'In the midst of life we are in death.' You—yes, even you, my child, could be carried off with all your sins upon you to face your Maker."

"I hadn't thought of that," I said, trying to move away from him without appearing to do so.

"No, indeed no. So . . . every night, you must kneel by your bed in your nightgown, and pray that all the naughty things you have done during the day . . . or even thought . . . may be forgiven."

I shivered. Tamarisk would have been able to laugh at all this. I should have caught her eye and she would have made one of her grimaces. She would say the man was "batty"—as batty as poor Flora Lane, but in a different way. He just went on about sins and Flora thought a doll was a baby, that was all.

But I had a great desire to get out of this house and I hoped I would never come into it again. I did not understand why this man frightened me so much—but there was no doubt that he did.

I said to Aunt Hilda: "Thank you so much for asking me. My aunt will be expecting me back and I think I should go now."

It sounded feeble. Aunt Sophie knew where I was and she would not be expecting me yet. But I had to get out of this house.

Aunt Hilda, who had looked uncomfortable while her husband was talking, seemed almost relieved.

"Well then, we mustn't detain you, dear," she said. "It was so nice of you to come. Rachel, will you take your guest to the gate?"

Rachel rose with alacrity.

"Goodbye," I said, trying not to look at Mr. Dorian.

It was a relief to escape. I wanted to run. I had a sudden fear that Mr. Dorian might follow me and go on talking about my sins, while he kept looking at me in that odd way.

Rachel came to the gate with me.

"I hope it was all right," she said.

"Oh yes . . . yes . . ." I lied.

"It was a pity . . ." She did not continue but I knew what she meant. If Mr. Dorian had not come in, it would have been an ordinary tea party.

I did say: "Does he always talk like that . . . about sin and everything?"

"Well, he's very good, you see. He goes to

church three times on Sunday, though he does not like the Reverend Hetherington very much. He says he leans towards Popery."

"I think he believes everyone is full of sin."

"That is how good people are."

"I'd rather have someone not so good. It must be uncomfortable." I paused. I was saying too much. After all, Rachel had to live in the house with him.

At the gate I looked back at the house. I had the uncanny feeling that he might be watching me from one of the windows and I just wanted to run as fast as I could to put a great distance between that house and myself.

"Goodbye, Rachel," I said and started off.

It was good to feel the wind on my face. I thought, he'd never be able to run as fast as I can. He'd never catch me if he tried.

I did not take the straight path home. That man had made such an impression on me. I wanted to wash it completely out of my mind but I could not. The memory of him remained. His dry hands that rasped when he rubbed them together, his intent eyes with the light lashes that were hardly perceptible, the way in which he moistened his lips when he looked at me. They aroused alarm in me.

How could Rachel live in the same house with such a man? But he was her uncle. She had to. I thought, as I had a hundred times before, how lucky I was to have come to Aunt Sophie.

Running into the wind seemed to wash away the vague unpleasantness. This was a strange place . . . fascinating in a way. One had the impression that weird things could happen here. There was Flora Lane with her doll, and Mr. Dorian with . . . what was it? I could not say. It was just an odd feeling of dread I experienced when he came near me and made me feel a special longing for Aunt Sophie's down-to-earth conversation and her protective love.

Lucky me, to have come to Aunt Sophie, and poor, poor Rachel! I would be particularly kind to her in future to make up to her for having an uncle like Mr. Dorian.

I had come round a long way and I could see the Lanes' cottage, not as I usually approached it, but from the back instead.

I made my way towards it. There was a wall round the garden. I could see over it, to the mulberry bush which Tamarisk had mentioned, and seated near it was Flora. Beside

her was a doll's pram and I guessed that the
doll was in it.

I leaned over the wall to look more
closely. She saw me and said, "Hello."

"Hello," I replied.

"Have you come to see Lucy?" she asked.

"Oh no. I was just passing."

"The gate is there . . . the back gate."

It sounded like an invitation and, spurred
on by my ever-present curiosity, I went
through the gate to where she was sitting.

"Shh," she said. "He's sleeping now. He
can be a little cross if anyone wakes him."

"I see," I said.

She was sitting on a wooden bench and
she made room for me to sit beside her.

"He's one for his own way," she went on.

"I can believe that."

"He won't go to anyone but me."

"His mother . . ." I began.

"Ought not to have had children. People
like that . . . going off to London . . . to
my mind they shouldn't have them."

"No," I said.

She was nodding and staring at the mulberry bush.

"There's nothing there," she said.

"Where?" I asked.

She nodded towards the bush. "Whatever
they say . . . mustn't disturb though."

"Why not?" I asked, because I was doing my best to find out what she was talking about.

It was the wrong thing to have said. She turned to me and her eyes had lost a certain calmness which had been there when I arrived.

"No," she said. "There isn't. You mustn't . . . it would be wrong. You shouldn't."

"All right," I said. "I won't. Do you sit here often?"

She turned her troubled eyes to me. Suspicion remained there.

"He's all right . . . my little baby. He's sleeping like an angel. Butter wouldn't melt in his mouth, you'd think." She gave a little laugh. "You should hear him in one of his paddies. He's going to be a tartar, that one. He's going to get what he wants in life."

Lucy must have seen me from a window of the cottage. She came out and I sensed at once that she was not pleased to see me sitting there talking to her sister.

She said: "It's Miss Cardingham's niece, isn't it?"

I told her I was and that I had been passing, seen Flora in the garden and had been invited in.

"Oh, that was nice. Were you going for a walk?"

"I have been to the Bell House and was on my way home."

"That was nice."

Everything seemed nice to her, but I sensed this was due to a certain nervousness and that she wanted me to be gone. So I said: "My aunt will be expecting me."

"Then you mustn't keep her waiting, dear," she said with relief.

"No. Goodbye," I said, looking at Flora, who smiled at me.

Then she said: "There's nothing there, is there . . . Lucy?"

Lucy wrinkled her brows as though she were not sure what Flora was talking about. I supposed she often said things which had no reasonable meaning.

Lucy walked with me to the gate.

"The Rowans isn't far. You know your way?"

"Oh yes. I know my way around very well now."

"Give my kind regards to Miss Card-ingham."

"I will."

I was off running again, feeling the wind in my hair.

A strange afternoon, I was thinking. There are some very mysterious people here and this afternoon I had encountered two of the strangest, and I now felt the need to get back quickly to dear *sane* Aunt Sophie.

She was waiting for me.

"I expected you back before now," she said.

"I saw Flora Lane in the garden and stopped to talk to her."

"Poor Flora! How was the party?"

I hesitated.

"I thought so," she went on. "I know what they're like at the Bell House. I feel sorry for poor Hilda. These good people who have their places booked in Heaven can be a bit of a trial on Earth."

"He asked me if I say my prayers every night. I have to ask for forgiveness in case I die in the night."

Aunt Sophie burst out laughing. "Did you ask if he did the same?"

"I suppose he does. They have prayers all the time. Oh, Aunt Sophie, how glad I am I came to you!"

She looked pleased.

"Well, I do my best to give you a happy time and, if we're a bit short on prayers, I hope some fun will be there. What about Flora? As crazy as usual?"

"She had a doll's pram and a doll in it. She thinks it is Crispin St. Aubyn."

"That's because she's back in the past

when she was his nurse. She still thinks she's there. Poor Lucy has a lot to put up with. But Crispin St. Aubyn is very good to her. He calls on her now and then, I believe."

"She talked about the mulberry bush and there being nothing there."

"She's full of fancies. Now, if I don't get down to the shops there'll be nothing for supper. Lily's left it to me today. What about coming with me?"

"Oh yes, please."

I held her arm as we walked down to the village shop.

I was filled with joy because I was realising what sad things can happen to children who lose their parents. There was Rachel, who had had to go to the Bell House and live with her Uncle Dorian; Crispin and Tamarisk, who had parents but they might have been orphans for all they cared. Of course, I had had a father who went away and a mother who was more concerned with what she had missed than the child she had. But I was the lucky one. Fortune had sent me to Aunt Sophie.

.   .   .

MISS LLOYD AND I were getting on very well together. I was far more interested in lessons than either of my fellow pupils. Miss Lloyd used to say: "We have history on our door-step, girls, and how foolish we should be if we did not take advantage of it. Just think, more than two thousand years ago there were people here . . . in this very place which we now inhabit."

My responses delighted her and perhaps it was because of this that one day she decided that, instead of sitting at our lessons every morning, we should take what she called occasional educational rambles.

One morning she took the trap and we drove across Salisbury Plain to Stonehenge. I was excited to stand there among those ancient stones while Miss Lloyd smiled at me approvingly.

"Now, girls," she said, "can you sense the mystery . . . the wonder of this link with the past?"

"Oh yes," I said.

Rachel looked somewhat bewildered, Tamarisk contemptuous. What was all this fuss about a lot of stones just because they had been standing there for a long time? I could see that was what she was thinking.

"Their age is assessed somewhere between 1800 and 1400 B.C. Think of that, girls! It was before Christ came that these stones were here. The arrangement of the stones, which are set in accordance with the rising and the setting of the sun, suggests that this was a place for the worship of the heavens. Just stand still and contemplate that."

Miss Lloyd was smiling at me. She knew that I shared her feeling of wonder.

After that I became very interested in the relics of ancient history which surrounded us. Miss Lloyd gave me some books to read. Aunt Sophie listened with approval when I told her of the fascination of Stonehenge, and that it was believed that the Druids had worshipped there.

"They were learned people, you know, Aunt Sophie, those Druids," I told her. "But they did offer up human sacrifices. They thought the soul never died but was passed from one person to another."

"I don't much like the thought of that," said Aunt Sophie. "And human sacrifices I like still less."

"Savages, I reckon," said Lily, who had overheard.

"They used to put people in cages which looked like images of their gods and they'd burn them alive," I told them.

"My patience me!" cried Lily. "I thought you went to school to learn reading, writing and arithmetic, not about a lot of hooligans."

I laughed. "It's all history, Lily."

"Well, it's a good thing to know what those people were like," added Aunt Sophie. "It makes you glad you didn't live in those days."

After that visit to Stonehenge I began to look about me for evidence of those who had lived here thousands of years before. Miss Lloyd encouraged me and one day she took us to Barrow Wood. This was quite close to the Rowans and I was delighted to have it so near.

"It is called Barrow Wood," Miss Lloyd explained, "because of the barrows. Do you know what a barrow is, girls? No? It is a grave. These in Barrow Wood were probably made in the Bronze Age. Doesn't that excite you?"

"Yes," I said, but a glazed look had come into Tamarisk's eyes and Rachel was frowning in an attempt to concentrate.

"You see," went on Miss Lloyd, "the earth and the stones have been piled up to make a mound. Beneath those mounds would be burial chambers. By the arrangement of the graves I imagine these must have been important people. And then, of course, the trees were allowed to grow round them. Yes, it must have been a special place . . . a shrine. The people buried here were probably high priests, leading Druids and the like."

I was thrilled because I could see Barrow Wood from my bedroom window.

"Barrow is the name which was given these tombs. *Tumulus* is another word for barrow. So this is Barrow Wood."

I went there often after that. It was so near. I would sit, contemplating the graves and marvelling that the people lying beneath had been there since before the birth of Jesus Christ. In summer the trees shut in the burial ground. In the winter one realised how close it was to the road.

One day when I was there I heard the sound of horse's hoofs on the road. I went to the edge of the copse and looked out. Crispin St. Aubyn was riding by.

There was another occasion when I encountered Mr. Dorian there. He came walking towards me and I felt numb with horror at the sight of him. When he saw me, a strange look came into his face and he hurried towards me. I had an immediate urge to get away from him as soon as possible. In this strange place he seemed more menacing than he had in the Bell House.

"Good day," he said, smiling.

"Good day, Mr. Dorian."

"Admiring the barrows?"

He was getting very close.

"Yes."

"Pagan relics."

"Yes, I have to run. My aunt is waiting for me."

And I ran, my heart beating wildly with incomprehensible fear.

I reached the road and looked back. He was standing at the edge of the wood looking after me, watching me.

I ran back to the Rowans, triumphant because I had escaped.

. . .

I WAS THINKING a great deal about Flora Lane. Perhaps one of the reasons was that I believed the doll she cherished was Crispin St. Aubyn, though it was hard to imagine he was ever a baby.

He was often in my thoughts. He was arrogant and rude and I did not like him, but I found myself making excuses for him. His parents had not loved him. Well, they hadn't loved Tamarisk either. I suppose there was a strong resemblance between brother and sister. They both thought everyone should do as they wanted.

Mr. Dorian also forced his way into my thoughts. There had been occasions when I had dreamed of him. Vague dreams they had been, with no real meaning to them, but I would wake up thankful to have left the dream, for with them came a vague feeling of fear.

Then I was by nature curious and interested in the life of Harper's Green. I often found my footsteps taking me in the direction of the Lanes' cottage. I had the impression that Flora liked to see me. Her face always lit up with pleasure when I called, "Good afternoon." I made a point of passing the cottage whenever I could—not after lessons, of course, because I had to go home to the luncheon Lily would have prepared, but when I walked in the afternoon I often did.

I would approach the cottage from the back and look over the wall. If Flora were sitting there in her usual place I would say, "Good afternoon"; she would always answer me, and only on one occasion had she looked away, as though she did not want to see me. Then I went on, but usually she would imply that she wanted me to come in.

I soon discovered that when I was not welcome was when Lucy was at home. I had quickly gathered that Lucy did not want me to talk to her sister. Flora knew this too. There was a certain cunning about her. She wanted to talk to me but she did not want to offend Lucy, so therefore my calling must be done when Lucy was out.

On this particular afternoon when I passed, I was invited to come in. We sat on the seat, side by side, and she smiled at me in an almost conspiratorial way.

She talked for a while. It was a conversation I did not entirely understand but she was very pleased to have me there.

It was mainly about the doll, but more than once she referred to the mulberry bush and kept insisting that there was nothing there.

Then suddenly she said that the baby was fretful that afternoon. It could be wind. He was sniffling a little too and there was a chill in the air.

"I'd better take him in," she said.

She stood up. I did the same and was preparing to say goodbye when she shook her head.

"No . . . you come."

She pointed towards the cottage.

I hesitated. I wondered whether I ought to go in. Lucy was certainly not at home or she would have been out by now.

I could not resist. After all, I had had an invitation to enter.

I walked beside her as she pushed the

pram to the back door and we stepped into the kitchen.

Gently she took the doll out of the pram murmuring, "There, there. It's a nasty little cold, that's what it is. He wants his cot. Yes, he'll be more comfortable there. Nanny Flora will see to that."

It was more uncanny in the cottage than it seemed out of doors, and I felt excited as I followed her up the stairs.

There were a nursery and two bedrooms. The cottage was large as such cottages go. One of the bedrooms was for Lucy, I presumed, the other for Flora and the nursery of course for the doll.

We went into this nursery and she laid the doll tenderly in the cot. Then she turned to me.

"He'll be better there, little angel. They get fratchetty when they've got a cold hanging about."

I was always embarrassed when she talked about the doll as though it were living.

I said: "It's a nice nursery."

Her face lighted up with pleasure and then a puzzled expression crossed it.

"It's not like the one we used to have." Now she was looking a little frightened. I guessed I must have reminded her of the one at St. Aubyn's, where she had nursed the real Crispin.

I tried to think of something to say. Then I noticed the picture. There were seven birds and they were sitting on a stone wall. It looked as though it had been taken from a book and framed.

I took a step closer and read the inscription beneath it. "Seven for a Secret," I read. Then I cried: "Why! It's the seven magpies!"

She was nodding enthusiastically. She had forgotten that this nursery was not like the old one at St. Aubyn's.

"You like it?" she asked.

"It must mean the seven magpies in the verse. I learned it once. What is it now? I think I can remember:

> "One for Sorrow,
> Two for Joy.
> Three for a girl,
> Four for a boy.
> Five for silver,
> Six for gold,
> And seven for a secret . . ."

She watched my mouth as I quoted the verse, and finished with me: ". . . never to be told."

"That's it," I said. "I remember now."

"Lucy made it," she said and touched the frame lovingly.

"She framed it, did she?"

She nodded. "Seven for a secret never to be told," she said. "It must never be told." She shook her head. "Never . . . never . . . never. That's what the birds are saying."

I examined it closely. "The birds look rather evil," I said.

"That's because it's the secret. Oh dear, he's waking up." She went to the cot and picked up the doll.

The room seemed to assume an uncanniness. I was filled with an eagerness to know more of her and to probe what was behind this strange delusion. I wondered whether, if she could be made to realise the doll was only a doll and that the baby she believed it to be was now a grown man, she might return to normality.

Then I was overcome by a desire to get away and I heard myself say: "I think I should be going now. I'll let myself out."

As I was about to descend the stairs I heard the sound of voices below. I was dismayed. I had not heard anyone come in.

"Flora!" It was Lucy's voice. She came out and was clearly astonished to see me descending the staircase.

"I've been with Miss Flora upstairs," I stammered.

"Oh . . . she invited you up here, did she?"

I hesitated.

"She has been . . . er . . . showing me the nursery."

Lucy looked rather angry. Then a man came into the hall. It was Crispin St. Aubyn.

"This is Miss Cardingham's niece," Lucy said. "Flora asked her in."

He nodded in my direction.

"I'll be going," I said.

Lucy took me to the front door and I went out.

I sped away.

What a strange afternoon that had been! I could not stop thinking of the seven magpies. They were rather sinister-looking birds. Lucy had evidently cut out the picture from a book and framed it for Flora. Could it be to remind her that there was some secret which had to be kept? Flora's mind was like that of a child. She might have to be reminded often of certain things. Perhaps the picture was just from a book she had loved in her childhood and Lucy had framed the picture for her.

In any case, it was very interesting, I was thinking, as I sped home to Aunt Sophie.

.   .   .

IT WAS A few days later when I discovered a side to Aunt Sophie's nature which I had not suspected before. At the Rowans there was a small room which led from her bedroom. It must have been a dressing-room, but she used it as a little study.

I wanted to speak to her about some trivial matter and Lily told me she thought she was in her study tidying a drawer, so I went up. I knocked on the bedroom door and, as there was no answer, I opened it and looked in.

The study door was open.

"Aunt Sophie," I called.

She came out and stood in the doorway.

There was something different about her. She looked sad, as I had never seen her before, and a tear was glistening on her eyelashes.

"Is something wrong?" I asked.

She hesitated for a moment and then said: "Oh no . . . nothing. I'm just a silly old fool. I've been writing to someone I knew in the past."

"I'm sorry I interrupted. Lily said she thought you were tidying a drawer."

"Yes, I did say I was going to do that. Well, come in, dear. It's time you knew."

I went into the study.

"Sit down. I was writing to your father," she said.

"To *my* father?"

"I do write to him now and then. I knew him very well, you see . . . when I was younger."

"Where is he?"

"He's in Egypt. He used to be in the Army, but he left all that. I've been writing to him over the years. It goes a long way back." She looked at me as though she were not quite sure of something. Then she seemed to come to a decision.

She went on: "I met your father first . . . before your mother did. It was at someone's house party. We were very friendly from the start. He was asked to Cedar Hall. That was when your mother came home from school. She was eighteen then and really beautiful. Well, he fell in love with her."

"But he left her!"

"That was some time after. It didn't work. He wasn't fitted to settling down. He was a very merry person. He liked the social life. He drank a little . . . not too much, but perhaps broaching on it. He gambled. He liked the ladies. He is not a very serious person. Well, they parted about a year after you were born. There was a divorce, as you know. There was another woman. He married her, but that didn't turn out very well either."

"He doesn't seem to be a very reliable sort of person."

"He had lots of charm to make up for it."

"I see. And you write to him."

"Yes. We were always good friends."

"Do you mean he might have married you instead of my mother?"

She smiled rather ruefully.

"He clearly preferred to marry your mother."

"You might have been my mother," I said.

"I suppose if I had been you wouldn't be who you are. We wouldn't want to change that, would we?"

She was laughing at me . . . her old self again.

"I don't know. Perhaps I shouldn't have been so plain."

"Oh nonsense! Your mother was a very beautiful woman. I was the plain sister."

"I don't believe you were."

"Let's forget about this plainness. I just want you to know that your father writes to me and he always wants news of you. He knows that you are here with me and he is very pleased about that. He is going to help with your education, which may be a little expensive if you go to that school with Tamarisk and Rachel, which I hope you will be doing in a few months."

"I'm glad he's doing that," I said.

"I would have managed somehow, but it is a help and is good of him to offer."

"Well, he is my father."

"He hasn't seen you since he left, but, Freddie, he would have done so if your mother would have let him. Perhaps now . . ."

"If he were to come home, you mean?"

"I don't think there is any sign of that just yet. But, of course, he may."

"Does it make you sad to write to him?"

"People get sentimental sometimes. I remember the days of my youth."

"You must have been very unhappy when he married my mother instead of you."

She did not answer and I put my arms round her.

"I'm sorry," I cried. "I wish he had married you! Then we should all have been together. He would have been here with us."

She shook her head. "He was not the sort to settle. He would have been off." Her lips curled into a rather tender smile as she went on: "And you are mine now, aren't you . . . just as though I were your mother. My niece

. . . his daughter. That's what I like to think."

"Do you feel better now that I know?" I asked.

"Much," she assured me. "I'm glad you know. Now let's start counting our blessings."

. . .

I KNEW I had plenty to count, especially when I compared my fate with that of Rachel. I often did that, because what had happened to us was similar. I was with my aunt and she was with an aunt and uncle. I had always been aware of my good fortune, but I did not realise the extent of it until I discovered something from Rachel.

I had always known she was afraid. She never actually said she was, for she rarely talked about her life at the Bell House, but I sensed there was a great deal to tell.

She and I were far more friendly than either of us was with Tamarisk. I felt protective towards her and I think she regarded me as a true friend.

She often came to the Rowans and we would sit in the garden and talk. I had for some time had the feeling that she wanted to tell me something and was finding it difficult to do so. I noticed that when we were laughing together and there was some reference to the Bell House a change would come over her, and I could not help being aware of her reluctance to leave me when we drew near the place and it was time for her to go home.

One day, when we were in the garden, I said to her: "What is it like at the Bell House? I mean *really* like?"

She stiffened and there was a long pause. Then she burst out: "Oh, Freddie, it frightens me."

"What?" I asked.

"I don't know . . . quite. It just does."

"Is it your uncle?"

"He's such a good man, you see. He is always talking about God . . . and to Him . . . like Abraham or one of those people in the Bible. How sinful a lot of things are . . . things that people wouldn't think of. I suppose that is because he is so good."

"It's supposed to be good to care about other people, not frighten them."

"When Aunt Hilda bought a comb for her hair he thought that was sinful. It was a nice comb and it made a difference when she put it in her hair. It was dinner time and we were at the table. I thought it looked very nice. He was angry. He said, 'Vanity, vanity, all is vanity. You look like the whore of Babylon!' Poor Aunt Hilda, she was quite white. She was so upset. He took the comb out of her hair and it fell round her shoulders. He was like an angry prophet in the Bible . . . like Moses when the people made the golden calf. He isn't like a person . . . not like one of us."

"My Aunt Sophie is kind and loving. I think that's better than quoting the Bible and behaving like Abraham. After all, he was ready to kill his son as a sacrifice when God told him to. Aunt Sophie would never have done that to make herself look good in God's eyes."

"You are lucky. Your Aunt Sophie is a darling. I wish she'd been mine. But, of course, my uncle is a very good man. We have prayers every day and they go on for a long time. My knees get sore. We have to pray for forgiveness and, because he is so good, he thinks we are all very bad and will go to Hell in any case, so it all seems so pointless."

"And he'll go to Heaven, of course."

"Well, he's always talking to God. But it's not that . . ."

"What is it?"

"It's the way he looks at me. The way he touches me. He said once that I was a temptress. I don't know what he meant. Do you?"

I shook my head.

"I try not to be there with him . . . alone."

"I know what you mean."

"Sometimes . . . well, once he came into my room at night when I was in bed. I woke up and he was standing there looking at me."

I felt cold suddenly and shivered. I knew exactly how she had felt.

"He said to me: 'Have you said your prayers?' I said, 'Yes, Uncle.' 'Are you telling me the truth?' he went on. 'Get out of bed and say them again.' He made me kneel down and he was watching me all the time. Then he started to pray in a funny sort of way. He was asking God to save him from the Devil's temptation. 'I fight, O Lord,' he said. 'Thou knowest how I fight to overcome this sin which the Devil plants in me,' or something like that. Then he put out his hand and touched me. I thought he was going to pull my nightdress off. I was terribly frightened and pulled myself away. I ran out and Aunt Hilda was just outside the door. I clung to her and she kept saying it was all right."

"And what did he do?"

"I didn't see, I just hid my face. He must have come out of the room and gone away. When I looked up he was gone."

"What happened then?"

"Aunt Hilda kept on saying it was all right. She took me back to my room, but I didn't want to stay there. She got into my bed with me and said she would not leave me. She was there all night. In the morning she said it was just a nightmare. My uncle had walked in his sleep. 'Better not mention it,' she said. 'He wouldn't like that.' So I didn't . . . not till now. Then she said, 'You could always lock your door in case he should sleepwalk again. Then you would sleep better,' she said. 'Nobody could come in then.' She took a key out of her pocket and showed me. I always have it with me. I make sure every night that I lock my door."

"I wish you could come and live with us."

"Oh, I should like that. Once . . . he was there . . . outside the door. He turned the handle. I jumped out of bed and stood there listening. He started to pray. He kept cursing the devils who tormented him just as the saints were tormented. He said he knew God did it to tempt him. Imps came in the form of young girls. He was half-crying. He would chastise himself, he said. He would purge himself of evil. He went away but I couldn't sleep, even though my door was locked."

"Oh, Rachel," I said, "I'm glad you told me. I knew there was something."

"I feel better now I've told you." She looked at the key and put it into her pocket.

"I have this," she said.

We sat for some time in silence, and I knew exactly how she had felt when he came into her room.

· · ·

THERE WAS A great deal of discussion about our going away to school. Aunt Sophie went to see Mrs. St. Aubyn and Rachel's Aunt Hilda went with her.

They were all so different. Aunt Hilda was meek and eager to please; Mrs. St. Aubyn made a play of showing an interest which she clearly did not feel; but Aunt Sophie was energetic and had already investigated several schools, and her choice had fallen on St. Stephen's. It was not too far away and she had seen the headmistress, whom she judged to be a sensible woman. She liked the tone of the school and felt it was the right one. There was no opposition.

It was May and we had to move quickly to start the term in September. It was Aunt Sophie who took us all into Salisbury to buy our uniforms and by the end of June everything was satisfactorily arranged.

We were very excited about it all—even Tamarisk—and we spent hours imagining what it would be like. We were a little apprehensive though, and we were all very pleased that the three of us were going together.

Then came that day which I am sure I shall never forget as long as I live.

It was July and the weather had been warm and sultry. Rachel and I had been to St. Aubyn's for afternoon tea. We had talked incessantly of school and it had been a very pleasant hour or so. Rachel was considerably happier at the prospect of leaving the Bell House and, of course, Tamarisk was always ready for a new adventure.

I had said goodbye to Rachel at the Bell House and did not want to go home immediately. Aunt Sophie would be shopping, so I decided to go the long way round by Barrow Wood.

I could not resist the temptation to go in and made my way to the barrows. I stood for a few moments, contemplating them. I loved the smell of the earth and the trees. It was very quiet except for the faint murmur of the light wind in the leaves.

I thought I should miss Barrow Wood when I went to school. I must not stay too long though. Aunt Sophie would probably be almost home by now.

I turned sharply and, as I did so, I tripped over a stone which was protruding a few inches from the ground. I tried to save myself from falling but I could not do so in time and crashed to the ground. My right foot was twisted under me and a pain was shooting through me. I scrambled to my feet, but I could not stand and sank back to the ground. I was dismayed. I should have been more careful. I knew there were odd stones jutting up in Barrow Wood. But what was the use of reproaching myself now? The important thing was how I was going to get home.

I touched my ankle and winced. It was swelling rapidly and was very painful.

I sat there, wondering what I was going to do.

And then it happened. He was there. He was coming towards me. He was staring at me and the look in his eyes terrified me.

"Poor little flower," he murmured. "You are hurt, little one."

"I fell down, Mr. Dorian. I've hurt my ankle. Perhaps you would go and tell my aunt."

He just stood there, staring at me. Then he said: "I have been led to this. It was meant . . ."

He was standing very close to me and I knew fear as I never had before. Some instinct told me that he was going to harm me in some way which I did not altogether understand.

"Go away! Go away!" I screamed. "Get my aunt. Don't come near me!"

He was laughing softly. "Poor little broken flower. She can't run away this time. Oh, it was meant. It was meant."

I screamed louder. "Don't touch me! I don't want you near me. Just go away and tell my aunt. Please . . . please . . . go away."

But he did not go away. His lips went on moving. He was talking to God, I knew, though I could not hear what he said. I was numb with terror.

"Help me, help me," I sobbed, and I let out a piercing scream.

But he was coming nearer. He was on the ground beside me and there was a terrible look on his face.

He seized me.

"No . . . no . . . no!" I screamed. "Go away. Help me! Help me!"

Then I was alert. I heard the sound of horse's hoofs on the road. I shouted with all my might.

"Help me! Help me! I'm in the woods. Please . . . please . . . help!"

I had a terrible fear that whoever was riding by would not hear me or perhaps would take no heed. There was no sound from the road now and I was here alone in Barrow Wood with this evil man.

Then I heard the footsteps. "My God!"

It was Crispin St. Aubyn.

He came towards me.

He shouted: "You swine!" and he picked up Mr. Dorian as though he were a puppet figure and he brought up his fist and gave him a blow in the face. I heard the crack of bone as he threw Mr. Dorian from him onto the ground.

Mr. Dorian sprawled there. He was quite still.

Crispin's eyes were blazing with anger. He ignored Mr. Dorian and turned to me.

"Hurt yourself, have you?"

I was sobbing and could only nod.

"Stop crying," he said. "It's all right now."

He stooped down and picked me up.

"He . . ." I began, looking towards Mr. Dorian who had not moved.

"He got what he deserved."

"You . . . you've killed him."

"No great loss. Hurt your foot, have you?"

"My ankle."

He did not speak. I looked over my shoulder at Mr. Dorian, who was still lying on the ground. I shuddered to see the blood on his face. But Crispin was carrying me off. He put me on his horse and mounted behind me.

He took me to the Rowans. Aunt Sophie had just arrived back with the shopping.

"She's hurt her ankle," Crispin explained.

Aunt Sophie exclaimed in horror, and Crispin carried me upstairs and put me on my bed.

"We'd better get the doctor," said Aunt Sophie.

They left me and I heard Crispin talking to her downstairs. He had said when they were on the stairs: "I have to tell you . . ." and then there was no more.

Aunt Sophie came back to me very soon, looking pale and disturbed, and I knew that Crispin had told her how he had found me.

She sat on my bed and said: "How are you feeling now? Does the ankle hurt?"

"Yes."

"We'll keep it up. I expect it's a sprain. I hope you haven't broken anything. Who would have believed . . . ?"

"Oh, Aunt Sophie," I said, "it was terrible."

"I'd kill him if I had him here," she said. "He's not worthy to live."

I grew up in that moment. I understood what might have happened to me but for

Crispin St. Aubyn. It was strange that he was the one to whom I had to be thankful. I could not stop thinking of the way he had picked up Mr. Dorian and shaken him. I would never forget the way Mr. Dorian had looked; his expression had been one of stricken horror and despair. I thought I had never seen such anguish on any face before. Crispin had been furiously angry; the manner in which he had flung Mr. Dorian from him made it seem as though he were throwing away some obnoxious rubbish. He had not cared if he had killed him. I wondered in horror if he had.

It would be murder, I thought. Then: Rachel would not have to be frightened anymore.

The doctor had come.

"Well, young lady," he said. "What have you been doing to yourself?"

He prodded my ankle and I was asked to see if I could stand. His verdict was that I had had a bad twist of the ankle . . . a nasty sprain.

"It will be a little time before you'll be able to put it to the ground with comfort. How did you do it?"

"I was in Barrow Wood."

He shook his head at me. "You'll have to watch where you're going next time."

He talked to Aunt Sophie about hot and cold compresses and, as soon as he was gone, she got to work on me.

She watched me anxiously. I knew she was thinking that what had happened to me was more than a sprained ankle and that, by great good fortune, I had been saved from greater harm.

Aunt Sophie was the sort of person one could talk to about anything, and she decided that it was better to talk than make a secret of my misadventure.

So I told her all about it: my fall, the sudden appearance of Mr. Dorian. I mentioned that I had been uneasy about him for a long time, and how he had talked of my saying my prayers in my nightdress.

"You should have told me," she said.

"I didn't know that it was important," I replied. Then I told her about Rachel.

"He's mad, that one," she said. "He sees sin everywhere he goes. It's what they call religious mania. I'm sorry for his poor wife."

"I think Crispin St. Aubyn has killed him. I think he's murdered him."

"I don't think that. Just a beating. I reckon it was what he needed. It might have taught him a lesson." Then suddenly she hugged me.

"I'm glad you're safe and well and unharmed. I'd never have forgiven myself if anything happened to you."

"It wouldn't have been your fault."

"I'd have blamed myself for failing to look after you. I ought to have known the sort he was."

"How could you?"

"I don't know, but I should."

She had my bed moved into her room. "Just till you've settled down a bit," she said. "You could wake in the night . . . and then I'd like to be near you."

And I did wake in the night, sweating from a nightmare. I was lying in Barrow Wood and he was coming towards me. He was there on the ground beside me. I was calling for Crispin. I felt arms about me . . . and they were Aunt Sophie's.

"It's all right. You're here in your bed. Old Aunt Sophie is here."

Then I found myself crying weakly. I could not think why. I was happy because I was safe and my dearest Aunt Sophie was here to look after me.

. . .

SILENCE BORN OF shock lay over Harper's Green. Then everyone was talking about the horrific events at the Bell House. We were a close community and that such a thing could have happened to one of its members sent a thrill of horror throughout the place. It was the sort of thing that happened to other people; one read about it in the newspapers, but to take place here in Harper's Green was difficult to believe.

The news first came to the Rowans through Tom Wilson, the postman, when he delivered the midday mail. I was in bed, for I was to be confined there for the next few days, but Aunt Sophie happened to be in the garden when Tom came.

When she came up to me her face was very solemn and she stood for a few moments regarding me.

Then she said: "A terrible thing has happened."

My thoughts were still in the wood, reliving my nightmare.

"Is it Mr. Dorian?" I asked. "Is he . . . dead?"

She nodded slowly and I immediately thought: Crispin has killed him. It is murder. Murderers are hanged. He did that . . . for me.

I believe Aunt Sophie guessed what was in my mind. She said quickly: "Poor Mrs. Dorian found him in the stables early this morning. He had killed himself."

"In the stables . . . ?" I stammered.

"He was hanging from one of the rafters —that is, according to Tom Wilson. He said Mr. Dorian came back to the Bell House yesterday and his face was bleeding. He had had a fall in the wood, he said. He was very upset. He went to his room and stayed there. She went up to him but he was at prayer and didn't want to be disturbed. She said he went on praying for hours in his room. She didn't see him that night and in the morning she realised he was not in the house. She happened to see that the stable door was unlocked. She went in . . . and found him."

She came to the bed and put her arms round me.

She said: "I didn't know whether to tell you . . . or what to do for the best. But you'd soon be hearing it in any case. You are so young . . . my darling . . . and you were concerned in this unpleasantness. It is all that I wanted to protect you from, but it is best that you should know because of your involvement. You see . . . this man . . . he wanted to be good. He wanted to be a saint, but he had certain instincts. He tried to suppress them and they came out in this way. Oh, I am making a mess of explaining."

I said: "It's all right, Aunt Sophie. I think I understand."

"Well, he failed and he was caught, he was

exposed. Thank God, Crispin St. Aubyn came along at the right moment. But this sad man could not face the fact that he had been discovered . . . so he killed himself."

She was silent for a moment. I was reliving it all. I believed it would always be there in my mind. I should never forget those moments of fear and horror.

"There is that poor woman, Mrs. Dorian . . . and Rachel. It will be terrible for them. And you were there . . . oh, it doesn't bear thinking of! So young . . ."

"I don't feel young anymore, Aunt Sophie."

"No. It is the sort of thing that makes you grow up. I don't know what will come out of this, but I don't want you to be involved in it. I am going to talk to Crispin St. Aubyn. I think I shall go along and see him."

She did not have to do that because he came to the Rowans. Aunt Sophie was with me when Lily came up to tell her that he was downstairs.

She hastily went to him. She had left the door open and I distinctly heard his voice, which was clear and resonant.

He said: "I've come to ask about the child. How is she? No worse, I hope?"

The child! I thought indignantly. I was not a child . . . especially now.

He had a long talk with Aunt Sophie and finally she brought him up to see me.

He looked at me and said: "Feel better now?"

"Yes, thank you."

"Sprain, was it? You'll be up and about in no time."

Aunt Sophie said: "Mr. St. Aubyn and I have been talking about what happened, and we have come to the conclusion that it would be better for everyone if nothing was said about what that man tried to do to you. The theory is that he had a bad fall and he came home in a distressed state. He shut himself in his room. Mrs. Dorian was upset because he would not see her all the rest of that day. In the morning she must have realised that he had gone out. She noticed the stable door was unlocked and went in. She found him there. It's clear—"

Crispin broke in: "He couldn't face up to people's knowing what he was really like. It shattered his pose as the holy man. He just could not face that, so he took his life."

"Yes," said Aunt Sophie. "There will have to be an inquest, and the verdict will be one of suicide—which it was. But Mr. St. Aubyn and I have decided that the wisest thing, for the sake of everyone concerned, is to say nothing of what happened in the wood. You fell over a stone and hurt your ankle. Mr. Dorian had a fall too. Say nothing of meeting him. I hate subterfuge, but there are times when it is necessary."

"Then," said Crispin, with an air of finality, "that is settled."

He seemed eager to be gone.

He turned to me. "You'll be all right now. No need to fear. He can't cause any more trouble."

He nodded to me in farewell and then Aunt Sophie took him down. I lay listening to the clip-clop of his horse's hoofs as he rode away.

. . .

THE INQUEST WAS brief; the verdict "suicide while the balance of his mind was disturbed." I could see that what Aunt Sophie and Crispin St. Aubyn had decided on was the best way. It would have been unbearably distressing for Mrs. Dorian and Rachel to know the truth and, as Aunt Sophie had said, it was better for me. So it was over quickly.

I wondered what it was like in the Bell House now. I could not imagine it without the overpowering presence of Mr. Dorian. It would be a different place altogether.

Mrs. Dorian's cousin came to help her and

Aunt Sophie suggested that Rachel come to stay with us until, as she said, "things settled down."

Aunt Sophie said: "We shall have to put a bed in your room, and you will have to share. That will get you ready for school, when you will be in a dormitory with others."

Rachel was delighted to come. She had changed. She was no longer afraid. We often talked far into the night until we fell asleep. We had both had frightening experiences with her uncle and we could not at first bear to talk of it. I remembered the warning I had had not to mention what had happened; but I could not get it out of my mind.

One night Rachel said to me: "Freddie . . . I think I must be very wicked."

"Why?" I asked.

"I'm glad he's dead."

"Well, he did it himself."

"I thought he was so sure about everything."

"I suppose he wasn't after all. He must have realised he wasn't as good as he thought he was."

"Do you think that was it?"

"Yes, I do. But it is not wicked to be glad. I am too."

There was a shared awareness that we had

both escaped a danger which had threatened us.

In September, Rachel, Tamarisk and I went off to school just as had been planned.

· · ·

IT WAS THE best thing that could have happened to us. It was a bridge for Rachel and me between an entirely new way of life and a past of haunted fears and shadows.

We gave each other courage in our new surroundings. Tamarisk was always cool and arrogant: she resembled her brother, I told myself. Rachel was like a different girl: she had lost that haunted look. I understood her feelings absolutely. We were the three friends; we shared a dormitory and we were in the same classes; and I, as well as Rachel, I was sure, began to grow away from that nightmare which could so easily have become a reality for us both.

During my first year at school my mother died. I went home for a short while in the middle of term to attend the funeral.

Aunt Sophie said: "It was for the best. She could never have recovered and it was no life for her."

I asked her if my father would come to the funeral. She shook her head.

"Oh no. He's far away and the divorce was

the end. When people like that part, they part forever."

"Have you told him?"

"Yes," she said, and I saw that look of wistfulness come into her face which I had seen when I had come upon her writing to him.

I shed some tears as the clods fell on the coffin. I thought how sad it was that she had been so unhappy, wasting her life in craving for what she could not have.

A few people came back to the house and we gave them wine and sandwiches. I was glad when we were alone.

"Well," said Aunt Sophie, "now you are all mine." And I felt contented about that.

Then I went back to school and life continued as before.

When we came home for the holidays, I went to see the Lanes and sat in the garden with Flora while the doll in the pram was beside her. She was just the same as ever; the cottage with its mulberry bush and the picture of the seven magpies had not altered one bit. I wondered if it ever occurred to Flora that the baby might grow up. But I supposed she had had that same doll for years and it would always be the baby Crispin to her.

There was change though at the Bell

House. I visited Rachel there and at first I thought the difference was due to the fact that one did not have to watch for Mr. Dorian to come creeping up on one at any moment. But it was more than that. There were new curtains of a light and flowery pattern. There were flowers in the hall.

Mrs. Dorian had changed more than anything else.

She wore her hair piled high on her head with a Spanish comb in it, a brightly coloured dress, cut rather low, and a necklace of pearls about her neck. She was another who was not grieving for the death of Mr. Dorian. For such a good man, he had made a lot of people unhappy.

I was no longer afraid of the house, but I did avoid looking at the stables when I went in and out.

So Harper's Green was back to normal. I was an orphan now—or, rather, half an orphan. My mother was dead, but in the last years she had become a hazy figure and in losing her I had gained Aunt Sophie.

I went back to the school life where what mattered was who was in the hockey team and what there was for dinner, and who was friendly with whom—schoolgirl triumphs and disasters.

THE ST. AUBYN'S BALL

So we were growing up. Two years had passed. I should be sixteen in May of the coming year.

Aunt Sophie said: "I reckon in a year or so you'll have grown out of school. I'm wondering what we'll do with you then. You'll have to get out and about a bit. When I was that age, there was a lot of talk about 'coming out.' There'll be parties and that sort of thing for Tamarisk, I reckon. As for Rachel, I don't know. Perhaps her aunt has ideas for her. I'll have a talk with her sometime."

I loved coming home for the holidays. Aunt Sophie was always at the station to meet me. There was no one to meet Tamarisk or Rachel, and Aunt Sophie had to be the universal guardian, as she had been since we started school. This was cheerfully accepted by Tamarisk and Rachel; and I felt very proud and gratified because she was my aunt.

When Tamarisk and Rachel had been delivered to their respective homes, I would go to the Rowans and there would be tea or lunch—whatever the time—and I would talk about school life, to which Aunt Sophie listened avidly; and Lily used to come in to hear it. It amazed me how funny events seemed to become when told in this way—far more than they had been at the time.

Lily said: "I reckon you have a rare old time at that school."

One day there was a fresh piece of news.

Aunt Sophie said: "By the way, there's a rumour—only a rumour, mind—that there might be wedding bells up at St. Aubyn's."

"Oh? Tamarisk didn't say anything about it."

"Well, you've just come home, haven't you? It's only blown up in the last month or so. It's a Lady Fiona Charrington, an earl's daughter, no less. So very right for St. Aubyn's. Even Mrs. St. Aubyn is bestirring herself. Well, it's about time Crispin was settled after that first disaster."

"Do you mean he is going to marry this Lady Fiona Charrington?"

"Nothing official. She came down to stay

at St. Aubyn's with her mama, and I believe he has visited the ancestral home. So it looks hopeful. Nothing definite, so far as I know though. Perhaps he's a little wary after the first . . ."

"Because he was married before, you mean?"

"That was supposed to be a disaster. Makes a man cautious, I expect. I shouldn't think he was the easiest person in the world to live with either. She left him and before she could enjoy the life she had chosen she was killed in that railway accident."

"Have you seen this Lady Fiona?"

"Oh yes, once. She was out riding with him. I wasn't exactly introduced. Just 'Nice morning' and 'Good day' *en passant.* She sits her horse well. She's not a beauty, but ancient lineage would make up for that."

"Tamarisk will know all about it," I said.

"The whole neighbourhood's agog."

"How interested they are in other people's affairs."

"Bless them. So little happens to them. They have to get a bit of excitement through others."

After that I kept thinking about Crispin and the way in which he had carried me away from that horrific scene. I had taken a special interest in him after that . . . well, before that, when he had made the unfortunate remark which had wounded my childish ego so bitterly. I should have liked to ask Tamarisk about him but I never did. One had to be so careful with Tamarisk.

One of my first visits when I arrived home was to go to see Flora Lane in the House of the Seven Magpies, as I romantically called the cottage to myself.

I fancied Lucy would rather I did not visit the house, but Flora liked me to, so I chose the times when I guessed Lucy would be out shopping and I could go in to see Flora and slip out without Lucy's knowing I had been.

On this occasion Flora was sitting in the garden close to the mulberry bush, the pram with the doll beside her. When she saw me her face lit up with pleasure. She always behaved as though I had never been away.

"I was expecting you," she said.

"Oh, were you? I only came home from school yesterday."

She looked vague and I went on: "Tell me what has been happening while I've been away."

"He's had the croup. In a real state he was. Pretty bad. I thought at one time I might lose him. It frightens the life out of you when they start that cough."

"He's all right now?"

"Right as a trivet. I got him over that. Mind you, it was touch and go. But he's a little fighter. Nothing's going to get the better of him!"

"I'm glad he's all right now."

She nodded and rambled on, describing the symptoms of the croup. Suddenly she said: "I'm going to take him up now. There's a touch of damp in the air."

She wheeled the pram to the back door of the cottage. I could not resist the temptation to follow her. I wanted to see those magpies again. Had I fancied there was something evil about them? Probably. It would be just like me to do so.

Tenderly she carried the doll up the stairs, with me in her wake. She sat in a chair, holding it, and there was an expression of great tenderness on her face.

I went close to the picture of the magpies. "One for sorrow . . ." I began.

"Two for joy," she said. "Go on, say it."

I did. She was before me with the last line.

"Seven for a secret . . ." She shook her head. "Never to be told." She looked very solemn and held the doll more closely to her.

There was an uncanniness about the scene. The words meant something very special to her. What secret? I wondered. Her mind was wandering, of course. Anyone who thought a doll was a baby could not be expected to have coherent thoughts.

I was alert suddenly. Someone was downstairs. I said: "Your sister must have come back."

She did not answer but continued to look at the doll.

There were footsteps on the stairs—heavy ones, not Lucy's surely.

A voice called: "Lucy! Where are you?"

It was Crispin. The door opened and he stood there, looking from me to Flora. His eyes went to the picture of the magpies.

Then it happened. Flora stood up abruptly. The doll fell from her arms and crashed to the floor. For a few seconds we all stared at the broken china face. Then Flora let out a wail of anguish. She knelt by the doll and clasped her hands across her breast.

"No . . . no!" she cried. "It's not. It's not. I didn't. It's a secret . . . never to be told."

Crispin went to her, pulled her to her feet. She kept sobbing: "I didn't mean . . . I didn't. I didn't."

He lifted her as effortlessly as he had once lifted me and carried her to her bedroom, where he laid her on the bed. He jerked his head to me, implying that I was to pick up the broken doll and take it away.

I obeyed and ran downstairs with the doll in my arms. I put it on the kitchen table and went back to Flora's room.

Flora was lying on the bed, sobbing. Crispin was not there but came in almost immediately stirring something in a glass.

He gave it to Flora, who meekly drank it.

"This will be better now," he said, more to me than to her.

I thought how strange it was that he managed to find whatever it was must be used to calm her when she was upset.

He said to me in a quiet voice: "It's all right. She'll calm down now. She will be asleep soon," and I was struck afresh by his knowledge of how to treat her.

We stood by the bed watching her. In less than five minutes she had stopped moaning.

"She doesn't remember much now. We'll wait awhile."

How strange it was to be here in this cottage with Flora lying on the bed and Crispin beside me. He must know the cottage well and its inmates. He must have gone straight to the place where Lucy kept the medicine her sister must need from time to time. He behaved as though he were master of the place. But then he was like that everywhere.

It was not very long before Flora slept.

Crispin looked at me, indicating that I should follow him downstairs.

In the kitchen he said: "What were you doing here?"

"I came to see Flora. I often do. She went upstairs and I went with her."

"Miss Lucy was not here."

"No. I expect she was shopping."

He nodded. "What we have to do now is get rid of that." He indicated the broken doll which was lying on the table. "It must be replaced at once. I am going into the town to buy one as like it as I can find. She will not awake until this evening. It must be there then. She must find a new one lying in the cot."

"But she will know . . ."

"She will be told that she had a bad dream. Miss Lucy will know how to deal with that. But there must be another doll in the same clothes. There is a toyshop . . . not in Harper's Green . . . we'll have to go farther than that. I shall write a note to Miss Lucy telling her what has happened and that we should be back in just over an hour."

"We . . . ?" I began.

"I want you to come with me to help choose the doll. We'll take the broken one with us and you will be able to choose it more easily than I could."

"I shall have to tell my aunt. She will be worried."

He looked at me thoughtfully. "I shall go back and get the trap. You go at once to your aunt. Tell her what has happened and that you are coming with me to choose the doll. You have seen the doll many times. I have never noticed it much, so I need your help."

I was excited. It was an adventure. I said: "Yes. Yes."

"Take the doll and I shall be with you very soon."

I ran home. Fortunately Aunt Sophie was in. Breathlessly I gave her an account of what had happened.

She looked puzzled. "I never heard the like! Good heavens! It will kill her."

"He's afraid for her."

"Dear me. What a to-do."

"I want to go with him. I couldn't bear anything to happen to Flora."

"Yes. You've got to get that doll replaced and quick about it. It's the sensible thing to do as he suggests."

Even before I had finished telling Aunt Sophie, he was there, waiting with the trap. I dashed out carrying the doll and climbed up beside him.

There were two horses and they travelled fast. I sat up in front with him. It was exhilarating . . . riding at breakneck speed to save someone's life, I thought. This was the second rescue in which we were involved together, and the manner in which he took command impressed me deeply.

He did not say much as we drove along, and in about thirty minutes we were in the town. He drove into an innyard where they seemed to know him and were very respectful.

He helped me down and we went off to the shop.

He laid the remains of Flora's doll on the counter and announced: "We want a doll. It must resemble this one."

"This kind has not been made for several years, sir."

"Well, the nearest. You must have something near."

We looked at dolls. He deferred to me, which gave me a sense of pride.

"It should not look like a girl," I said. "The broken one had its hair cut off. And these clothes have to fit."

It took us some time to find something which was sufficiently similar to the broken doll to be passed off as the same one; and even then I was unsure.

We put the clothes on the new doll and came out of the shop.

"We must get back at once," he said; and so began the journey home.

"The hair is the right colour," I said, "but we shall have to trim it. This one looks too much like a girl."

"You can do that, or Miss Lucy will."

I wanted to do it. I wanted to remain in this adventure as long as I could. As we reached the cottage Lucy came out. She looked very worried.

"It's all right," said Crispin. "We have found a replacement." Crispin patted her arm. "It will work," he went on, "as long as the doll is there when she wakes and she doesn't notice the difference."

"I'll put it in the cot," said Lucy.

They let me cut the hair and when this was done the new one did not look too dissimilar.

Lucy took it and went upstairs. Crispin and I were alone in the kitchen. He was looking at me intently and I wondered if he was still thinking that I was plain.

He said: "You were a great help." I glowed with pride. "Miss Flora is very sick in the mind," he went on. "We must be very gentle with her. That doll to her is a baby."

"Yes, I know. She thinks it is you when you were a baby."

His face creased into a smile. Anyone less like a doll I could not imagine.

"She will have to be carefully treated after this. Let's hope she doesn't remember what happened. It would disturb her very much."

Lucy came down. "She is sleeping peacefully," she said. "I shall keep my eye on her. I must be there when she wakes."

"That's right," he said, and smiled at her in a manner which I could only call tender. It surprised me very much, for I had never seen him look quite like that before. I was continually being surprised by him.

He is very fond of her, I thought. But then, of course, she had been his nanny after Flora became ill.

Now he was looking at me.

"I daresay your aunt is expecting you home by now," he said.

"Yes, she will be," I said reluctantly.

"Well, goodbye, and thank you for all you have done."

It was a kind of dismissal, but I was glowing with pleasure as I ran home.

. . .

I COULD NOT resist going to the House of the
Seven Magpies. It was two days later. Flora
was sitting in her usual place in the garden,
the doll's pram beside her. I called over the
wall and she welcomed me with a smile.

"How is . . . he . . . this afternoon?" I
asked tentatively.

"Sleeping nicely. The little monkey woke
me up at five this morning. There he was,
gurgling and chuckling to himself . . . once
he'd wakened me, of course."

I went over and looked down at the doll.
The clothes and cutting of the hair had
helped a good deal, but I was surprised she
did not appear to have noticed the difference.

"He looks as well as ever," I said cautiously.

A shadow came over her face. "There was
a nightmare," she said, her lips beginning to
tremble.

"A nightmare," I said. "Then don't talk of
that. They are best forgotten."

"It's all right." She looked at me appealingly. "I didn't, did I? I held him tight, didn't
I? I couldn't have let my baby come to any
harm . . . not for the world."

"No, of course not, and he is perfectly all
right. You only have to look at him . . ." I

stopped myself. That was not the right thing
to say.

She was staring at the mulberry bush. "It
was a nightmare, wasn't it?" she said appealingly. "That was all."

"Of course it was," I reassured her. "We
all have nightmares at some times, you
know."

I was thinking of those awful moments in
the wood before Crispin came . . . and after.

"You too?" she said. "But you weren't
there."

I wondered what she meant. I had been
there when she dropped the doll; but I
thought it best to agree with her.

I said: "It's all right. Just look at him.
There's nothing wrong with him."

"No," she murmured. "Nothing wrong.
He's here . . . he's been here all the time."

She closed her eyes. Then she opened
them very wide and said: "It's when I
look at him . . . I see him . . . his little
body . . ."

Her thoughts were jumbled and, clearly,
dropping the doll had unnerved her.

I just said: "Well, everything is all right
now."

She smiled and nodded.

I talked to her for a while until I thought it

was time for Lucy's return. Then I said goodbye and that I would come again soon.

As I came out of the cottage I saw Crispin St. Aubyn. I had not gone far when he was beside me.

"So you have been to the cottage," he said. "I think our little subterfuge worked."

"I don't think she has completely forgotten."

"Why do you say that?"

"She seems disturbed."

"How?" he asked sharply.

"I'm not sure. It was the way she talked."

"What did she say?"

"Something about his not being there but here."

"Her mind's unhinged. You can't take what she says seriously."

"No. But there seems to be a pattern to it."

"What do you mean? A pattern?"

"I mean that what she says one day seems to be linked with what she may say the next."

"You seem to be a very discerning young lady."

Young lady! I liked that. Not just the child anymore. I felt he would have more respect for a young lady than he would have for a mere child.

"Well, I often go to the House of the Seven Magpies."

"Where?"

"I mean the Lanes' house."

"Why did you call it that?"

"There's a picture in the nursery . . ."

"So you named the house after the picture?"

"I think it has a special meaning for Flora."

"What did you call it?"

"The Seven Magpies. You have been up there in that room. You must have seen it. It's seven magpies sitting on a wall."

"What is so special about it?"

"The rhyme. Flora said it came from a book and Lucy cut the picture out and framed it for her. You may know the rhyme about the magpies. 'One for Sorrow, Two for Joy,' and all that. And seven are for a secret which must never be told. Flora knows it. She has said it to me more than once."

He was silent for a moment. Then in a cool voice he said: "And you think there is something significant about that?"

"Yes, I do. It was the way Flora looked when she told me."

"Is that why you are so interested?"

"I suppose it is . . . partly. I am very

sorry for Flora. I think there is something worrying her."

"And you want to find out what it is?"

"I like discovering things."

"Yes, I see you do. Sometimes though . . ." He stopped and, as I was obviously waiting for him to go on, he added, "Sometimes it can get you into trouble."

I was surprised. "I can't see . . ."

"One often does not see trouble coming until it has caught up with one."

"Is that true or just what people say to the inquisitive?"

"I daresay that in certain circumstances it could be true."

We had reached the Rowans.

"Goodbye," he said.

I went in, thinking about him. I hoped all through that holiday that I would see him again and that he might seek me out to talk to me. But he did not. Tamarisk told me that he had gone abroad. I could not help wondering whether Lady Fiona had gone too.

. . .

SOON AFTER THAT, we went back to school. Our last term had begun. I wondered now and then what was going to happen when we finished. I had been seventeen last May. That was quite a marriageable age, Tamarisk said. She thought there would be a lot of entertaining at St. Aubyn's and it would all be for the purpose of launching her. Rachel was a little unsure.

There was a certain amount of entertaining at the Bell House now. It had completely changed. In fact, I said to Aunt Sophie, I believed Mrs. Dorian was trying to make everything as different as possible so that she could forget her husband.

Aunt Sophie agreed with that.

When the news leaked out that there was to be a wedding, Harper's Green was astounded. It was not that of Crispin and Lady Fiona. That had been expected and had not happened. It was Mrs. Dorian who took a new husband.

This was Archie Grindle—a widower of about fifty who had farmed in the district for many years. He had now given up his farm to his two sons, and was to live in the Bell House with his new wife.

He had a rotund figure, a red face and a booming laugh. He was as different from Mr. Dorian as Rachel's Aunt Hilda—now Mrs. Grindle—was from her old self. There was only the stable which was the same and nobody liked to enter it because of grim reminders.

Aunt Hilda continued to wear bright

colours and a comb in her hair; she laughed a great deal. And Rachel liked Archie, so that everything was a complete contrast to what it had been before.

But to me the spirit of Mr. Dorian lingered and I wondered what he would think if he knew what was happening in his old home. I should never forget him because I had played a big part in his tragedy.

Aunt Sophie was very amused and glad, for, as she said, Hilda deserved a bit of life after all she had gone through; and now she was taking it with both hands.

The wedding had caused a great deal of stir in the neighbourhood.

"One wedding sparks off another," prophesied Lily.

But there was still no news of an engagement between Crispin and Lady Fiona.

. . .

SCHOOLDAYS WERE OVER, and that provided a problem for our respective guardians. Mrs. St. Aubyn did not care to disturb herself greatly in order to launch her daughter into society; Rachel's aunt had no idea how to; and Aunt Sophie, who had, owing to her own youthful experience at Cedar Hall, lacked the means.

Aunt Sophie called a meeting. They must do what circumstances permitted.

While this was going on, I did see Crispin now and then. He noticed me and smiled in a manner which I convinced myself was conspiratorial. After all, we had our dramatic encounter, though that was never mentioned, and we had also worked together over the new doll.

I still visited Flora Lane. Lucy was never very welcoming, so I timed my visits to avoid her, reminding myself that it was Flora whom I went to see and she was always glad I came.

At length it was decided that there should be a ball. Aunt Sophie would help to organise it. It would have to be held at St. Aubyn's, that being the only suitable place—and there was actually a ballroom in the house.

Mrs. St. Aubyn was quite interested then. It was like the old days of what Aunt Sophie called "Riotous Living." We were all excited about it. I guessed Crispin would be there. He would have to be for his sister's ball—although it was really for the three of us.

Lady Fiona's name had not been mentioned for some time and I believe she was forgotten in the neighbourhood. The marriage of Rachel's aunt and Archie Grindle was the nine days' wonder at that time.

I was quite often at the Bell House now. It had become a friendly, delightful place. There was only the grim stable to remind me. I believed the others did not think about that as much as I did. The stables were never used because there were no horses at Bell House. Once I went inside, I let the door shut behind me and I stood for some seconds looking up at the rafters. It was horrible. He seemed to materialise. His body was limp . . . but his eyes looked at me with the same frightening look which had terrified me when I was lying helpless on the ground in Barrow Wood.

I turned and ran out. It was silly. He couldn't hurt me now. He was dead. He had killed himself because he had been discovered and he could not face living with that.

Shivering, I ran home to the Rowans, promising myself I would never enter that place again. The episode was over, to be forgotten, if that were possible. Crispin had rescued me and we had become friends . . . of a kind. But it was, of course, the affair of Flora's doll which had done that. But I imagined that he did not dislike me.

Tamarisk had once said that people liked those for whom they had done good turns because every time they looked at them they thought how good they themselves were. Well, he had saved me from something terrible, so perhaps Tamarisk was right and when he saw me he remembered what he had done for me.

There was little talk of anything now between us girls other than the ball. Aunt Sophie took us into Salisbury to buy material for our dresses. I chose a bluish mauve, Tamarisk flame red, and Rachel a cornflower blue. Aunt Sophie was a little wistful, thinking no doubt of the court dressmaker who would have made her gown for her coming-out ball. I had heard all about such things from my mother. The village dressmaker, Mary Tucker, would be entrusted with ours.

"She'll do a good competent job," said Aunt Sophie. "How I wish . . ."

I was more and more at the Bell House. Archie Grindle was very jolly and there was no doubt of Aunt Hilda's happiness. She went about the house singing and revelled in the pretty dresses she now possessed. I never ceased to marvel at the change.

Daniel Grindle was frequently there. He was Archie's eldest son who had taken over the farm with his brother Jack.

Daniel was tall and rather awkward, never seeming to know where to put his hands. I liked him. I called him the Gentle Giant, for he was tall and broad; he spoke little and his father told us that he had a way with animals such as he had never seen in any other living person.

"My grandfather had it," said Jack Grindle. "Dan takes after him."

Jack was shorter and inclined to be fat like his father and, like him too, had plenty to say for himself. They both gave the impression of enjoying life.

It was Jack Grindle who was responsible for the introduction of Gaston Marchmont into our circle.

Gaston Marchmont made a great stir and both Tamarisk and Rachel were constantly talking of him. He was tall, slender—willowy almost—and very good-looking in, as Tamarisk said, a worldly way. His hair was dark, almost black, and his eyes dark brown. He was elegant in the extreme.

Jack had met him on the Continent; they had travelled across the Channel together and, because Gaston Marchmont was going to put up at an hotel for a little while, Jack suggested that he come and stay at Grindle's Farm for a few days.

Jack seemed to think it was a great condescension on Gaston's part to do this. Not that Gaston implied it. Far from it. He was

all gracious charm. But I could see why the
Grindles—who were humble folk, though
quite affluent and properous—allowed
themselves to think such a grand personage
as Gaston Marchmont was doing them an
honour by staying with them.

Jack lost no time in introducing this fascinating gentleman into local society. We
learned that Gaston's mother had been
French—hence the name Gaston. He had
been settling his affairs in France and was
now concerned with the estate he had inher-
ited through his father in Scotland, for his
father had died recently.

His mode of dress revealed good taste and
natural elegance. His suits were cut according to Savile Row, Tamarisk told me, and in
his riding gear he looked godlike; he was
charm personified. Mrs. St. Aubyn immediately became very fond of him. She flirted
gaily with him and he responded gallantly.
He was constantly saying that he would have
to go to Scotland, but everyone—including
Jack Grindle—was urging him to stay a little
longer.

"You tempt me," he said, "and I am so
weak."

Tamarisk said he must stay on for the ball,
or she would never forgive him.

"My dear young lady," he replied, "I cannot refuse the appeal of those beautiful eyes. Just till the ball, then."

She and Rachel went on talking continuously about Gaston. I did not. I was a little piqued, I think, because, though he did not exactly ignore me, few of his compliments came my way. He did include me when he talked of us as the Three Graces, but that was just politeness; and I noticed that his eyes were rarely on me and that Tamarisk and Rachel received most of his smiles.

He was, of course, an extremely attractive man. Crispin seemed dour beside him and the Grindle young men country bumpkins. That was unfair. The Grindle young men were very pleasant indeed and I thought the gentle, kindly smile of Daniel was more agreeable than the charm of Gaston Marchmont.

Mary Tucker worked on our dresses in the St. Aubyn's sewing-room and one day, when we went for a fitting, and they were as usual talking about Gaston Marchmont, I said: "I don't think he means half what he says."

"He does mean some of it," retorted Tamarisk. "You're only jealous because he doesn't take much notice of you."

I pondered that. Was I?

Rachel was the first of us to have a real admirer. It was Daniel Grindle. Rachel was very pretty in a rather helpless, feminine way, and Daniel was the sort of man, I decided, who would want to protect people.

I noticed the dreamy look in Daniel's eyes when he watched Rachel. So did Tamarisk. She could not understand why any young man could look at someone else when she was there. It was a tender look. I had seen him look like that on one occasion when I went to the farm and he was holding a new-born lamb in his arms.

"Well!" said Tamarisk. "He's only a farmer."

"There is nothing wrong with that," Rachel defended him fiercely. "And he's a good one. Aunt Hilda is very pleased that she married his father."

"Do you like him?" Tamarisk demanded of her.

"He's all right," said Rachel.

"Would you marry him?"

"What a question!" cried Rachel.

"You would! You would! Well, he might be all right for you."

Rachel did not answer. She was too embarrassed.

I guessed Tamarisk was comparing Daniel with Gaston Marchmont.

She went on to talk about him. She was so glad he was staying for the ball.

"I told him I'd never forgive him if he didn't stay, and he said, 'You leave me no alternative.' Wasn't that nice?"

"He does say the nicest things," admitted Rachel.

"He's a wonderful rider," went on Tamarisk. "On a horse he looks absolutely part of it . . . like one of those old gods."

"He looks like a cross between a highwayman and a cavalier," I said. "I could just imagine him saying, 'Stand and deliver!' or riding into battle against Cromwell."

"I always hated Cromwell," said Tamarisk. "Horrid old spoilsport. Closing theatres and things . . . I hate spoilsports."

"I don't think you could call Gaston Marchmont one of those by any stretch of the imagination," I said.

"I should think not!" said Tamarisk, smiling secretly.

She went on talking of him. He was an aristocrat, there was no doubt of that.

Rachel smiled dreamily, and I said: "Since he's so wonderful, I wonder he bothers to stay here."

"Perhaps," said Tamarisk mysteriously, "he has his reasons."

. . .

IT WAS ONLY a few days before the ball. Our dresses were made. Tamarisk told me that plants would be brought in from the greenhouses to decorate the ballroom and there would be a supper laid out in the diningroom—a buffet from which guests could help themselves. An orchestra had been engaged. Her mother was taking a little walk in the gardens every day so that she would be strong enough to attend the ball. She had had a special dress made for the occasion; the invitations had all gone out. It was the first time there had been a ball since Crispin's wife had died.

"Everything will be different now," she declared. "I'm of age. Even Crispin will have to realise that."

I went to see Flora. I sat in the garden near the mulberry bush and talked to her about the ball. I did not think she followed what I was talking about but she liked to hear my voice. Every now and then she would break in with a comment such as, "He was a bit restless last night. I think that tooth is troubling him." But it made no difference. I just went on talking and she sat there smiling and seemed really pleased that I was there.

When I left her I met Crispin. I think he was on his way to call at the cottage as I knew he did from time to time, for if there was anything wrong it was always attended to with the utmost promptness.

I cherished the memory of how concerned he had been when Flora broke the doll. I liked to think he cared so much for his old nannies.

"Hello," he said. "I can guess where you've been."

"She seems to like me to go."

"When Miss Lucy is not there?"

I flushed a little. "Well," I repeated, defending myself, "Flora seems to like me to go."

"Does she confide in you at all?"

"Confide? No, not really."

"You mean she does in a way?"

"Well, she does say odd things at times."

"What sort of things?"

"I think perhaps about the mulberry bush. She keeps saying something isn't there."

"Isn't there?"

"Yes. She keeps looking at it. I'd say she was a little worried about something there."

"I see. Well, it is good of you to call on her, being preoccupied as they all seem to be about the ball."

"Everyone is looking forward to it."

"Including you?"

I nodded. "I think it will be fun."

"And I hear the dashing hero has promised to attend."

"You mean . . . ?"

"You know whom I mean. Is that going to make it especially agreeable for you?"

"I think people are pleased that he is coming."

"People? Does that include you?"

"Yes, of course."

"I see. Well, I must not keep you."

He smiled at me, lifted his hat and bowed slightly.

Then he went on to call on the Lanes.

·   ·   ·

IT WAS THE day before the ball. I went over to the Bell House to see Rachel.

She looked different. There was a certain radiance about her. I thought she was about to confide in me, but she appeared to hesitate. I was reminded of that other occasion when she had been so scared and had turned to me. She was very different from Tamarisk; she was withdrawn, diffident, keeping her secrets.

I had another look at her dress. I had looked at my own fifty times.

"You'll wear it away looking at it," Lily had commented wryly. "Take it from me, love. You'll look a treat in it."

I was apprehensive. Would anyone want to dance with me? We had practised our steps again and again and we were quite proficient now; but what worried me was partners. Tamarisk would have plenty, not only because of her charm and good looks, but because the ball was taking place in her home and her mother was the hostess, in spite of all that Aunt Sophie had done to make it possible; people would feel it a duty to dance with Tamarisk. And Rachel would be all right. That helpless fragility had its appeal. But myself? Perhaps Jack Grindle would ask me, or Daniel. Crispin? I could not imagine what his dancing would be like.

Suddenly Rachel said: "Daniel has asked me to marry him."

I stared at her in amazement. The thought immediately came into my mind: she is the first of us to receive a proposal of marriage. Tamarisk wouldn't like that. She'd think she ought to be the first.

"How exciting!" I cried.

"I don't know. It's difficult."

"He is very nice and kind. You'd get on well with him. Have you said yes?"

She shook her head.

"Why? Don't you like him?"

"Yes, I do. Very much. We've always been friends, even before his father married my aunt, but of course we've seen a lot of each other since. A little while ago . . ." She stopped and frowned. "I . . . er . . . I do like him very much," she finished.

"I know," I said. "It's too soon. We've only just left school. Of course, some people marry when they are very young. And you have known each other for a long time."

"Yes, but it's different . . ."

"What have you said?"

"I hated telling him I couldn't. He looked . . . well, you know, so nice. He's always been kind to me. I felt safe with him . . . after . . ."

I knew exactly what she meant. I thought of her in that bedroom, hearing footsteps coming . . . pausing outside her door— most fortunately locked the second time— hearing his heavy breathing outside. She wanted to feel safe after that—as I did after those terrifying moments in the wood.

"You see," went on Rachel, "he thought it was all right. We'd been such friends."

"It will be all right. It's just because it's too soon. You're not ready yet."

She was staring into space.

"I don't think I ever can now . . ."

"But you like him a lot."

"Yes . . . I do . . . but . . ."

"You just need time," I said, thinking that

was just the remark Aunt Sophie would have made. "Wait till Tamarisk hears!"

"I shan't tell her. Please don't say anything about it, Freddie."

"Of course not. But I should love to see her face. She likes to be the first in everything."

I was smiling. I was convinced that Rachel would marry Daniel. It would be so right, married to Aunt Hilda's stepson. I was sure she would be as happy as Aunt Hilda was. It would be a wonderful ending after all they had suffered in a Bell House dominated by Mr. Dorian.

. . .

THE BALLROOM AT St. Aubyn's looked splendid. Potted palms and flowering shrubs had been brought in from the greenhouses and scattered around in artistic fashion; the floor had been polished with French chalk; there was a dais at one end and on this were the musicians in pale pink shirts and black dinner jackets. It was all very grand and awesome.

Mrs. St. Aubyn, miraculously restored to health for the occasion, greeted the guests. There was only one concession to her previous state: she sat regally in an ornate chair

which people approached with great defer-
ence.

Aunts Sophie and Hilda hovered round
her as though to remind people that their
protégées were of equal importance to Tamarisk; but, of course, this was St. Aubyn's
Park and Mrs. St. Aubyn was seen as the
main hostess. The ball was one in which Rachel and I had been privileged to join.

Rachel and I sat on either side of Tamarisk; and Aunt Sophie was beside me, Aunt
Hilda beside Rachel. I felt much less confident than I had in my bedroom when both
Aunt Sophie and Lily had declared that I
looked quite beautiful.

"The Belle of the Ball, that's what you'll
be," Aunt Sophie had said.

And Lily commented: "Well, Miss Fred, I
never thought a dress could do all that for a
girl. You look a real treat, you do."

However, beside Tamarisk, flamboyant in
flame-coloured chiffon, and Rachel in soft
blue *crêpe de Chine,* I realised that I was far
from being the Belle of the Ball, and what
looked "a treat" in my bedroom might look
less delectable in an elegant ballroom.

As soon as the dancing began Gaston
Marchmont was standing before us. He
turned his eyes upwards and said something
about a trio of enchantresses. Then he asked

Tamarisk if she would honour him. It was what she expected, as the important Miss St. Aubyn; and she was gracefully whisked away as the Grindle brothers came up. Daniel then danced with Rachel and I went off with Jack.

Jack danced well. He commented on the excellence of the floor, the size of the ballroom, and that he expected, now that Tamarisk was growing up, there would be more such occasions as this. It was light, trivial conversation.

When the first dance was over, Gaston Marchmont danced with Rachel, Tamarisk with Daniel and I with a middle-aged friend of the St. Aubyns whom I had met once before.

I guessed that I should dance next with Gaston. He would have to dance with the three of us, he would decide, and I felt a little irritated. I did not want to be selected as a matter of protocol, or duty, whatever it was. I knew he would not really want to dance with me.

When my partner took me back I was surprised to see Crispin talking to the aunts.

He stood up when he saw me approaching and, just at that moment, Gaston Marchmont came back with Rachel. Rachel looked flushed and happy.

"That was very pleasant," said Gaston. "I must compliment you, Miss Rachel, on your skill on the dance floor."

Rachel murmured something and the music for the next dance was beginning. I saw Gaston's eyes on me, and he was about to speak when Crispin laid his hand on my arm and said firmly: "This is promised to me."

We moved onto the floor. I saw Gaston's startled look as we did so.

Crispin was saying: "I hope I have not disappointed you by snatching you from the arms of the fascinating Marchmont?"

I laughed. I was indeed very pleased and excited.

"Oh no," I said. "He was only going to ask me because he thought he ought to."

"Are you sure that he is so mindful of what is expected of him?"

"In that way, I am sure he is."

"Are you being a little cryptic? You think in other matters he might not be so eager to carry out his duty?"

"I didn't mean that at all. I just thought he would always behave, as he thought, impeccably in social matters."

"I see you have not been quite so deeply impressed as the others have. I am glad of that. I am afraid I don't dance as well as he does. He really is adept. Talking of dancing, you might find me a little clumsy. Shall we sit down? I think that would be more comfortable for you."

He did not wait for my reply but led me to two seats among the potted palms.

We sat and watched the dancers in silence for a few seconds, and I saw Gaston dance round with one of the guests.

Crispin's eyes followed him and he said: "Yes, an adept. Tell me, how do you think Miss Flora likes the new doll we found for her? Do you think she has accepted it?"

"At times I do. At others . . . I'm not sure. I fancy she looks sometimes as if she knew it is only a doll. Her face puckers up."

"Yes?"

"Well, just that."

"Did it before? I mean, her face pucker up?"

"I'm not sure. I think it might have."

"Poor Flora!" He was silent for a while, then he said: "You still pay your periodic visits to the cottage then."

"Yes."

"It's difficult to talk with all this noise. We'll have supper together. I'll come for you then. Do you have a card or something?"

I gave him my dance programme and he scribbled his initials on that space for the dance before supper.

"There," he said. "You'll have plenty of chances to dance with people who know how to do it. But that one is mine."

I was disappointed that he had only asked for that dance, and at the same time his manner was somewhat peremptory. He had not exactly asked but taken for granted that I should agree. That was typical and reminded me of Tamarisk.

I could not resist saying: "Do you always tell people what they should do?"

He looked steadily at me, raised his eyebrows and smiled.

"It is a way of getting what one wants quickly," he said.

"Does it always work?"

"Alas, no."

"Suppose I had already promised the supper dance?"

"You hadn't, had you? It was not booked on your programme."

"Well, it's only just started and . . ."

"So, it's all right then, isn't it? I thought we'd have supper together. I want to talk to you."

I felt pleased about this and I noticed that, when he took me back to my chair, several people looked at us with interest.

I danced once with Gaston. He came up soon after Crispin had brought me back.

Crispin had then departed. I think he had no desire to dance, which he rather despised, no doubt because he did not do it well.

I saw him later in conversation with a man who, I think, was one of the estate managers, and later with an elderly man who, I had heard, had an estate some miles from St. Aubyn's and who had brought his wife and daughter to the ball.

Gaston was such a good dancer that he made me feel I was one too.

He told me I looked charming and my dress was his favourite colour. I guessed that when he danced with Tamarisk flame-red was his favourite, and when he was with Rachel it would be cornflower blue. Well, he might not be sincere, but he did try to please, which was different from Crispin.

He talked about St. Aubyn's Park and Crispin. It was a very large estate, was it not? Probably one of the biggest in Wiltshire.

"Tamarisk tells me that you are interested in an odd couple who have a cottage on the estate."

"Do you mean Miss Lucy and Miss Flora Lane?"

"Are those their names? What is all that about a doll one of them carries around and thinks is a baby?"

"That is true."

"Strange, isn't it?"

"It's been going on for a long time."

"Thinks the doll is the lord of the manor?"

"When he was a baby, she was his nurse."

"And he looks after these sisters with very special care."

"They were both his nannies at one time. People feel like that about their nannies. It's very kind of him to take such care of them."

"Bountiful indeed. Tamarisk says you get along with the mad one well and that you have a very special interest in it all."

"I am sorry for them."

"You have a kind heart, I see, and you visit them often. Tamarisk tells me that you go there when the other sister—not the crazy one—is away, and you're hoping to find out what made the poor old thing lose her reason."

"Tamarisk told you that!"

"Is it not so?"

"Well . . ."

"Of course," he said, "we all like to get to the bottom of these things. And it must have been something that turned her brain, don't you think?"

"I don't know."

"Perhaps through your research you will discover it."

The dance had come to an end.

"We must dance again," he said. "This has been most enjoyable. I expect you are fully engaged."

"There are one or two," I said, and he conducted me back to my seat.

After that I danced with several young men and I wondered why Gaston Marchmont was so interested in the sisters. I supposed Tamarisk had talked about them in her usual dramatic way. She always exaggerated. And, of course, Flora and her doll were unusual.

I soon forgot Gaston. I was waiting impatiently for the supper dance. I was afraid that Crispin might have forgotten, but as soon as the dance was announced, he was there.

He took my arm and led me onto the floor where people were beginning to dance. We went round the room once, then he said: "We'll go now and get the table we want. Otherwise we might have to share with others."

He led me to the two chairs where we had sat before. A table had been set up beside them. It was laid with glasses and cutlery.

"This will do," he said. "Put your programme on the table to warn other people that it is already taken. Then come along with me and we'll get some food."

A long table had been set up on trestles in the dining-room. There were candles set at intervals and an abundance of food—cold chicken, salmon, various meats and salads. It looked deliciously tempting. We were the first to arrive.

Crispin led the way and we helped ourselves to what we wanted. When we returned to the table there was a bottle of champagne in an icebucket standing there.

The music had stopped and people were now leaving the ballroom for the dining-room.

"What foresight!" I said. "To be the first."

"Indeed. We have avoided the crowd and here is our table with everything waiting for us."

He sat opposite me. One of the servants had come to us and was pouring the champagne.

Crispin looked searchingly at me and raised his glass.

"To Frederica," he said. "Her coming out. Are you pleased to have left childhood behind?"

"I think so."

"What do you propose to do now?"

"I haven't thought much of that."

"Most girls want to get married. That seems the ultimate goal. What of you?"

"I hadn't thought of that."

"Oh come. All girls think of it."

"Perhaps you don't know all girls. Only some."

"And perhaps you are right. In any case, here you are on the threshold. Your first ball. How did you enjoy it?"

"Very much."

"You sound surprised."

"One really doesn't know how it will go. Suppose no one asked you to dance?"

"That would put you in an awkward position. I'll swear you don't like to wait to be asked. You would like to be the one to do the asking."

"Anybody surely would."

"Then you could ask Gaston Marchmont to dance with you."

"I wouldn't do that."

"Oh? I'd forgotten that you are not as impressionable as some. Very discerning—that is you."

"I hope . . . a little."

"And then I come along and demand you leave the supper dance for me." He was looking at me intently. "You and I have had some unusual encounters, haven't we? Do you remember when we went and bought the doll? And then . . . there was that affair in Barrow Wood."

I shuddered. Did I remember? It was something I should never forget. I could be transported there at a second's notice. It was always ready to leap out and confront me.

He put his hand across the table and held mine briefly.

"I'm sorry. I shouldn't have mentioned it."

"It doesn't matter," I replied. "But it is not something I can forget."

"It was a terrible experience. Thank God I happened to be passing!"

"He died . . . because of it," I said. "I can't forget that."

"It was the best thing that could have happened to him. He hadn't the courage to face up to the fact that he had betrayed what he really was when all the time he was putting on that saintly mask to hide the man beneath."

"He must have been very desperate when he went into the stable and hanged himself."

"Don't think of it in that way. Only be glad that I came along when I did. I can have no regrets."

"Do you never feel that he died because he knew you despised him? There in the wood I thought you had killed him. You left him there. That did not worry you?"

"No. He was a coward . . . a hypocrite, setting himself up to be a saint when he could behave like the lowest animal. I can only rejoice that I came along when I did and in what happened after as a consequence. The best thing he did was to rid the world of his obnoxious presence—and, my dear Frederica, your well-being was far more important than his miserable life. Look at it that way and you'll have no soft feelings for the miserable creature. The world is well rid of him. I would have been justified in killing him, but it was much more convenient that he did it himself."

There was no sympathy in his face, but I could not help telling myself that through it all Mr. Dorian had *wanted* to be good.

Crispin went on: "Forgive me. I shouldn't have brought this up. I wanted to be sure that you weren't brooding on it. You must not, you know. Life can be ugly sometimes. You have to realise this. Remember what is pleasant and cut out of your mind what is not."

He was smiling at me now very benignly and I remembered Tamarisk's saying once that when people had rescued someone from something horrid they liked them because they reminded them of how good and noble they themselves were.

"Would you like more salmon?" he asked.

"No, thanks."

"I'd like to hear more of what you think about Miss Flora. She talks to you, doesn't she?"

"A little. But I've told you, it doesn't make much sense."

"And you think she might realise sometimes that the doll has been changed?"

"It really wasn't very much like the old one, was it? She had had the first one a long time and they make different styles now."

"But she hasn't actually said . . . ?"

"No. She just looks puzzled . . . but then she often has before."

"As though she is trying to remember?"

"In a way. But perhaps more as though she is trying *not* to remember."

"As though she is trying to tell you something."

I hesitated and he was watching me intently.

"Yes?" he queried. "As though she is trying to tell you something."

"There is that picture in the nursery," I said. "She is always looking at it and when she does her lips move. I can see she is saying to herself . . . 'a secret never to be told.' "

"So it is that picture . . ."

"I don't know. It's what it stands for, I suppose."

I remembered my conversation with Gaston Marchmont earlier in the evening, and I went on: "Something must have happened to her to make her lose her senses . . . something very dramatic. Perhaps it concerns some secret which must never be told."

He was suddenly quiet and stared down at his plate as I went on.

"I think it must have happened a long time ago when you were a baby. It frightened her so much that she can't accept it. Perhaps it was her fault and she is pretending it didn't happen . . . and she wants to be back in those days before it did. That's why she wants you to stay a baby."

He said slowly: "That's an interesting theory."

"I should have thought if something *had* happened, people would know about it. Unless it was something only Flora was aware of. It is rather mysterious. Once or twice I've heard her mention a Gerry Westlake."

"Gerry Westlake?"

"I think that was the name."

"What did she say about him?"

"She just said his name."

"There are Westlakes in the neighbourhood. A middle-aged couple with a daughter who is in service somewhere and there was a son who went abroad. Australia or New Zealand, I think. I don't know much about them."

"Well, I've only heard her murmur his name once or maybe twice."

"I think she rather likes you."

"She likes me to call, I'm sure."

"Only when Miss Lucy is away."

"I get the impression Miss Lucy doesn't like people to call. Perhaps she thinks they might upset Flora."

"But you don't let that deter you."

"Well, I quite like talking to Flora and I know she likes to talk to me. I don't see any harm in it."

"And you are naturally curious by nature."

"I suppose I am."

"And you are intrigued by the secret of those magpies, and you are wondering if it is at the root of what has robbed poor Miss Flora of her wits."

"I have an idea that it might have been due to some terrible shock. These things happen."

"And Miss Frederica Hammond has become a part-time sleuth and is determined to solve the mystery."

"That is an exaggeration."

He laughed at me.

"But containing a grain of truth?"

"Well, I suppose anyone would be interested."

"And particularly some." He lifted his glass. "I suppose I should wish you well in your endeavours."

"If the cause of something is known, there is more chance of putting it right."

"Might the truth not be too horrifying to disclose? In which case it might make everything worse."

"I suppose that is a possibility."

"We've talked about others all the time. Tell me about yourself. What do you do when you are not visiting Miss Flora?"

"It is so recently that I left school, I have not really settled to anything yet."

"There will be other occasions like tonight. They will keep you busy. I believe several events are being planned for my sister, and I daresay you and Rachel Grey will be joining in them."

"The three of us have been together ever since I came to live here."

"You have been happy in Harper's Green?"

"Very happy. My Aunt Sophie has been wonderful to me."

"I was sorry to hear about your mother."

"It was sad because she never enjoyed life.

My father had gone and she would have liked to go back to her old home, but it had been sold. She wasn't happy living in a small house where she could see it all the time."

"So Harper's Green was a happier place to be in."

"I was very lucky to have Aunt Sophie."

"Your father . . . ?"

"I have never seen him. He and my mother parted."

He nodded. "These things happen."

I wondered if he were thinking of the wife who had left him.

"Well, when you marry I hope you will be as happy as you are now in the Rowans."

"Thank you. I hope you will be happy too."

"You know what happened. There are few secrets in Harper's Green apart from the one which claims so much of your attention. My wife left me. Perhaps one could not blame her for that." He spoke rather bitterly and I felt I should change the subject, but I could not think of anything to say, and we fell into silence.

Then I waved my arm, indicating the room.

"What a lot of trouble it must have taken to prepare all this."

"We have a very good housekeeper and

butler. They are practised in this sort of
thing and were glad to have an opportunity
to show their skills." He went on: "She left
me for someone else and then she was killed
in a railway accident."

"It must have been a terrible shock for
you."

"What? Her elopement or her death?"

"Both," I said.

He did not answer. I said rather clumsily:
"Never mind. You might find someone else."

I was thinking of Lady Fiona, who was
said to be so suitable, and it occurred to me
that the conversation was taking a rather unusual turn which was embarrassing us both.

"Oh yes," he said. "Had you anyone in
mind?"

I had to go on. "There was some talk
about a Lady Fiona."

He laughed. "People do talk, don't they?
We are good friends. There was never a sug-
gestion of marriage. She has, as a matter of
fact, married recently. I was at her wedding.
Her husband is a friend of mine."

"So it was just gossip."

"There is always gossip. Depend upon it.
If people think a man should settle down
they will try to find a wife for him."

I was amazed at the relief I felt.

People were leaving the tables now and the clock was striking midnight.

"Alas," said Crispin, "this pleasant interlude is coming to an end. Thank you for talking to me."

"I have enjoyed it so much."

"And you did not mind my insisting that you join me?"

"It was the best part of the evening," I said frankly.

He smiled and, rising, led me to a group who were forming a ring in the centre of the ballroom. The orchestra played "Auld Lang Syne" and we all joined in the singing, clasping hands and shaking them with fervour.

Archie Grindle drove Aunt Sophie and me home before taking Rachel and her aunt back to the Bell House.

Lily was waiting to greet us.

"I've got some hot milk waiting for you," she said. "And how was the ball?"

"It was very good indeed," said Aunt Sophie. "That hot milk will be nice. It will help us to sleep after all the excitement. Where are we having it?"

"Kitchen," announced Lily. "Come on. It's all but ready."

So we sat there drinking milk and answering Lily's questions.

"I reckon they were fighting each other to dance with you," said Lily.

"That is a slight exaggeration," Aunt Sophie told her. "But there were plenty of partners. And what do you think? She was monopolised by the lord of the manor."

"Get away with you!" said Lily.

"It's true. He doesn't go in for dancing much, but it was the supper dance with our young lady and he booked it well in advance to make sure of it. Isn't that right, Freddie?"

"Yes, it was."

"Well, I'll be jiggered," cried Lily.

"And there he was, plying her with champagne."

"You don't say! Champagne! That's heady stuff."

"It was all very grand, I can tell you. I remember balls at Cedar Hall. At one time they terrified me. I was always afraid of being a wallflower, till I told myself I didn't care a jot and if the young men didn't want to dance with me, well, I didn't want to dance with them either."

"That's the spirit," said Lily. "Silly young things. Didn't know what they were missing, I reckon. Well, it wasn't like that with Miss Fred by all accounts."

"By no means. What did Crispin St. Aubyn talk about, Freddie?"

I thought back. "It was really mostly about the Lanes," I said. "He is interested in them and he wanted to know what I thought about Flora."

"He really is very good to them," said Aunt Sophie.

She sat sipping her milk, looking back in her mind to those days at Cedar Hall when, I supposed, the partners came to my mother and not to her.

I agreed with Lily that they were indeed silly young things.

And I loved Aunt Sophie more than ever.

The Elopement

The day after the ball Tamarisk and I were invited to tea at the Bell House. I could never enter the place without marvelling at the change in it. I had the impression that the object had been to remove all trace of its previous occupant. There was only the grim stable door to remind me. It was locked, I saw, and I wondered whether anyone even went in there now.

I was soon immersed in conversation. Tamarisk told us of her triumphs. The ball had been a great success. Her mother was delighted; she had said it was quite like old times and they must do it again.

Tamarisk had danced six times with Gaston Marchmont. Wasn't it a shame, though, he was going off that very day to Scotland to deal with his estates there.

"Will he ever come back, I wonder?" I said.

Both Tamarisk and Rachel looked at me in amazement.

"Of course he will!" cried Tamarisk.

"He must," said Rachel.

Daniel came in while we were having tea. He sat down near Rachel and I asked if he had enjoyed the ball.

"I believe it went off very well," he replied cautiously. "Everyone seemed to think so."

"It was a great success," Tamarisk assured him.

Aunt Hilda came in and I kept thinking of her as she used to be, with that apprehensive look on her face, without the pretty dress and the comb in her hair. How different Mr. Grindle must be from Mr. Dorian. Crispin was right. What was good for so many people could not be wrong.

I noticed Tamarisk was cool with Daniel. She could not forgive him for paying more attention to Rachel than he did to her.

Jack Grindle joined us. He told us he had driven Gaston Marchmont in the trap to the station and had seen him on the train to London.

"He'll be going straight to Scotland," he said. "There seems to be some business up there which he has to settle."

"He'll be back," put in Tamarisk confidently.

"I imagine he's a very busy man. He says he'll come again and stay awhile. He enjoyed his stay very much," went on Jack, "and it was fun having him. He livened us all up a bit."

"He certainly did," agreed Tamarisk, with a smile.

I wondered if she knew more about Gaston Marchmont's plans than the rest of us.

Perhaps she did, for three weeks later Gaston Marchmont did return. He went to the Grindles' farm and asked if he could stay awhile. If it were not convenient, he could of course put up at an hotel but he had so enjoyed staying with them before, so perhaps for a little while he could be with them.

Jack said they would be delighted and certainly he must stay with them. They would be quite hurt if he did not.

· · ·

IT WAS SOME five days since Gaston Marchmont had returned. I had seen very little of him during that time. I was helping Aunt Sophie in the garden when I heard the sound of horse's hoofs and the next moment Lily came running into the garden.

"Mr. St. Aubyn's here," she said. "He wants to see Miss Fred."

Crispin was already coming into the garden.

"Tamarisk has gone," he said. "Have you any idea where?"

"Gone!" cried Aunt Sophie. "Gone where?"

"That's what I want to find out." He was looking at me. "Do you know where she might be?"

"I? No."

"I thought she might have told you."

"She hasn't told me anything."

"Well, she is not at home. She must have left late last night. Her bed hasn't been slept in."

I shook my head. "I saw her yesterday and, yes, she did seem excited."

"Didn't you ask her what about?"

"No. She usually tells people if there is something going on, so I didn't think much about it."

He was clearly anxious, and realising that I could not be of any help, he left.

We talked about it all through the morning.

"This is a funny business," said Aunt Sophie. "I wonder what's happened. She's up to something, I reckon."

We speculated on where she could have gone without coming to any reasonable conclusion. I expected her to turn up later. She might have left in a fit of pique. Perhaps she had quarrelled with her mother.

Then Jack Grindle reported that Gaston Marchmont had also gone. He had not just disappeared as Tamarisk had. He had left a note to say that he had been called away on urgent business and would explain when he returned, which he hoped would be shortly.

People immediately linked the disappearance of Tamarisk with that of Gaston Marchmont and speculation was rife.

I walked over to the Bell House to see Rachel. Aunt Hilda told me she was in the orchard. The garden of the Bell House consisted of some two acres. There was a sizeable lawn, which, if there was some reason why the church garden parties and fêtes could not be held at St. Aubyn's, had on those rare occasions provided a substitute. Parts of it were quite wild and trees grew thick near the orchard, which was a favourite haven for Rachel, I knew.

I found her there and as I approached, I called out: "Have you heard the news?"

"News? What news?"

"Tamarisk and Gaston Marchmont have

disappeared. They must have gone together."

"Oh no!" she cried.

"It is rather a coincidence . . . both going off like that at the same time."

"They can't be together?"

"Why not?"

"He wouldn't . . ."

"He danced with her more than anyone else at the ball."

"That was because he had to, because the ball was given at St. Aubyn's. He had to dance often with Tamarisk."

"*I* believe they are together."

"We'll know when Gaston comes back. I'm sure he will come back."

"But they are both missing . . . together!"

"There must be some explanation."

She was staring into the little stream which ran through the orchard. Her expression was one of intense apprehension. It might have been desolation.

.   .   .

SHE WAS RIGHT. He did come back, and with Tamarisk.

Tamarisk was radiant. There was a gold ring on the third finger of her left hand. Life was wonderful, she declared. She was Mrs.

Gaston Marchmont. She and Gaston had eloped and gone to Gretna Green, where you could get married without any fuss; and that was how she and Gaston had wanted it to be. They had not wanted to wait for the fuss and preparation necessary for a conventional ceremony. They wanted to be together without delay.

Harper's Green was in a state of great excitement. It was the most dramatic event since Josiah Dorian had hanged himself in the Bell House stable.

"The things that happen in this placc!" said Lily. "It makes you wonder what's coming next."

Aunt Sophie said it was an odd business.

"Why did they have to elope? If he's all he makes out to be there wouldn't be any objection. Planning a grand wedding would have been a real tonic to Mrs. St. Aubyn, and I can't believe that Tamarisk wouldn't have liked that. It looks a bit fishy to me, as though the gentleman might not want too much probing."

Gaston Marchmont stayed at St. Aubyn with the bride. That was to be until he had sorted out his affairs and they could get a home of their own.

The day after their return, I met Crispin

riding back from Devizes. He stopped when he saw me and dismounted.

"Are you sure," he asked, "that you didn't know of Tamarisk's plans?"

"Absolutely sure."

"So she gave you no hint?"

"Of course not."

He was looking very angry.

I said: "I think she is very happy, isn't she? It was what she wanted."

He stared ahead, his mouth grim. "She is completely ignorant," he said. "This is an impulsive act which could ruin her life. She is just out of school."

I felt my indignation rising. That was what he thought of me. A child just out of school.

"But they are in love!" I said.

"In love!" he retorted scornfully.

"You may not believe it but some people do fall in love."

He looked at me impatiently. "If she gave you a hint of what was in her mind, you should have warned me, or someone."

"She didn't, I keep telling you, and if she had, why should I have reported it to you? You would have tried to spoil it for them."

I walked away. I felt very upset. He did not care for people's feelings. I had begun to think that he was interested in me—only mildly though—but I supposed it was only due to the fact that I visited Lucy and Flora Lane. He was still the same man who had said in my hearing, "Who is the plain child . . . ?"

. . .

I HAD NOT seen Rachel since Tamarisk's return, and one afternoon I called at the Bell House.

I found her where I had expected, in the orchard by the stream. I was horrified by her air of dejection.

I sat down beside her and said, "Rachel, what is it?"

"You have heard that Tamarisk and Gaston are married."

"Everyone is talking about it."

"I just could not believe it, Freddie. When they went away together . . ."

"I suppose we might have guessed it was something like that."

She was silent, and I said: "Rachel, were you in love with him?"

I put an arm round her and she shivered.

I went on with sudden inspiration: "And he let you believe . . ."

She nodded.

"I never thought he was sincere," I said. "He talked in that extravagant way to all the girls, and, for that matter, to Aunt Sophie and Mrs. St. Aubyn. One just knew it didn't really mean anything."

"It meant something to us," said Rachel.

"Do you mean . . . ?"

"He told me he loved *me* and all the time it was really Tamarisk."

"He danced a lot with her at the ball and they had supper together."

"I thought that was just because . . ."

"Didn't you realise that all those flattering compliments didn't mean a thing?"

"It wasn't like that, Freddie . . . not with us. It was something serious. And then he just went off and married Tamarisk."

"Poor Rachel. You didn't understand. It didn't *mean* anything."

"It did. It did! I know it did."

"Then why . . . why did he marry Tamarisk?"

"I suppose it was because she is who she is. She's rich, isn't she? She is bound to be. She's a St. Aubyn."

"Well, if that's the reason, you're well rid of him. He's not like Daniel. Daniel really loves *you,* not anything you can bring him."

"You talk like an old aunt, Freddie. You don't understand."

"I understand that he led you to think he was in love with you and then went off and married Tamarisk."

She said desperately: "Yes, yes. That's what he has done."

"Well then, you are well rid of him. It is Tamarisk whom we should be sorry for."

"I would do anything to be where she is."

"Be reasonable. Daniel loves you. You like him. He'll be a good husband because he is a good man. Oh, I know he doesn't dance well and travel around and know how everything should be done in top circles. That doesn't count for much. It's goodness . . . fidelity."

"Don't go on like that, Freddie. It's like some sermon. I can't bear it."

"All right," I said. "But I'm glad it wasn't you he married. Actually, I think Tamarisk has made a big mistake. Crispin St. Aubyn thinks so too."

We sat for a long time staring at the stream and saying nothing.

I felt very uneasy about Rachel.

•   •   •

MRS. ST. AUBYN roused herself. Marriage at Gretna Green was all very well, but she would like to see a proper wedding in our own church.

Both Tamarisk and Gaston were quite agreeable, and this was arranged.

Mrs. St. Aubyn's health had improved

wonderfully. She had been planning more balls for Tamarisk in an endeavour to launch her daughter into society, but Tamarisk had forestalled her by making the process unnecessary.

The wedding, of course, would not be all that she desired; if she had had more time, it would have been better, but she wanted to get the ceremony over as soon as possible just in case there were those who felt the simple marriage which had already taken place was no true one.

Banns were read in church. I was a bridesmaid; and the Reverend Hetherington conducted the ceremony. Tamarisk wore a wedding gown made of silk and lace which her mother had worn at her wedding, and Mrs. St. Aubyn, though not quite well enough to attend the church, received the guests at the reception at St. Aubyn's afterwards.

Now no one could doubt that Tamarisk and Gaston Marchmont were well and truly married.

Rachel had not been in church. She was not well, we were told. She was closer to me than Tamarisk had ever been, and I was anxious about her. I could not get out of my mind the memory of her sitting by the stream with that look of abject misery in her eyes. All the time I was at the reception, thoughts of her kept intruding into my mind.

Aunt Sophie and I had returned home afterwards and still I was thinking of Rachel. I had a premonition that something terrible might happen.

Dusk was falling and I knew I could not rest until I saw Rachel. I slipped out of the Rowans and ran all the way to the Bell House.

I had to pass by the stables. As I did so, my heart bounded with shock. The stable door had been kept locked and now it was unlocked.

I paused and looked at it. I felt a great revulsion. The place filled me with horror. I felt that if I pushed open that door and went in I should see Mr. Dorian hanging there. I would see those frightening eyes looking at me accusingly. They would seem to say to me it was because of you this happened to me.

That was foolish. It was not because of me. Crispin had made that very clear. I was foolish to think like that.

As I stood hesitating, there was a slight breeze and the door moved. I heard the faint creaking sound as it did so.

Why should someone open the door now?

Why had I been aware of this strange impulse to come to the Bell House?

I had a feeling that Rachel was in danger and needed me.

I steeled myself. I went to the stable door. I pushed it open and went in.

"Rachel!" I cried.

She was sitting on the floor and there was a rope in her hands.

"What are you doing?" I cried.

She said fiercely: "What are *you* doing here?"

"I had to see you. I felt you were calling me. Then I saw the stable door was open."

"You should go away."

"No, I won't. What are you doing in this awful place?"

She looked at the rope in her hands and did not answer.

"Rachel!" I cried.

"He did it," she said. "It seemed the only way to him."

"What are you talking about?"

"Freddie, I don't want to be here anymore. I can't. It's too awful."

"What are you saying?"

"I can't bear it. I can't live through what will have to come."

"You're talking nonsense. People have to live through whatever comes. It's Tamarisk and Gaston Marchmont, isn't it? He made you believe you were the one. Well, I reckon you're lucky not to be involved with him. Think of that."

"You don't know what you are saying."

"You mustn't think of this," I went on. "This dreadful place . . . I can't bear it. Let's get out of here. Come with me. Let's go to the orchard and talk."

"There's nothing to say. There is nothing that will make any difference."

"Perhaps we can think of something."

She shook her head.

"Well, I'm going to try," I insisted. "But not here. I can't endure this place. Come with me. Let's get out of here."

I took the rope from her hands and threw it into a corner. I put my arm through hers.

"Have you got the stable key?" I went on.

She took it from the pocket of her dress and gave it to me. I led her to the door. I looked back at those rafters, almost expecting to see him there leering at me.

I shut the door firmly, locked it and put the key in my pocket.

"Now," I said, "we'll go to the orchard where we can talk."

We sat there. She was shivering and I was trying not to think of *her* body hanging limply from those rafters. Would she have done it? She was in a mood to. She really was so wretched that she did not want to live.

I had come in time. I had known I must go to her. There was a very special friendship between us. I was here to look after her.

"Tell me all about it," I said firmly.

"It's worse than you think. You think I have just been jilted."

"Did he say he would marry you?"

"Well, not exactly . . ."

"Implied it?" I said.

She nodded. "I thought we were going to be married. That was why . . . it all seemed so natural. You see, Freddie, it's not only that he's married Tamarisk. I . . . I'm going to have a baby."

I was astounded. I stared at the stream in horror. I dared not look at Rachel for fear she should see how shocked I was.

"What . . . what are you going to do?" I stammered.

"You saw what I was going to do. It seemed the only way."

"Oh no. That's not the way."

"How else?"

"People do have babies."

"They are supposed to be married. Then it would be wonderful. If you are not . . . it's terrible. You are disgraced forever."

"Not forever. It comes right in the end sometimes. Tamarisk doesn't know?"

"Of course not. Nobody knows but myself . . . and now you."

"Not . . . him? He doesn't know?"

"No."

"He is . . . despicable."

"It's no use talking like that. It doesn't help."

"That's true. He's married to Tamarisk now. Oh, Rachel, what can we do?"

"I don't see any way out of it, Freddie. That's why . . ."

"You must not do that. Everyone would know. So what difference does it make?"

"I shouldn't be here to care."

"There must be a way."

"What? I don't know of one."

"Suppose you told him?"

"What good would that do?"

"Oh, poor, poor Rachel! But we'll think of something. It's a pity it isn't Daniel."

"Daniel!"

"Daniel is such a good man. He would never be like Gaston Marchmont, who is callous. I don't know how anyone can care for him."

"He is very charming . . . different from other people."

I was not listening to her, for an idea had

struck me. I wanted to think about it, and keep it to myself until I had.

"I can't see any way out," said Rachel. "And, Freddie, I can't face it. I can just imagine the fuss . . . the scandal . . . everyone in Harper's Green talking about it."

I said: "Don't do anything yet. Don't say anything. Will you promise me this? You won't do anything until I see you tomorrow. Will you promise me that?"

"What are you going to do?"

"There might be a way out of this."

"What do you mean?"

"I don't know yet. I just want you to promise me one thing. That you won't do anything until you hear from me."

"When shall I hear?"

"Soon. I promise you."

"Tomorrow?"

"Yes, tomorrow. This is a secret. Please don't do anything yet. I think there might be a solution."

"You're not going to see Gaston?"

"No. Certainly not! I never want to see him again. Please trust me, Rachel."

"Really, Freddie, I can't see . . ."

"Look here. Why did I go into the stables just then? It was because something made me. I knew it was important that I should. It is because there is something special between us. I have an idea that this can work out. Please do as I say. Trust me, Rachel."

She nodded. "Till tomorrow then."

I left her then. I felt the key in my pocket as I ran from the Bell House to Grindle's Farm.

I prayed all the way, let Daniel be there! Please, please, God, let him be there.

My prayer was answered. He was the first person I saw when I reached the farmhouse.

"Oh, Daniel!" I panted. "I am so pleased to see you. I must talk to you. It's very important."

"My dear Freddie . . ." he began.

"It's about Rachel," I said. "I am very, very worried. Where can we talk?"

At the mention of Rachel's name he looked alarmed.

"Come into my workshop," he said. "It is just here."

I went with him. In the room there were two stools and a bench with tools lying on it.

"Now," he said, "what is it?"

"She . . . was going to kill herself."

"What?"

"Daniel, I'm afraid she will. She is very, very unhappy. I know you love her. So do I. She is my best friend. I couldn't bear it if . . ."

"What is all this about?"

"It's Gaston Marchmont."

He turned pale and I saw his fists clench.

"What has he done?"

"He's married Tamarisk."

"And Rachel?"

"She thought he would marry her."

"My God," he said quietly.

"Yes, he's a . . . philanderer. He courted Rachel . . ." I hesitated. I was praying silently again. Please, God, let me do this right. I have to explain to him . . . for Rachel. Let me do it the right way and let him understand. It's the only way. If he won't help, she'll kill herself.

I steeled myself afresh. "She . . . she is going to have a baby. I found her in the stables where Mr. Dorian hanged himself. Something led me there. We're very great friends. Daniel, I would do anything I could for Rachel. I thought you might too."

He stared at me unbelievingly. I thought, he is shocked. He is horrified. He doesn't love her as much as I thought he did.

"She can't face it, Daniel," I pleaded. "She can't face it . . . alone."

"In the stables," he muttered. "Where the old man . . ."

"That must have been why she thought of it. She was going to do it, Daniel. If I hadn't gone in . . ."

"Rachel . . ." he murmured.

"She was so unhappy. Oh, how I hate that man!"

The silence seemed to go on for a long time. Then I said: "If only he hadn't come here. I thought perhaps you might love her enough. You did ask her to marry you."

"She didn't accept me. It was because of that man . . ."

"People make mistakes about other people, Daniel. If you really loved her . . . I thought you did. It's why I came. I'm sorry now. I thought if you really loved her, you could marry her. Then it would be all right about the baby."

I was going too far. That sense of the important part I must play—had been chosen to play—in this tragedy was fast disappearing. I was trying to arrange other people's lives. It was arrogant. It was meddling . . . and Rachel's life was at stake.

I heard myself saying: "I suppose you think it is no business of mine. But she is my friend. I care about her . . . so much. I just can't let her kill herself when there is a way out."

Daniel spoke then. "You're a good girl," he said. "You did right to come to me."

"Oh, Daniel, did I? You will then? Oh, thank you . . . thank you."

He said: "I'll go and see her."

"There isn't much time. I was afraid to leave her. Daniel . . . will you come now?"

"Yes," he said. "I'll come now."

He sat me in front of him on his horse and we went to the Bell House.

When we arrived and had dismounted, he said: "Go home now, Freddie. I will go to Rachel. I shall come to see you before I go back to the farm."

"Oh, Daniel . . . thank you . . . thank you."

My lips were trembling. I was still praying inwardly that he would do what I wanted him to.

He looked at me for a few moments and I could see that he was very moved.

Then he kissed me lightly on the forehead and said, as he had before, "You are a good girl."

He turned away, and I went home and straight to my room. I did not talk to anyone of what had happened . . . not even Aunt Sophie.

•   •   •

A MONTH LATER Rachel and Daniel were married. It was a quiet wedding, as there was just enough time for the banns to be read in church. I was well aware that in due course people would be nodding their heads and whispering that the reason for haste was now clear.

Daniel was happy and I was glad. I felt very proud of myself for thinking of this solution, and extremely gratified because it had come to pass. I was old enough and wise enough to have realised that Daniel was an unusual man. And how fortunate it was that he had been at hand to set this matter right. I had witnessed that rare phenomenon, an example of selfless love, and I thought what a lucky girl Rachel was to have inspired it.

I tried to tell Rachel this, and she agreed with me. She said she would never forget what Daniel had done for her—and without reproaches of any sort. She was going to try to make up for that for the rest of her life.

And Tamarisk? What was her life going to be?

She and Gaston continued to live at St. Aubyn's. Gaston paid a great deal of attention to Mrs. St. Aubyn who, I was told, had become very fond of him. There was a coolness between him and Crispin. Crispin, I believed, was of a suspicious nature, and would be asking himself why Gaston had wanted such a hasty wedding.

I wondered what he would have said if he

had known that the baby Rachel was going to have was Gaston's.

I had been roughly awakened to the ugly side of life in Barrow Wood some years before. Now it seemed I had extended my knowledge.

Rachel had certainly married in unusual circumstances, but what of Tamarisk? She might be contented now, but what would her life be with such a man as Gaston?

I often thought of those girls we had been at the ball, dreaming of "coming out" and courtship, marriage and the ultimate goal of living happily ever after. How often was that dream attained, I wondered.

There was Rachel with this as yet unborn baby. For her there would be memories. And Daniel—kind Daniel—self-effacing as he was, surely when the child came he would sometimes think of Gaston and Rachel together.

But Tamarisk. She must live her life with the man who, while he was claiming undying love for her, was making love to someone else.

Crispin's manner towards Gaston was so cool that I began to wonder whether he had discovered something. It occurred to me that Gaston might be capable of any deceit. What of those grand estates in France and

Scotland? Did they really exist? Had he wanted to secure Tamarisk and her fortune before it was found out that he was not what he had made himself out to be?

It seemed plausible that this might be so.

I went to see Tamarisk. She had changed a little. She looked more sophisticated. She laughed a good deal and was full of gaiety, but I did wonder whether part of it was assumed. She insisted that life was wonderful. But did she do this too vehemently?

I asked her if she and Gaston were going to live at St. Aubyn's.

"Oh no," she answered. "We're pondering. Such fun! We're not quite sure where we want to live. St Aubyn's will do very well until we've decided."

"I should think it would do very well indeed!" I replied. "You won't live abroad, will you? Those estates in France."

"Oh, you've forgotten. Gaston sold those. We might buy another there."

"And Scotland?" I went on.

"Those are in the process of being sold. At the moment we shall be here. My mother is pleased about that. She adores Gaston."

"And Crispin?" I asked.

"Oh, you know Crispin. He never adores anything except the estate."

Was she happy, or was there a hint of uneasiness which she was trying to disguise?

As for me, there was a certain amount of uncertainty. Aunt Sophie had thought there would be more balls at St. Aubyn's to which eligible young men would be asked. Tamarisk's marriage had put an end to that.

I was caught up by Miss Hetherington. I must, she said, "pull my weight" and do what I could for the good of Harper's Green. That meant I must join the sewing circle, making garments for the poor and naked people of some remote part of Africa. I must help promote the bazaar and the annual fête. I must join in the organising of the cake-judging competition and become a member of the flower arranging class.

Aunt Sophie was amused at first, and then a little thoughtful. It was not what she had planned for me.

I said: "I feel I ought to do something. I mean, take a post of some sort. After all, I'm a bit of a drain on you."

"Drain! I never heard such nonsense."

"Well, you can't be as well off as you were before I came. So it must be something of a burden."

"No such thing. You're a bonus."

"And you are a darling," I replied. "Yet I

do want to do something. Earn a little money preferably. You give me so much."

"You give me so much too. But I do know what you mean. You don't want to stultify, become a martyr to village life, become another Maud Hetherington."

"I have been wondering what I could do. Perhaps get a post as a governess or companion."

Aunt Sophie looked horrified. "Granted there is little else a genteel young lady can do. But I can't see you as the governess to some wayward child or fractious old woman."

"It might be interesting for a while. After all, I am not like some. I could leave if I did not like it. I do have a little money of my own."

"Put the idea out of your head. I'd miss you too much. Something will be resolved."

The time for the birth of Rachel's baby was almost with us. I went over to see her.

She said: "It's impossible not to be happy about this baby. I love this child deeply, Freddie. It's strange, when you think . . . ."

"It's not strange at all. It's natural. The child is yours, and when it is born it will be Daniel's. Only the three of us know, and we shan't tell."

"A secret," she said, "that must never be told."

My thoughts immediately went to the nursery in the Lanes' cottage and the seven birds in the picture.

"The old verse," I said.

"I know," said Rachel. "I always wondered what that secret was. What do you think the poet had in mind?"

"Just any secret, I suppose."

She nodded thoughtfully.

That reminded me that I must go to see Flora soon. Poor Flora. The passing of time meant nothing to her. She lived permanently in the past.

Rachel was saying: "I am trying to put all that behind me. I was silly to believe in him. I can see it so clearly now. I believe he married Tamarisk for her money."

"Poor Tamarisk," I said.

"Yes. I can say that now."

"And you, Rachel, have someone who truly loves you."

She nodded. She was not completely happy, I knew, but she had left a long way behind that girl whom I had found in the stable with a rope in her hands.

. . .

SOON AFTER, I called on Tamarisk again. She was wearing a tea gown of lavender silk and lace and looked beautiful.

"And what are you doing here, Freddie?" she wanted to know.

"I have just left the sewing circle."

She grimaced. "How exciting!" she said ironically. "Poor you! I don't suppose Maud Hetherington lets you off lightly."

"She's a hard taskmaster."

"How long are you going to let her rule you?"

"Not much longer. I'm thinking of taking a post."

"What sort of post?"

"I haven't decided yet. What do young ladies of some education and very small means do? You don't know? Well, I'll tell you. They become governesses or companions. It's a very humble condition, but, alas, the only thing available."

"Oh shut up," cried Tamarisk. "And look! Here's Crispin."

He came into the room and said to me: "Good afternoon. I saw you arriving and I guessed you had come to see Tamarisk."

"She has just been telling me she's thinking of being someone's governess or companion," said Tamarisk.

"Looking after other people's children or ministering to some old woman."

"Teaching children could be rewarding," I said.

"For the children who would benefit from your tuition perhaps. But for you? When a governess is no longer needed, off she goes."

"That would apply to any employment, surely?"

"The period of a governess's usefulness is necessarily limited. It is not a career I would recommend."

"There is little choice. There would appear to be only two openings—governess or companion."

"The second could be worse than the first. People who need companions are more often than not querulous and demanding."

"It may be that there are some pleasant ones."

"It would not be my choice if I were a young woman in search of a career."

"Ah, but then you are not."

Tamarisk laughed. He shrugged his shoulders and we talked of other things.

Shortly afterwards he left and I went back to the Rowans. I sat at my window, looking out at Barrow Wood.

. . .

AUNT SOPHIE WAS having tea in the drawing-room when I came in. I had been to the church to help with the flower decoration, supervised by Mildred Clavier, who had French ancestry on one side of her family and was therefore noted for her good taste.

I was tired—not so much from physical fatigue but through a sense of futility. I was wondering, as I did twenty times a day, where I was going.

To my surprise Crispin was with Aunt Sophie, and she was looking rather pleased.

"Oh, here's Frederica," she said. "Mr. St. Aubyn has been talking to me. It's an idea he has."

"I'm sorry I disturbed you," I said. "I didn't know you had a visitor."

"This concerns you. Come and sit down. You'd like a cup of tea, I know."

She poured it out and I took it. Then she smiled at Crispin.

"It's just an idea I had," he said. "I thought it might be of interest. You may have heard of the Merrets. He was one of the two assistant managers on the estate. Mrs. Merret was a great help to him in his work. They are leaving for Australia at the end of next week. His brother is farming over there and has persuaded them to join him. At last they have decided to do so."

"I did hear something of them," I said.

"A good fellow, Merret. Someone's taking over his work, so that is not the point. It was just Mrs. Merret. She was a great help to him in his work and therefore to us."

"Wives often are," commented Aunt Sophie, "and rarely get the credit until they are no longer there."

He smiled rather grudgingly. "Yes, you could say that. Merret was excellent, but Mrs. Merret had a way with her. I suppose you would call it the feminine touch. Merret might have been a bit gruff at times. He was a man of few words and when he talked he spoke his mind, whereas she knew how to handle people. She also knew what was right for the cottages . . . those Elizabethan ones on the edge of the estate. She made sure that they did not lose their character, whereas Merret might have had something done, if he could get it at a low cost, which wouldn't have been right for them. She made the tenants feel proud of their places. You see what I mean?"

Aunt Sophie was sitting back in her chair looking a little smug, while I was wondering what this was leading to.

"The fact is," went on Crispin, "hearing you talk about becoming a governess or companion, I thought this might suit you better."

"Suit me? What do you mean?"

"I thought you might care to take over Mrs. Merret's work. It would mean getting to know something about the properties, but most important, the people. Dealing with them tactfully. James Perrin is taking over Merret's work, and you'd be working with him. What do you think?"

"I'm just astounded. I'm not sure what I should be expected to do, and whether I would be capable of it."

"Well, you were always interested in old buildings," said Aunt Sophie. "And you've always got along well with people."

"You could try it," said Crispin. "If you didn't like it, you could give it up. You could see Tom Masson about a salary. He deals with that sort of thing. Why not give it a try? I think you might like it better than tiresome children or querulous old ladies."

"I think I should have to know more about it," I said. "I am not sure that I have the qualifications."

"That will soon be discovered. I think you might become really interested. Some of the properties on the estate go back a long way. We have to make them comfortable enough to live in without spoiling the old features.

People are beginning to value these old places. They're solid. They knew how to build well in those days. See how they have stood up to the years."

"I can't imagine what I should have to do."

"It's simple. You get to know the people. You go round in your official capacity and they'll talk about their dwellings. You listen sympathetically. We have to keep them in good order. They ask for all sorts of things. You will explain why this or that could not be done. You'll see. In any case, you won't know whether you want to do it until you have tried, will you?"

"It sounds very interesting to me," said Aunt Sophie.

"When would you want me to start?" I asked.

"The sooner the better. Why don't you go along and see Tom Masson and James Perrin? They'll give you all the details."

"Thank you," I said. "It was good of you to think of me."

"Of course I thought of you," he said. "We need someone to take Mrs. Merret's place."

When he had left and we sat back listening to the sound of his horse's hoofs on the road until they died away, Aunt Sophie laughed.

"Well!" she said, "what did you think of that?"

"I can hardly believe it."

"It sounds a cosy sort of job."

"It's amazing. How should I know anything about property?"

"Why shouldn't you learn? He's what I'd call a cryptic sort of fellow."

"What do you mean by that?"

"You can't be sure what he's getting at. I imagine there's something behind most things he does."

"And what's behind this?"

She looked at me knowingly. "It's my opinion that he takes an interest in you. He doesn't like the idea of your going away. The talk of governessing has put this into his mind."

"You mean he is creating this job just to keep me here? That's a bit wild, even from you, Aunt Sophie."

"He's bound to have his reasons. I am sure he has some idea that he has to keep an eye on you. It's somewhere in the past . . ."

"Do you mean Barrow Wood?"

"That's something none of us is likely to forget, and it applies to him as much as any of us. Let's say, because of what happened, he takes a special interest in you and he doesn't think it would be a good thing for you to go off on some wildcat scheme."

"Wildcat scheme! Being a governess!"

"He thinks it is, and he did save you, remember. People feel these things quite strongly after something like that happens."

"It's hard to imagine he could feel very strongly about anything except the estate."

"He's thinking of the estate now. His precious Elizabethan cottages and all that."

We were thoughtful for a while.

I said: "I must say, I feel rather interested in all this."

"So do I," said Aunt Sophie.

. . .

THE NEXT DAY, I went over to the St. Aubyn Estate Office to see Tom Masson. He was a tall, middle-aged man with rather a brisk manner.

"Mr. St. Aubyn told me you would be coming," he said. "He thinks Mrs. Merret was a great asset in her husband's work, which she undoubtedly was, and we shall miss her. You'll be working with James Perrin as a sort of assistant. Mrs. Merret will be here shortly. It is better for you to talk to her about what your duties will be."

"I shall like that," I said. "At the moment

I feel a little vague about what is expected of me."

"I do not think you will find it over-arduous. We found things ran more smoothly with her around. It's better for you to talk direct to her. Meanwhile, we'll settle other details."

He told me about the rules of the estate. Hours of duty would be flexible. Someone might want to see me at any hour of the day, and I would be expected to be available for emergencies. There would be a horse at my disposal and, if I needed it, a pony and trap. We discussed salary, and he asked me if I had any questions. I had not. I felt there was so much for me to discover.

Mrs. Merret arrived.

"Oh hello, Miss Hammond," she said. "I hear you are going to take over my job."

"Yes, and I am eager to know what is expected of me. I'm not altogether sure."

She had a very pleasant face and an easy manner. I could see why people liked her.

She said: "It began like this. I started helping my husband and I found certain things which I thought weren't quite right with the tenants. I got more and more interested. There are several tithe cottages on the estate and we have to make sure the tenants keep them in order. I suppose some feel they are only theirs while the job lasts and that makes them careless. You have to see that they report what is wrong so that things don't get beyond repair. Then you get the complaints and quibbles. You have to sort them out, of course. You have to get to know the people . . . those who have a real grievance and those who have a habit of complaining and grumbling. I always tried to keep them happy. I'd make them proud of their places. There's a lot in that. One of my jobs was to make sure they got a hamper for Christmas with the things they needed. I found people with a cupboard full of blankets which they'd been getting year after year when they were short of coal. People are proud . . . some of them. Then, of course, there are the cadgers. You want the worthy ones to get what they want and for which they are too proud to ask. Am I giving you some idea?"

"Oh yes indeed."

"You get to know them in time. We aim to have a happy estate. That's the best way to keep things working well. I'll give you my notebooks. There are little snippets about people in them."

"Thank you."

"Don't worry. There'll be plenty for you to do. I daresay Mr. Perrin will find lots. My husband did for me. He really does need an assistant, and I am sure you will find yourself fully occupied."

"It seems a rather unusual sort of job."

"To employ a woman, you mean? The men sometimes think we're not up to it. Mr. St. Aubyn isn't like that. He said I understood people and it was something to do with the feminine instinct. You'll be a success, I'm sure."

She handed me the notebooks. I glanced through them and saw there was a brief reference to Mulberry Cottage.

"That's the Lanes' place," I said.

"Poor Flora. I didn't have much to do with them. Mr. St. Aubyn himself keeps an eye on them. That is his wish."

"I know he looks after them very well."

"Miss Lucy was his nurse at one time— and Miss Flora before that. It's a very sad affair."

"You must have known them for a long time."

"Since I married and came here."

"So you've always known Miss Flora as she is now?"

"Oh yes. She went like that when Mr. St. Aubyn was a baby."

"I often wonder whether something couldn't be done for Miss Flora."

"What do you think could be done?"

"I wonder if it could be brought home to her that the doll she treasures is not a baby —only a doll."

"I don't know. Surely her sister would have done it if she thought it was any good. She looks after her very well."

I asked how she felt about leaving.

"Mixed feelings. My husband is keen to go. He thinks there are great opportunities out there. His brother went and he has a flourishing property now. Land is cheap, and if you work hard they say you can do well."

"It's a great challenge, I suppose," I said.

She agreed.

Mr. Perrin arrived and I had a long talk with him.

He was young, in his early twenties, I imagined. He had a friendly, happy smile and I knew at once that I should have no qualms about working with him.

He said: "You can help with the accounts. Not that there is much of that in our department, but they come along now and then and figures are not my strong point. And there are letters. Merret tells me that there will be plenty to do and I'll need all the help I can get."

"I fear I have no experience."

"Well, we shall get along, I am sure."

When I went home Aunt Sophie was eagerly waiting to hear the outcome. I told her that there really did seem to be a job to be done and that her notion that Crispin wanted to keep me here was just another flight of fancy.

"It is no sinecure," I told her firmly. "I think I am going to be very busy."

"Well, I'm glad," she replied. "I certainly did not want you to go away. And I didn't think that governessing would have suited you very well."

DANIELLE

So I was working for the St. Aubyn estate.

On the first morning James Perrin was very helpful. I was given certain papers to read, looked at some of the account books and wrote a few letters under his direction. He showed me a map of the estate, which was larger than I had thought it to be.

"Why don't you ride over to the cottages," he suggested. "You know, the row of Tudor ones on the edge of the estate. You can tell people you are taking over from Mrs. Merret. They were all very fond of her. She had a sympathetic nature and I can see you have the same, which is of course why Mr. St. Aubyn chose you for the job. I tell you what . . . I'll come over with you and introduce you."

I thought that was an excellent idea.

"What sort of horse do you like?" he asked as we walked over to the stables.

"Nothing too sprightly. I have only ridden since I came to Harper's Green. That's just over five years ago."

"Oh, I see. Well, we'll find the right mount. He or she will soon get to know you. I'll talk to Dick or Charlie—you can trust them to know what's best."

He did and we were soon riding through the estate. He showed me several places of interest which he thought I should know about.

"There's a great deal of work involved in a place like this," he said. "I haven't been here long but I can see it is well looked after by Mr. St. Aubyn. I gather his father let it go rather badly."

"Yes, I have heard that."

"So it is a jolly good thing for the estate that he didn't take after his father. Most of the houses on the estate are St. Aubyn property. But Mr. St. Aubyn's father sold some of the farms. Grindle's, for instance. They bought their place and Archie Grindle made a good thing of it, too."

"He recently married the aunt of a friend of mine," I told him.

"Oh yes. He's gone to live at the Bell House, but the sons run the place well.

We're coming up to the Tudor cottages, which I thought we would concern ourselves with this morning."

The cottages looked very beautiful in the sunshine, with their ancient red bricks, latticed windows and overhanging gables. I could believe that the interiors would be dark. There were six of the cottages, each surrounded by a little ground. I had seen them many times. They were known as the Old Cottages.

"They are beautiful," I said.

"They knew how to build in those days. Think how they have stood up to the elements all these years . . . just little places like that. They are marvellous. Of course, some people complain that they get little light."

"You couldn't possibly change those windows."

"It would be criminal, don't you agree?"

"I certainly do. Of course, it's so pleasant to have the light, but in places like that you would have to put up with the inconvenience for the sake of beauty."

"You'll soon get to know the tenants. Mr. St. Aubyn likes a contented community. He says that's the way to get them to work well. Lots of these people work on the farms . . . tithe places, most of them . . . except the old faithful servants who will be sure of their homes until they die. First we'll call on Mrs. Penn. We know she'll be in. Poor old soul, she's bedridden now. Her husband worked for the estate and she was cook up at the house. Visitors mean a lot to her. The door's on the latch most of the day and her daughter-in-law pops in with a hot meal at midday. She's a bit of a whiner, but who wouldn't be?"

He lifted the latch of the door and called: "Mrs. Penn. James Perrin here with Miss Hammond. May we come in?"

"Seems you are in," said a high-pitched voice.

He grinned. "Well, say you're glad to see us."

"Come on in," she said, "and shut the door."

The bed was close to the window so that she could look out. She was old and wrinkled; her white hair was in two plaits and she was propped up by pillows.

"So Mrs. Merret's off to Australia," she said. "Outlandish sort of place. Used to call it Botany Bay. Prisoners went there."

"That's in the past, Mrs. Penn," said James Perrin cheerfully. "It's quite different now. Very civilised. After all, *we* were running about in caves at one time . . . little more than monkeys."

"You get along with you," she said and peered at me. "I liked Mrs. Merret," she added. "She listened to what you had to say."

"I promise to listen," I said.

"It's a pity she's gone."

"I'm here to take her place. I shall be the one to come and see you now."

James had brought two chairs from the other side of the room and we sat down.

"You'll tell all your little grievances to Miss Hammond now," said James.

"Well," Mrs. Penn announced, "you tell that Mrs. Potter that I don't like seed cake. I like a nice jam sandwich . . . and not jam with pips in it. They get under your teeth."

I wrote this information down in a notebook which I had brought for the purpose.

"What's the local news, Mrs. Penn?" asked James and, turning to me: "Mrs. Penn is a fount of knowledge. People come in here and talk to her, don't they, Mrs. Penn?"

"That's right. I like to hear what's going on. There was trouble here last Saturday night. That Sheila . . ."

"Oh, Sheila?" Once more James turned to me with an explanation. "That's Sheila Gentry, in the last of the cottages . . . the one right at the end of the row, I mean. Mrs. Gentry died about nine months ago and Harry Gentry hasn't got over it yet."

"He worried too much about that Sheila," explained Mrs. Penn. "Mind you, he's got something to worry about there. She's got a flighty look about her, that one. And not fifteen yet. I reckon he'll have a rare to-do with her one day—and that day not far distant."

"Poor Harry Gentry," said James. "He's one of the grooms. Quarters over the stables are full just now, that's why he's in one of the cottages. We'll call, but I'd hardly think he'll be there just now. Well, Mrs. Penn, you've met our young lady."

"She's a bit young," said Mrs. Penn, as though I were not there.

"Her youth is not going to affect her ability to do the job, Mrs. Penn."

Mrs. Penn grunted. "All right then," she said. "Remember, dear, I've got my birthday coming along soon and they'll be sending the cake like they always do from the house. Tell them, no seed. Jam sandwich and no pips in the jam!"

"I will," I promised.

The door opened and a woman looked in.

"How are you, Mrs. Grace?" asked James.

"Fine, sir. I don't want to interrupt."

"It's perfectly all right. We were just going. Lots to do just now."

Mrs. Grace came in and was introduced. "The head gardener's wife and Mrs. Penn's daughter-in-law."

"And you're Miss Cardingham's niece. I remember when you came here."

"I was about thirteen then."

"And you're one of us now."

"I feel that I am."

"We must be going," said James, so I shook hands with Mrs. Grace and we left.

I said: "Poor old lady. It must be sad to be bedridden."

"The daughter-in-law looks after her and I think she enjoys being waited on. That's the Wilburs' cottage. Dick does carpentering jobs and Mary works in the kitchens, so I doubt either of them will be around now. We'll knock and see."

We did and he was right.

"That's old John Greg's place. He'll be in his garden, I reckon. He used to work in the gardens until a few years back. He spends all his time now in his own."

We called and were shown prize roses and vegetables. We were both presented with a cabbage, and I was told that the old oak tree in the garden was keeping the sun off some of his herbs. He'd like it trimmed, but it was a ladder job and his rheumatics weren't up to it.

I made a note of this and said I would ask one of the gardeners to look at it.

And so we went on.

There was one I remembered above the others, and that was Sheila Gentry. Her father was working and she was alone in their cottage. She was a very pretty girl with brown curly hair and mischievous eyes. She gave me the impression that she was looking for adventure.

"I expect they'll find a place for her in the house," James told me. "Her mother worked up there when they needed extra help. She was a good pastry cook, I believe."

Sheila let us in and said her father was at work. She took good stock of me, I noticed. She told me she had left school and was keeping house for her father, but she didn't want to do that forever.

When we left, James said: "You can understand how Harry Gentry's got his hands full with a girl like that."

I agreed that I could.

As we came away from the cottages I said, "What about the Lanes' place?"

"Oh, they're a case on their own. You know about Flora."

"Oh yes, I've visited her often. Should we look in now?"

"Why not?"

"I feel sure Flora will be there if Lucy isn't."

"Mr. St. Aubyn himself looks after them. He has a special interest, you know, because they were his nurses when he was a child."

"Yes, I know."

We went through the garden gate. Flora was seated there. She looked a little startled to see us together.

I said: "I've come in an official capacity today."

She looked at me uncomprehendingly.

And almost immediately Lucy came out of the cottage.

"I heard you were taking on the job," she said. "You needn't include us."

"I know Mr. St. Aubyn takes good care of you," James told her.

"He does indeed," Lucy said.

"I wanted you to know that I'm taking Mrs. Merret's place," I explained.

"That's nice," said Lucy. "She's always been such a nice lady, without prying . . . if you know what I mean."

I did know what she meant. I had betrayed too much curiosity. I must remember to call when Lucy was not there . . . just as I had in the past.

. . .

JAMES PERRIN WAS very helpful to me during those first days. He made me feel that I was useful, otherwise I might have believed, as I had in the beginning, that there was no real job for me.

James had a small apartment over the estate office. It consisted of three rooms with a kitchen and the necessary facilities. The Merrets' cottage was being redecorated for a married couple who had been awaiting accommodation.

I soon became very interested in the estate as James initiated me into the working of it, and I could understand why Crispin was so absorbed in it. I would come home and tell Aunt Sophie the fascinating details and she would listen intently.

"All those people working there!" she said. "Just think! It provides a living for them. And then there are people like old Mrs. Penn who are in their homes for life, looked after by what they call 'the Estate,' which in a way means our Mr. Crispin. He is the great benefactor."

"Oh yes, he keeps it in working order. Imagine what it was all like before he took over. His father neglected the place and all those people must have been in danger of losing their livelihoods."

"He has a habit of appearing at the right moment," said Aunt Sophie soberly.

One day Crispin came into the estate office and saw me sitting at my desk beside James, who was showing me one of the account books.

He called out: "Good morning." He looked at me. "All going well?"

"Very well," replied James.

I said: "Mr. Perrin has been very helpful."

"Good," said Crispin and went out.

The next day James and I rode out to one of the farms.

"It's a question of a faulty roof," James had said. "You may as well come. You can meet Mrs. Jennings. It's your job to be on good terms with the wives."

On the way we met Crispin again.

"We're going to Jennings's farm," James told him. "Trouble with a roof."

"I see," said Crispin. "Good day," and he left us.

It was the following day. I had been down to the cottages to see Mary Wilbur, who had scalded her arm while working in the St. Aubyn kitchen.

Crispin was riding towards me.

"Good morning," he said. "How is Mrs. Wilbur?"

"She's a little shocked," I answered. "She has been rather badly scalded."

"I looked in at the office and Perrin told me where you had gone."

I was expecting him to ride on, but he did not.

Instead, he said: "I'd like to know how you are getting on. I was wondering if we might have lunch somewhere together . . . somewhere we could talk more easily. Would you care to do that?"

I usually brought a sandwich with me and ate it in the office. I could always make myself a cup of tea or coffee in James's kitchen. James was often out of the office, but if he were in he joined me.

I said: "That would be very agreeable."

"There's a place I know on the Devizes road. Let's go that way and you can tell me how things really are."

I felt elated. There were times when I believed Aunt Sophie's initial reaction to his offer of a post on the estate was true and that he had done it because he did not want me to go away. My pleasure now was in his interest which occasionally I felt to be there; but at other times, I believed my work was necessary and he felt nothing but indiffer-

ence towards me. But since he had asked me
to lunch I did begin to wonder whether there
might be a little truth in what Aunt Sophie
had thought.

The way led past Barrow Wood, and that
place must always affect me deeply. Neither
of us spoke as we rode by it. The trees
looked sombre and through them I caught a
glimpse of one of the graves. I thought, I
shall never forget. It was indelibly imprinted
on my mind and it always would be.

Crispin was saying: "The inn I'm thinking
of is The Little Vixen. Have you seen it?
There's a signpost of a very appealing little
fox outside."

"I think I know it. It stands back from the
road."

"They have good stabling there and they
do a simple but wholesome lunch."

He was right. It was very wholesome. We
ordered ham.

"They cure it themselves," said Crispin.
"They keep a small farm and run it well.
They grow their own vegetables."

With the ham we had lettuce, tomatoes
and potatoes baked in their jackets.

He asked if I would like wine or cider and
I said that wine would make me rather
sleepy perhaps and I must work that afternoon.

He smiled and said: "That applies to us both. Let's go for the cider."

When the food was served he said: "Now tell me how the work is really going."

"Very well, thank you. Mr. Perrin is very kind and helpful."

"I have noticed that you work well together."

I looked at him steadily and said: "Yet sometimes, I feel . . ."

"What do you feel?" he asked.

"Mrs. Merret helped her husband as many wives might. It was not really her own job, one might say. She was just . . . an adjunct."

He raised his eyebrows. "I don't think she would be flattered if she heard that."

"I know she was very popular and things ran smoothly, but sometimes I feel this work that I am doing was really created . . . well, to give me something to do."

"You mean there isn't enough to keep you occupied?"

"I have been occupied, but sometimes I think it might be a little contrived. I mean, do you really want someone going round the estate to discover that Mrs. Penn prefers jam sandwich to seed cake?"

"Is that what you have discovered?"

"It is one of the things, yes."

He started to laugh.

"It may seem amusing," I said hastily, "but I should like to know frankly whether what I am doing is really worthwhile or . . . you were taking pity on me. You knew I wanted to do something."

"Your aunt did not want you to go away."

"No. And I did not want to stay to be a burden to her."

"A burden? I've always thought she was overjoyed to have you with her."

"She is not a rich woman."

"I did not know she was in financial difficulties."

"She is not. She is quite comfortably off."

"Then why should you be a burden?"

"It is . . ."

"Your pride?" he asked.

"If you like, yes. I have a little money of my own. My mother's house was sold, which was to pay for my schooling. However, my father did that, and the money was invested and provides a small income for me."

"So you have your independence," he said. "But village life was a little dull for you."

"One wants to *do* something. You have the estate. You are very well occupied. Can you understand that I want to do something more than arrange flowers and sew for the needy?"

"I understand perfectly."

"Tell me about the work I am doing."

"It is more suitable for you than being governess to some squalling brat."

"Well-brought-up children are not brats, and I should think they rarely squall."

"It's an undignified position for a proud young woman, and I could not allow you to be in such circumstances if I could help it."

"You not allow it?"

"I was mindful of the effect it would have on you. Believe me, it would be quite wrong for you."

"How could you know?"

"Put it down to experience of the world. I have always felt governesses and ladies' companions have sad lives. They depend on the moods of children and, very often, demanding old people. No, I said, that is not the life for Frederica Hammond."

"So you created this job for her?"

"It is a job that is well worth doing. Mrs. Merret proved that. I did not have to create this job. It was there and, miraculously, you were there too to fill it."

I looked at him searchingly and he smiled. Then suddenly he put out his hand across the table and took mine. He patted it gently.

"I suppose," he said, "I have a special interest in you."

"You mean because of Barrow Wood?"

"Perhaps," he answered. He released my hand as though he were rather embarrassed to find himself holding it.

"Does it still bother you?" he went on.

"At times I remember."

"For instance, this morning, going past?"

"Yes."

"One of these days you and I will go there. We will stand there, where it happened, and exorcise the memory. You must forget it."

"I don't think I ever shall completely."

"Well, it didn't happen, did it?"

"He killed himself," I said.

"He was unbalanced. You can't judge those people by ordinary standards. It was best the way it happened. Look at the change at the Bell House. Mrs. Archie Grindle is a happily married woman. So is Rachel. Good came out of evil. Look at it that way."

"I suppose you are right."

"And now I am going to make you forget all that, and stop worrying about what you are doing on the estate. It is worthwhile, I assure you. I am a businessman. I do not do things that are not worthwhile for my business."

He seemed like a different person from the man I had known, and I was suddenly happy. I still believed he had contrived that job for me. What did he know about the lot of governesses and companions? Very little, I was sure. He had found this for me because he wanted to keep me there.

"There is ginger pudding with custard, and apple and blackberry tart with cream, and blancmange. I'll say the apple and blackberry tart."

"I'll say that too."

When it arrived he said: "There is something I want to talk to you about. It's Tamarisk. You don't see so much of her now, do you?"

"I am working and she is married."

"Of course. I am a little uneasy about her. Well, perhaps more than a little."

"Why?"

"I fancy everything is not going well."

"In what way?"

He frowned. "I think her husband is not all he made himself out to be."

"What do you mean?"

"Perhaps I should not be talking to you of this, but I think you might help."

"How?"

"She might confide in you. You were schoolgirls together."

"She used to talk a great deal about herself, but recently . . ."

"I believe she would again. See her and find out how she is feeling. I fancy everything is not as we hoped. In fact, I know . . ."

I waited for him to go on, and after a pause he said: "You and I have been through that experience of which a short time ago we were talking. Am I right in thinking it makes a special bond between us?"

"I think it might."

"I am sure it does. You see, there are so few of us who knew. Your aunt, you and I were the only ones. It was right that the secret should be kept. It is always right for secrets to be kept when a lot of good can be done through secrecy. And for those who are involved, there is a special feeling."

"Yes?"

"You and I . . ." He smiled at me warmly, almost appealingly.

I said quickly: "You can trust me with a confidence."

"Very well. I said I was unhappy about this marriage. In the first place I did not like it. I saw no need for all that haste. I thought it was just romantic nonsense. He was out to impress her with an elopement and so on. Now there seems to be a different aspect.

The fact is that I have been making enquiries. There were no estates in France or Scotland. I doubt whether his name is Gaston Marchmont. I have not checked this out fully yet, but I believe him to be a George Marsh. He is an impostor . . . an adventurer."

"Poor Tamarisk. She was so proud of him."

"She is a foolish girl. She has been easily duped. Well, now she is married to him. He is a liar and a cheat, and, alas, her husband. He knew that I should make enquiries so he arranged the elopement before I could discover the truth. Now she is married and we have to accept him. Of course, it may be that he will settle down. We've got to give it a chance. If she is happy with him . . ." He shrugged his shoulders. "That is something I am eager to know. I fancy she is not entirely happy. It may be that she is realising he is not the fine gentleman he tricked her into believing he was. But if he is prepared to turn over a new leaf, settle down . . ."

"You will find him work on the estate?"

"That's what it might come to. But I should be very wary about that. I should have to be sure of his intentions first. As you can guess, in my eyes he would be wide open to suspicion. It is an uneasy situation. That is why I want you to sound out Tamarisk. Discover what her feelings are. Is she really in love with him? We have to find a reasonable way out of this miserable situation."

I wondered what he would say if he knew that Gaston Marchmont was the father of Rachel's child, who was soon to be born. I could not tell him. That was Rachel's secret and not mine to divulge.

I said: "I am not sure that Tamarisk would confide in me."

"You can try. I think it is very necessary to find out exactly how things are going. I am very much afraid there might be unpleasantness."

"I will do what I can," I promised.

"Thank you." He sat back in his chair and smiled at me.

"This," he said, "I feel sure, has been a very satisfactory morning's work."

. . .

THE NEXT DAY I went to see Tamarisk.

"How are you?" I asked.

"Wonderful," she answered. "Everything is perfect."

"And Gaston?"

"He's as marvellous as ever." She laughed as she spoke and I wondered whether she were telling the truth.

"And you are working," she went on. "Doing something called 'Tenant Relations.' It sounds very important. And are you getting on well with James Perrin?"

"Who told you that?"

"There's no need to look guilty, or is there? You know how things get round in a place like this. You are seen together a good deal, they tell me."

"We work together."

"It sounds very pleasant."

"It is. But tell me about yourself. You really are enjoying married life?"

There was a slight pause, which I did not fail to notice, before she said: "It's blissful."

I knew then that I was not going to get any confidences. If anything was wrong, she was not prepared to admit it yet.

"I suppose you will soon be getting a place of your own," I said.

"Yes, of course. But we're comfortable here for the time being. My mother adores Gaston. He knows just how to please her. She would make a great fuss if we suggested going."

"Where do you propose to live when you do?"

"We're thinking. Perhaps we'll travel first. Gaston wants to show me Europe. Paris, Venice, Rome, Florence and all that."

"It sounds wonderful. So married life really is good?"

"I've told you, it's wonderful. Why do you keep going on about it?"

"I'm sorry. I just wanted your assurance."

"Are you thinking of embarking on it yourself?" she asked archly.

"The thought had not entered my mind, for obvious reasons," I said tersely.

I came away depressed. There was a change in Tamarisk. She was not quite natural, and instinctively I knew she was not the light-hearted girl who had been so confident that everything in the world would come right for her.

I knew now that Gaston Marchmont was a philanderer. He had completely bemused both Tamarisk and Rachel. He was a plausible rogue. Crispin knew him for what he was, but the knowledge had come too late. Poor Tamarisk! At least Rachel was loved by a good man, but I feared she was not completely happy either.

I went back to the estate office by way of the old cottages, my thoughts filled with Tamarisk and Crispin's anxieties about her.

As I approached the row of cottages, to my surprise I saw Gaston himself. He was standing by the Gentrys' cottage, talking to Sheila.

As I approached he came towards me.

"Hello," he said jauntily.

"Good afternoon," I replied. "I've just been with Tamarisk."

"Good. That will please her. And how are you? A busy lady these days, I hear. It suits you. You look blooming."

"Thank you," I said coolly.

"May I walk with you?"

"I am just going to the office."

"Been playing truant, have you?"

"By no means. My hours are flexible."

"That's the best way of working. I was just passing when I saw the little girl. I think she lives here. I was asking about her father."

"Oh, is he indisposed?"

"I thought I heard he was ill, but it seems to have been someone else."

I felt uncomfortable to be with him. I knew too much about him to be able to talk normally, and I was glad when I reached the office.

. . .

IT WAS TIME for Rachel's baby to arrive, and I visited her frequently.

For some weeks she had seemed to be in that state of serenity which I had noticed before in pregnant women, and she thought of little but the baby and was longing for its arrival.

But now that the time was coming very close, I was aware that a certain apprehension had come to her.

Our friendship had strengthened since her marriage. Both she and Daniel regarded me as their greatest friend, I knew. Rachel said to me once: "Do you realise what a big part you have played in our lives? Suppose you hadn't found me? Suppose I had . . . ?"

"Life is like that all the way through, isn't it? Certain things happen because people are in a certain spot at a certain time."

"But what you did was wonderful."

"I was over-bold. I hesitated for a while but something told me that Daniel loved you enough, was strong enough. You are lucky to be his wife, Rachel. He is the one who has done so much for you, not I."

"Daniel feels the same as I do about you."

"I am glad. It is gratifying to take a bold step and be right."

"We have been so lucky, and, but for you . . ." She shivered.

"You are doubly lucky because you realise how lucky you are. So many people don't."

"It will soon be over now. There is one thing, Freddie."

"What is that?"

"Daniel has been marvellous, but . . ."

"But what?"

"It's the baby. If it were his, it would be the most wonderful thing. But it isn't. Nothing can alter that, however good he is . . . however much he pretends."

"Pretends?"

"To love the child. He is going to remember. I am afraid that he might hate it . . . no, not hate it. He wouldn't hate anyone, let alone an innocent child . . . but he will look at it and be reminded. Then I shan't be able to bear it. Already I love this child. It doesn't make any difference that it has no right to be there. It is my baby and I know I shan't be able to bear it if Daniel doesn't love it too."

"Daniel is a good man, one of the best."

"I know. He'll try, but it will be there. It's going to remind him every time he looks at it. It must, mustn't it?"

"He has always known."

"It will be different when it is actually there. I want everything to be right for this baby. I think I love it more because it is going to need special love and care from me. I'm longing for it, and yet dreading seeing Daniel's face. He can't hide his feelings very well. I wonder how he'll be when the child is born. Freddie, you're our closest friend. Nobody knows about Gaston and me . . . only you. Everyone thinks the baby is Daniel's and that is why we had to marry so quickly. They whisper about that and some pretend to be shocked, but they think we redeemed ourselves by marrying in time. You are the only one who knows the truth, Freddie. You see what I mean. We can talk freely."

"You've got to forget about Gaston. That is all over. You have to count your blessings. Because of it you married Daniel, and that was the best thing you have ever done . . . for both of you. You have to think of the good things, Rachel."

"I know. But what I wanted to say was this. Will you be here when the baby is born? I want you to be with Daniel. I want you to tell him that I love him very much. Make him see that I was young and foolish and easily flattered. I know all that now. He is such a modest man. He thinks that Gaston is so much more attractive than he is. He would not be so to me now. I should see right through him. I want Daniel to know that, and I am afraid he doesn't. I want you to be with him when the baby is born. I want you to tell him what I have told you. You could make him understand perhaps."

"I will be there, Rachel," I said. "I shall do my best."

She leaned towards me and kissed my cheek.

. . .

A FEW DAYS later, when we were at breakfast, one of the men from Grindle's Farm came to tell me that Mrs. Godber, the midwife, was at the farm and Mrs. Daniel's baby was expected that day.

I went to the office and told James what was happening and that I should be at Grindle's Farm if he wanted to get into touch with me about some urgent matter.

I went to Rachel immediately.

She was lying in bed looking pale and a little frightened.

"Oh, Freddie," she said, "I'm glad you're here. I knew you'd come."

"How are you feeling?"

"All right. It's starting. Is Daniel here?"

"Yes. We shall be together."

Her face twisted suddenly and Mrs. Godber was immediately at the bedside.

"You'd better go now, Miss," she said to me. "I've sent for the doctor. That sounds like him now."

I smiled at Rachel and went off. I met Daniel on the stairs.

I said: "She asked me to be here."

"I know," he said. "Is it going to be all right?"

"Of course. You've got the good Mrs. Godber. She has a great reputation, and the doctor has just come. Where shall we go?"

"We could go into my office. We could wait there. How long will it be?"

"I don't think there are any fixed times for this sort of thing. We shall have to be patient."

"It's hard to be."

He took me to a small room on the first floor. Ledgers and books on farms, farming and animals lined the walls. There was a desk with writing materials covering it; there were also several chairs.

"I didn't want to be with any of the others," he said. "Rachel's aunt will be here soon. She is very good, but she fusses. It upsets me."

"You don't mind my being here?"

"No . . . no."

"Rachel asked me to be with you. She's worried about you."

"About me?"

"Well, they say some husbands suffer as intensely as wives on such occasions."

"I think she is going to be all right."

"I'm sure of it. She is young and strong and there haven't been any complications.

People are having babies every day, you know."

"Yes . . . but this is Rachel."

"She'll be all right."

"I pray she will be."

"She is very happy now, Daniel, you have made her very happy."

"Sometimes I wonder. I see a sadness in her eyes. I think sometimes she looks back . . . with regret."

"You know the reason for that, Daniel. She looks back and regrets what happened before. She wishes beyond everything that this child was yours."

"So do I."

"And she worries. This is her child, Daniel, part of her."

"Before anything else, I want her to be happy," he said earnestly.

"She will be and so will you be . . . if you let yourselves be."

"But she will always look back, and I . . ."

"You must look forward, Daniel. You have done so much for her. You have shown her clearly how much you love her. No one knows that more than she does. You've got to go on doing that. You've got to forget what went before. You've got to make this child your child, too. That is what she is afraid of: she thinks you will remember, and it will make a barrier between you and the child which will spoil the happiness you have built up together."

"I shan't be able to forget who the child's father is."

"The child will be yours from the moment it is born. That is how you have to see it."

"I can't do that. Could you if you were in my place?"

"I should try. I should try with all my strength, otherwise the happiness will not be there."

"I know you are right," he said. "And what of Rachel?"

"It will depend on you, Daniel. It is not difficult to love a small child. And this is Rachel's. Remember that. It is here because you love her so much."

"You have done a great deal for us. I shall never forget how much."

"I think you and Rachel have been very lucky, Daniel," I said.

We sat silently, each aware of the clock ticking away the seconds. He was wondering, as I was, how long we should have to wait.

It was not until early evening that the baby was born. The doctor came down to us. One look at his face told us that all was well. He was beaming.

"You have a little girl, Mr. Grindle," he said. "A healthy little girl."

"And . . . my wife?"

"Weary but triumphant. You could see her for a few minutes. Most of all she wants a rest now."

We went up to the bedroom. Rachel looked pale but, as the doctor had said, triumphant. Mrs. Godber was holding the child wrapped up in a shawl and only a red and wrinkled face was visible.

She put the bundle into Daniel's arms.

I waited in trepidation. So much depended on this. Rachel was watching him closely.

"She's beautiful," he said. "Our baby."

It was just right. I felt my eyes fill with tears.

Rachel was looking at me. "Freddie, you came then."

"Of course I came. I wanted to see the baby. You can't monopolise her, Daniel."

I held the child in my arms—this little creature who had such an effect on their lives—and all the time I was saying to myself, it's going to work out. All is going to be well.

. . .

THERE WAS THE usual excitement in Harper's Green. Births and deaths were the very stuff that life was made of. Everyone was interested in the new baby at Grindle's. There would be a christening at the church. The newcomer was very welcome, in spite of her rather precipitate arrival.

I was spending a good deal of time with Rachel. I would walk over at lunch time and have a light meal with her. The baby was thriving.

"Daniel really loves her," Rachel told me. "How could he help it? She is the most perfect baby."

I agreed that she was. Her looks had improved since the first time I saw her and she was looking more like a baby now than a wrinkled old gentleman of ninety. She had blue eyes and dark hair and, fortunately, no resemblance so far to Gaston Marchmont.

The question of names was discussed at length.

"If she had been a boy," said Rachel, "I should have called him Daniel. It would have made Daniel feel that the child was his as well."

"That would have been a good idea. I am sure Daniel would have liked that."

"I have an idea that he already looks on

her as his. Freddie, I think I should call her after you."

"Frederica! Oh no! Fred . . . Freddie . . . just think of it! I wouldn't call a child of mine by my own name."

"You have been so close to us in all this."

"No reason why the poor child should be burdened with my name. I've got an idea. There's a girl's name. It's French, I think, but that wouldn't matter. It would be near, and I do think it is a lovely idea. I'm thinking of Danielle."

"Danielle!" cried Rachel. "It's almost Daniel. But I think it ought to be Frederica."

"No, no. That would be wrong. In a way it would be a reminder. We want to make a complete break with the past. She is yours and Daniel's . . . that is the point. She must be Danielle."

"I see what you mean," said Rachel.

In due course the Reverend Hetherington christened Rachel's baby. Most of Harper's Green were at the church; and after the ceremony, with proprietary pride, Daniel carried Danielle back to Grindle's Farm.

MURDER IN HARPER'S GREEN

Since I had been working for the estate, I had little spare time to give to the sewing circle and the rest, and even Miss Hetherington understood that. She approved of what I was doing, for she thought that women should play a more prominent part in business and general affairs.

Aunt Sophie was, of course, delighted.

"It was just what you needed," she said. "I can't be grateful enough to Crispin St. Aubyn for suggesting it."

She enjoyed hearing details of what I discovered from the tenants. She liked James Perrin, and he was asked to tea on several occasions.

In fact, several people exchanged glances when they saw me with James, and I guessed what was in their minds. I felt faintly embarrassed about this.

I visited Tamarisk now and then, but she was not exactly welcoming. I guessed everything was not going smoothly, and she did not want to talk about what was wrong. I was often at Grindle's Farm. The baby was flourishing and both Daniel and Rachel were obviously delighted with her.

It was a Saturday afternoon, a free time for me unless there was some problem which had to be dealt with, and since it was some time since I had called on Flora Lane, I thought it was time I did so.

I approached the cottage from the back. There was no one in the garden. The empty doll's pram was standing by the wooden seat in which Flora usually sat. Then I noticed that the back door was open and presumed she had gone in to get something.

I went to the door and called: "Is anyone at home?"

As I did so, Flora came out, carrying the doll, and to my amazement, Gaston Marchmont was with her.

"Hello," said Flora. "You haven't been for a long time."

"I see you have a visitor."

Gaston Marchmont bowed.

"I was passing," he said. "I spoke to Miss

Lane and she has shown me the nursery where she tends her precious child."

Flora smiled down at the doll in her arms.

My amazement must have been obvious. It seemed so strange to me that she should be friendly with Gaston to such an extent that she invited him into the house. It had taken me several meetings before I had that privilege.

Flora put the doll in the pram and sat on the seat. Gaston and I were on either side of her.

"You didn't expect to see me here," said Gaston to me.

"No, I did not."

"I take an interest in the estate and all who live on it. After all, I am a member of the family now."

He spoke with a certain insolence, I fancied.

"I like to know what's going on," he continued.

"It's a long time since you've been," said Flora again.

"I don't get so much time now that I am working," I explained.

"Miss Hammond is a very unusual lady, you know," put in Gaston Marchmont. "She is a pioneer. She is out to prove something which we should have learned about a long time ago. The ladies are as good as the men —only better."

Flora looked vague.

"He's got a touch of that cold he has. Never quite got rid of it. I took him up to give him a dose of that stuff. It's made with herbs. That makes it better, doesn't it, precious?"

Gaston raised his eyebrows and looked at me, as though he found this amusing. Knowing so much about him, I felt contempt for him swelling up in me.

"What a pleasant nursery Miss Lane has created up there," he said.

I thought, this could not be the first time he had called on her. I supposed he looked in as I did and when talking to him she had conceived the idea that the baby was not well and needed this medicine. She had gone up and he had followed her.

"It was so good of Miss Lane to show me the nursery," Gaston went on. "And thank goodness little what's-his-name is better now. Have you, Miss Hammond, seen those venomous-looking birds on the wall?"

I felt myself turn cold at the sudden intense curiosity I saw in his eyes.

The birds had had a certain effect on me, reminding me of the old rhyme, of a secret which must never be told. And he had felt the same.

"The magpies," said Flora. "Lucy put them in a frame for me. They show you it's a secret . . . never to be told. That's what they are saying."

"Do you know the secret?" asked Gaston.

She looked at him in horror.

"You do," he said triumphantly. "Suppose you told us. That would be fun, wouldn't it? We would never tell. Nothing to worry about."

Flora had begun to tremble.

I whispered to him: "You are upsetting her."

"Sorry," he murmured. "What a beautiful day it is. Just right for sitting in the garden."

I could see how much he had upset her and that could not be lightly set aside.

I said: "I think we should be going. I just came to see how you were," I went on to Flora. "Your sister will be back soon, I daresay."

Gaston was looking at me steadily.

I repeated firmly: "Yes, I think *we* should go."

Flora nodded. She looked at the doll in the pram and started to push it backwards and forwards. Then she stood up and wheeled it towards the cottage.

"Goodbye," I said.

She did not turn but muttered: "Good-bye."

He went with me to the gate.

"Phew," he said as we walked away. "She's quite mad."

"She's deranged. You shouldn't have talked about those birds."

"She talked about them. She took me up there and showed them to me. She didn't seem to mind."

"You have to be careful with people in her state."

"She really is . . . far gone. Thinking that doll is a baby! It's supposed to be Crispin, of all people. That makes it madder than ever. There he is, strutting round, cock of the walk, and she thinks he's a china doll!"

"She was his nurse. She is still . . . living in those days."

"I pity the poor sister."

"They are very fond of each other and Crispin is very good to them."

"I think you are blaming me for that scene."

"Well, it was because you talked about secrets and all that."

"I thought that if she could unburden her-self . . . all that talk about secrets . . .

struck me that that was what she had on her mind . . . or what was left of it."

"I think it is better to leave her alone . . . to go along with her . . . pretending with her that the doll is a baby. That is what her sister does, and Crispin too. They know her best. Her sister was there when she lost her senses, and Crispin . . . well, he has known her for a long time."

"Knew her as his dear nanny, I suppose."

"Not Flora. He was a baby only a few months old when she had to give up, and that was when Lucy took over."

"Extraordinary story, isn't it? Interesting, though. All I wanted to do was cheer the old girl up a bit, now that I'm taking such an interest in everything."

"You're thinking of staying here then?"

"That, my dear Miss Frederica, is in the hands of the gods."

I was glad when we reached the Rowans and he left me to go on to St. Aubyn's.

· · ·

AUNT SOPHIE SAID to me one morning at breakfast: "Gerry Westlake is home."

"Who is Gerry Westlake?" I asked. The name seemed vaguely familiar.

"You know the Westlakes. They have one of those houses in Cairns Lane."

"And Gerry?"

"He's their son. He went away years ago. Twenty . . . no, more than that . . . twenty-six years ago. That's more like it. He was quite a boy then. About seventeen or so. Went to Australia rather suddenly. Decided he wanted to emigrate. No, it wasn't Australia. It was New Zealand. Had a friend out there, by all accounts."

"I wonder how the Merrets are getting on in Australia?"

"They're bound to write to someone sooner or later, then it will be passed round. I daresay all will be well. They were both hard workers."

When I reached the office, one of the first things James said was: "The Westlakes' son is home."

"Aunt Sophie was saying something about him. Gerry, isn't it. Did you know him?"

"Good heavens, no. I don't think I was born when he went away. But lots of people in Harper's Green remember him and they're all talking about his return, of course. I have to go over that way to see about some repairs and I thought I'd look in on the Westlakes and meet the young man. Why don't you come with me?"

I hesitated, knowing that people were talking about our being rather frequently together. I liked James very much, but I did not care that my name should be linked with his. I wondered if he knew of the gossip and found it disconcerting.

I said: "Is it justified?"

"But of course. It's a good opportunity for you to meet Mrs. Westlake. Her husband is one of the part builders we employ—only part-time now he is getting on a bit. There's always some work of that nature to be done on the estate. I'd like to hear what Gerry's got to say."

So I set out with James.

The Westlakes' residence was a neat little house with a well-kept garden and we had a pleasant morning.

Mrs. Westlake brought out her elderberry wine and I met Gerry—a pleasant man with a wife and a daughter of about my age.

They told me it was their first visit to England and Gerry explained how he used to do odd jobs on the estate. It was just after his seventeenth birthday that he decided to go to New Zealand. It had been a hard decision to make, but he had felt there was more scope for him in a new country. He had a friend who'd gone out there and they had been writing to each other. It was that which had decided him.

He was frowning slightly as he looked back over the years.

"It was the right thing for you, I suppose," I said.

"Oh yes, though it wasn't easy at first. But young people were wanted out there and there were facilities for emigrants. I went out steerage, of course . . . a bit primitive, but who cares for that at seventeen. It was exciting. And there was my friend waiting for me. He was ten years older than I and in the end it worked very well."

Old Mrs. Westlake smiled at her son. "You were quite fond of one of the girls over here," she said. "It was all to the good that you went."

"Yes," said her husband. "Poor girl. She went a bit strange after you left."

"It wasn't because of me, Mother!"

"Well, I reckon there was something wrong before that. You were a handsome lad though, son."

Gerry looked uneasy.

"It was all a long time ago," he said. "How is . . . Mr. Crispin St. Aubyn?"

"I believe he is very well," I said.

"In good health, is he?"

"I have not heard otherwise, have you, James?" I asked.

"Never," said James.

"A fine figure of a man, I suppose."

"That is exactly how I would describe him," said James. "Wouldn't you?" he asked me.

"Yes, I would," I replied.

"Tall, upstanding, sound in every way," murmured Gerry.

"Absolutely."

Gerry laughed and seemed well pleased.

Mrs. Westlake senior had brought out some little cakes to go with the wine.

"This is indeed a celebration," said James.

"Well, Mr. Perrin," said old Mr. Westlake, "it is not every day we have a son come home from New Zealand to see us."

That was a very interesting morning.

. . .

I WAS GOING to call on Flora and, to my dismay, when I was close to the cottage I met Gaston Marchmont.

"Good afternoon," he cried gaily. "I'll guess where you're going. Do you know, I thought I'd look in myself."

"I see," I said blankly.

"I think she likes visitors. She always seems to. I'm really sorry for the old girl."

"I don't think her sister wants people there."

"Is that why you call when she's away? 'When the cat's away . . .' and so on?"

I felt irritated and just at that moment I saw Gerry Westlake coming through the gate. He too had been visiting the cottage. That was very odd.

"Hello," he said.

I returned his greeting and, turning to Gaston Marchmont, went on: "This is Mr. Gerry Westlake."

"I know," said Gaston. "It must have been very pleasant to return to the old country to see your family."

"It was," said Gerry.

"And you will be leaving soon?" I asked.

"Tomorrow. It's been good, but all good things come to an end, alas."

Gaston said: "I daresay you'll be coming again soon."

"It's a long way and we've been saving up for this for years."

"Well, good luck," said Gaston.

"And a safe journey back," I added.

He left us.

As soon as I saw Flora, I knew something was wrong. Her eyes looked wild, her face distorted.

"Flora!" I cried. "What has happened?"

She stared at me blankly and shook her head from side to side.

"Tell me, Flora, what is it?"

She stared at the doll in her arms. "It's not
. . . it's not . . . It's only a doll," she murmured.

Suddenly she threw the doll from her. It
lay across the pram, inanimate, smiling its
china smile.

I could not believe this. Flora was coming
back to reality.

Everything seemed very still around us. I
was aware of Flora's tortured face and the
avid curiosity in Gaston's.

"Why?" he said to her. "Why has it
changed?"

I laid my hand on his arm to restrain his
questions. And then I saw Lucy coming into
the garden.

"What's happened? What's happened?"
she cried.

"It's only a doll," said Flora piteously.

Lucy's eyes were filled with fear. Her lips
moved as though she were praying. She put
her arm through Flora's.

"Come along in, dear," she said. "It's all
right. Nothing's changed."

"It's a doll," whispered Flora.

"You've been dreaming," said Lucy.

"Only a dream?" whispered Flora. "It was
only a dream."

Lucy looked over her shoulder at us.

"I'll take her in," she said quietly. "I'll soothe her down. She has these turns."

She went into the house with Flora, leaving Gaston, with me, looking after them as they went.

I said: "Come on, we must go."

We went through the gate and out to the road.

"What do you make of that?" he said.

"I suppose she has flashes of reality."

"Sister Lucy didn't seem very pleased about that one."

"She is very anxious about Flora. What a terrible responsibility it must be."

"She had just had a visitor," said Gaston. "I think there must have been some revelation. I wonder what our pioneering colonist had to say to her."

I could not stop thinking about Flora and a few days later I called on her. Lucy was at home on this occasion.

"It was good of you to call," she said.

Flora was in the garden, the pram containing the doll with her.

"She's well now, aren't you, dear?" said Lucy to her.

Flora nodded. She was pushing the pram backwards and forwards.

"This rocking gets him off to sleep sooner than anything," she said.

It seemed that everything was back to normal.

Lucy came with me to the gate.

"She's recovered," she said. I thought "recovered" was hardly the right way to describe it. For a moment Flora had been in the present time. Could that not have been a good thing?

"She's been like this before," Lucy told me. "It's not good for her. She's not well after. She gets over-excited. Gets nightmares. I have some soothing medicine for her from the doctor."

"She seemed for a moment as though she were seeing things as they really are."

"No, it isn't quite like that. She's better as she is now. She's quiet and contented, really."

"Something must have provoked it," I suggested.

Lucy lifted her shoulders.

I went on: "I wondered if it had anything to do with Gerry Westlake?"

Lucy looked startled. "Why ever should it?"

"I just wondered because he had been to see her. We saw him leaving."

"Oh no. He's been away, it must be twenty-seven years or more."

"I do hope she will be all right."

"Thank you. I shall see to that."
I walked soberly home.

.   .   .

I WAS DISMAYED when I saw Tamarisk. I had guessed that all was not well after my conversation with Crispin, and I had tried to win her confidence. My dislike of Gaston Marchmont was increasing. Moreover, there was something about his interest in Flora which made me uneasy. He seemed to be amused by her affliction, and the fact that he was visiting her disturbed me.

On this occasion Tamarisk was not so guarded as she had been. I could see that she had been crying. She must have realised that it would be futile to continue the pretence that all was well.

"Tamarisk," I said, "why don't you tell me? It helps sometimes."

"Nothing will help."

"Is it Gaston?"

She nodded.

"You've quarrelled."

She laughed. "We're always quarrelling. He really doesn't make any effort now."

"What went wrong?"

"Everything. He said I was a fool and he preferred Rachel. He said she was a simpleton and knew it. I was one too, and didn't.

That was the only difference between us. Crispin hates him and he hates Crispin. I think he hates me too. He has a violent temper and I thought he was so charming . . ."

"Poor Tamarisk!"

"I don't know what to do. I think Crispin would like there to be a divorce."

"On what grounds? You can't divorce people just because you suddenly find that you don't like them as much as you thought you would."

"Adultery, I expect."

"On what evidence?"

"I'm sure we can find some. He said he was Rachel's lover before we were married. He said he would have preferred her. I know why he married me. It's because of all this. He thinks I'm rich. Well, I do have something, of course. He'd like to own all this. He's envious of Crispin. He says my brother doesn't know how to live."

"And I suppose *he* does . . . making people unhappy . . . cheating, lying."

I could not stop thinking of what she had said about Rachel. What if this were known? It would be an end to the happy life at Grindle's. And what of little Danielle, who was such a joy to them? I could not bear it if he spoilt that. But he must not, he would not. He would be putting himself in such a bad light—the man who seduced and deserted a young trusting girl!

"Crispin is trying to think of some way to get rid of him. He has been cheating all the way. Even his name. He hasn't any estates, either. He's a penniless adventurer. Oh, Fred, I'm so ashamed."

"Well, I don't suppose you're the only one who has been taken in by him. He was very plausible."

"He drinks too much. That's when lots of things are revealed. He talks a lot about Rachel. He said he could get her to leave everything and go away with him if he wanted to."

"That's nonsense!"

"I know. But I think it's true about them. I know she was very keen on him."

I said: "Rachel is happily married. She has a child. I am sure she would despise him if he made advances to her."

"She'd be the good little wife, of course. And there is the baby. She must have been very friendly with Daniel at the time too."

I had to stop this. I said quickly: "What are *you* going to do, Tamarisk?"

"I don't know. I think Crispin will find some way. He's very clever and he's working on it. I don't think he'll tolerate having Gaston in the house. Gaston still gets round my mother with that flowery talk about her being as beautiful as a young girl. She's on his side, but that won't help him. I am sure Crispin will do something soon."

I was thinking of Crispin. I thought I ought to tell him that Tamarisk had confided in me to some extent.

When he came to the office, I had the chance of telling him.

"Good," he said. "Can you meet me at The Little Vixen at one o'clock for lunch?"

I said I would be there.

. . .

I TOLD HIM what Tamarisk had said.

"What can you do about it?" I asked.

"The best thing would be to get rid of him. But that is impossible. He is not going to relieve us all by departing. The only other way is divorce. It's not entirely satisfactory, but I see no other way out."

"On what grounds?"

"Adultery, I daresay. I feel sure from what we know of him we could find evidence somewhere."

Not Rachel, I thought. That would be unbearable. But that happened before his marriage. It would not count. But it would be revealed if there were probings, suggestions. Rachel's happiness must not be sacrificed.

"Do you know for sure that he is promiscuous?" I asked.

"I'm fairly sure of it. As a matter of fact, I am having him watched. It is highly secret. He has no idea, but if he suspected . . . well, he would be warned."

"Do you think you will find something?"

"He's reckless. Although he is sharp, with an eye on the main chance, he can be foolish in many ways. He married Tamarisk because he thought she would provide a comfortable life for him, which so far she has done; but the strain of keeping up the pretence of being a loving husband has been too much for him. He is clever, but not quite clever enough. Frederica, I must get him out of the house. I am so glad that Tamarisk has started confiding in you. She talks to me very rarely and then with restraint. You can let me know exactly what she feels. We must meet often."

He smiled at me very warmly, and I felt a glow of pleasure, as I always did when he showed an interest in me.

"Are you still getting on well with Perrin?" he asked.

"Oh yes. He is very kind and helpful."

"You know I have a special interest in you, Frederica?"

"After Barrow Wood. Yes. I understand

that." I could not resist adding: "Though before that you were hardly aware of me."

"Oh, I was aware of you when you first came to St. Aubyn's for lessons."

"I shall never forget the first time I saw you," I said.

"Yes?" he asked.

"It was on the stairs. I was with Tamarisk and Rachel. We came down and you were about to go up. You nodded briefly and when you were still in earshot you said in a voice which we all heard distinctly: 'Who is the plain child . . . ?'—meaning me."

"No," he said.

"Yes, it's true."

"It rankled?"

"Very much so. Aunt Sophie had to spend a long time soothing my wounded vanity."

"I'm sorry, but I can't believe that. What I really meant was, 'Who is the interesting child?' "

"When one is thirteen years old, it is rather hurtful to be called a child, and plain is the final insult."

"You have never forgiven me."

"Well, I believe I was plain."

"I remember you had two plaits, very severe, and a penetrating look."

"And you had a penetrating voice."

"Believe me, I am very sorry. It was foolish . . . and obtuse. I should have recognised you as a very attractive young lady. The plainest people often turn out to be the real beauties, the ugly duckling, you know, turned into the swan."

"There is no need to make excuses. I was plain. And, do you know, I began to take an interest in my appearance after that. So you see, it was all right in the end. You did me good."

He put his hand across the table and held mine firmly in his.

"That's what I want to do," he said. "Always."

I thought then that he was going to say something else, but he hesitated and appeared to change his mind.

"This is a pact then," he said. "We are going to meet often. You will tell me what you discover and we shall see if we can find a way out of this."

We chatted then about the estate, of which I was becoming quite knowledgeable. That pleased him and he became very animated.

When we parted, he said: "I am anxious about Tamarisk, but we'll find some way out, and at least we have had a very pleasant time together."

. . .

I FREQUENTLY CALLED at Grindle's Farm. Danielle was an enchanting child and I took a very special interest in her. Rachel was happy too. I think she was succeeding in forgetting the past and one of the main reasons was her absorption in Danielle.

Alas, this contentment did not last.

Soon after Crispin and I had talked in The Little Vixen, I went to see Rachel and realised that all was not well.

"Freddie," said Rachel, "he's been here. Gaston has been here."

"Whatever for?"

"He said he wanted us to be friends again."

"What impertinence!"

"Oh, Freddie, it was awful. I'm frightened."

"What happened?"

"He said, 'You used to love me, remember?' I told him to go away. I did not want to see him ever again. He was horrible. He tried to put his arms round me. I was frightened."

"How did he get in?"

"He just called. One of the maids brought him to the sitting-room, where I happened to be at the time. I thought he would never go."

"Did you tell Daniel?"

"Yes. He was very angry. I think he would kill him if he saw him. It is not often Daniel is angry, but then he was. Oh, I do hope Gaston never comes here again. If he does . . ."

"He can't harm you."

"I am thinking about Danielle."

"Did he guess?"

"Yes. I told him when I was going to have a child and I could see then that he didn't care . . . only that it shouldn't go and spoil his plans for Tamarisk."

"He can't hurt you now, Rachel."

"He could tell people Danielle was his child. He could make a terrible scandal. Think what that would mean to her. People would talk of it for years. Oh, Freddie, what a mess I have made of everything!"

"It will be all right. There's nothing he can do."

She clung to me. "I'm so afraid. I'm terribly afraid."

I did not tell her so, but I was too.

. . .

How I HATED that man! He caused misery wherever he went. I had thought everything had been comfortably settled when Daniel accepted and cherished the child. I could clearly see what harm Gaston could do to them. I railed against him to myself. If only he would go away! As if he would! He liked the luxury he enjoyed at St. Aubyn's too well. He had schemed to marry Tamarisk and establish himself there—and he meant to stay. He would fight to stay and he would not care what happened to anyone else as long as he had what he wanted.

There was a new development which caused a stir in the neighbourhood. Harry Gentry had discovered that Gaston Marchmont was paying attention to his daughter Sheila. The girl was barely sixteen. Harry Gentry had come upon them together in the woodshed in his garden.

It was clear to Harry what Gaston's intentions were towards his daughter and Harry was enraged. He declared he would kill the man. Gaston had tried to make excuses, but Harry had gone into the house and come out with a shotgun which he used for shooting rabbits.

Gaston escaped and Harry fired into the air to warn him what would happen if he came near Sheila again. The neighbours had heard the shots and had come out to witness the scene.

People were now talking of the trouble at St. Aubyn's. It had been very romantic, running away to Gretna Green, but look at the result of such goings-on. Mr. Crispin must be wondering how they were going to get rid of the fellow.

Rachel was growing more and more frightened. She could not bear that scandal should touch her family. Gaston Marchmont would not care. He would make trouble for anyone if he thought there was any advantage in it for himself.

Crispin came to the office one afternoon when he knew James Perrin would not be there.

"This goes from bad to worse," he said. "We really must get rid of this fellow."

"Have you any idea how?" I asked.

He shook his head.

"He's philandering around. So perhaps it won't be difficult to find something against him."

I trembled for Rachel. I wanted to make him see how important it was to spare her from becoming involved, but I could not without her permission to tell, and I knew she would never give that.

He sat on the edge of the desk, swinging his leg, while he stared ahead, frowning. His attitude was one of despairing frustration. I understood his mood perfectly, because I shared it.

"You said you were having him watched," I said.

"Yes. But that little flutter with Sheila is hardly any help."

There was a knock at the door. "Come in," called Crispin.

One of the labourers from the home farm entered.

"I was passing the cottage when Miss Lucy called to me," he stammered. "She said to come and tell you, sir, right away, will you go there? Something's happened."

Crispin said: "I'll come right away."

He ran out and leaped onto his horse.

"I'll follow you," I said, "in case I can be of any help."

When I arrived I ran into the cottage. Flora was with Lucy and Crispin in the kitchen.

Flora looked frantic, and Lucy said again and again: "It's all right, Flora. It's all right."

Crispin was also trying to soothe her, but Flora could not be soothed.

She was crying: "He took the baby. He took him. He was going to hurt him. He said he would if I didn't . . . if I didn't . . ."

"Don't cry," said Crispin. "It's all over now."

She shook her head. "No, no. He said, 'Tell . . . tell . . . and you shall have the baby back.' "

"And you told," said Lucy in a flat voice.

"It's not a secret anymore. Never be told . . . but it was the baby . . . he was going to hurt the baby."

I knew instinctively of whom she was speaking. It was Gaston, of course. Hadn't I seen him here several times? He had been interested in Flora. Intrigued . . . determined to discover that secret which was never to be told. And he had found a way of learning what it was. Oh, poor Flora! She had shown him the picture of the magpies just as she had shown me, and he had determined to force the secret from her.

Why was he so interested in Flora's rambling? I wondered. Why, when he was only concerned with that which could bring advantage to himself?

Lucy took Flora to her room. Crispin stayed behind to help, and I left them, since I could be of no use.

All through the day I thought about what had happened, and that night I had a frightening dream. I was in Barrow Wood, lying helpless on the ground and Mr. Dorian was coming towards me. I called out for help. There was a murmur in the trees. It wasn't

Mr. Dorian who had come to me. It was the seven magpies. They settled on a tree and watched malevolently; and I was struck with terror, as I had been by Mr. Dorian.

I awoke in a panic. It was only a dream, a muddled, silly dream. How could I have been so frightened by a few birds?

The day passed. I wanted to see how Flora was, but I guessed I might not be welcome. I hoped Crispin might come into the office, but he did not. I was glad James did not notice my preoccupation.

The next morning, when we were at breakfast, the postman called. If he had time to stop for a cup of tea when he came, Lily gave it to him in the kitchen. On this occasion, she brought him in to us. Her eyes were round with that horror and excitement which only bad news can bring.

"Tom's just told me," she said, "that Gaston Marchmont's been found shot in the shrubbery at St. Aubyn's."

I felt suddenly faint.

"Yes," went on Tom. "He was found this morning in the shrubbery. You know, near the back of the house. One of the gardeners found him there. Must have been there all night."

"This is going to be a bit of a how-de-do," said Lily.

I heard myself stammer: "How? Who?"

"That," said Tom, "is something they'll have to find out."

. . .

So, IT HAD happened. There were several people who had wanted him out of the way. I was very much afraid, for I feared someone I knew might be guilty of murder.

My first thoughts had gone to Daniel. I could not believe that that gentle man could be capable of murder. It was unbearable. It would mean the end of Rachel's happiness.

Harry Gentry? He had threatened Gaston Marchmont with a gun. He had actually fired it.

Tamarisk? She had come to hate him. He had deceived her; he had humiliated her. She was unpredictable, reckless and above all things she hated to be humiliated.

Crispin hated him. He had said more than once that he would like to be rid of him. He was a menace to everyone. He had even disturbed poor Flora. He created unpleasantness wherever he went.

Not Crispin, I kept saying to myself. That would be unbearable beyond everything.

For the first time, I faced my true feelings for him. He had attracted me from the moment I saw him; and when he had made that unfortunate remark, it had hurt more because it came from him. Barrow Wood? Well, that had affected us both deeply. For myself, I could never forget his wrath when he had thrown Mr. Dorian from him. Nor could I forget his tenderness when he turned to me and picked me up. How I had enjoyed those lunches at The Little Vixen! I had tried to disguise from myself how much I looked forward to his coming to the office.

But there was a barrier there, something which I could not understand. Sometimes I saw a warmth in his attitude towards me—I could imagine that he cared about me—then there would be that aloofness. Perhaps I was half in love with him, but there were times when I felt I did not know him entirely. That aloofness was not only for me, though. It was for everybody. He had a fanatical devotion to the estate. I supposed that was understandable. It was a great responsibility. It was as though there was something on his mind . . . some secret.

Secrets! I was looking for secrets everywhere. It was due to those visits to the Lanes' cottage and that haunting picture of the magpies. I had even dreamed of them.

Aunt Sophie talked of little else but the death of Gaston Marchmont, but then everyone in Harper's Green was naturally talking about it.

Who killed Gaston Marchmont? That was the question on everyone's lips. There was expectancy in the air. Everyone believed that they would know the answer soon.

Lily was sure it was Harry Gentry.

"He had it in for him," she said. "Ever since he caught him with young Sheila. She was ready enough, I'll warrant. If you ask me, it was six to one and half a dozen to the other. Well, he got his comeuppance and it'll be a lesson to her."

"I hope poor old Harry hasn't got himself involved with that," said Aunt Sophie. "It's murder, whatever way you look at it. He's hot-tempered, I know, but I doubt he'd lie in wait, cold-bloodedly like that. He'd have too much sense. No, I reckon it's someone from that man's past. I reckons he's got one."

Aunt Sophie was soothing. She had an idea that I was worried about Crispin. She may have understood my feelings better than I did myself. She knew very well that Crispin had hated Gaston Marchmont and was hoping to get him out of St. Aubyn's. I liked to think that someone from his past had murdered Gaston Marchmont.

. . .

OVER THE NEXT few days the police were constant visitors to Harper's Green. Accounts of Harry Gentry's threats had leaked out and he was questioned several times. It seemed he had an alibi. He had been painting a neighbour's house until nine o'clock that evening when Gaston was shot, and after that the neighbour had gone to the Gentrys' cottage with Harry. They had had a beer and a sandwich made by Sheila, and they had played poker till past midnight.

It was reckoned that the shot which had killed Gaston had been fired between ten thirty and eleven that night. So Harry Gentry was, as they said, "in the clear."

I went to see Rachel. I was glad that her connection with Gaston was not generally known. Daniel, Tamarisk and I were the only ones in the secret.

She was very relieved to see me. "I knew you'd come sometime," she said.

"I wanted to come before . . . but I was not sure . . ."

"Freddie, you don't think it was Daniel?"

I was silent.

"It's not true," she burst out vehemently. "He came in in the late afternoon and was in the house till morning. Jack was here. He can prove it."

"Oh, Rachel, I've been so worried."

"So have I . . . or would have been if I didn't know that Daniel had been here all that time. It happened that night between ten and eleven, wasn't it? He'd been lying there . . . dead . . . all that time."

"Why should Daniel come into this?" I said. "Why should Gaston be connected with you? No one knows that there might be a motive."

"They mustn't know, Freddie. Oh, they mustn't know."

"No one knows about you and Gaston but us, and . . . er . . . Tamarisk."

She looked at me in dismay.

"He told her," I said. I went on quickly: "She wouldn't say anything. She wouldn't want it known that while he was courting her he was making love to you. It's all right. There's nothing to worry about. Aunt Sophie thinks it might have been someone from his past. A man like that would surely have a shady past. He must have made enemies. He has, in the short time he has been here, made many."

"Oh, Freddie, I know it's wrong, but I'm glad he's not here anymore. There would never have been any peace. I'm glad. I'm glad."

"I understand how you feel. I can really

see no reason why you should be connected with this."

She put her arms round me and clung to me.

"I'm glad you're here, Freddie. I'm glad you're my friend. Daniel often says what a wonderful friend you have been to us both. When I think . . ."

"Don't think of that. Forget it. It isn't going to matter now. You are free of him. I just wanted to make sure that Daniel was not . . ."

"He wasn't. I swear he was here all the time."

I wanted so much to believe her. I did while I was with her, but when I went away, I thought how much Daniel must hate him because Rachel had once loved him. The child he loved was not his. And then Gaston had come back to threaten.

He was innocent. She had sworn he was innocent. But then a little voice within me said, well, she would, wouldn't she?

· · ·

I WENT TO see Tamarisk. I was told that she was in her room and not seeing anyone.

"Will you tell her I called?" I said. "If she wants to see me I could come at any time."

I hovered while the maid went upstairs. She came down hastily just as I was leaving.

"Mrs. Marchmont says she will see you, Miss Hammond." She looked at me and shook her head. "Poor lady. The police have been pestering her again. She's taking this badly."

"I know what it must be like," I said. "I won't stay long unless she wants me to."

Tamarisk was lying on her bed. She was fully clothed but her long fair hair was loose about her shoulders. She looked very pale.

"So you came, Fred," she said.

"I wanted to before, but I wasn't sure whether you'd want to see anyone. I was almost turned away today."

"I didn't want to see most people. But I'd like to talk to you."

I sat down by the bed.

"Isn't it awful?" she went on.

I nodded.

"I can't believe that I shall never see him again. I can't believe he's dead. The police have been here. They keep asking questions. They've interviewed Crispin . . . my mother . . . some of the servants. My mother is very unhappy. She was really fond of him."

"Tamarisk, how are you feeling?"

She stared ahead of her and I noticed the sullen droop of her lips.

She said: "I know I mustn't say this . . . but it's only to you. I'm glad. That's the truth. I hated him."

I was startled and she smiled wryly. "I didn't tell the police that, of course. They might have thought I was the one who did it. I can tell you there were times when I might have done it."

"Don't talk like that, Tamarisk!"

"It's unwise, isn't it? In fact, it's almost as though they suspect me . . . although they haven't said so in so many words. I've been an awful fool, Fred. But you always thought I was, didn't you? I believed all he told me. And while he was telling me he wouldn't look at anyone else, he was carrying on an intrigue with Rachel."

"Tamarisk, please don't talk of that. Think of what it would mean to her and Daniel. And there's the baby."

"But it's true," she said.

"Listen, he did a lot of harm while he was alive. He's dead now. Let that be an end to it."

"An end of it! What about this pestering by the police?"

"That's inevitable. This is a case of murder. What did the police say to you?"

"Oh, they were very polite. One talking to me very gently and the other making notes in his little book. I had to tell them about our marriage and how I'd known him only a short time. They knew he had come here under a false name. They knew something of him. Apparently he had been in trouble . . . under another name. It's so humiliating to think I was so taken in."

"Never mind. Lots of people are taken in at some time and you were very young."

"It will be in all the papers. I wonder who did it. They say Harry Gentry was with a neighbour of his when Gaston was killed. I was here all the time. So was Crispin. At one time I wondered whether Crispin . . ."

"Of course he wouldn't! He has too much sense."

"I suppose so. But he did hate him. In any case, he was here. I suppose we shall know one day. The police will find out, won't they?"

"I daresay they will. They usually do."

"I'm glad you came, Fred. I like talking to you. Nothing lasts, does it? This will be over sometime. Then I shall be free."

"Tamarisk, I hope everything turns out all right."

"I know you do. You cheer me up. I guessed you'd come along with your wise old sayings. 'Every cloud has a silver lining.' 'Good cometh out of evil.' 'When this blows over everything will be different.' It will be a new start. I'll have to forget. And one thing I keep telling myself is, I'm free."

Yes, I thought. You are lucky to be free of him. There must be several people to rejoice that Gaston Marchmont was dead.

. . .

THE NEXT MORNING when the postman arrived with the mail, he had more news for us.

Lily brought him in while we were having breakfast.

"There's something going on up at St. Aubyn's," he told us. "They're digging up in the shrubbery."

"What for?" asked Aunt Sophie.

"Don't ask me, Miss Cardingham. But the police are there."

"What can that mean?" murmured Aunt Sophie. "What do they expect to find?"

"Reckon we'll know soon enough."

When he had left we went on talking about it and the first thing James Perrin said when I saw him was: "Have you heard? There's an investigation going on."

"They are digging in St. Aubyn's. The postman brought the news while we were at breakfast."

"This is a distressing business."

"It must be something to do with the murder. I don't know where this is going to end. There are so many rumours going round and strangers all over the place hoping for a peep at the spot where a murder was committed."

"I wish that man had never come here."

"I don't suppose you are the only one. It's strange. Nothing happens for years and then it changes. There was poor old Dorian's death, the elopement, the coming of this man, and now murder."

I wondered what James would have thought if I had told him about what had happened in Barrow Wood.

"I hope Crispin's all right," said James.

"What do you mean?" I asked fearfully.

He was frowning and did not answer. I thought, he suspects Crispin. A memory of Crispin in Barrow Wood came to me—the look in his eyes when he had picked up Mr. Dorian. I had said later: "You might have killed him," and he had replied that that would be no loss. Was that how he had felt about Gaston?

I was glad to get home that day. Aunt Sophie was waiting for me. She had something of importance to say to me. Before she could speak the thought flashed into my mind, what have they found in the shrubbery?

But what she said was: "Crispin called. He wants to see you. It's important."

"When?" I asked eagerly.

She looked at the clock on the mantel-piece. "In about half an hour."

"Where?"

"He's coming here. He knew what time you'd be home. He said he'd call back. You can talk to him in the sitting-room."

I said: "What has happened about the shrubbery?"

"I don't know."

"Are they still digging?"

"No. They've stopped, I believe. Well, he'll be here soon. He said he wanted to talk to you alone."

I washed, combed my hair and waited. Then I heard the sound of his horse's hoofs and Aunt Sophie brought him into the sitting-room.

"Would you like a glass of wine?" asked Aunt Sophie.

"No, thanks," said Crispin.

"Well, I'll be around if you want anything."

When she left us together he came to me and took both my hands in his.

I said: "Please tell me . . . what has happened?"

He released my hands and we sat down.

He said quietly: "They've found the gun. It was buried in the shrubbery not far from where the body was found. It's obviously the one. No doubt of it."

"What made them look?"

"They noticed the ground had been recently disturbed."

"Does it help them?"

"It's one of the guns from the gunroom at St. Aubyn's."

I stared at him in dismay.

"And what does that mean?"

"That someone took the gun from the gunroom, used it and, instead of putting it back, buried it in the shrubbery."

"Whatever for?"

He shrugged his shoulders.

"Do they think it was someone from the house?" I asked.

"That does seem one conclusion."

"But why should someone in the house take a gun and not put it back there?"

"That's a mystery."

"What do they think it means?"

"I don't know. Until they have found the guilty one, they suspect everyone. It is obvious now that it was someone who had access to the house."

"So the idea that it could have been an enemy from the past is no longer plausible."

"An enemy from the past?"

"Oh, it was just something Aunt Sophie suggested. She thought that a man like Gaston Marchmont must have made enemies wherever he went and she thought it possible that one might have caught up with him."

"It's an interesting theory. I wish it were true."

"What's going to happen now?"

He shook his head.

"You're worried?" I said.

"I am. It brings it closer to the house. But why on earth did someone take the gun and then bury it . . . not very neatly, either? It was a strange thing to do."

"Perhaps they'll find out."

He turned to me. "I have been wanting to talk to you for a long time. Perhaps this is not the time to do it, but I feel I can't wait any longer."

"What did you want to say to me?"

"You must have known for some time that I am very interested in you."

"You mean, after that terrible thing happened . . ."

"That too. But before that. Right from the beginning."

"When you noticed the plain child?"

"That has been forgiven and forgotten. Frederica, I love you. I want you to marry me."

I drew back in amazement.

"I know this is hardly the time," he went on, "but I could not keep it to myself any longer. I have been on the verge of saying it many times. I feel that so much time is being wasted." He looked at me searchingly. "Do you want me to go on?"

"Yes," I said eagerly, "I do."

"Does that mean . . . ?"

"It means that I like to hear it."

He had risen and drew me to my feet. He held me tightly in his arms and, in spite of all the fear and suspicions I was experiencing, I was happy.

He kissed me eagerly, fiercely even.

I was breathless with emotion. I felt I must be dreaming. So much that was strange had happened recently, and this was as unexpected as any.

"I was afraid to face up to my feelings," he said. "What happens in the past has an effect, doesn't it? You think everything is tainted. But now . . ."

"Let's sit down and talk," I said.

"Tell me first, you do care for me?"

"Of course I do."

"I'm happy then. In spite of this . . . I'm happy. We'll be together. Whatever it is, we'll face it."

"I am rather bewildered," I told him.

"But you knew how I felt!"

"I wasn't sure. When I talked about going away you kept me here."

"Of course I couldn't let you go."

"I hated the thought of leaving."

"Yet you planned to do it."

"I thought it would be best."

"I have been rather arrogant, haven't I?"

"Standoffish. Aloof."

"It was a sort of defence." He laughed suddenly. "And now . . . in the midst of all this . . ."

"Perhaps," I said, "because of all this."

"It had to come out. I couldn't keep it to myself any longer, Frederica. What a dignified name you have!"

"Yes, I have often found it so. My mother gave it to me because she was so proud of the family. There had been several Fredericks who had won honours—generals, politicians and such. She would have preferred me to be a boy. Then I should have been plain Frederick."

Why were we talking in this way of things

that did not matter? It was as though we were trying to put off something frightening. I kept remembering his anger, his fury against Mr. Dorian, the manner in which he had spoken of Gaston and his desire to be rid of him. He had chosen this moment, in the midst of all this turmoil, when it had been discovered that the murder weapon had been found in his shrubbery, to propose marriage to me.

I wanted to ask him why.

He said: "I've been in love with you for a long time. More than anything, I want you to love me too. I could not believe you could, though. I am not a charmer like . . ."

His face darkened and the fear was back with me.

I said: "Crispin, I love you. I want to marry you, and I want everything to be perfect between us now and always. I want to know everything about you. I don't want there to be any secrets between us."

I was aware of a slight withdrawal and the pause before he said: "Of course, I want the same."

There was something he was holding back. I prayed inwardly that he might not be involved in this terrible affair. I could not bear it if he were.

It seemed to me that he was begging me

to speak of our love and nothing else, that he was asking me to put aside everything but this wonderful revelation that we loved each other.

He said, almost pleadingly: "It is wonderful that you care for me. And you care about the estate too." He frowned and waved his hand. "All this . . . trouble . . . will be over soon. They'll find out who did it and settle it. We've got to forget it. We shall be together and it will be wonderful. You have changed me, you know, my darling. You have changed my outlook on life. I was melancholy. I didn't believe in the good things. I want you to understand . . . about my first marriage."

"That was a long time ago."

"It had a great effect on me . . . on what I became. It was only after I was in love with you that I began to escape from it. You must understand. I shall have no peace until you do."

He held my hand tightly and went on: "I was very young. Eighteen, getting on for nineteen. I was at the university and a company of players came to the town. She was one of them. She must have been twenty-five at that time. She admitted to twenty-one. I went to the show . . . some musical comedy . . . song and dance show. She was in the front line of the chorus. I thought she was beautiful. I was there on the first night . . . and the next . . . I sent flowers. I was granted a meeting. I was completely infatuated."

"It has happened to many young people before."

"That does not excuse my folly."

"No, but it is comforting to know you were not the only one."

"You will always make excuses for me like that, won't you?"

"I suppose people do for those they love."

He drew me to him and kissed me.

"How glad I am that I told you! I really can't believe you love me. You will take care of me forevermore."

"You are the strong man. It is you who should take care of me."

"I will with all my strength . . . and . . . in my weakness you will be there."

"When you want me," I told him.

There was silence for a few moments while he held me close to him and kissed my hair.

"You were telling me," I reminded him.

He was sober immediately.

"I am so ashamed of it, but you must know me as far as . . ." He hesitated and I felt that fear touch me once more.

"I want to know everything, Crispin," I said firmly. "Please don't hold anything back. I will understand . . . whatever it is."

There was again that brief hesitation.

"Well," he went on, "against the advice of my friends, I married her. I gave up my studies. After all, I had the estate. I had always been interested in it. I thought I would settle down. Kate . . . I don't think that was her real name . . . there was no truth about her. It was all false. Kate Carvel. She was bored with the estate. She didn't want to live in the country. I was disillusioned. I realised very quickly what a terrible mistake I had made. And to see oneself as a fool at the age of nineteen is a very humiliating experience. It maims you . . . for life, sometimes. It did for me until you appeared. Then, I hope, I began to change."

"I am so glad of that, Crispin."

"I don't want to make excuses for myself, but no one ever really cared for me before except Lucy Lane. That was why I was so easily duped by Kate. She was good at pretence. My parents had never been very interested in Tamarisk or me. They were so absorbed by their own way of life, which didn't include us. Lucy was always wonderful to me."

"And you have been wonderful to her."

"I have only done what was natural."

"I think you have looked after her splendidly . . . and her sister too."

"I was so relieved when Kate went away. I can't explain how I felt."

"I can understand."

"You've heard about the accident. I was called to identify her. She was very badly injured. Fortunately there was a ring which I had given her before we were married. It had been in the family for years. It had a crest on it, very delicately carved. I have the ring now. It was enough. There was also a fur cape with her initials worked in the lining. That episode was over."

"And you must forget it."

"I can now. The fact that you love me has restored my faith in myself."

I laughed. "I had always believed that was the last thing you lacked. In fact . . ."

"I was arrogant, as we agreed."

"Well, perhaps."

"You don't have to watch your words with me, my dearest. I shall want the truth from you."

"And I from you," I replied, again conscious of that little qualm of fear.

"I had the estate," he went on. "I gave myself up to that entirely. You have no idea how it helped me through that time."

"I understand perfectly."

"It will be wonderful. We'll be married . . . as soon as this affair is over."

"I do hope it soon will be. James was saying that there are strangers round the place, curious to see where a man was murdered."

"Ah, James." He looked at me intently. "He's a good fellow, James."

"I know."

"He has a fondness for you. I can tell you, I have been jealous of him at times."

"There was no need."

"People would say he will make an admirable husband."

"I am sure he will to someone one day."

"Do you have any strong feelings for him?"

"I like him."

"Liking can grow into something stronger. But that growth is stunted now. Assure me this is so. You will find I am in constant need of reassurance."

"You shall always have it."

He stood up suddenly and, drawing me to my feet, held me tightly against him so that I could not see his face.

"There we are," he said. "Explanations over. You know of my past and you still want to marry me. I could dance round this room, but you have already had experience of my dancing and I know you did not have any great opinion of it."

"I shall certainly not be marrying you for your ability to dance," I said lightly.

His face was against mine and I longed to be able to still the fears that would keep intruding. If only they would go, how happy I could be.

I said: "Aunt Sophie will be getting very curious. Shall we call her and tell her?"

"Yes, do. I want everyone to know."

Aunt Sophie came in.

"We have news for you," I said. "Crispin and I are engaged to be married."

She opened her eyes wide and her joy was apparent.

She kissed me and then Crispin.

"God bless you both," she said. "I knew . . . I just knew. But you were such a long time about it!"

. . .

WHEN CRISPIN HAD left, Aunt Sophie and I sat together in the sitting-room and talked.

She told me how delighted she was.

"I always thought there was a lot of good in Crispin," she said, "and when I saw you two together, I knew how it ought to be. He found that job for you, didn't he? That was a sign all right. It made me laugh. Of course, he did have that first marriage of his. It was rather sad. He was so young, and one of the saddest things about life is that when you are young you think you know everything, and when you get older you learn how little you know. But everything that happens is experience, and at least when you've had one bad blow it teaches you not to do it again. I'm so happy for you, Freddie, and for myself. You'll be here—a stone's throw away. It's the best thing that could have happened. I've always been scared that one day you would go away."

I told her about the find in the shrubbery. She was decidedly sobered and I saw some of the joy go out of her face.

"A gun from the gunroom!" she cried. "What on earth does that mean?"

"No one knows."

"It would seem that someone from St. Aubyn's fired that shot."

"Someone could have got in and taken the gun."

"It would seem to be someone who knew the place pretty well."

"There are a lot of people who do."

"And why bury it? Why not put it back?"

"It's a mystery. Oh, I do wish this wretched business was over."

"It won't be until they find who killed that man."

She was looking at me with anxiety in her eyes.

I wanted to shout at her: it wasn't Crispin. He was in the house all the time. People don't kill their brothers-in-law just because they don't like them.

I could see the thoughts chasing themselves round and round in Aunt Sophie's mind. Why had Crispin chosen this time to ask me to marry him?

. . .

IT WAS THE day of the inquest. Crispin and I had not officially announced our engagement. We decided that it was not yet the time to do so, and Aunt Sophie had agreed with that.

Suspicion hung over Harper's Green. The discovery in the grounds of St. Aubyn's, having made headline news in the newspapers, was being discussed everywhere. I could imagine that all sorts of bizarre conclusions were being arrived at. We were all very uneasy.

I went to the office in the morning. James was very thoughtful.

"This is a horrible business," he said. "I can't bear to see the sightseers round the place. They are all trying to get a look at the shrubbery. I wish they could find the murderer and have done with it."

"There'll be even more publicity when they do," I reminded him. "And there'll be a trial."

"I do hope no one here is involved," he said uneasily. "Poor Mrs. Marchmont! This must be a trial for her."

"She keeps to the house," I remarked. "And it certainly is very upsetting for her."

"She will have to go to the inquest, of course—and poor Harry Gentry too. And the servants—some of them, in any case. I wonder what effect this will have on the estate."

"What effect should it have?"

"I was thinking, if they never find the murderer, it's going to make for a lot of uneasiness. I often thought of getting my own place. It would be small to start with. My own farm, I mean . . . a place to manage, all of my own. There's nothing like being one's own master."

"I suppose not."

"One could rent at first and perhaps in time buy." He was looking at me expectantly.

"At the moment," I said, "you are doing

very well here. Oh, I do wonder what will happen at the inquest."

"I wish they hadn't found that gun buried in the shrubbery."

"I was hoping it was someone not known to us," I said. "Someone from his past."

"Which must have been a shady one. Yes, that would have been a very good solution."

I don't know how I got through that day. I left as early as I could.

Aunt Sophie was waiting for the verdict as eagerly as I was. I was sure that Crispin, knowing my anxiety, would come immediately to the Rowans.

He did.

"The verdict," he told us, "is murder, of course. Murder against some person or persons unknown."

"What else could it be?" said Aunt Sophie.

"What now?" I asked.

"The police will be as busy as ever," said Crispin. "We all had rather a gruelling time on the stand. Poor Tamarisk was most upset. Harry Gentry stood up to it all very well. He had, of course, threatened Marchmont and fired his gun—though into the air. And it had been witnessed by several people. But, of course, the gun which fired the fatal shot was not his. Marchmont was revealed as a very unpleasant type, but that doesn't give anyone a right to murder him. We haven't heard the last of this. The matter of the gun caused a great stir of interest. It appears to level it down to someone in the neighbour-hood. They asked me a lot of questions about the gun and the gunroom. We don't use them much now. There used to be a lot of shooting on the estate. The odd point was that someone took the gun and buried it. Whereas, if it were someone who had access to the house, it would have seemed so much easier to put it back."

"It points to someone who could get into the house but didn't live there," I said with a certain relief.

He smiled at me, understanding my thoughts.

"I believe that is the impression they had," he said. "There is more to come, I don't doubt. I am afraid we haven't seen the last of this miserable business, but at least the inquest is over."

A Ghost from the Past

We were in late September and there was to be a dinner party at St. Aubyn's at which Crispin and I would announce our engagement.

"It is what my mother will want," said Crispin. "There has always been a certain amount of formality in the family."

People were still talking of the murder. Far from stemming interest in that morbid subject, the inquest had increased it. "Some person or persons unknown." There was something sinister about the very phrase. In the shops and every household the question was "Who killed Gaston Marchmont?"

Suspicion rested on one or two people: Crispin was one of those, so were Tamarisk and Harry Gentry, though more than one clung to the belief that it was someone from

Gaston's past. After all, why should not someone have got into the house, taken the gun and not had an opportunity of putting it back? There was a certain plausibility in the theory.

Meanwhile, there was the dinner party and there would be another piece of news to startle the community.

Mrs. St. Aubyn joined us for dinner. Her health had improved so much since the arrival of Gaston that she had ceased to be the invalid she had been before. He had flattered her so blatantly, telling her she had the appearance of a young girl, that she had begun to behave like one. She had made a habit of dining at table with the family and she could not slip back into invalidism so soon after his departure. I thought to myself, he has done some good, then. She must have been the only person who mourned him, for there was no doubt that she was genuinely saddened by his death.

Guests at the party were the Hetheringtons and friends in the neighbourhood, including the doctor and his wife and from Devizes a lawyer who represented the family. Aunt Sophie, of course, was present.

Crispin sat at the head of the table and I was on his right hand. Mrs. St. Aubyn sat at the other end and, although she looked very sad, she was very different from the invalid who had taken most of her meals in her own room. Tamarisk also was present. She had changed a great deal; she had lost that careless manner of the past and was no longer the light-hearted girl.

The ghost of Gaston Marchmont seemed to hover over us all, and although a great effort was made not to refer to past events and to be as we all had been before, that was not possible.

The meal was over when Crispin rose and, taking my hand, said simply: "I have an announcement to make. Frederica—Miss Hammond—and I have decided to marry."

Congratulations ensued, and we drank the champagne which the butler had brought up from the cellars.

I could have been very happy but for that hovering ghost. I wondered if it would ever leave us in peace.

Later in the drawing-room I found Tamarisk beside me.

"I did not need the formal announcement," she said. "I knew, of course, what was in the air."

"Was it so obvious?"

"Quite. Particularly since you went to the office. He arranged that, of course."

"It was good of him."

"Good! He was thinking of himself," she said.

"Tamarisk, how are you?"

"I don't know. Sometimes I'm miserable. Sometimes I'm ashamed. Then I'm afraid. Then I'm glad . . . glad that he's gone . . . and yet in a way he is still here. He always will be until they find out who killed him. I wish . . . oh, how I wish I had never seen him."

I put my hand over hers.

"We're like sisters in a way," she said. "That's something I find cheering."

"I'm glad."

"Rachel, you and I. The three of us . . . we were always together, weren't we? It seems that you have done better than any of us. You and Crispin. Who would have believed Crispin would be in love, and with you?"

"Rachel has a very happy marriage."

"Poor Rachel."

"She's all right. She's happy now. But, Tamarisk, what about you?"

"I shall be all right too when this is all over. If only it had been someone we didn't know who had killed him so that we could forget. They will be hovering till they find out. The police, I mean. They don't just forget it after an inquest."

"We have to go on as if it hadn't happened."

"Some people think I did it. They always will. You see what I mean about it's being there always."

"It won't be. There'll be an answer."

"But what if the answer is something we don't want it to be?"

"What do you mean?"

"You know what I mean. We're going to try to be happy. Or pretend we are. Perhaps we might even succeed for a time. And then it will be there. It will pop up, Fred. They've got to find out who did it. It will never be finished until they do."

Aunt Sophie was coming over to us. She was smiling brightly. She was very pleased, but behind her smiles I could detect a certain anxiety.

Oh yes, indeed, the ghost of Gaston Marchmont was with us on that night.

. . .

IT AMAZED ME to realise the interest there was in our proposed marriage; and I did not only mean among the inhabitants of Harper's Green. That, of course, I fully expected.

It was a few days after the dinner party. When I went down to breakfast Aunt Sophie was already seated at the table. She was reading the morning newspaper and when she greeted me I detected the dismay in her face immediately.

"Good morning, Aunt Sophie." I went to her and kissed her. "Anything wrong?"

She shrugged her shoulders. "I suppose it's nothing, really."

"You look upset."

"It's just this."

She pushed the newspaper over to me as I sat down beside her. There was a picture of Crispin on the front page.

"What is this?" I cried.

"They must have taken it sometime during the investigations. The press is usually lurking somewhere. That's Inspector Burrows with him. The one who was here, remember?"

I read:

To marry. The engagement is announced of Mr. Crispin St. Aubyn to Miss Frederica Hammond, who has been a neighbour of his for some years. Mr. St. Aubyn is the Wiltshire landowner on whose estate the body of Gaston Marchmont was recently found. The gun from which the fatal shot was fired was taken from the St. Aubyn gunroom. This will be Mr. St. Aubyn's second marriage. His first wife was Kate Carvel, the actress, who was killed in a railway accident soon after the marriage.

Aunt Sophie was watching me.

"Why do they want to bring all this up?"

"I suppose they think people want to read it," said Aunt Sophie.

"But that first marriage . . ."

"Oh, I suppose it adds a further touch of drama."

"Why should people want to hear all that?"

"The case was publicised nationally, of course."

Yes, I thought, this paper was not the local one. It would be circulated all over the country. I thought of the thousands who would be reading that item.

It will be forgotten in time, I told myself. But there would always be some to remember. There really was no escape.

. . .

CRISPIN HIMSELF WAS not very disturbed by the newspaper notice.

He said: "Until this thing is settled they will keep their eyes on us. We have to forget it. Let's think about pleasant things. I don't see any reason for delay. Let's make it soon.

My mother is already making plans. She says it must be a wedding in the St. Aubyn's tradition. I mustn't forget that I'm the head of the family and all that. Personally, I'd go for the quickest way. I just want to be with you . . . to make sure we are together . . . always."

"I want that too," I said. "But I suppose the wedding is going to attract more attention from the press."

"I'm afraid we shall have to accept that."

"Perhaps we should wait a little . . . not too long. But in case there is some development."

He looked aghast.

"Some discovery," I went on. "Some revelation."

"Oh no!" he cried vehemently. He was frowning deeply, and I put my arms round him and held him close to me. He clung, almost as though he were asking for protection.

"Never leave me. Do not talk of delays."

I was deeply touched. I felt as though I were trying to reach out to him and could not quite do so. I was deeply aware of some barrier between us, and I said: "Crispin, there is something . . ."

"What do you mean?" Did I fancy I detected a note of fear in his voice?

"There should not be any secrets between us," I said on impulse.

He drew back. He was himself again—the man in command of any situation.

"What do you mean, Frederica?" he repeated.

"I just thought that there might be something important that I did not know."

He laughed and kissed me. "This is the important matter . . . the most important matter in the world to me. When are we going to get married?"

"We should talk to your mother and Aunt Sophie."

"I think Aunt Sophie will be amenable."

"She will go along with anything we decide, of course, but she did say, that in view of . . . everything . . . we should not have the grand ceremony your mother wants. It is too soon after that trouble."

He was silent.

"She is right," I persisted. "Your brother-in-law is dead. It's a death in the family. It is usual to wait a year after that."

"Impossible! It was no great bereavement."

"It was murder. I think we should offend a lot of sensibilities if we celebrated what should be a joyous occasion too soon after that. What construction would people put upon it?"

"Do we care?"

"I think we have to remember it is a delicate situation. Crispin, we have to remember that until the case is solved some may be thinking all sorts of things about people."

He was thoughtful. "You don't mean you think we should wait a year?"

"Not as long as that, no. But shouldn't we see how things go?"

"I long to get away," he said. "Darling, where shall we go?"

"Anywhere will do."

"Away from this place . . . all the speculations . . . all the memories of it. I want to think of us and nothing else."

"It sounds blissful."

Again I had that idea that he was trying to reach out to me, to tell me what was on his mind. A terrible fear came to me and it would not go away. What part had he played in this murder, I kept asking myself. Why did he not tell me what was on his mind? Could it be that he dared not?

I thought how happy I could be if we could be together and there was nothing between us and our happiness, if I could think of the future with hope and confidence. But I could not rid myself of images of that body in the shrubbery and the gun which had been taken from the gunroom at St. Aubyn's.

Crispin continued to talk of our honeymoon. Italy was always a favourite place. Was it not one of the most beautiful countries in the world? So much of the past still survived there. Florence, Venice, Rome. Austria was inviting. We could go to Salzburg, Mozart's birthplace. France? The châteaux of the Loire. He had always wanted to see Château Gaillard with its memories of Richard Coeur de Lion.

But while we discussed them all I could not stop thinking. There is something. He cannot entirely hide it. I can see it in his eyes.

Why will he not tell me? I can't ask him because he does not admit to its being there. But, knowing him, loving him, I am aware of it.

· · ·

LILY WAS PROUD of me.

"The big house, eh? Mistress of all that! My word, you'll be too grand to come and see us at the Rowans."

We laughed at her.

"You don't think that, Lily, you know very well," I retorted.

"Well, of course not. You'll always be our little Miss Freddie, won't she, Miss Sophie?"

"Yes, she will. When we are doddering old ladies and she herself a mature matron, she will always be our little Miss Freddie."

Aunt Sophie often talked about the past.

"I remember Crispin as a boy," she said. "A nice lad. And the way he looks after those Lanes . . . that's a credit to him. I used to see him now and then. His parents were hardly ever here. They were always gadding up to London or the Continent . . . letting the place go to rack and ruin. It was a mercy they had a good manager. And when Crispin took over, that was the best thing that could have happened to the place. That was when he was married. That brought him out of the university and got him into the estate. It was time, too. It's a funny thing, but there is always good in something. That marriage of his brought him home and the estate has prospered ever since."

"You must have seen his wife often."

"Oh yes, I saw her. My goodness, what a shock it was! Disaster from the start. I just wondered how he could have done it. Folly of youth, I suppose. She seemed a lot older than he was . . . more than she'd admit to, I reckon."

"Was she very beautiful?"

"Not to my mind. All rouge and powder and hair too gold to be natural. As soon as I set eyes on her I knew it wouldn't last long."

"I want to know about it, Aunt Sophie."

"You've nothing to fear from her, my dear. Sometimes in these second marriages the second wife gets fancies about the first. Thinks the husband is hankering after the past. That's something you'll be spared. He was glad to be rid of her. Everyone knows that."

"What was it like at St. Aubyn's when she was there?"

"She wanted parties and that sort of thing."

"Like Crispin's parents."

"They were abroad most of the time and it wasn't like that with her at all. The parents' kind were elegant affairs. These were noisy, rowdy. Lots of music hall people, I think. People in the neighbourhood didn't like it much. There was quarrelling, too. Poor Crispin. He soon saw what he'd let himself in for. Then she got bored with it all and went off. Soon after that there was the crash and she was killed. Happy release, people said, for Crispin."

"I think all that had a great effect on him."

"Bound to. He seemed to shut himself

away. Thought of nothing but the estate. One or two people had their eyes on him."

"You mean like Lady Fiona?"

"Perhaps. There were others. He didn't seem to want any of them. Not until he fell in love with you. Oh, Freddie, I believe everything is going to be wonderful for you. He's changed a lot. He's losing that haunted look. That proud sort of arrogance. It's a defiance against fate. He seemed to have come to the conclusion that he was a fool to have got caught as he did. He despised himself, and all that self-assurance was a shield to hide behind."

"Yes," I said. "I am sure you are right, but I think there is something between us though . . . something which prevents my getting as close to him as I should like."

"That's it, dear. It will take some time for him to break completely from the past. But he's on the way and I am so happy about this. I am sure it's right for you and your happiness is more important to me than anything."

"Dearest Aunt Sophie, I don't know how to begin to thank you for all you have done for me. Ever since I came to you here you have been wonderful to me."

I saw the brightness of tears glistening in her eyes.

"Dearest child, you are my own niece and . . ."

"And my father's daughter? Tell me, have you written to him?"

"I have told him of your engagement."

"Will he be interested? After all, he doesn't know anything about Crispin. He doesn't really know me."

"He knows you well from my letters. He is always anxious to know about you. He has now gone right away to an island on the other side of the world."

"I thought he was in Egypt."

"He left some time ago. It's a remote sort of place called Casker's Island. It seems to have been discovered by a man called Casker some years ago. Few people have ever heard of it. I searched the map in vain. But I did find it in one atlas. Just a little black dot on the sea. I suppose it is too insignificant to be mentioned in most."

"What is he doing there?"

"He's with someone called Karla. Polynesian, I think. He mentions her now and then. I can't think why he left Egypt. I suppose there is some reason, but he hasn't told me."

"I think it is wonderful that you have kept in touch all these years."

"We were great friends. Still are, and I suppose always will be," she replied.

. . .

CRISPIN AND I were together almost every day. He took me round the estate and we were greeted with congratulations everywhere we went. He was anxious for me to learn more about it. My spell in the office had taught me a good deal and I was already quite knowledgeable. It was his life and he was eager for me to share it. And I fervently wanted to.

We were very happy during those days. Crispin had changed subtly. I was discovering new facets in his character, and they delighted me. He had a great capacity for enjoyment which had previously been suppressed. Life seemed now to be full of amusement; we were constantly laughing and it was the laughter of happiness.

I thought, everything will be all right now.

We called at Grindle's Farm. Rachel was delighted to see us and Danielle was produced to be admired. I had a few moments alone with Rachel and she told me how happy she was for me.

"And you are not worried anymore?" I asked.

"Only occasionally it comes back. I suppose that is inevitable. I wish they could find out who killed Gaston and settle it once and for all. I don't think we shall be entirely at ease until they do. The police don't seem to be so interested anymore."

"I expect they will call it one of those unsolved crimes. There are many of them, I am sure."

"Yes. They just fade out of people's memories in spite of the fact that they were so interested in them at the time. That's how it will be. But how I wish it could all be settled."

"So do we all."

Crispin and I rode off together.

They were such happy days until I noticed the change in him. I knew him so well now and it was hard for him to deceive me. I fancied there was a false note in his laughter and I caught an anxious expression in his eyes now and then. He was preoccupied with some problem, making any effort to pretend all was well.

"Is anything wrong?" I asked.

"No. Nothing. What should be?"

How I wished he would tell me everything. That vague uneasy feeling was back with me. I thought it had gone forever.

I wanted to say: there must be complete trust between us. Tell me what it is that is bothering you. Let us share it.

There were times when he cast off this

anxiety. Then I asked myself if I had imagined it.

It was some days later when he said he had to go to Salisbury on business and would be away for the day. I wished that I could go with him but he said he would be engaged with various people during the day and I should be left alone.

"It's only for a day," he added.

But when we said goodbye that evening he held me tightly to him as though he were very reluctant to let me go.

"I shall see you the day after tomorrow," I said.

"Yes," he said, still holding me tightly.

"You don't seem to want to let me go," I said lightly.

He replied fervently: "I shall never let you go."

. . .

THAT MORNING AUNT Sophie said to me: "I am going into Devizes this afternoon. Why don't you come with me?"

"I think I ought to go and look in at the office," I replied.

She nodded. "Oh well, never mind. I shall take the trap. There are one or two things I want to get. I'll be back before evening."

I went to the office. James Perrin was

there. He had changed towards me since my engagement to Crispin had been announced. He was quieter, more reserved. I knew that in his rather sober way he had contemplated marrying me. I should never have done so even if there had not been Crispin, but I liked him very much all the same.

He talked about the tenants and how concerned he was about the north-facing walls of some of the cottages.

"I think they will have to be carefully looked at," he said.

He was going to do this now and I was glad that he did not suggest I accompany him.

I asked him about the place he was considering renting.

"I'm giving that one a miss," he told me. "There'll be something else when the time comes. As a matter of fact, someone has already taken the place I was thinking of."

I was glad when it was time to go home. I realised afresh how empty the days were without Crispin.

When I arrived home Aunt Sophie was not back. Well, she had said before evening. I supposed something had delayed her.

It was nearly seven o'clock when she returned and I was beginning to get anxious about her. She looked tired and rather strained.

"Are you all right?" I asked anxiously.

"I'm exhausted. It's a long journey. I'm going straight to my room."

"Shall I get Lily to bring something up?"

"No. I don't really want anything to eat. I had something in Devizes. Really, I'm worn out."

"What happened?"

"Nothing . . . nothing. I'll tell you about it sometime. Just now I want my bed more than anything. I'm getting too old for this sort of thing."

"Can I do anything?"

"No . . . no. I'll be better in bed."

"You're sure Lily can't bring you something? Some hot milk?"

"No, no." She was frowning. That was so unlike her.

She went to her room and I went to see Lily.

"She's back then," said Lily. "I'll see about dinner."

"She doesn't want anything. She's gone straight to bed."

"She must have had something in Devizes."

"She looks worn out and she just wants to go to bed."

"Doesn't want anything! I'll take up some milk."

"She firmly said she doesn't want anything. All she wants is bed and sleep."

It was a gloomy evening. It started to rain and there was thunder in the air. I had expected Aunt Sophie to come back and tell me with her usual vivacity all about the visit to Devizes. This was most extraordinary, and I was worried about her.

I could not resist going to her room. She was lying in her bed, her eyes tightly closed, but even so she looked unlike herself. I was afraid she was going to be ill.

I went to Lily. I said: "I hope she's all right. I just crept in to look at her."

"So did I," said Lily. "She is just worn out. Exhausted, that's what. It'll teach her a lesson. She's always doing too much."

I had to be satisfied with that.

I went to my room. It was about half past nine. How different everything seemed without Aunt Sophie. I could not bear anything to happen to her.

I sat by my window looking out. The clouds were louring. I could see Barrow Wood. It looked particularly menacing in this light, but it always did to me . . . even in sunshine. From the distance came the rumble of thunder. It had been a very unsatisfactory day. I kept saying to myself, I should have gone to Devizes with her.

I undressed and got into bed. I could not sleep. Then suddenly I thought I heard a footstep. It was nothing, I told myself. The Rowans was an old house and the boards creaked at times; one frequently heard them in the quiet of the night. But was that the sound of a door being quietly opened?

I put on my dressing-gown and slippers, went to the door, opened it and listened.

Yes, someone was downstairs. Could it be Lily? She had said she would have an early night, but perhaps she had gone down to the kitchen for something.

I decided to go and see. So I went downstairs to the kitchen and quietly opened the door. On the table was a lighted candle on a stick and sitting there was Aunt Sophie.

There was a look of abject misery in her very attitude. She was leaning forward, her face cupped in her hands, staring ahead of her.

"Aunt Sophie," I said.

She stared at me in alarm.

"What has happened?" I asked.

"Oh," she said. "I couldn't sleep. I thought I'd come down and make a cup of tea. It might help."

"There's something wrong, isn't there?"

She was silent.

"You must tell me. What is it?"

Still she did not speak.

"We can't go on like this," I said. "I know something is very wrong. You have to tell me."

"I don't know what to do. Perhaps I was mistaken. No, I wasn't. But perhaps."

"Mistaken about what? Where was it? What was it you saw? Was it in Devizes?"

She nodded. Then she turned to me and put her arms about me. I knew she had decided she must tell me.

She said: "I saw them. They came out of the hotel together."

"Who, Aunt Sophie?"

"I keep telling myself it couldn't be. But I know it was."

"You must tell me everything."

"It was Crispin. He was with Kate Carvel."

"His wife? She's dead."

"It gave me a terrible shock. I thought I must be dreaming. But it was. She's not the sort you forget. There couldn't be any doubt."

"But you couldn't have seen her, Aunt Sophie. She's dead. She died in a railway accident a long time ago."

Aunt Sophie looked at me steadily. "I

didn't know whether to tell you or not. I've been trying to make up my mind ever since. I couldn't face you. I had to be by myself."

"You must have imagined it."

"No. I couldn't be mistaken. She had the same gold hair. She's not changed. She's just as she was . . . and they came out of the hotel together. They stood there and then they got into a cab."

"It simply can't be true."

"Well, I saw it. What can you make of that?"

"It must have been someone else."

"There couldn't be two like her in the world. It was Kate Carvel, Freddie. It means . . . she's alive."

"I can't believe that."

"She's his wife. He married her. Oh, Freddie, how can he marry you?"

I sat at the table, limp with horror and fear, trying to grasp the implication of all this. I could only keep repeating to myself, it isn't true.

A great clap of thunder startled me. I was bewildered, uncertain. The night lay ahead of me. The clock on the mantelpiece told me it was only half past ten. Tomorrow I would see him, but how could I live through the night? I must see him now. I must hear from his own lips that Aunt Sophie had made a terrible mistake.

I stood up and said: "I am going to see him."

"Tonight?"

"Aunt Sophie, I can't go through the night not knowing. I have to find out . . . now . . . if you were right."

"I shouldn't have told you. I knew I shouldn't."

"You should. It is better for me to know. I am going now."

"I'll come with you."

"No. No, I must go alone. I must see him. I must know."

I went to my room and put on boots and a heavy coat. Then I ran downstairs and out into the night, through the rain to St. Aubyn's. I rang the bell and a manservant opened the door.

"I want to see Mr. St. Aubyn," I said.

He looked amazed. "Come in, Miss Hammond," he said, as Crispin came into the hall.

"Frederica," he cried.

"I had to come," I said. "I had to see you."

"It's all right, Groves," said Crispin to the servant, and to me: "Come in here."

He took me into a small room leading

from the hall and attempted to take off my coat, but I kept it on. I had not waited to dress properly.

"I had to come," I burst out. "I had to know if this is true. I could not wait."

He was looking at me in alarm. "Tell me what it is," he said.

"Aunt Sophie was in Devizes today. She is very upset. She said she saw you there with Kate Carvel."

He turned pale and I knew in that moment that Aunt Sophie had not been mistaken.

I said: "It was true then?"

He seemed to be grappling with himself.

I went on: "Please, Crispin, I must have the truth."

He said: "It's all right. Everything is going to be all right. We're going to be married. I tell you, it will be all right."

I knew he was not telling the truth. I thought, he tells me what he wants me to believe. A great fear came to me then.

"Everything is settled," he went on. "I have arranged everything. Everything is going to be just as we planned."

"You said you were going to Salisbury," I reminded him. "Yet Aunt Sophie saw you in Devizes."

He was silent and I knew that he had been

to Devizes to meet Kate Carvel and there was no doubt now that Aunt Sophie had seen them together there.

He laid his hands tenderly on my shoulders. "Look," he said, "there is no need for you to worry about any of this. I have arranged it all. You and I are going on as we planned. I could not endure it otherwise. Nor will I. I am determined on that."

"If you are going to have secrets from me, Crispin, if I am not to be told what I know affects you deeply, there can never be true closeness between us. I must know the truth. Aunt Sophie saw you coming out of the hotel with the woman whom you married. She is supposed to be dead. How can she be if she were with you in Devizes?"

His arms slipped round me and he held me tightly. "I will tell you what happened, but it isn't going to make any difference. She is silenced. I could arrange that, and I did."

"Silenced!" I cried in horror.

"I see I must tell you everything. A few days ago I had a letter from her."

"I knew something had happened," I cried. "Oh, Crispin . . . why didn't you tell me?"

"I couldn't. I feared what this would mean. I am determined that at all costs I will not lose you. Frederica, you must not leave me. She wanted money. She always wanted money. That is why it is an easy way out . . . to silence her, to keep her quiet . . . to stop her preventing us . . ."

"But she is there. She is your wife."

"She read the announcement of our engagement. That is what started it. But for that she would never have known. I would have gone on believing her dead. None of this would have happened. When I received the letter I did not know what to do."

"Why did you not tell me? I want to know everything."

"I couldn't tell you. I had to make sure that everything could go ahead as we planned. It was a mistake on my part to see her in Devizes. It was too near here. I ought to have thought of that. I arranged to meet her in that hotel. It was terrible. I hated her. I hated myself for ever being involved with her. I was so thankful when she left me, and when I heard she was killed I naturally thought I would never see her again. It was the end of the most idiotic mistake a man ever made."

"But she was not dead."

"No. She explained all that."

"But you had identified her after the accident."

"There was a ring and a fur stole which I

had given her. The girl I saw was badly injured . . . facially. I could not have said she was really Kate, but the ring and the stole seemed to clinch the matter. They were considered adequate identification."

"Crispin, was it because you wanted to be sure?"

"I felt certain. The ring and the stole . . . they were enough. She told me she had sold the ring and the stole to a fellow actress, a girl who had left home a year or so before to try her luck in the theatre. It seemed that either she had no family or they had lost touch. Her death was unnoticed. Kate had seen the account of the death of my wife in the newspaper and decided to do nothing about it. No doubt she thought she might make profitable use of it at some time. That was the way her mind worked. So when she saw the announcement of our engagement in the paper she decided to use the situation to her advantage."

"And you, Crispin?"

"One thing I was certain of. I was not going to let her spoil my life again. I arranged to meet her at the hotel in Devizes. She was there. God, how I hated her! She laughed at my dismay. She had a way of laughing which made me want to kill her. She thought she had caught me. She said she would never agree to a divorce and that, if I tried that line, she would fight with all her might against me. I saw there was only one way to deal with her. I would give her money to go away and never come near me again."

"You believed she would do that!"

"I told her that if she ever came back I would call the police and she would be charged with blackmail."

"And you really thought that would stop her?"

"I think it might."

"But if you are ready to submit to blackmail once, why should you not be again?"

"I know how to deal with her."

"Crispin, don't you see, this is wrong?"

"What else is there to do?"

"To accept the truth, I suppose."

"You know what that would mean?"

"Yes, I do. But it is here. It is no use pretending it isn't. She is not dead. You have actually seen her."

"She has gone away. She assures me she is going to Australia. She says I shall never hear from her again."

"You believe that!"

"I want to."

"But you can't believe it because you want to. She's a blackmailer and you have given way to blackmail. Don't you see . . . if you went through a form of marriage with me it could be no true marriage. She would know it. She would be back . . . with an even greater reason for blackmail."

"I'll deal with her if she does. I have found you. For the first time in my life I have been happy. I know what I want for the rest of my life. I love you, Frederica, and I will do anything . . . just anything . . . to keep you."

I was shaken by the violence of his emotion. I was bemused by what I had heard. I rejoiced in the power of his love for me—but I felt more strongly than ever that I did not know him. He was revealing a side of his character which I had not known. I felt now, as I had before, that much was hidden from me.

I said: "You were going through with our marriage in spite of this?"

"Yes," he said.

"And you were not going to tell me?"

"I could not risk telling you. I could not be sure what you would do. I love you. I want you and I did not think beyond that. You will be my wife in every way . . . no matter what ceremony. That is words. My feelings for you go deeper than any words."

I could only say: "You would have kept it from me."

"Only because I was afraid you might not agree."

"I think," I said slowly, "that is what shocks me more than any of this. I feel there are secrets which I do not know."

"Secrets?" he said with alarm in his voice, which made my heart leap in fear.

"Crispin," I said, "why don't you tell me everything? Just as you have told me this."

He said: "There is nothing more to tell."

I did not speak, but I thought: you have told me this because you could do nothing else. Aunt Sophie saw you and if she had not I should not have known. I should have gone through a form of marriage with you. And you would have let me do that. You would have deceived me as far as that.

"Frederica," he was saying, "my darling, I love you. You know how much. It sounds so inadequate. I want you with me night and day . . . forever. There is nothing . . . nothing on earth which can hurt me if I am with you."

"I feel stunned," I murmured, "bewildered."

"It is the shock, but you will not have to worry. I shall look after everything. We'll tell no one about this. It's no one's affair but ours. It concerns only us. She will go away and if she ever comes back I shall know how to deal with her."

I could only think, his mind is full of secrets. He would have kept this from me. If we are to be close, how could this be?

I did not know what to say. I must get away, I must think. Nothing was as I had believed it to be.

One thought kept hammering in my brain: he would have married me and said nothing . . . knowing this. It would have been another secret in our lives.

Another secret? What was the other?

I thought of Gaston Marchmont walking into the shrubbery, lying dead there, killed by a gun from the St. Aubyn gunroom.

Crispin would talk to me of his love. It was love which had made him act as he did. I wanted that love. I rejoiced in the depth of it. I wanted to believe that it would be there forever. I dared not. I must get away. I must think rationally. There were many questions I must ask myself.

"Crispin," I said, trying to speak calmly, "I have to think about this. It has been a great shock. I must go home."

"Of course, my darling," he said. "You must not worry. You are going to leave everything to me." He held me fast and kissed me tenderly. "I'll take you home."

"No, no . . . I'll go back alone."

"It's late. I shall come with you. The rain is teeming down. I'll get the carriage. I'll drive you back."

I let him go. From the porch I watched him and, as soon as he disappeared, I ran out.

He was right. The rain was falling heavily. There was thunder overhead; lightning streaked across the sky. And I ran. My hair was falling about my face—a damp cloud; my clothes were soaked. I had not stopped to put much on under my coat. I was unaware of my condition. I could only think that a chance happening in Devizes had revealed something of which I should have been kept in ignorance, though it concerned me deeply.

He would not have told me, I kept saying to myself.

I reached the Rowans, where Aunt Sophie was waiting for me. She looked very frightened.

"You're soaked to the skin," she cried. "Come along in quickly. You shouldn't have gone."

She was hustling me to my room, getting off my wet clothes, running off and coming back with towels and blankets.

She called to Lily: "A fire."

"God help us!" said Lily. "What is all this in aid of?"

"She's been out in the rain."

"God give me strength!" prayed Lily.

I was shivering. I was not sure whether it was due to the cold. I suppose I had never in my life faced such a shock.

They brought hot water bottles to my bed; a fire was soon blazing in the grate. Blankets were piled on my bed and Lily was trying to force hot milk down my throat.

I pushed it away. I could only lie there shivering.

They were up with me all night, hovering about me, and in the morning they went for the doctor.

I was quite ill, he said. I had caught a bad chill. We must be careful that it did not turn into congestion of the lungs.

· · ·

MY ILLNESS WAS, in a way, not without its advantages. My mind was in a turmoil. I was often delirious. I thought I was married to Crispin but I could not be happy. I had seen the shadow of a woman whom I had never met but who was clear to me; she hovered continually in the background. I might be married to Crispin but I was not his wife. She was his wife—an ever-menacing figure. I longed to be with him. I wanted to say, as he did, let's forget she came back. If Aunt Sophie had not been in Devizes on that day it would have happened differently. I should not have known anything about it.

Sometimes I wanted to lie in my bed, feeling limp and tired, too weak to think of anything. There was a certain comfort in that. I was lying in limbo. I could take no action. I was too ill to do anything.

Aunt Sophie was constantly there. So was Lily. There were flowers in the room. I believed I knew who had sent them. I did not see him, though I know he came, for once or twice I heard his voice.

There was a time when I thought I heard Aunt Sophie say: "It's better not. It might upset her." Then I heard his voice pleading.

I wondered if he would come in spite of Aunt Sophie, but he did not. He would be remembering that scene which had taken place before I had run off through the storm.

I was getting better. They were trying to make me eat. I had grown very thin, said Lily. That was no way to be, but if anyone knew how to tempt an appetite, she did.

She would bring some tasty dish to my bedside. "Now eat this up or you'll worry your poor Aunt Sophie into her grave." So I would eat it.

As I grew better, I went on asking myself what I must do. I was very uncertain. I could not imagine life without Crispin. Sometimes I felt weakly acquiescent. I wanted to let him take care of everything. Then I thought of what he was prepared to do and keep secret from me, and I said to myself, I feel as if I shall never truly know him. There are things he is holding back. It is like a screen which comes down between us. It was not only this. There was something else.

Aunt Sophie was sitting by my bed.

She said: "You're getting better. My word, you have given us a fright."

"I'm sorry."

"My dear, I wish I could have borne it for you."

I knew she meant more than my illness.

"What am I going to do, Aunt Sophie?" I said.

"Only you can decide. You can go the way he wants, or . . ."

"I shouldn't be truly married to him."

"That's so."

"If there were children . . . We should never be sure when she was coming back."

"That is a point."

"And yet, I can never be happy without him."

"Life changes, my dear. If you have doubts, you should hesitate. That's why I think you should get away from here. When you are close you can't see things clearly. This is something you can't hurry into. You need time. It's wonderful what time can do."

"I feel so tired," I said. "Aunt Sophie, I want to listen to him. No one will know. We could go through with this."

"It is not lawful. If you had been in ignorance of the fact that he had a wife living, you could not be blamed. But you would go to the altar knowing that he has a wife living."

"I must not do it."

"What you must do is get away and think. You would not be well enough yet. We'll have to talk about it . . . again and again. I know you can't face losing him. I understand well how you feel, my dear. Perhaps we shall find some way."

.   .   .

IT WAS A few days later when the letter came.

Aunt Sophie sat by my bed.

She said: "It's from your father."

I started up, staring at her. I saw the hope in her eyes.

"I wrote to him right at the start of all this. I guessed how it would go. It takes a long time for letters to get here. He must have sat down and written right away. He wants you to go to him."

"To go to him? Where?"

"I'll tell you what he says. 'This place is right on its own. The rest of the world seems far away. There'll be sunshine and everything will be different. A new way of life, something you have never dreamed of before. Here she can think and perhaps see which way she has to go. It's time I met my daughter. It must be nearly twenty years since I last saw her. I am sure it is right for her. Persuade her, Sophie . . .' "

I was aghast. I had wanted so much to see my father, and now he was suggesting that I go to this remote island.

She dropped the letter and looked at me steadily.

"You must go," she said.

"How?"

"You take a ship at Tilbury or Southampton . . . somewhere like that, and you just sail away."

"Where is this island?"

"Casker's Island? Almost on the other side of the world."

"This sounds preposterous."

"It's not impossible, Freddie. You have to think about it. I see it as an answer. You should know your father."

"If he had wanted to see me he could have done so before this."

"He wouldn't while your mother was alive, and after that . . . well, he has been far away. But now you need help and he is there to give it."

"But suddenly to be presented with a proposition like this . . ."

"It's what you need. You want something to come between you and all this uncertainty. You have to come to a decision and you'll do it better away from it all."

"So far!"

"The farther the better."

"Aunt Sophie . . . suppose I do go . . . you'd come with me?"

She hesitated. Then she said firmly: "No, there is too much for me to do here. He didn't suggest that I should go."

"You mean I should go alone? I thought you liked my father."

"I did. I do. But I know this is not the time."

She had turned her head away because she did not want me to read her thoughts.

As for myself, I felt bewildered. This was such a sudden proposition. The idea of leaving England, of going off to some remote island, and, as Aunt Sophie said, on the other side of the world, in those first moments seemed too wild to be taken seriously.

Casker's Island. Where was it? It was just a name. And to see my father, whom I could not remember, but who over the years had kept up what I supposed was a desultory correspondence with Aunt Sophie, in which she gave him news of his daughter!

They had been good friends in the past and the friendship had never really died. She had always insisted that he was interested in me, but he had never made any effort to see me. Was that due to the animosity between him and my mother? But now my mother was dead and he was on some remote island. I had thought I should never meet him. And now he was inviting me to Casker's Island to get right away to consider which way I could turn.

. . .

AUNT SOPHIE BROUGHT maps to my bedside.

"Here it is," she said. "This is Australia. See this little speck in the ocean? That's Casker's Island. Too small and insignificant to be marked on some maps. Look, there are several other little dots. That would mean other islands. Just imagine being there, with all that sea around you!"

"It would be a very strange experience."

"That is what you need just now. You need to get right away to something entirely new."

"Alone?" I said.

"You'll be with your father."

"I shall have to think of getting there. It's so far away."

"These things can be arranged. People say that a sea change does you all the good in the world."

"I am so unsure."

"Of course you are. It takes some thinking of. He so much wants you to go, Freddie."

"After all this time? How can he?"

"I've read it in his letters. He has been waiting for so long. I know it is best for you."

"If you came too . . ."

"That would be a reminder. You want a complete change. I think you are beginning to think about it seriously."

Crispin came. I held out my hands to him.

He took them and kissed them fervently. I made up my mind then. If I stayed I should do as he wanted. I thought of our life together, living under the shadow. When would she come again, asking for money? It was inevitable that she would. It would always be there—that threat, that fear. It would spoil our chances of happiness. Passionately I wanted children; I believed he did too. What of them? And yet, how could I let him go? He looked so sad, so bewildered. That pleading look in his eyes unnerved me.

"I have been so worried," he said.

"I know."

"You ran out in the rain. You left me. And then they wouldn't let me come to see you."

"I am better now, Crispin, and I am going away."

He looked stricken. "Going away?"

"I've thought a lot about it and I think it's best. I've got to get away for a time. I've got to think about this."

"No," he said, "you must not go."

"I have to, Crispin. I don't know what to do."

"If you love me . . ."

"I do. But I have to think about this. I have to know what is for the best."

"You'll come back."

"I am going to my father."

He looked astonished. "He lives far away, doesn't he?"

"Yes. I shall be able to think there."

"Don't go! What shall I do? Think of me."

"I am thinking of us both. I'm thinking of the future."

I do not want to dwell on that scene. It hurts too much even now. He pleaded with me. I almost gave way. But the conviction was strong in me. I had to go.

Aunt Sophie wrote to my father and I enclosed a letter to him in with hers. I wanted to see him. After all these years he would become a real person to me—not just a fantasy.

Aunt Sophie threw herself wholeheartedly into preparations, though I knew how sad she was that I was going away. I caught her with tears in her eyes and there were times when we wept together.

She said: "But it's right. I know it's right."

. . .

TAMARISK CAME TO see me.

She said: "So you are going away?"

"Yes."

"To . . . the other side of the world."

"More or less."

"I know something has gone wrong with you and Crispin. It's because of that, I suppose."

I was silent and she went on: "That's obvious. You were going to marry him, and now you are going away. How can you disguise the fact? I suppose you don't want to talk about it."

"That's right," I said. "I don't."

She shrugged her shoulders. "So you are going off alone. Isn't that rather a daring thing to do?"

"You, Tamarisk, to talk of daring!"

She smiled faintly. "Fred, I want to come with you."

I stared at her in amazement.

"Don't say I can't. Nothing is impossible. You make up your mind to do something and you go and do it. Remember Miss Blake at school? 'Girls . . . if you make up your minds that you are going to succeed, if you work hard to achieve that end, you will.' Fred, I must come with you."

"But this is all . . ."

"I know. So sudden, you are going to say. But it is not, really. I've wanted to get away for a long time, and now this has come along it is exactly what I want. I can't stay here, Fred, I can't endure it. Every day is a reminder. There are things here all around me . . . things I want to forget. I can't escape them . . . here. Every time I look at the shrubbery . . . it's horrible. If they found out who had done it, it would be different. There is suspicion and of course everyone thinks of the wife. We know he was unfaithful. He was a cheat and a liar. Who would suffer most from that? His wife. Why shouldn't she have gone into the gunroom, taken that gun and shot him?"

"Stop it, Tamarisk! You're getting hysterical."

"I have to get away. I can't stand it here anymore. I'm coming with you. You can't go alone. You need someone. We've always been friends. Write to your father and tell him you can't travel alone and you have a friend who desperately needs to get away."

I was silent, trying to imagine what this would mean. I knew that she needed to get away. That was very clear. She was in the midst of this tragedy. She lived with it as Crispin did. I knew her mood, and I was wondering whether it might not be good to have a companion.

She read my thoughts.

"It's easily arranged, Fred. It would be good to be together. Oh, I feel so much better. Life has been wretched for a long time . . . ever since I realised the mistake I had made . . . and then he was killed. Please let me come with you."

"Let's think about it."

"I don't need to think. I know I want to come. When I heard you were going, I wanted to go too. It was like a heaven-sent opportunity. Oh, Fred, let me have a chance of getting away from all this . . . to start again. Please, Fred, *please!*"

"Let's talk about it with Aunt Sophie."

Her face fell.

"She is very understanding," I said. "She'll know exactly how you feel and she'll want to help."

"All right."

I called Aunt Sophie. When she came, I said to Tamarisk: "You tell her."

She did so, pleading eloquently, explaining her wretchedness, her inability to come to terms with life at St. Aubyn's, where there were constant reminders and that terrible mystery hanging over her.

Aunt Sophie listened gravely. Then she said: "Tamarisk, I think you and Freddie should go together. I can see you need to get away. I have been worried about Freddie's going all that way on her own. I think you can help each other."

In that impulsive way which was typical of Tamarisk, she ran to Aunt Sophie and put her arms round her.

"You're a dear," she said. "Now, what do I do? I shall have to book a passage, shan't I . . . at once?"

"The first thing is to write to Freddie's father and tell him she is bringing a friend. We can't wait for his reply. There won't be time.

I am sure there will be no objection, for he has already said he wished someone was travelling with her. But perhaps you need a little time, Tamarisk, before you make up your mind."

"I have been considering it for so long and I know it is what I want."

"Then we must see about your passage immediately."

"This is wonderful. I feel different already." She kissed us both. "I shall go now. I have so much to prepare. I love you both dearly. You are the best friends I ever had. Bless you both. When do we leave?"

"We'll have to see about that," said Aunt Sophie. "In any case, it's settled that you go together."

When she had gone, Aunt Sophie said: "I thought it had changed her, but she's just the same underneath. It's good to see her recover a little of her old ways. Poor girl, she's had a bad time. I think they call it a baptism of fire. She was too eager for life. She grasped it with both hands before she was ready and she's got badly scarred. I'm glad she's going with you. There'll be two of you. That's a weight off my mind."

. . .

So it was arranged. We were to leave England in a month's time. Tamarisk chafed against the delay. She was a constant visitor at the Rowans now. There was so much to discuss.

She had changed a great deal and cast off that melancholy which was so alien to her nature. She helped me, too, for she brought such enthusiasm to our preparations that I could not help being affected by it.

It was by this time early January and time for our departure.

Crispin was very downcast. He said that if I went away he feared I would not come back. I tried to explain again. I needed time to think clearly and this was something I had to do. There was so much at stake. I often thought of our being together and the temptation to stay was great, but always I would see those children we both wanted. Even Crispin must understand that.

It was a very sad parting.

I said: "I have a feeling that I shall come back soon, Crispin, and that we shall know what to do."

That was small comfort to either of us.

Aunt Sophie and James Perrin were to travel to the ship to see us off. Crispin did not come. We knew that that would have been too harrowing for both of us.

Dear Aunt Sophie was rather sombre, though trying hard not to show it; and James Perrin was very kind. I realised that he had cared for me, and I believed he was thinking that, as something had gone wrong between Crispin and me, in due course I might turn to him. That was touching, and comforting in a way.

We spent one night in London. The next day we went to Southampton, and there at the dockside I said goodbye to Aunt Sophie and James.

Aunt Sophie was near to tears. So was I. I was going away from everything I loved and leaving a future which only a short time before had been opening out to me. But Aunt Sophie's resolute smile was reassuring me that what I was doing was right. On that remote island with my father I should see the way I must go.

"We have to get on board now," said Tamarisk with a trace of impatience.

So there was the last farewell, the embrace with Aunt Sophie and the firm handshake with James, who impulsively leaned forward and kissed me.

"Thank you, James," I said.

"You'll come back soon," he said. "I know it."

Once more Aunt Sophie and I clung together.

"How can I ever thank you for all you have done for me, dear Aunt Sophie?" I said.

She shook her head and smiled. "Just be happy, my love. You will be home one day, I know it."

So we said goodbye and Tamarisk and I stepped aboard *The Queen of the South* which was to carry us far away to the other side of the world.

Outward Bound

We found our cabin, which was on the boat deck. It was small, but we had expected that. There were two beds, each against a wall with a space between so that we should be able to lie in bed and see each other. There was one porthole. We had a dressing-table with a mirror above it, a wash basin and a wardrobe. I could see that we should be rather cramped for our clothes, as Tamarisk had brought quite a wardrobe with her.

Our luggage had not yet arrived, and when we had examined the cabin we went out to inspect the ship.

There was bustle everywhere. There seemed to be a great many people hurrying in all directions. Piles of luggage lay in the foyers of the decks awaiting delivery to the cabins. We mounted the companion way and inspected the public rooms. There was a smoking-room, a reading-room, a music room and another room in which dances and such entertainments could be held. We were very impressed.

As we returned to our own deck, we saw stewards delivering the luggage.

"I wonder if ours is there," said Tamarisk. She inspected the pile.

"The labels tell you where they are going," she commented. "Look at this one. 'J. Barlow, Passenger to Melbourne.' I wonder what J. Barlow is like? 'Mrs. Craddock, Passenger to Bombay.' I don't see ours. I wonder if it is in our cabin now. Oh, just look at this! 'Luke Armour, Passenger to Sydney and Casker's Island.' "

She turned to me, her face alight with interest.

"Imagine! He's going to our island! There can't be many people on board who are doing that."

"It's nice to know there is one."

"Luke Armour. I wonder what he's like?"

"I think it is very possible that during the voyage we may discover."

We returned to our cabin to find that our luggage was there. We unpacked, washed and went down to dinner. We sat at a long table with several others. There was some conversation and we learned a little about our fellow travellers, but they were too tired to talk a great deal and, like ourselves, had been overwhelmed by the effort of getting on board.

As soon as we could, we returned to our cabin.

The movement of the ship told us that we had set sail, and we lay in our beds talking until Tamarisk's voice grew more and more drowsy and at length faded away.

I lay sleepless, thinking of poor Aunt Sophie's tear-filled eyes when she had said goodbye, and of James Perrin, who had made up his mind that I would soon be back.

But chiefly I thought of Crispin, with that look of hopeless longing and pleading, which I knew I should carry with me forever.

. . .

As I LOOK back on those first days, they seem a little hazy to me. There was the adventure of getting to know the ship, on which we were continually losing our way. There were so many rooms to explore, so many people to meet, so much that was new to us.

I remember well the roughness of the sea after that first night. Tamarisk and I lay in our beds and felt at times that we should be thrown from them, and then we wondered whether we had been wise to come.

But that passed and we were on our feet again, ready to take an interest in our surroundings. I was greatly comforted to have Tamarisk with me, and I am sure she felt the same about me.

We were assured by Jane, our very attentive stewardess, that we should feel differently when the weather changed. The Bay was noted for its habit of playing tricks, but she had known it smooth as a lake.

"It just depends on the way the wind blows. Well, ladies, we'll soon be out of it, and when we are, you can start enjoying yourselves."

She was right, of course. The turbulence passed and the adventure began. It did not take me long to realise that, although I could not stop myself yearning for Crispin, to plunge into an entirely new and unusual experience was the best way to distance myself from it so that I might see it more clearly. It was also gratifying to see how Tamarisk was benefitting from the adventure.

We dined each day at the long table with several others and were soon all chatting together in a friendly fashion. Most seemed eager to talk of their experiences on other ships and to tell us where they were going.

Very many of them would be leaving the ship in Bombay; they were in the service of the Government or Army and were going back to India after a spell of leave. Most of them were experienced travellers.

There were some who were visiting relatives in Australia or Australians who were returning home after staying with family or friends in England. We had yet to find anyone who was going to Casker's Island, apart from Luke Armour, and he was just a name on a luggage label to us at that stage.

The captain was genial and made a habit of talking to the passengers whenever he had an opportunity of doing so. He liked to hear where everyone was going. When he heard we were bound for Casker's Island he raised his eyebrows.

I told him we were visiting my father there.

"Is that so?" he said. "Not many of our passengers go there. I suppose you have it all fixed. You'll be leaving us at Sydney, of course. There's a ship leaves the same day for Cato Cato and from there you'll get the ferry boat to Casker's. Quite a journey!"

"Yes, we had heard that."

"No, don't get so many people going there. I think the ferry might not leave very frequently from Cato Cato. It takes goods over, and passengers if there are any. But you are going to your father, you say. I suppose he'd be in some business there. Copra, I'll guess. There's a lot of business from the coconuts. People don't realise what a useful product they are. I believe they produce the main industry for Casker's."

"I don't know. I only know he's there."

"Well, we'll take care of you till Sydney. Then we shall be there for a few days before we start the homeward run. How are you liking my ship?"

"Very much."

"Everyone looking after you, I hope?"

"Yes, very well, thank you."

"That's good."

After he had left us, Tamarisk said: "It seems our captain thinks we are going to one of the most remote places on earth."

.   .   .

WE HAD ARRIVED at our first port of call, which was Gibraltar. And by this time we had made the acquaintance of Major and Mrs. Dunstan, who were going out to Bombay where the major would join his regiment. They were seasoned travellers, having made the journey to and from India several times. I think Mrs. Dunstan was a little shocked to find two inexperienced young women travelling alone and was determined to keep an eye on us.

She told us that when we reached Gibraltar, if we wanted to go ashore, which she was sure we would, it might be a good idea if we accompanied her and her husband. A small party would be going from the ship; they would hire a guide and see a little of the town. We were delighted to accept.

I awoke in the morning to look through the porthole and see the Rock of Gibraltar looming up ahead of us. It was an impressive sight. We hurried on deck for a better view, and there it lay before us, in all its glory, like a defiant fortress at the entrance to the Mediterranean Sea.

Major Dunstan came and stood beside us.

"Magnificent, isn't it? Never ceases to make me proud that it is ours. The ship will move round to the west, I expect. You'll see. Oh yes, we're moving now."

We stood there watching. We were now on the west side of the peninsular on which Gibraltar stood. The slope here was more gradual and tiers of houses stood above the defensive wall. As we came into the bay we could see the dockyard and the fortifications.

"Have to defend the place," said the major. "Busy down there, isn't it?"

I gazed in wonder at the small boats which were coming in to greet the ship. From one, several small boys were looking up appealingly at us.

"They want you to throw coins into the water so that they can swim around and catch them. Shouldn't be allowed. It's a dangerous practice."

I felt sorry for the boys. They looked so eager. A few passengers did throw down coins and they darted about like fishes, triumphantly holding up the coin when they had retrieved it. We could see the town now. It looked colourful and interesting. Neither Tamarisk nor I had seen any place like it before.

The major was saying: "We have to go ashore in one of those little boats. The ship is too big to get closer. You'll be safe with us. You have to watch these people—they are inclined to overcharge the tourists."

We crossed in one of the little boats under the care of our friends the Dunstans, along with the rest of the party. It was an exhilarating experience, and I could forget everything just for the moment, and I knew it was the same with Tamarisk. It was good for us both to have such respite, however brief.

Ashore, we were caught up in the crowds. Several people from the ship were there, mingling with the natives. The Moors in their loose robes and Fez hats or turbans gave an exotic atmosphere to the place. Other nationalities were there—Spanish, Greek as well as English. They all seemed to make a great deal of noise, shouting to each other as they passed along.

In the narrow streets, stalls had been set up. There were all sorts of goods on display—trinkets, rings, bracelets, necklaces, leather goods—capacious bags of the softest kind with patterns tooled on them very delicately. There was bread being baked in cavern-like shops; some loaves were on display decorated with little black seeds. There were Fez hats, turbans and straw hats; shoes, sandals such as were worn by the Moors, some with pointed toes curled upwards, and soft leather slippers.

Tamarisk paused by one of the stalls. A hat had caught her eyes. It was made of straw, rather like a boater, and trimmed with blue ribbons and a bunch of forget-me-nots.

She picked it up. The salesman was alert, while Mrs. Dunstan looked on in mild amusement.

"You can't wear that, my dear," she said.

To tell Tamarisk she could not do something, I knew from the past, always made her determined to do it.

She put on the hat. The man at the stall watched her, his black eyes wide with admiration. He put his hands together and raised his eyes to the sky. It was obvious he meant to convey the impression that he was overwhelmed by the beauty of Tamarisk in the straw hat.

It did make her look young, and she reminded me of Tamarisk the schoolgirl. The nightmare of the last months had left her untouched . . . for the moment.

"It's fun," she said. "I must have it. How much?"

Mrs. Dunstan was at her side, and a little bargaining ensued, until Mrs. Dunstan, with an air of authority, clinched the deal and sorted out the money which Tamarisk had been able to change. Tamarisk set the straw hat on her head, putting the small toque which she had been wearing into a bag, and we went on.

It was the major who said we must see the Barbary Apes. That was essential. We should have to climb a bit, as they inhabited the higher slopes.

"You'll find them amusing. They've been here for hundreds of years. We like to see them flourishing. There is a legend that while the apes are here the British will be too. The two will go together. A lot of nonsense, of course, but these things have an effect on people."

They were certainly amusing, lively creatures, with alert inquisitive eyes, accustomed to visitors, for as the major had said, when you come to Gibraltar you must see the apes.

They approached us almost mischievously, coming close, clearly without fear. They apparently liked attention and seemed to glean as much amusement from the visitors as the visitors did from them.

"Be careful of anything you're carrying," warned Mrs. Dunstan. "They have a way of snatching things and running off."

Just as she spoke, one came very close. We did not see him at first, then Tamarisk gave a sudden cry, for he had whipped her hat from her head and was running off with it.

"Well!" stammered Tamarisk, and we could not help laughing at her dismay.

"It was very colourful," said Mrs. Dunstan. "It must have caught his eye. Never mind. It's gone now."

We walked on and had not gone far when a man ran up with Tamarisk's new hat in his hand.

He was laughing.

"I saw what happened. You lost your hat. The ape was so quick. They are very human, these creatures. He stopped near me. He was looking back at you. That gave me the opportunity. I snatched it from him."

"How clever of you!" cried Tamarisk.

Everyone was laughing. Others came up and joined us.

"It was the funniest thing," said one of the ladies. "The ape looked so bewildered. Then he seemed to shrug his shoulders and run off."

"It's a becoming hat," said its rescuer, smiling at Tamarisk.

He was tall, fair-haired and pleasant-looking with a manner which was immediately likeable.

"I don't know how to thank you," said Tamarisk.

"It was so easy. The wily ape only had possession of his prize for a few seconds."

"I'm glad to have it back."

"Well," said Mrs. Dunstan, "all's well that ends well. I shouldn't put it on again, Tamarisk, if I were you. This time there might not be a gallant rescuer at hand."

We moved on and the man attached himself to us. I had no doubt that he was among the party of sightseers from the ship.

Mrs. Dunstan confirmed this by saying: "You *are* on *The Queen of the South,* of course."

"Yes," he said. "It seems that most of the people in Gibraltar today are from *The Queen of the South.*"

"It's always so when the ship calls," added the major.

"I think it is time we descended a little," said Mrs. Dunstan. "Perhaps a little refreshment would be a good idea. What about that place we went to last time, Gerald?" she addressed the major. "Do you remember? You liked those special pastries they had?"

"I remember them well," replied the major. "And I am sure everyone would like to sample them. We can watch the world go by while we refresh ourselves."

We descended, and the hat rescuer was still with us. We found the café and about six of us went in and sat where we could look out on the street. The fair man sat between Tamarisk and me.

Coffee and the special pastries were ordered and the major, looking at the newcomer, said: "It's amazing that one can be on a ship in a fairly confined space and not know a number of one's fellow travellers."

It was clearly an invitation to the young man to introduce himself.

"I'm Luke Armour," he said. "I am going to Sydney."

Tamarisk and I looked at each other in delight.

"That's interesting . . ." she burst out.

Mrs. Dunstan was looking at her as though to say, in what way?

Tamarisk explained: "We saw your luggage label on the first day we got on the ship. Your bags were piled up with the others. We saw you were going to Casker's Island."

"That's right," he said expectantly.

"The point is," said Tamarisk, "so are we."

"Really! How interesting! You must be the only ones apart from myself. Why are you going there?"

"My father lives there," I said. "We are going to see him."

"Oh," he replied.

"Do you know it well?" I asked.

"I've never been there."

"People always look amazed when they know we're going there," said Tamarisk.

"Well, nobody seems to know very much about it. I've tried to find out but there doesn't seem much to know. All I learned is that it is an island which was discovered by a man named Casker about three hundred years ago. He lived there until he died. Hence, Casker's Island. Your father lives there, you say?"

"Yes, and we are going to see him."

He looked at me questioningly, as though wondering why I knew so little about the place since my father lived there. But he must have guessed that my relationship with my father was not a usual one and he was too polite to probe.

"Well, it is interesting to find someone who is going to this little-known place."

"Rather comforting," commented Tamarisk.

"I agree," he said, with a warm smile.

We were both happy to have discovered the identity of Luke Armour and to have found him so pleasant.

He was very knowledgeable and told us that when he visited places he liked to learn as much about them as possible. That was why he was frustrated at being unable to discover much about Casker's.

"It is wonderful to see the world," he said. "One has heard of places from school lessons but it is seeing them in reality which brings them to life. I like to think of Tariq ibn Ziyad coming to this place years ago—in 711, I think. That would be nearly twelve hundred years ago. Just think of that! And the English thought Jabal Tariq—Mount Tariq—was too foreign for their liking and Jabal Tariq was translated into Gibraltar.

And now the place is in British hands—the only entrance to the Mediterranean from the Atlantic Ocean—guarded as one of the most important fortresses in the world."

"That's true," said the major, "and long may it remain in our hands!"

"And now," said Mrs. Dunstan, "if everyone is finished, I think it is time for us to return to the ship."

We were very tired that evening. Tamarisk and I lay in our beds talking about the day's adventures.

"It was wonderful," said Tamarisk. "The best I've had since . . ."

"It was interesting," I agreed.

"The most marvellous moments were when Luke Armour came up with the hat and when he said that his was the name on the luggage label. And he's going to Casker's! Isn't that wonderful?"

"Well, we knew he had to be on the ship somewhere."

"But that he should be the one to retrieve my hat from that odious little monkey. It was wonderfully dramatic. And when he said who he was, I wanted to burst out laughing. He's nice, isn't he? There's something about him . . ."

"You don't know him yet."

"Oh, but I shall," she said. "I am determined to—and I don't think he will be averse."

. . .

WE DID SEE a good deal of him after that. He did not offer to tell us why he was going to Casker's and we did not ask him. We knew that, as we were all going there, we should know in due course.

We gravitated towards each other. We used to meet on deck; then we would sit and talk. He knew a great deal about islands. He had spent a few years in the Caribbean and on one near Borneo, but Casker's was more remote than any of these.

By the time we reached our next port, which was Naples, we were on friendly terms and it was natural that he should suggest that we should accompany him to the ruins of Pompeii. Mrs. Dunstan, having by now cultivated the acquaintance of Luke Armour, thought it was quite in order for us to go with him.

It was a most interesting day, and Luke Armour was an instructive companion. He had said he liked to know something of the places he visited and he talked very vividly and made me, at least, feel I was back in that tragic year of A.D. 79 when Vesuvius had erupted and ruined the thriving city, along with Herculaneum and Stabiae. The remains seemed to come to life, and I could picture those people and the panic of bewilderment and not knowing where to turn to escape the destruction.

When we returned to the ship Tamarisk remarked: "What a serious man our Luke Armour is! He seemed to care so much about all those ancient ruins and the people who had lived there."

"Didn't you think they were interesting?"

"Yes, but he does go on. It's all in the past, isn't it?"

"He is serious-minded. I like him."

"The way we met him was fun . . . but now he seems . . ."

"He is certainly not frivolous, but I should have thought you would have learned to be a little wary of people who are all charm on the surface with not very much of value beneath."

Afterwards, I was sorry I said that. It had an effect on her. She lost a little of her high spirits for several hours, and when we were next with Luke Armour she was very charming to him.

· · ·

WE WERE BOTH looking forward to going through the Suez Canal and were not disappointed. I was enchanted by the golden banks and the occasional glimpse of a shepherd tending his flock. Such were like the pictures in the Bible we had had at Lavender House. We saw the occasional camel making its disdainful way across the sandy soil and people in their long robes and sandalled feet added a picturesque touch to the scene.

It was pleasant to sit on deck and watch this as we slowly passed by.

Luke Armour came to sit beside me.

"Inspiring, isn't it?" he said.

"It's a wonderful experience. I never thought I should see it."

"What a feat—making such a canal! And what an asset to shipping!"

"Indeed, yes."

"Well, we are getting on with our journey."

"You must be accustomed to travel. Imagine what an experience it is for those who have not done it before."

"There is something very special about the first time in doing anything."

"That's so. I wonder what the other ship will be like?"

"Not as big as this one and less comfortable, I imagine. *The Golden Dawn,* which will take us to Cato Cato, may be similar, though much smaller. And I have had some experience of ferries. They are not so good."

"You must have done a great deal of travelling in your business."

"To outlandish places, yes. Your father too."

I hesitated. Then I decided I should tell him, for he would know in due course, as he was bound for Casker's Island.

I said: "I have never seen my father. He left home when I was too young to remember. He and my mother were divorced. She died some time ago and I live with my aunt. Now I am going to see him."

He nodded gravely, and we were silent for a while.

Then he said: "I daresay you are wondering what my business is. I am a missionary."

I was astonished, and he laughed. "You feel a little shocked?"

"Shocked? Why should I be?"

"People sometimes are. I think I look like an ordinary man going about an ordinary business. They don't expect me to be what I am."

"I suppose it is very laudable."

"I see it as my destiny—as it were."

"So you go to these far-off places."

"To bring people to the Christian faith. We have a mission in Casker's Island. There are only two people there—a brother and sister, John and Muriel Havers. They have recently set it up and are having difficulties. I am going out there to help get things in order, if I can. I did this in another place . . . and now I am going out to this one to try to do the same."

"It must be very gratifying if you are successful."

"Everything is gratifying if one is successful."

"But this particularly so."

"We try to help the people in every way. We teach them hygiene, how to grow crops suitable to the land—well, to lead good and useful lives in general. We are hoping to set up a school."

"And the natives are friendly?"

"Usually, although they can be a little suspicious at times. That's very understandable. We want to show them the Christian way of life—how to forgive their enemies and love each other."

He began to talk of his plans and his ideals. I liked his zeal.

"I am very fortunate," he said. "I am able to do the work I want to do. My father left me a small income, so I am more or less free. This is the way of life I have chosen."

"You are fortunate to know what you want to do with your life," I said.

"And you and Mrs. Marchmont?"

"Well . . . there was trouble at home and we thought this would help."

"I knew there was sadness there—even for Mrs. Marchmont."

He waited, but I did not tell him more, and shortly after that I left him.

I found Tamarisk in the cabin, waiting to go out.

I said: "I've just had a talk with Luke Armour. He told me he is a missionary."

"What?"

"A missionary who is going to work on Casker's Island."

"You mean, convert the natives?"

"Something like that."

She grimaced. "Do you know, after the way he retrieved my hat, I thought we were going to have some fun with him."

"Perhaps we shall."

"I had no idea," she said. "I thought he was just an ordinary man. I think I shall call him St. Luke."

"That seems, shall we say, a little blasphemous."

"But a missionary!" she murmured under her breath.

She was disappointed.

. . .

THE DAYS WERE passing. We had slipped into a routine, and one day was very like another until we came into port; and then there would be times of activity during which we would be absorbed by new impressions in a world that seemed very far away from Harper's Green.

My friendship with Luke Armour was growing. He was charming and a diverting companion. He told amusing stories of the places he had visited and rarely spoke, unless pressed, of his dedicated calling. He told me once that, when people discovered it, they were inclined to change towards him, sometimes avoiding him; others expected him to preach to them. He had noticed that Mrs. Marchmont's attitude seemed different since she had known.

Tamarisk had certainly been a little taken aback. She had been so delighted by the manner in which he had rescued her hat from the ape. She had said to me that it was an interesting way to begin a friendship, and she had thought there might be fun in developing the acquaintance, particularly as he was going to Casker's Island. I was amazed that, after her recent experiences, she could contemplate a somewhat flirtatious relationship, for I was sure she was wondering how there could be such with a missionary.

I thought then: all that has happened to her has not changed her.

The Dunstans left us at Bombay. We said goodbye to them with some regrets on both sides, I think. They had been good friends to us and helped us considerably by initiating us into the ways of shipboard life.

After they left, Tamarisk and I went ashore with a party of acquaintances. We were struck by the beauty of many of the buildings and appalled by the poverty we witnessed. There were beggars everywhere. We wanted to give but it was beyond our means to help all those who crowded around us; I felt I should be haunted for a long time by those pleading dark eyes. The women in their beautifully coloured saris and the well-dressed men seemed indifferent to the plight of the beggars, and the contrast between wealth and poverty was both distressing and depressing.

We had an adventure in Bombay which might have been disastrous. We were passing through the narrow streets with the party from the ship. The Dunstans had impressed on us that it was always unwise to go ashore without ship companions and we should never go alone. Stalls had been set up in the streets, and such places always caught the attention of Tamarisk. I must say, the goods looked intriguing. There were displays of silver articles and sari lengths beautifully embroidered, trinkets and all kinds of leather items.

Tamarisk was interested in silver bangles.

She picked some up and tried them on and after that decided she must have them. There was some difficulty about the money, and by the time the transaction was completed we found that the rest of the party were out of sight.

I seized Tamarisk's arm and cried: "The others have gone. We must find them at once."

"Why?" said Tamarisk. "We can get some conveyance to take us back to the ship just as easily as they can."

We started along the streets. We had been with a Mrs. Jennings who had once lived in Bombay and knew the place well; she had taken charge of us all. Now that we had lost sight of the party, I could not help feeling apprehensive.

There were crowds everywhere and it was not easy to make our way through the press of people. When we reached the end of the street, I still could not see any of our party. I looked round in dismay, for there was no sign of any vehicle which might take us back to the ship.

A small boy ran into me. I was startled. Another dashed by. When they had disappeared, I saw that the small bag in which I was carrying our money was no longer on my arm.

I cried: "They have stolen our money. Look at the time! The ship will leave in just over an hour, and we were asked to be on board half an hour before she sailed."

We were both panic-stricken now. We were in an unknown country with no money; we were some way from the ship and had no idea how to get back to it.

I asked one or two people the way to the dock. They looked at me blankly; they had no idea what I was talking about. Desperately I searched for a European face.

Possibilities flashed into my mind. What should we do? We were in a desperate situation—and all because we had been absorbed in Tamarisk's purchase.

We went up another street. There was a wider road ahead of us.

I said: "We have to try this."

"We didn't come this way," replied Tamarisk.

"There must be someone who can tell us the way to the docks."

And just at that moment I saw him.

I cried out: "Mr. Armour!"

He came hurrying towards us.

"I met Mrs. Jennings," he said. "She told me you'd strayed in the market there. I said I'd come and look for you."

"We lost our money," said Tamarisk, in great relief. "Some horrid boys stole it."

"It's unwise to be on your own."

"Oh, how glad I am to see you!" cried Tamarisk. "Aren't you, Fred?"

"I can't tell you how glad! I was getting more and more terrified every moment."

"Afraid we'd sail without you? Which would have happened, of course."

"You are our saviour, Mr. Armour," said Tamarisk. She took his arm and smiled up at him. "Now you will get us back to the ship, I know."

He said: "We shall have to walk a little and then we can get a ride. There's nothing just here. But we are not so very far from the docks."

My relief was immense. The prospect of being left alone in this place had daunted us both; and now here was our rescuer, suddenly coming upon us with the news that he had come to look for us.

"How did you find us so soon?" asked Tamarisk.

"Mrs. Jennings said they had lost you in the market. I knew the place and guessed you'd come out where you did—from Mrs. Jennings's description. I thought it best to hang about there for a few minutes. And, you see, it worked."

"It is the second time you have come to my aid," Tamarisk reminded him. "First the hat and now this. I shall expect you to be at hand at the next time of danger."

"I hope I shall always be at hand to help you when you need me," he said.

I was almost happy as we mounted the gangway and stepped on board. It had been a miraculous rescue and I still shivered to contemplate the alternative. I was glad, too, that it was Luke Armour who had saved us. I was liking him more and more.

So was Tamarisk, although she still referred to him as St. Luke.

. . .

SHE HAD CERTAINLY changed towards him. On one or two occasions I found her sitting on deck with him. I usually joined them and we would have a pleasant time together.

We were getting near to the time when we should leave the ship, and Tamarisk admitted that she was glad we should not be the only ones going to Casker's Island, and that it would be good to have St. Luke there. He was resourceful and would be of great help.

She told me that he had even talked to her about what he was going to do on Casker's Island. He had no idea what he would find there, but he believed it would be different from any other place he had known. The mission was in its infancy and the initial stage was always the most difficult. They had to make the people understand that what was being done was in their interest and not for the sake of interference.

"He's an unusual man," said Tamarisk to me. "I never knew anyone like him. He is very frank and honest. I told him about myself, how I had been infatuated with Gaston . . . about my marriage . . . and everything . . . even how Gaston had been found dead. He listened with great attention."

"I suppose," I said, "it is a story which would attract most people's attention."

"He seemed to understand how I felt—that frightful not-knowing . . . and wondering who . . . and also myself being under suspicion. He said the police could not have suspected me, or they would not have let me leave the country. I told him that it had seemed as though we were all cleared . . . myself, my brother and the man whose

daughter he had seduced . . . everybody.
That was what made it so difficult for us all
. . . not knowing. I said that I thought it
was someone from Gaston's past, someone
who had had a grudge against him. He
promised he would pray for me, and I replied that I had prayed for myself without
much effect, but perhaps he would be listened to more than I would, being on better
terms with those above. He was a bit withdrawn after that."

"You shouldn't have said it."

"I knew afterwards, but I meant it, in a
way. He is such a good person, and I suppose it is logical to suppose he would get a
hearing more easily than someone like me.
If there is any justice, he would. He's the
sort of person whose prayers ought to be answered, and I reckon he prays as much for
others as he does for himself. He's a nice
man, our St. Luke. I really like him."

We were sailing up the Australian coast—
first Fremantle, then Adelaide and Melbourne—and that brought us very near to
our departure from *The Queen of the South.*

At last we reached Sydney, whose
splendid harbour Captain Cook had said was
one of the finest in the world. It was magnificent, passing through the Heads, to see that
town, which not very long before had been

merely a settlement, stretching out before us.

There was little time for us to see much, for the bustle of approaching departure prevailed throughout the ship. There were goodbyes to be said to the people whom we had sailed with all those weeks, with whom we had sat down to meals three times a day. I said to Tamarisk: "We do not see our close friends at home as often as that." And now they were going out of our lives forever and most of them would become just a memory.

Luke Armour had become very businesslike. He wanted to make sure that all our luggage was conveyed to *The Golden Dawn* and that we should all go aboard together.

It was a pity we could not see more of Sydney—a very fine city, we realised, from what little we could observe. However, the most important thing to us was to proceed satisfactorily on our journey.

"How very efficient our holy man is!" said Tamarisk. There was always a note of mockery in her voice when she talked of Luke. She liked him; it was just that she could not regard a man who followed his calling as being like other men.

At last we had boarded *The Golden Dawn* and were on our way. She was a cargo ship first and foremost, and it was only occasionally that she carried passengers.

We had a rough crossing of the Tasman Sea, when we spent most of our time in bed, before we reached Wellington. Our stay there was brief, as it depended on the amount of goods to be taken on and off. Then we were on our way to Cato Cato.

There followed a leisurely day at sea. The weather was calm and hot and it was a great pleasure to sit on deck and look out on a smooth and pellucid sea in which one glimpsed, here and there, flying fishes rising gracefully from the water and, now and then, a shoal of dolphins at play.

We sat on deck with Luke and learned of his childhood, which had been spent in London. His father was a businessman who had done well in financial circles. He wanted both Luke and his elder brother to join the business, but Luke had had other ideas. On his father's death, he had been left sufficient money to follow his inclination, and the elder brother had taken over the business.

Luke had not liked his father's business, but he admitted that it enabled him to do what he wanted with his life. As his brother had complied with their father's wishes, he felt he could go his own way with a clear conscience.

"So," said Tamarisk teasingly, which was typical of her manner to Luke, "you do not like your father's business, but you admit that because of it you can spend your time doing what you want. How does that suit your conscience?"

"I see your point," he said with a smile, "but I believe in life one must apply simple logic. My income, which enables me to work as I want, comes to me through a business in which I do not wish to work. But I can see no logical reason why this money should not help to promote something I believe in."

"I suppose," said Tamarisk grudgingly, "I shall have to say that sounds like good sense."

"I hope you will never say anything to me which you do not believe."

And that was how the days passed. Tamarisk kept up a friendly badinage with Luke which they both seemed to enjoy.

And in due course we came to the island of Cato Cato, where we were to leave *The Golden Dawn* and await the ferry which would take us to Casker's Island.

. . .

CATO CATO WAS a small island, but when we arrived it was full of activity. There were shouts of welcome as *The Golden Dawn* sailed in. Little boats came out to meet the ship and the passengers were taken ashore before the unloading of goods began.

We were surrounded by shouting and gesticulating people. They were obviously excited by the arrival, and all were eager to show us what they had for sale. There were pineapples, coconuts, carvings on wood, and stone images of what appeared to be mysterious and malevolent-looking gods or warriors. Tall palm trees grew in abundance, and the surrounding vegetation was lush indeed.

Luke said that the first thing was to find a hotel where we could stay until the ferry arrived, and as soon as we were settled somewhere he would make enquiries as to when it could be expected.

We found a man who was eager to be our guide. He spoke a little English, but he depended to some extent on a kind of mime.

"Hotel?" he said. "Oh yes. I show. Nice hotel . . . lord and ladies . . . nice hotel. Ferry he come. Not this day." He shook his head vigorously. "Not day."

He had produced a wheelbarrow, onto which our luggage was loaded. Pushing his way through the little crowd which was beginning to assemble about us, he signed to us to follow him. Several children, without a scrap of clothing to cover their brown bodies, stared at us in wonder as we went, and our guide kept turning his head to make sure we were behind him. "Come follow," he shouted.

Resolutely he wheeled the barrow to a white stone building a few hundred yards from the shore.

"Fine hotel. Very good. Best in Cato. You come. You like."

We went into a room which was several degrees cooler than outside. A large woman with a very dark skin, brilliant black eyes and dazzling teeth smiled at us.

"I bring, I bring," said our guide. "Lord, ladies . . ." And then he began to talk volubly in their native tongue.

The woman went on smiling as she directed her attention to us.

"You want stay?" she asked.

"Yes," Luke told her. "We have to stay until the ferry comes to take us to Casker's Island."

"Casker." She blew with her lips. "Oh no. Best here. I have two . . ." She held up her fingers. "Two rooms?"

"Two rooms would suit us very well," said Luke, and turning to me: "You two will share?"

"We did on the ship," said Tamarisk. "Let's see what they are like."

We were very speedily settled and as there was no choice we gratefully accepted what there was. The plump lady seemed very pleased by our arrival, and her only regret was that we were waiting for the ferry.

The rooms were small and somewhat primitive, but there were two beds in each. It would only be a short stay. There were mosquito nets over the beds and the fat lady was very proud of these, which was obvious when she pointed them out to us.

At length the guide went off happily with the air of a man who has done a worthwhile job.

We discovered that the ferry was due on Friday, and as this was Wednesday we considered that we were fortunate that our stay should be so short.

It seemed strange to be on dry land after so long at sea. It was all so new to us that we were eager to get out and see a little of the island, which we guessed could not be so different from Casker's, as they were no great distance from each other.

We went to our respective rooms and took from our baggage the few things we should need during our short stay.

Tamarisk thought it was all very exciting. "I liked the fat lady," she said. "She was so pleased that we had come, and sorry because we were not going to stay long. What better welcome could you have than that?"

· · ·

THE FERRY CONNECTING Cato Cato and Casker's Island paid more or less regular visits, taking to both islands goods which had come out from Sydney. It was also one source of conveying the mail.

We settled in and prepared to wait. The heat was intense, but at least it was a little cooler in our rooms than outside.

We were exhausted after our arrival, and had a meal of some unknown fish and fruit. As, by that time, it was getting late, we decided to have an early night, for we should have to explore, if we wished to, during the morning or evening, for we realised the heat would be too great at midday and in the afternoon.

Tamarisk was soon asleep, but I lay awake listening to the sound of the waves and the strains of a musical instrument which someone was playing some little distance away.

I wondered what Crispin was doing at this moment. And Aunt Sophie? She would be asking herself what could be happening to me. And soon I should see my father. It was what I had always wanted. But how I should love to be back in England.

"If only," I kept saying to myself, "if only that woman had never existed. If only she had never come back."

This was not the way. I had to put a distance between myself and all that. I had to think which way I was going, what I should do with my life.

One thing was certain. I should never forget Crispin.

I glanced at Tamarisk. She looked beautiful in the moonlight, her hair spread over the pillow; the mosquito net under which she lay made her skin look translucent. It was easier for her. She had longed to get away, and her one desire was to escape to forget. She had changed a little, but often the old Tamarisk looked out. This journey was what she had needed, and she was succeeding in loosening the bonds which held her to the past.

I believed I never would.

.   .   .

THE NEXT MORNING we explored Cato Cato. Our presence excited a certain amount of curiosity among the natives, although they were not completely unaccustomed to Europeans. Tamarisk's golden hair received a good deal of attention. One woman came up and touched it. None of them attempted to hide their curiosity. They stared at us openly, laughed and giggled as though they found us a cause for hilarious amusement.

The heat was intense, and we stayed in the hotel after lunch. We sat looking out on the scene, just waiting for the time to pass.

"Not long, now," said Tamarisk. "Soon we shall be there. I do hope it won't be as hot as this place."

"Probably not much difference," said Luke. "You'll get used to it. One does."

"You'll have your work . . . your important work," said Tamarisk. "What shall I do?"

"You might like to come and give me a hand. I daresay I shall find something for you to do."

Tamarisk grimaced. "I don't think I am quite the right type, do you?"

"I am sure you could make yourself so."

They were smiling at each other.

She appealed to me. "Can you see me doing good works?"

I said seriously: "I believe you could do anything if you wanted to enough."

"There, you see, St. Luke. There is hope for me yet."

CASKER'S ISLAND

*A*t last, to our relief, it was Friday morning and the ferry boat was seen approaching. People hurried to the shore. Our guide of the first day came to us with his barrow, and when the ferry came in we were ready waiting for it.

There were no special quarters on the ferry. We were told it would leave in the afternoon of that day and would arrive at Casker's the following afternoon—providing all went well.

There was a great deal of noise on the shore as we prepared to leave. We had been delayed because everything depended on how long it took to get the cargo on board. We were the only passengers who were to sail to Casker's Island.

I could see that the arrival and the departure of boats was a great event in the lives of the islanders, something which relieved the monotony of the days, and of course they never knew what strangers would arrive with it—people like ourselves who, by their very difference, made a diversion.

In due course we set sail, and that night I sat on deck with Tamarisk and Luke, hoping that we might get a little sleep. The sea was calm, benign and murmured softly as it washed against the side of the ferry. The night air was balmy and very pleasant. Every now and then I caught a phosphorescent gleam as a shoal of fish swam by.

Almost on the other side of the world was all that I cared for most. There were times when I told myself I had been a fool. I should have been one of those who lived boldly. I had lost Crispin because I was afraid to stay. And what now? I could never forget. What a fool I had been to think I might.

The other two were dozing, and I could only gaze on the quiet waters, and everywhere I looked I seemed to see Crispin's face.

It was mid-afternoon of the next day. I was sitting on deck when there was a shout from one of the ferrymen. He was waving his hands excitedly and indicating land on the horizon.

"Casker's Island," he cried.

And there it was—a brown and green hump in a calm blue sea.

Several of the sailors were on deck to prepare for our approach. Luke and Tamarisk, with me, were beside them. I was filled with emotion. After all these years I was about to see my father.

Luke understood my feelings and laid his hand on my arm.

"This will be an important day for you," he said.

I nodded.

"It is good that you will be together."

"This island looks remarkably like Cato Cato to me," said Tamarisk.

And as we grew nearer it certainly did. A number of brown-skinned people had gathered on the shore. They wore brightly coloured robes and beads about their necks and ankles. There came the sound of a musical instrument similar to that which I had heard on Cato Cato. Naked children were running in and out of the sea, shouting with delight. Women with babies strapped to their backs —and some with them simply clinging to them—were waiting at the water's edge.

They screamed with delight as the ferry drew near.

"We have to see to the luggage," said Luke.

"Aren't we lucky to have the Saint to look after us?" said Tamarisk.

"We are indeed," I replied.

The luggage was found. We were ready, and as we stepped off the ferry a big man with a somewhat officious manner came towards us. He wore white cotton trousers and a blue shirt.

"Missie Hammond. Missie Hammond," he was chanting.

"Yes, yes," I cried. "I am here."

His big dark face broadened in a dazzling grin. He put his hands together and made a little bow. "Missie Karla. She say come. I take."

"Oh, thank you. This is wonderful!" I cried. "There is some luggage, and I have two friends here."

He was grinning and nodded. "Leave Macala. He do all."

I turned to Tamarisk and Luke. "I think my father must have sent him to meet us."

I had expected him to be there himself. There was probably some reason why he was not, I told myself, and he had sent this man.

"Karla?" Tamarisk was saying. "Who is Karla?"

The man Macala snapped his fingers in an imperious manner.

"Mandel," he called. "Mandel," and a boy of about ten years came running up.

Macala reverted to his own tongue and the boy listened eagerly and nodded. Then he turned to us. "You come. Follow."

He led us to a cart which was drawn by two donkeys.

"I take," said Macala.

"To Mr. Hammond?" I asked.

He nodded. "I take."

He indicated that we get into the cart.

"We won't go without our luggage," said Tamarisk.

At that moment the boy appeared. He was carrying one of our bags. He set it down and pointed backwards.

Macala nodded and, turning to us, grinned reassuringly.

"I get," he said.

"Shouldn't we help?" asked Luke.

"If you go with them you will leave us," pointed out Tamarisk. "This is all very strange and, after all, we are more important even than our luggage. I should have thought your father would have been here, Fred. He can't live far away."

I did not answer.

We need not have worried about the luggage. Macala returned in a short time with the boy and another tall man. Between them they carried all our bags.

We had a little of the currency we had used in Cato Cato, and the man and the boy were overcome with joy when we gave this to them.

Then we set off, the cart trundling along through lush vegetation, and in less than ten minutes we saw the house. It was raised a foot or so from the ground on props, and there was only one floor. It was long and squat, made of white wood, and brightly coloured flowering shrubs grew profusely round it.

As we approached, a door on the porch opened and a woman stood there. She was strikingly handsome, tall, statuesque. Her black hair was coiled loosely about her head, her face was less dark than most we had seen since our arrival on the island; it was very smooth, and she had large luminous eyes, and her smile, showing those perfect white teeth, was welcoming.

"You are Frederica," she said, looking not at me but at Tamarisk.

"No," I said. "I am."

She spoke English with a light lilting accent which was attractive.

"You have come at last. Ronald is so eager to have you here."

She spoke my father's name with the accent on the first syllable. I was wondering who she was.

"This is my friend Mrs. Marchmont, who travelled with me."

"Mrs. Marchmont," she said. "We're happy that you have come."

"And Mr. Armour, who has helped us along the way. He is going to the mission."

Her brows knitted together for a moment, then she was smiling again.

"I am Karla," she said.

"We heard that the man . . . Macala . . . was sent by you."

"Yes."

"My father is here?"

"He is so happy that you are come."

I looked round expectantly and she went on: "But come in. We do not want to stand here."

She led the way into a room which was cool after the heat outside. There were several windows. They were open, but there was a mesh over them which I presumed was to prevent the insects coming in. The furniture appeared to be made of light-coloured wood, which I supposed was bamboo.

"You must see your father first," she said.

She looked at Tamarisk and Luke in a rather puzzled way. Her face was very expressive. One could almost read her thoughts. She was thinking that I should be alone when I met him.

Luke said in that quiet, understanding way which was typical of him: "We can wait here. He'll be eager to see you. Perhaps we could meet him later."

I thought it was all rather mysterious and there must be some explanation for it.

Karla looked relieved, smiling gratefully at Luke, while Tamarisk sat down in one of the bamboo chairs. Karla turned to me and said: "Come."

She took me through a passage and, stopping before a door, opened it. She said in a very gentle voice: "She is here."

He was sitting in a chair before the window. He did not even turn his head, which seemed very strange.

I followed Karla into the room, and I stood beside his chair. Although he remained seated, it was obvious that he was very tall. His whitish hair had a tinge of gold left in it; his features were classically regular. He had been—and still was—a very handsome man. He said, in one of the most musical voices I have ever heard: "Frederica, my daughter, so you have come to see me. At last you are here."

He put out a hand. "I can't see you, my dear. I am blind."

My lips trembled as he went on: "Come close."

He stood up then and reached for me, putting his hands on my shoulders and lifting them to feel my face, exploring it with his fingers. Then he kissed me tenderly on the forehead.

"My dear child," he said, "for so long I have waited for this meeting."

. . .

HE RECOVERED FROM that emotional scene more quickly than I did, and said he must meet Tamarisk and the young man who had been so helpful. I went to them and told them my father was eager to meet them. I explained that he was blind.

They were astounded, but when he met them he seemed light-hearted and lively— very much the man I had expected him to be from Aunt Sophie's description of him.

He welcomed Tamarisk warmly and said how glad he had been when he had heard she was to accompany me; and most courteously he thanked Luke for his care of us during the voyage.

We sat and talked and Karla brought in a fruit drink. She joined us, and I noticed how watchful she was of my father, making sure the table for his glass was near him.

There was so much I had to discover about his household, and I could see that Tamarisk was full of curiosity.

Luke eventually said he must get on to the mission, where they would be expecting him.

"Macala will take you if you don't mind the old cart," said Karla. "It is the best we have. The poor old donkeys are a trifle ancient, but they will have to do until we replace them. They've done good service."

"The mission house is about half a mile along the road from here," said my father, "so we shall be close neighbours. Whatever made you decide to come here?"

"It was offered me and I accepted," said Luke.

My father nodded. "You will be welcome if you want a meal at any time, won't he, Karla?"

"He will," she answered.

When Luke had gone, my father said: "Poor young man. But he seems earnest. I hope things don't go too badly for him."

"You don't seem to think very highly of the mission house," I said.

"I suppose it's all right, as such places go. Converting the heathen is a very demanding occupation . . . unless, of course, the heathen are desirous of conversion."

"And these are not?"

He lifted his shoulders. "I daresay they like things the way they are. It's easy if the spirits are in their favour, and they can always placate them with some little offering. They don't understand all that 'love your neighbour as yourself.' They are concerned with looking after themselves. They can't spare much time for their neighbours."

"Luke is a very good man," I said.

"We call him Saint Luke," added Tamarisk.

My father smiled. "Yes," he said. "There is an aura of gentleness about him. I hope you see a good deal of him."

We were shown our rooms. They were side by side. Everything was in light wood. There were a few rugs on the wooden floors, and the windows were screened by the mesh. Wash basins and ewers were in each bedroom, and I discovered later that water had to be drawn from the well near the house. It was no less primitive than conditions had been in Cato Cato. Two families lived in hut-like dwellings in the grounds and they acted as servants. Considering the circumstances, I could see that everything had been done to provide the utmost comfort.

What I wanted most was to talk to my father alone. Tamarisk seemed to realise this and after we had had a meal, which was served under Karla's supervision, she said she felt very tired and would like to go to her room. That gave me the opportunity I needed.

He took me to the room where I had first met him.

"This is my sanctum," he said. "I am here a great deal. Karla says you are a little puzzled and I should explain everything to you."

"Who exactly is Karla?"

"This is her house. She is the daughter of an Englishman and a native woman. Her father came here and set up a large coconut plantation. He did not marry her mother but he thought a lot of Karla. She is a very clever woman . . . and attractive. In fact, she is a very wonderful person. I knew you two would like each other from the start. Don Marling, her father, left her this house, the plantation and a fortune when he died. She is a power in this place."

"And you share this house with her?"

He smiled. "We are very great friends.

She brought me here when"—he touched his eyes—"when this was happening to me."

"Aunt Sophie used to tell me about you. She did not mention that you were blind."

"She did not know. I did not tell her."

"But you were writing to her. And I thought you were in Egypt until I was coming here to see you."

"I was in Egypt. In the Army at one time, you know. And then . . . I left. I did all sorts of business deals out there . . . and in other places. It's in the past. No sense in dwelling on a misspent youth."

"Was it misspent, then?"

"I enjoyed it, so how could it have been. I was stating the general view rather than my own."

"I want to know so much about you. All these years I knew I had a father, and I had never seen you. I knew very little about you until Aunt Sophie told me."

"You mustn't trust her. She would be too lenient with me."

"She always spoke of you with great affection. She was always fond of you."

"I was fond of her, too. She kept me informed of your progress. I was very glad when you went to live with her."

"It was wonderful for me."

"I liked to think of the two of you together, comforting each other. Sophie was adept at the art of comforting . . . always."

There was a deep regret in his voice, and I wanted to ask him more about their relationship. I knew that she had loved him; I fancied he had loved her, too. There was so much I had to learn. I could not expect to know it all at once.

"I want to hear more about Karla," I said. "So this is her house, and we are her guests."

"I live here too."

"As her guest?"

"Not exactly." There was a brief silence, and then he went on: "You have probably heard about my rather chequered career. Your mother and I, we parted. You know why."

"You were not happy together."

"She was well rid of me. We could never have been happy together. I was by no means a saint . . . not in the least like your Luke. I am afraid I am rather different, and with a man like me there must be . . . relationships."

"You and Karla?" I asked.

He nodded. "We share the household."

"You could have married . . . or couldn't you?"

"Well, yes. I am free now. She was mar-

ried once . . . married for her money, I
suppose. Perhaps not entirely, but it would
have been an incentive, I daresay. He might
have robbed her, but he didn't because she is
a shrewd businesswoman. He died. Yes, we
could marry, but here . . . it is not the
same as an English village, where the neighbours keep a sharp look-out to make sure
society's laws are observed. Karla does not
think of marriage. Nor do I. But that does
not prevent our enjoyment of each other's
society. Now, you are not shocked, daughter?"

"I don't think so. I guessed that was how it
might be. She is a very kindly person."

"She is half native, half Anglo-Saxon. It
makes an interesting combination. I met her
in Egypt. She has travelled somewhat. I liked
her freshness, her frankness and her happy
disposition. Live for the day, that is her doc-
trine, and I suppose it is mine. We were
friends in Egypt, and then when my affliction
began to descend, she looked after me. I was
in a low state. I feared blindness, my dear
Frederica, as I had never feared anything in
my life. I even went so far as to pray: 'Dear
God, leave me my eyes and take everything
else.' And the Lord ignored my request, but
He gave me Karla." He gripped my hand
tightly for a moment. Then he went on:

"Karla was wonderful. She is the eternal mother. Why do such women not have children? She was with me through my despair. She was very important to me. And she brought me here to this house left to her by her doting father. She is rich by island standards; she owns thousands of highly productive coconut trees. She is a businesswoman and looks after the plantation as well as any man could, and she looks after me like a mother. Besides her coconuts, she has my eternal gratitude. Frederica, I could never have come through to accept my blindness without her."

I said: "Aunt Sophie would have cared for you. You could have come back to us."

He shook his head. "No," he said. "Though I know she would. But I could not go back to her. There were times when I thought of it . . . before the blindness began to come on. You see, in the first place . . ."

"I know. She told me. She thought you would marry her, and you married my mother instead."

"So you see . . ."

"She would have understood."

"It wouldn't have worked. I really was not worthy of Sophie. I could never have lived up to what she would expect."

"She wanted you for what you are."

"But she had my daughter—a much better bargain."

"And it is Karla who looks after you. You share her house . . . her life."

"It is what she wants."

"And you are happy here?"

He was silent for a few seconds. "Well," he said at length, "I have a good life. And now I have come to terms with this. There are compensations in all things. I am overjoyed when I recognise a footstep. I say, 'That is Macala coming . . . or young Mandel.' I know Karla's footsteps. I am acutely aware of the inflection in people's voices. And so I get through my days. I think of the pleasures of the past, and there were many of them. The unpleasant things I try to dismiss. I am often able to do that. It is quite an art, you know. Sometimes I say to myself, 'You are blind. Perhaps your most precious possession has been taken from you, but there are these compensations.' Then I count them. I have the love of Karla, and now my daughter has come all the way across the world to see me."

. . .

A WEEK HAD passed and I felt that I had been a long time on the island.

At night I would lie awake and wonder about Crispin and Aunt Sophie, and I would ask myself if I had been right to come. It had been a wonderful experience to meet my father and to be aware of an immediate rapport between us, which made me feel that I had known him all my life. That was because of Aunt Sophie. I could see that he must always have had a way of winning people's affection. He already had mine.

I had many conversations with him. We would sit under the trees listening to the gentle rise and fall of the waves and he would talk about his life. It was very clear that he was happy to have me there.

It was at night when the great longing for home would come to me and I could not shut out the memory of Crispin's face when he had pleaded with me not to go. I could hear his voice saying, "I will find a way. There must be a way." I would try in vain to shut out the memory of the shrubbery at St. Aubyn's and the thought of Gaston Marchmont lying there.

The island was a beautiful place but, I supposed, like most tropical islands—waving palm trees, lush foliage, heavy rain showers and burning sunshine, carefree people, lazy, seeking no other way of life.

I was amused by Tamarisk's interest in the

place. I think this was largely due to the deep desire she had to get away from home. I did not believe that she was guilty of her husband's murder but, as she said, the wife in such cases generally comes in for a certain amount of suspicion.

She would laugh a great deal at the antics of the children, and there was no doubt that they were particularly interested in her. There were usually one or two following her wherever she went. Some were bold enough to come up and touch her white arm and her hair, which she often wore loose about her shoulders.

She had always enjoyed being noticed, and she showed her appreciation and quickly became the children's favourite. ◄

We would explore the island. We would pause to look at the potter squatting near the shore as he made clay pots—platters and drinking vessels. To his delight, we bought some. A group of children—Tamarisk's admirers—watched the transaction in glee.

Other salesmen were squatting on mats made from coconut fibre. There might be passengers when the ferries came in and they wanted to be ready for these prospective customers. What they had to offer were mostly carved images, paper knives and beads.

We were warned to be careful of snakes and not to go through the thick undergrowth without a guide.

We had, of course, visited the mission house—a bleak place like a barn with a thatched roof. There was little to make it inviting. The walls were plain, and the only adornment was a crucifix hanging there.

"What a dreary place!" said Tamarisk to Luke, who was showing it to us.

There was a cupboard at one end of the room and a blackboard on an easel.

"It is meant to be a schoolroom," said Luke.

"Where are the pupils?" asked Tamarisk.

"They have yet to come."

Luke had introduced us to John Havers and his sister Muriel. They had been on Casker's Island for two years and they admitted that they had made little progress, being mainly ignored by the islanders.

"It was different in our previous place," said John Havers. "That was bigger and not so far away from everywhere. Here one has to start right from the beginning, and the people do seem rather indifferent."

"That is why Mr. Armour has come," went on Muriel.

"And you don't have any pupils yet," I said.

"Some come but they don't stay. I used to give them cakes at eleven o'clock if they came in the morning. I tried to teach them, but I am sure they were only waiting for the cakes. They would eat them, smile and then run off."

"Bribery," commented Tamarisk lightly.

"I fear that is what it amounts to," said Muriel Havers.

"Poor little things," said Tamarisk afterwards. "But I don't think they would want to be taught by Miss Havers, however good those cakes were."

Meals at Karla's were always merry affairs. Karla's and my father's personality made that inevitable. The food was lavish, and we were waited on by numerous servants who moved soundlessly in and out on bare feet.

Both Karla and my father talked of the life they had led in Egypt. There always seemed some amusing anecdote to relate, and we would sit on long after the meal was over.

"Poor Luke," said Tamarisk one day. "Think how different it must be at the mission with the Havers."

"They are good people," said Karla, "but they are sometimes too good to know how to laugh. Life is too serious for them. I pity them."

"Could we ask them here to dinner?" asked Tamarisk.

"Oh my!" cried Karla. "I am sorry. I should have thought to ask them."

"As a matter of fact," said my father, "I was thinking that we should have asked your friend Luke immediately. He was so good to you on the journey out."

"Of course we must," replied Karla. "And I will ask Tom Holloway to come too."

"Tom Holloway," my father explained, "is the manager of the plantation. He's a good sort, don't you agree, Karla?"

"He is a very good sort, but he is a little sad and life is not meant to be sad."

"We should like to meet him, shouldn't we, Tamarisk?" I said.

"But of course," was her response.

"We will do it tomorrow," said Karla.

"Would they be able to come on such short notice?" I asked.

Karla gave one of her frequent loud bursts of laughter.

"They don't get many invitations to dine out, I can tell you. They'll come."

"Social life on Casker's Island is a little restricted," added my father. "They'll come."

Before they did, my father told me a little about Tom Holloway.

"He had been in England, importing the mats which were made from one of the products of the coconuts. What uses that old coconut can be put to! Well, one of the products is the fibre to make mats and rugs and such like. Tom Holloway sold them all over England. Then his wife died in child-birth and the child with her. He couldn't get over it. Karla met him now and then on business and she was appalled by the change in him. You know her nature by now. She sees someone in trouble and she has to help. Well, she had this idea that Tom wanted a complete break with the past, so she offered him the job of managing her plantation, and to her surprise he accepted."

"And did it help?"

"I think perhaps a little. It's two years now —or nearly that—and he's the faithful sort. I think he forgets for a time, and he is very keen on the plantation. He's learned how to handle these people. He enjoys the work. Karla would like to see him settled—which isn't easy over here."

"What a fine woman Karla is!"

He nodded, looking pleased.

. . .

THE DINNER WAS a success, though Luke was a little dejected, I noticed. The happy optimism he had shown on the ship was slightly less bright. John and Muriel Havers talked earnestly of the mission, but I could not help feeling that they had very little understanding of the people among whom they were living.

I remarked to my father afterwards that they seemed to regard the people as savages rather than ordinary simple folk who might not care to have other people's ideas thrust upon them. I fancied too that Muriel did not approve of my father's relationship with Karla.

Tamarisk was very amused; and when they had gone and we had retired, she came to my room to discuss the evening.

"What did you think of it?" she asked.

"That it went very well. I think Luke was glad to get a good meal."

"Poor dear," said Tamarisk lightly. "He's a disappointed young man, I fear. I am not surprised—living in close contact with that dreary pair."

"They are not exactly dreary. Just out of their depth, I think."

"Out of their depth! They're missionaries, aren't they? They ought to be in their depth. An island right away from everywhere and the population in need of conversion! Poor Luke! We'll have to see him more often and cheer him up."

"I think we should."

"I wonder what your father thought of it all."

"I shall hear in due course. And how do you feel now, Tamarisk? About everything?"

"I don't think about it all the time now."

"That's good."

"Do you?"

"I think a lot."

"There was no need for you to go away like that."

"My father wanted to see me."

"You were just engaged to Crispin. Oh, I know you don't want to talk about it. *I* had to get away. Gaston was *my* husband and he had been murdered."

"I understand. Of course I understand. I felt I had to get away too."

"Because of this thing that happened? You don't know anything about Gaston, do you?"

"No. No. It wasn't about that."

"You're cagey," she said.

I did not answer but left it at that.

At the same time I did feel that, whatever this adventure was doing for Tamarisk, it was not much help to me.

· · ·

THE NEXT MORNING Tamarisk and I went out together. We had not gone far when we were seen by three or four children who were squatting on the ground playing some game. As soon as we approached they rose and ran towards us, their eyes on Tamarisk. They went into fits of uncontrollable giggling.

"I am glad," said Tamarisk, smiling, "that I amuse you so much."

That made them giggle the more. They watched her expectantly, as though waiting for her to say something else.

We walked on and they followed. We went down to the shore past the men squatting on the ground with the mats on which their goods were displayed.

We paused before the potter. There were two tall vases on his mat. They were simple, but beautiful. Tamarisk admired them while the owner surveyed us through amused eyes. What was it about us that they found so funny? I wondered. The way we looked, the way we spoke, our general behaviour, which was different from theirs?

Tamarisk picked up the tall vases and the children closed in round her, watching excitedly.

She held the vases out to the man enquiringly, and he named a price.

"I'll have that one," said Tamarisk.

"What are you going to do with it?" I asked.

"You'll see. I want the other one, too."

There was great excitement. Several of the women and more children came up to watch. The man on a nearby rug with his carved images looked hopeful and envious.

"You carry this one, Fred," she said. "I'll take the other. I want the pair."

"I don't see what you are going to do with them."

"I do," said Tamarisk.

One of the children jumped into the air with glee. The others pressed round while money was exchanged.

"Come on," said Tamarisk. "This way." The children followed us in procession. Several more had now joined us, as she led the way to the mission house.

She pushed open the door and stepped into the hall.

"There!" she said triumphantly. "This is where they are going to be. We shall fill them with water from the stream, then one by the door, and the other . . ." She looked round the room. "Yes, over there between the two windows. Now I want some beautiful flowers. The red ones. Red's a lovely colour. It's warm and friendly. Come on, we will fill them with water."

The children came with us to the stream. They were jumping up and down with an excitement they could not restrain.

"And now the flowers." She turned to the children. "Come on. You're going to help me instead of laughing at me. We're going to pick flowers. Red . . . like this one . . . and mauve like this for the other. There are plenty of them here."

She was right about that. The flowers grew in abundance. She picked some and made the children understand that they must do the same. She had one group picking red and the other mauve.

Then we all went back to the hall. Tamarisk knelt before the vase into which she put the red flowers. The children watched her in wonder and kept running up to her with flowers.

"That's lovely," she cried. "Here, that's a good one."

She took a flower from a little girl who hunched her shoulders and laughed with glee as it was put into the vase.

Finally Tamarisk stood up and exclaimed: "What a beautiful vase of flowers!" She clapped her hands and all the children began to clap too.

"Come on," said Tamarisk. "Now we will do the mauve flowers."

The children were delighted. They fought together to be the ones who took the flowers to her. She arranged them with some skill in the vase and they looked beautiful, but no more so than those laughing happy children.

When she had finished the children clapped their hands, and at that moment Muriel Havers came in.

"What on earth!" she began, staring about her. I doubted she had ever seen so many children in the hall. They all turned to look at her and smiled, but they could not let their eyes stray long from Tamarisk.

"I thought the flowers would liven it up a bit," said Tamarisk.

"They do, they do," said Muriel Havers. "But the children!"

"They just came in to help," said Tamarisk.

There was a certain triumph in her voice. I thought, she *has* changed. Something has happened to change her.

. . .

WE HAD NOW spent three weeks on the island. The days seemed long and yet time flew by.

Often I said to myself, what am I doing here? I should go back. I kept thinking of what would have happened if Aunt Sophie had not seen Kate Carvel in Devizes that day. How different my life would have been then. I should be with Crispin, in blissful ignorance. No, it would not have done. She would appear again. It would be a life of fear, of blackmail and pretence. Crispin's words kept echoing in my ears. "Something will be done." He would have kept it secret. He was a man of secrets. Had I not always felt that? But I loved him; with all my heart I loved him, yet there were times when I would say to myself, but you do not know him. There is much that he keeps hidden.

Then I would say, I must go back. I cannot bear to stay away.

Tamarisk seemed to adapt herself more easily than I could. But she was escaping, leaving nothing that was essential to her happiness. Her family had never been close to her. Her mother had neglected her in her youth and there was no great love between them. She was proud of Crispin and liked him in a sisterly way. But that was all. There were no firm ties pulling her away. I could well imagine that in time she would tire of the island and its people . . . but now it was an amusing novelty and what she needed.

She had been mildly interested in Tom Holloway at first, but he was too serious to hold that attention. He was still grieving for a dead wife too much to be interested in Tamarisk. She was amused by Luke, "that good man," as she often called him with a note of mockery in her voice. I think she felt faintly protective towards him, which was unexpected in her. Usually she looked to men to protect her.

However, she did go often to the mission house. The children all gathered there as soon as she appeared and, of course, that endeared them to her. They fought to get near her and giggled at everything she did or said.

"They seem to expect me to entertain them," she said. "I must say they are very appreciative. Luke is amused . . . and as for Muriel and John, they say it is good to get the children into the mission house, no matter what the reason."

She bought some more pots from the potter.

She said: "He greets me like a queen every time he sees me. The children keep bringing flowers to me. I told them a story the other day. They didn't understand a word of it, but they all listened as though it were the most breathtaking tale that ever was told. You should have seen them! It was Little Red Riding Hood, actually. Miming mostly. You should have seen the excitement when the Big Bad Wolf arrived on the scene. They laughed and cheered and kept stroking me and pulling my hair. I can tell you, it was a riotous success. Muriel says it should have been Bible stories. Well, I might try that, but for the moment it is Little Red Riding Hood, and they will have no other. They know when the wolf is coming and pretend to be frightened. They go round on all fours shouting, 'Wolf! Wolf! Big Bad Wolf' . . . and the native equivalent, too. I can tell you, it is all great fun."

I was very pleased to see her so interested, and I knew it delighted Luke.

A ship came to the island. It was much bigger than the ferry, and there was great excitement. Tamarisk and I went down to the shore. There was noise and bustle everywhere. Little boats went to and from the ship, and a few passengers came ashore. They came over to talk to us, and told us they were doing a trip round the islands from Sydney. They had been to Cato Cato and some others, but one island, they said, was very like any other.

They were amazed that we were staying here for a visit.

The children hung around and watched us talking together. The potter sold more cups and platters that afternoon than he had in a month. Carvings, straw mats and baskets were also sold.

There was an air of sadness among the watchers on the shore when the ship departed.

The ship had brought some mail to Casker's, and there was a letter from Crispin and one from Aunt Sophie.

I took them to my room because I guessed that reading them would be something I must do when I was alone.

Crispin first:

My dearest,

How I miss you! Will you come home? Leave everything and come now. I know I am going to settle this matter one way or another. I am going to make her agree to a divorce. I can divorce her. She deserted me to go off with a lover. I have all the evidence I need. I have set a lawyer working on it.

I cannot tell you how dreary it is here without you. There doesn't seem to be any point in anything. What I want is for you to take the next ship home. Even then, think how long it would take. But if only I knew you were on the way.

It is going to be all right, though: I am going to find a way out of this mess. If only she had stayed away . . . forever. But never doubt that I shall find a way. And when I have, if you haven't returned, I shall come out there to get you.

I know you are unhappy—as I am. In a way I am glad you are. I couldn't bear it if you ceased to care for me. I would never have left you, you know, whatever had happened. I beg of you, come home soon.

Your aunt is missing you very much. I know she is very unhappy. I think she agrees with me that you should never have left us.

My love forever,

Crispin

I knew from Aunt Sophie's letter that she too was questioning the wisdom of my departure. She wrote:

We miss you very much. Poor Crispin is most unhappy. He really loves you, Freddie. This separation is breaking his heart, I can see. He is not one to love lightly. When he loves, his feelings go deep. I fancy he is a little cross with me because I told you I had seen Kate Carvel. He has to blame someone, poor dear. He says he will find some way of getting rid of her. He speaks with such conviction that I believe he will. After all, she left him. I don't know what the position is exactly, but I pray that all will come right.

He needs you, Freddie. You would think that he was in complete command, able to look after himself. On the surface he is, but I know how he is suffering. It seems to me so cruel that one action taken impetuously in youth can spoil a life. But he won't let it, and I fancy he is a man who gets his own way.

Dearest child, I hope you and your father are getting along happily together. I have no doubt of it—knowing you both so well. He is delightful, isn't he? Do let me know.

And, Freddie, I believe you should think of coming back. Your father wanted to see you. Is he ill? I should like to have news of him. Don't keep anything from me. I sense something is wrong in his letters. It was one reason why I urged you to go, although I did think it would be better for you to be away until Crispin had sorted this thing out.

But now you should think about coming home. I know you have only just got there, but if you could write and tell me when, I think that would help Crispin a great deal.

Take care of yourself, my love.

God be with you, and much love to you,

A. S.

I read the letters several times. I thought of the many miles which separated us and that I must go back soon.

. . .

My father said to me: "You have heard from home?"

"Yes."

"It's saddened you. You are homesick, aren't you?"

"I suppose I am."

He put his hand over mine and held it for a moment.

"Should you tell me?" he said.

So I told him. I told him everything from the beginning: my first meeting with Crispin, when he had made that unfortunate remark; of Barrow Wood, my work in the estate office and the love which had grown up between us. I told of the return of Crispin's wife and our shattered plans; and I explained that Crispin had wanted to go ahead and had planned not to tell me.

"Yes, and that shocked you," said my father. "I think that is the root of the uncertainty. You love him very much, don't you?"

"Yes, I do."

"And at the same time you are not entirely sure of him."

"I am sure that he loves me. But . . ."

"But . . . ?" he prompted.

"There is something. I can't explain it. It's there. Even before this . . . it was there."

"Some secret?"

"I suppose that is what it is. It sometimes seems like a barrier. It is because we are so very close, because I know him so well that I am aware of it. But at times I feel I just can't get beyond it."

"Why did you not ask him?"

"It seems strange, but there has never been any mention of it. It is something which is on his mind, something he does not want me to know. And then this happened and he admitted that he would have gone on with our marriage without telling me that he was not in a position to marry me. This other thing seemed more real to me then."

"You have explained," he said. "I think you love him without completely trusting him. Is that it?"

"I feel there is some secret he will not tell me . . . something important."

"About his first marriage?"

"No. He believed, as everyone else did, that his wife was dead. That was why it was such a shock when she returned . . . as much of a shock to him as to any of us."

"So it is something of longer standing. Some dark and shameful secret. You think this of him, and yet you love him?"

"Yes. It must be so."

"Love is more important than anything else on earth, you know. 'Faith, Hope and Charity, and the greatest of these is Charity.' And charity is love. It's true. If you have love, you need very little more."

"I want to know what this thing is."

"It was there when you promised to marry him. Yet you were happy and thought of spending your life with him."

"Yes. When I was with him I could forget these misgivings. They seemed vague, fanciful and silly."

"Some people are afraid of happiness. They regard it with suspicion. It is too wonderful to be real, they think, and they look for flaws. Have you done that, do you think?"

"Perhaps. But I am not sure. There *is* something there, and it haunts him."

"He will tell you. When you are married

to him and he has lost his fear of losing you, he will tell you."

"Why should he be afraid to tell me now?"

"For the same reason that he was not going to tell you his wife had returned. Because he fears above all things to lose you."

"It is dishonest."

My father smiled shrewdly and said: "It is love, and did we not agree that there is nothing in life so wonderful as true love?"

. . .

I WROTE TO both Crispin and Aunt Sophie. I had not told Aunt Sophie that my father was blind. I sensed that he would have done so himself had he wanted her to know. The letters would be ready next time a boat called to take them back to Sydney, where they would have to make the long journey to England. It would be a long time before they reached their destination.

I was convincing myself that I must go home. They were both asking me to and, whatever the outcome, I must be there.

Tom Holloway was a frequent visitor. Karla welcomed visitors. Luke and the Havers often came now. Karla was sure they did not get enough to eat at the mission house. They employed only two servants and Karla feared that Muriel was too concerned with the spirit to think much of bodily needs.

Luke was always overjoyed to come. The optimism he had shown on the ship had faded considerably. There were many alterations he wanted to make to the mission house, and this presented a difficulty, as he did not want to override the Havers, who, although they were not the most forceful of people, had firm ideas.

Tamarisk had already lured the children into the mission house, and many of them were regular visitors now. But they came to see Tamarisk, and although she gave them the story of the Good Samaritan, they still demanded Little Red Riding Hood and the Big Bad Wolf.

Poor Luke! He was so dedicated, so anxious to do the work he felt needed to be done.

One afternoon Tom took us over to see the plantation. There were Tamarisk, Luke and myself. As we walked through the tall trees we saw the kernels of the nuts exposed to the sun, and Tom took us into the shed where they were making the coconut matting which formed a large part of the business, and to the office where his assistant sat working.

We saw his living quarters. They were

quite spacious and well-furnished. I guessed Karla would have arranged that. He had one servant, who brought us a fruit drink, and as we sat on a verandah looking out over the plantation, Tom asked about the mission and Luke explained the indifference of the people and the difficulty of getting through to them.

"Language is a problem," said Tom. "It's easier for me. I show them what to do and they do it. These people who work for me are the aristocrats of the island. They earn money, but it is not all of them who want to. Some prefer to lie in the sun. It is the heat which forms their characters. It makes them light-hearted and easy-going unless they are roused to anger. Then they can be dangerous."

"That's true enough," said Luke. "There were two of them quarrelling the other day. It was over some trivial matter about a piece of land. One said it was his, and the other laid claim to it. There were curses and knives flying. It looked like a fight to the death until someone called in the big chief."

"Oh yes," said Tom. "I know who you mean. Olam. A little old man with very fierce eyes. They are very strange eyes. There are white rings round the pupils.

Some disease, most likely, but it is because of this that he has his power."

"It was settled at once," went on Luke. "I was amazed at his power."

"He is the wise man. I have qualms about him. His judgement in your case evidently solved the matter satisfactorily. It's not always so. He can be quite . . . terrifying. He is reckoned to have special powers. If he tells a man he will die, generally he does."

"I have heard of that," said Luke. "It's dangerous."

"I have to be wary of him. Keep on good terms with him. I send him little presents from time to time. That keeps him my good friend."

"What a lot one has to learn about these people," said Tamarisk. "A pity they are not all like the children—they are sweet."

"Tamarisk gets along well with them," commented Luke.

"It's the colour of my hair which attracts them," said Tamarisk. "It's so different from theirs."

"Most of them just want a pleasant life," Tom explained. "They'll work for a while, but you mustn't expect too much from them. They enjoy their work here. They take a certain pride in it. Olam doesn't object because I show due respect to him, so all is well at the moment. Last year, some special season which is important to them went off very well. It will soon be here again. I am prepared for it. But my first year was rather tricky."

"What happened?" asked Tamarisk.

"While it's going on, they don't come to work. I didn't know this at first and was annoyed, for I had had no warning. There are all sorts of rituals. There was chanting through the days and nights and they danced with long spears. Where they keep them, I don't know. One doesn't see them from one season to the next. Old Olam is much in evidence. In fact, he organises the whole show. They dance round, stamp their feet and look fierce. I was on the point of going to look where they were when Karla arrived. She explained to me that it would be wise for me to keep out of the way during the two days it was going on. We couldn't help hearing the chanting all through the night, which was disturbing. When it's over they all settle down and everything is as it was."

"What are they supposed to be doing?"

"It's like a preparation for some battle—a sort of practice perhaps to keep them in trim in case they are attacked by people from another island."

"That's not likely," said Luke.

"Not now, with all these ships plying back and forth and some of the bigger islands belonging to Britain and France. But they keep on the ceremony. It is invoking the spirits to come and fight for them. And, of course, it is the wise old Olam who remembers these things and keeps the tradition going."

"Isn't it fascinating?" said Tamarisk. "Do you feel scared, Mr. Holloway, living right in the midst of it?"

"We are all in the midst of it," said Tom.

"Yes, but you more so. You are surrounded by them."

Tom shrugged his shoulders. "No," he said. "They are gentle people. It is only when they are provoked that they might be dangerous, and I am not likely to provoke them."

"What we have to do is show them a different way of life," said Luke. "Teach them that they must love their neighbours. I think, with God's help, we shall do that."

"I am sure you will," I said.

Then Tom asked about the mission. He had heard some children were going every morning.

Tamarisk laughed. "To hear Red Riding Hood and pull my hair."

"It's a good start," said Luke, smiling at her affectionately.

"It's fun," replied Tamarisk. "I'd like to meet old what's-his-name. Olam, is it?"

"Rest assured, he will be aware of you," said Tom.

I said: "I think it is wonderful the way in which those children have taken to you, Tamarisk."

"As I told you, it is Red Riding Hood they appreciate, or perhaps more likely the wolf."

"Not entirely. They liked you before that."

She laughed, flashing her eyes from Luke to Tom. "Oh, I am a very popular person, you must know."

Just at that moment, one of the men came running up to the balcony.

"What has happened?" cried Tom rising.

"Master. He fall. Jaco . . . he fall from tree. He lie." The man lifted his shoulders and shook his head backwards and forwards mournfully.

"Show me," said Tom, and we all followed him out to the plantation.

A boy of about twelve years was lying on the ground, crying out in pain. His leg was twisted under him.

Tom held his breath in dismay, and Luke said: "It looks as though he has broken his leg."

He knelt beside the boy. "Poor little chap." He said: "Painful, is it?"

I don't think the boy understood the words, but the sympathy in Luke's voice soothed him a little. He lifted wide, frightened eyes to Luke's face.

"It'll be all right," went on Luke. "I can see to this. I want a stout stick and some bandages."

"I'll get those," replied Tom. "Stay here with him."

Luke turned to the boy. "I'm going to try to move this. It'll hurt. I'm going to put it back in place. Tamarisk, put your arm round his shoulders. That's right."

I stood there helplessly watching them. Several of the men had gathered around. They were all gabbling together.

Luke had the boy lying flat on his back, and it was obvious that the bone was broken.

"I wish I had something to give him," said Luke. "Where's Tom?"

"He'll be back soon, I'm sure," I said. "Here he is. He's got the things you wanted."

I watched Luke as, with deft fingers, he set the leg. I remembered his saying, some time before, that his training included lessons in first aid. He said, at the time, that at least he could do something in an emergency.

The boy was obviously in less pain now. He was gazing at Luke with touching gratitude.

"I want to get him back to the mission," he said.

"We'll get one of the carts to take him," said Tom.

He stood up and shouted something to the watchers in their native tongue. Several of them immediately ran off and in a short time returned with a cart.

"We'll have to be very careful not to jolt him," said Luke. "We want pillows and something for him to lie on. We must get him safely to the mission. Muriel has had some training in nursing, and she can make a proper job of it."

"It's wonderful!" cried Tamarisk. "I do hope he'll be all right."

"If we get it properly set, he will be," Luke assured her.

The boy was carefully carried to the cart, where he lay stretched out. Tamarisk sat at his head, I at his feet. She stroked his forehead and murmured comforting words. The boy looked at her in a sort of wonder. She looked very beautiful with the compassion on her face.

Tom led the donkey, making sure that the passage was as smooth as it possibly could be, and when we reached the mission house, Muriel and John were there to help.

Muriel said the boy should go into her room. She would make herself up a bed in one of the others in the building. She knew exactly what to do and took charge. He had broken his fibula, she said. It was a simple fracture. He was young, his bones would soon heal.

She seemed happy to have something to do and showed an efficiency which I had never seen in her before.

Afterwards Tamarisk and I went home and told my father and Karla what had happened.

"And you think it will be back to normal in time?" asked Karla.

"There should not be any difficulty."

"That will be wonderful," said Karla, her eyes shining. "There was one man who had a fall like that, and he's been a cripple ever since."

. . .

IT WAS THAT night when the drums started. They were faint at first and then grew louder. The sound of musical instruments came floating over the air.

As we sat at dinner, Karla said: "This will

go on all night and tomorrow and the next night."

"Tom was telling us about it," I said. "I think he feels a little uneasy."

"It's one of the old customs, isn't it, Karla?" asked my father.

"Yes. It goes back many years. It's a sort of war cry, a preparation for attack."

"But what are they going to attack?" I asked.

"Nothing . . . now. But at one time there was always fighting—tribe against tribe. It's different now. The islands are at peace. They have been taken over and some sort of order brought in. But in the past they had always to be ready. This is an exercise in readiness . . . letting the spirits know that they are waiting if attacked."

"And what about old Olam?" asked Tamarisk. "He fascinates me."

"He's very old. He would remember those days. They all revere him. He's rather like the old witch doctor. He has that sort of power. They are all in awe of him and everyone must show due respect."

"I'd like to see him," said Tamarisk.

"I doubt you will," Karla told her. "His hut is in the centre of the settlement close to the plantation. He doesn't emerge very often, except at times like these. People consult him from time to time if they are in difficulties, and he gives them directions which must be obeyed. No one dares cross him."

"I believe he can be a rather terrifying sight in all his war paint," said my father.

"Have you seen him?" I asked Karla.

"Oh yes. For ceremonies he has two blue stripes painted across his forehead and feathers on his head."

"Will he be there tonight?" asked Tamarisk, her eyes speculative.

"You must not try to see him," said Karla quickly. "There would be trouble if you were detected. We live here. We must respect these people."

"Of course," said Tamarisk demurely.

· · ·

ALL THROUGH THE night I could hear the strains of the instruments and beneath it the intermittent beating of the drums.

There was something hypnotic about them.

I thought longingly of home. "I will go," I promised myself. "I will talk to my father in the morning. He will understand. He said that love was all-important and he was right." Of course, my father had not led an exactly moral life, but then it was not always easy to know what was right and what wrong.

I could not sleep. I would doze for a few minutes and then wake to the distant murmur of the sea and the throbbing of the drums.

Suddenly I was wide awake. Something was happening outside the house. I looked out of my windows and saw people there. I hastily put on a dressing-gown and slippers and at that moment Tamarisk came into my room.

"What's going on?" she asked.

"I don't know. I've just woken up."

We went out together. Karla was by this time at the door. As the men saw her they began to shout. I did not know what they were saying, but Karla answered them.

She turned to us.

"Trouble at the mission," she said. "I must go."

Tamarisk looked disturbed. She took a proprietorial interest in the mission.

Karla started off, and we followed her. We ran all the way to the mission, and there was an amazing sight. The torches gave out an eerie light. There was a crowd of men, and at the head of them the man who, I knew, was Olam.

He seemed enormous, but that was due to his tall feather head-dress, which gave him the appearance of some fierce predatory bird. I looked at his face, which was like nothing so much as a distorted image from a nightmare, for painted across his forehead were the two blue stripes which Karla had mentioned, and there were red lines down his cheeks. Two tall men stood beside him, their faces painted, though less luridly than that of Olam himself. They were carrying spears, and I felt a great fear grip me, for their anger appeared to be directed against the mission.

Luke had come out. He was standing on the balcony in front of the door. On one side of him stood John and on the other Muriel.

When Karla appeared, there was a momentary silence. She made her way to the balcony steps, Tamarisk and I following. She stood there beside Luke.

"What is it?" she asked.

"It's something to do with Jaco, it seems," said Luke. "I gather they want him. He can't stand on his feet. I can't understand what it is they are asking."

Karla held up a hand. It was amazing what dignity and authority she maintained.

She addressed the crowd, and we guessed she was asking them what they wanted of the mission. They began shouting, but Olam held up his hand and they were immediately silenced.

He spoke to Karla and she replied. Then she turned to Luke and the Havers.

She said: "They want Jaco. He has some special duties in tonight's celebration. He has trained for it and he has to be there."

"He can't stand on that leg," said Muriel. "It's imperative that he rests it. How can the bone set, otherwise? He can't move."

"They want him," said Karla.

"They shall not have him," replied Luke.

Karla was frowning. "They won't understand," she said. Then she addressed the crowd. I knew she was explaining to them that Jaco had broken his leg and that the people at the mission were mending it but it was not ready yet.

There was silence and the crowd began to talk together excitedly.

"They want him brought out," said Karla.

"He is sleeping peacefully," said Muriel firmly, "and he cannot be brought out here. He has to keep that leg in position and still."

Karla tried again. She talked for a long time. Then she turned to Luke.

"They say you claim you can make him well. You have special powers. They want to see him."

Luke replied: "We will not allow him to be brought out. To stand on the leg at this time would be disastrous. Can you make them understand that?"

"They believe in magic, certainly. I can see that they are not sure whether you have greater powers than their spirits. When old Mahe fell he was crippled for life, and you say you can save Jaco from that. They are wavering. They have doubts of you, and yet they know the white men have powers which they do not possess. Olam is pondering as to what he should do. This is a matter of great importance to him. He is the one with the power, and you are promising them a miracle. We must go very carefully. Olam might bring his men in and take Jaco away with them."

"We shall not allow him to do that," said Luke.

Karla lifted her shoulders. "The three of you . . . myself . . . these young ladies? Look at those people out there . . . armed with spears. What do you think will happen? We have to bargain. But it may be that they will insist on taking the boy."

"No, no, no," said Luke.

Karla turned to the crowd. She told us afterwards what she said. She made a bargain. The mission people said they could cure Jaco. They could make his leg as new, but they must have time. Their spell would not work in a day or two. Olam and the rest, in time, would see what they could do. But if they insisted now, if they did not leave Jaco in the hands of the white men, he would be crippled all his life. He would hate those who had spoiled his life, and there would be bitter resentment throughout the island. They should go away. They should find someone who could be at the ceremony and perform those duties which would have been Jaco's. Jaco must be given a chance to see if the white man's cure was a good one.

There was a great deal of whispering among the crowd.

Then Karla turned to Luke. "He wants you to swear to cure Jaco."

"Of course, we'll swear to do everything we can to cure him."

"It's only a simple fracture," added Muriel. "I can't see that anything can go wrong. The boy is young, his bones are strong. It is almost certain that he will make a complete recovery."

"They want you to swear," said Karla, looking intently at Luke, "to swear on your blood. You know what that means?"

"What?" asked Luke.

"If he is not completely cured, you will die yourself."

"I die?"

"You will fall on your spear if you have one, or you will walk into the sea and not come back. It's an oath they want. If your gods fail you, as you did not hand over Jaco to take his part in the sacred ceremony, you will have failed to honour your oath. The only thing you can do then is die."

"I've never heard such nonsense," said Muriel.

"It's either that or they take Jaco now."

"They are not going to take Jaco," said Luke firmly. "All right. Tell them, I swear on my blood."

Karla told them and turned back to Luke. He was asked to hold up his right hand while they chanted what sounded like a dirge.

Then Olam inclined his head and, turning, led his followers away.

We were left standing on the balcony, bemused, but relieved because the torch-led gathering was disappearing into the trees. All we could see was the flickering of the flames as it gradually receded.

Luke spoke first. "What a show!" he said.

"It was horrible," replied Tamarisk.

"We certainly saw a bit of local colour," commented Luke.

Tamarisk said: "There isn't any doubt, is there? Jaco's leg will get better."

"It will be all right as far as I can see,"

answered Muriel. "So long as he doesn't get up and do some damage."

"I wish it were over," said Tamarisk.

"Do you think they'll come back?" asked Muriel.

"No," said Karla firmly. "The matter is ended for tonight. You have made your pact. Olam is satisfied. He does not want to quarrel with the mission. At the same time, he does not want his authority undermined. This is a challenge. If the boy recovers completely, you will have done good work. Such a thing would bring people to you more quickly than anything else. I hope the boy did not hear all that was going on."

"He had some pain last night and I gave him a little laudanum to help him sleep," Muriel told us.

"That's good," said Karla. "He shouldn't know there was all this fuss. It might upset him." She looked from me to Tamarisk and went on: "I think we should try to get a little sleep before morning."

Tamarisk laid her hand on Luke's arm.

"It's all right," he said. "I'll defeat the witch doctor."

"That boy's leg must be all right," said Tamarisk earnestly.

"There is no earthly reason why it should not be," insisted Muriel.

"Come," said Karla. "Your father will be anxious."

"He will know something is happening," I said.

We made our way back to the house, where he was waiting up for us.

"What happened?" he asked.

"It was old Olam."

"The ceremony?"

"He wanted to take the boy Jaco there."

My father grimaced.

"Sit down awhile," he said. "I don't think any of us is going to get much sleep tonight. What about a spot of brandy? You all seem as if you could use it . . . all of you."

Karla said: "You're right when you say if we go to bed we shan't sleep."

We went to my father's study and Karla poured out the brandy while she told my father what had happened.

"Old Olam in all his war paint. I don't like that."

"The spears were terrifying," said Tamarisk. "And they held them as though they were ready to charge. Karla was wonderful."

My father turned in her direction and smiled. "You calmed them down, did you?"

Karla sipped her brandy. "I'd like to see that boy on his feet again," she said.

"He's going to be all right," said Tamarisk.

"I do hope so," my father murmured.

"It was rash of Luke . . ." I began.

"What else could he do?" demanded Tamarisk. "It was the only way."

"It was all very dramatic," I put in. "It was as though they were play-acting . . . all that paint on their faces and the spears and the torches."

"In a way they were," agreed Karla. "But you must understand them. This is the important part of the year for them. They go back into their past. They become as they used to be—great warriors who spent most of their time fighting each other. Olam is a sort of chief and holy man combined. They look up to him and fear to offend him. They believe him to be in touch with spirits. He is an old man. He is revered. They bring him gifts of food and the products of their work. He lives out his life in comfort. He would not want that to change. There is no doubt that he is clever. He has set himself apart from the rest. It is possible that now he is hoping that Jaco's leg will not be set. He could not perform such a miracle himself. Therefore, you will understand, he would prefer others not to be able to either."

"Do you mean he will try to prevent it?" asked Tamarisk.

"He has certain powers over these people," said Karla. "Some time ago he told a man he would die, and that night the man did die."

"How could that be?" asked Tamarisk.

Karla lifted her shoulders. "I do not know how—only that it happened. It may be that the man died because he had absolute faith in Olam."

"But now," said my father, "these natives are growing away from the superstitions of the past. Now that the ferries and ships come here, the new world is encroaching and the old shibboleths are fading away. These people have changed a great deal in the last few years."

"That is so," said Karla, "but it would not take a great deal to send them back into the past. Nothing must happen to Jaco. His leg must be cured. Otherwise . . ."

"You mean Luke would be in danger?" cried Tamarisk.

"We should not allow him to die," said Karla, "but they would expect it. Oaths are sacred in their eyes."

I felt sick with horror.

Tamarisk said: "Jaco must be watched all through the night as well as the day."

"Most certainly he shall be," said Karla.

"You must make sure no subversive suggestions are put before him," insisted my father.

"Everything will be all right," said Karla. "I feel sure of it."

She lifted her glass and we drank.

There was no point in going to bed, so we sat on, talking desultorily for a while, but I could not get out of my mind the memory of that scene, and it was useless to pretend otherwise.

So we sat on. The dawn was not far away, and all the time we could hear the beat of the drums.

.   .   .

THE NEXT MORNING Karla, Tamarisk and I went to the mission. As with us, the three of them had not gone to bed that last night. The Havers looked a little tired, but Luke was as normal.

"What a night!" he cried. "That old man in his war paint! What a sight! I thought at first the Ancient Britons had come to Casker's in their woad."

"Thank goodness they went away," said John. "At one time I thought they were going to force their way in and carry Jaco off."

"Does he know about it?" asked Karla.

"Nothing," said Muriel firmly. "We thought it better that he should not."

"I am sure you agree with that, Karla," I said. "We were saying that we did not want him to have contact with anyone until his leg is right."

"That might be difficult," said John.

"Not if we make it a rule, a part of the miraculous cure," replied Luke.

"I fear Olam might do something to prevent the cure," said Karla.

"Why?" asked John.

"Because he doesn't want someone to be able to do what he can't."

"If all goes well, we can show them what we can do for Jaco, and this will be a great boon to the mission," declared Luke, his eyes shining.

"Yes," agreed Karla. "That would make a lot of difference. You will have proved to have something to offer, and you will win their respect."

"But," murmured Tamarisk, "suppose something went wrong?" She was looking at Luke with frightened eyes.

"Then," said Luke, "I shall go to old Olam and ask him which of his spears I should take into the jungle."

"Don't joke!" said Tamarisk almost angrily.

"Everything will be all right." Muriel spoke with conviction. "It's a simple fracture, and I shall ban visitors until I know all is well."

. . .

DURING THE WEEK, we had news from the mission every day. Karla cooked special dishes for Jaco, and the boy was having a most enjoyable time. He could never have been so cossetted in his life. I was sure he was telling himself it was not such a bad thing, to break a leg. Regular meals at the mission and delicacies sent to him by Karla had an effect on him. His body filled out; his eyes were bright; he was clearly in a good state of health and enjoying the attention he received.

Tamarisk and I were there when the splints were removed. He was perfectly healed, and there was no sign of a break. His limbs were stiff and he needed a few exercises which Muriel made him do—and there he was, none the worse for his fall.

On Karla's advice, we made an occasion of this. It was the way to fix it in everyone's memory. A courteous message was sent to Olam. That evening at sundown, if he would be gracious enough to come to the mission house, the boy Jaco would be handed over to his people.

What a scene that was! Olam came,

painted and befeathered, and with him his followers. They carried spears and torches, as they had before.

First, on the advice of Karla, a gift was presented to Olam. It was a china figure of a tiger which Karla had produced. Olam accepted it graciously and presented Luke with a bone necklace on which was a carved pendant. This he placed round Luke's neck.

Karla, Tamarisk and I, with the Havers, stood on the balcony and watched the presentation ceremony. Then, wearing the necklace, Luke came up the steps to the balcony, went into the house and came out, holding Jaco by the hand. Jaco, a little more plump than when they had last seen him, in radiantly good health and delighted to be at the centre of such attention, stood before them. Suddenly he leaped into the air, turned a somersault and ran out into the crowd.

There was a gasp of wonderment. Then there was silence as the men bowed their heads, lifting them after a few seconds to look at Luke, whom they believed to be the creator of the miracle. Poor Muriel, who had set the leg so expertly, was not considered by them.

She did not mind. I knew she had been very perturbed that Luke should have entered into such an agreement with one whom she thought of as a savage.

However, it had all worked out very well and we were deeply gratified.

We all went back to the mission hall, changed now by the vases of flowers, which seemed to fill every possible space.

We sat down at the table and Luke began to laugh.

"It worked out wonderfully," he said. "Everyone played their parts so well, including young Jaco."

"This is the best thing that could have happened for the mission," I said.

Luke was smiling at Tamarisk. "There are other good things," he said.

Then we were all laughing, perhaps a little too heartily, because we had suffered some frightening moments since this affair had begun. It was in fact the laughter of relief.

I could not help wondering what would have happened if something had gone wrong and Jaco's leg had not healed. The same thought must have occurred to Tamarisk, for she said very sternly to Luke: "You must not in future swear rash oaths to medicine men, witch doctors or whatever they call themselves."

. . .

THE DRAMA OF Jaco's leg had temporarily dominated everything about us, and when it was over the days seemed empty. I realised I had been away from home a long time. When the ferry called I would hope for mail, but it took so long to reach us and any news letters contained would be very much out of date.

I was with my father a great deal. He liked to sit outside the house where I could see the sea and the men with their goods squatting on their mats, their eyes on the horizon, watching for the ferries.

My father told me that when he had first come here he had not completely lost his sight. He had had a blurred view of the sea and shore, so it was easy for him to picture the scene.

One day he said: "You are not happy here, daughter." He usually called me daughter. It was as though he were revelling in the relationship.

I replied: "You and Karla have been so good to me. You have done everything . . ."

"But we have not been able to do enough. Nor shall we ever be able to. Your heart is back in Harper's Green. You know that as well as I do."

I was silent.

"You must go back," he went on. "Nothing is ever resolved by running away."

"You knew of this before I came," I said. "Aunt Sophie told you much about me."

"Yes, I know. She never told me about the Barrow Wood incident. She no doubt thought that would have disturbed me too much. Sophie was always protective."

"You should have gone back to her."

He shook his head. "No . . . not because I needed to be cared for. How could I have done that?"

"There is no need to ask yourself for reasons. She would have cared for you."

"I know. But I could not do it."

"She does not even know that you are blind."

"No."

"When I go back, do you mind if I tell her?"

"You must tell her. Tell her I am happy enough. Tell her that, although I cannot see, I have found much in life to live for. There are compensations from these afflictions. I can hear better than I ever did, I can distinguish footsteps, the inflections in voices. It amuses me to do that. Don't let her pity me."

"I won't. I shall tell her that, in spite of being blind, you are not unhappy."

"That is true. I could not ask for better care. Tell her about Karla. She'll understand. She knows me well. She knows in her heart that it would never have been right for us. I would never have conformed. I think you understand that now."

"I think I do."

"I have been a wandering rogue. I would never have settled until forced to—as I am now. You have seen my life here. It is not bad, is it? The old man of the island. No, that is Olam. But I am lord of all I survey, for I survey nothing. That is life. Karla is right for me. She understands me. She is fond of me. We are alike in our ways. The moralist would say it is all wrong, but I have had a happy life. It isn't fair, is it? Your poor mother! Such a good woman and such an unhappy one."

"She settled her heart on the unimportant things in life. She mourned for the grandeur of the old days. That was what made her unhappy. It killed her in the end."

My mind went back to that day when she was so angry because she was not to arrange the flowers. It was not even that she greatly wanted to; she needed to be acknowledged as the lady of the manor—although she was not.

"Ah, you see," he said. "That is life, I suppose. We make our own way through it. What is right for one is not for another. Perhaps there is a lot of luck in it, and I have been lucky. But here I am, blind, my careless youth behind me, and yet I have someone to care for me. Would you not say I am a lucky man?"

"Yes, I would, but perhaps you deserve your luck."

He laughed aloud. "That seems an odd sort of justice to me. I am as contented as I could be in the circumstances, spending the rest of my life in contemplation and living through the lives of those around me. Perhaps it is not such a bad idea. Which brings me to you and your affairs. What are you going to do?"

"I have been thinking of little else."

"I know."

"I shall have to go back."

He nodded. "You must go. You love this man and you are capable of that true love, the faithful, everlasting sort. It's the best, really. The other—well, it is light, amusing, gratifying, exciting, but the lucky ones are those who find the true variety. I think you and your Crispin have it. Should you let all that slip through your fingers? I know I would not. But perhaps I am not a good example for you to follow. You love Crispin.

You should be with him. You should not allow obstacles to stand in the way of true love."

"Crispin is determined to find a way."

"He will, and you are afraid of some side of his character which bothers you—that secretive bit. Perhaps that is what makes him fascinating. After all, it is exciting to discover new depths in those around one. That is what makes new acquaintances so amusing. Perhaps some people grow tired of each other's society because there are not enough surprises. You are still worried about the mysterious affair of the man in the shrubbery. You think Crispin holds something back from you. You suspect him of certain actions, perhaps, but whatever you think he might have done, you still love him, do you not? You have come here and learned that, whatever he has done, you cannot be happy without him. My dear daughter, that is enough. You love him."

"So . . . you think that is enough?"

"We are talking of love . . . true love. It must prevail. It is the most important thing in the world."

"So I must go home."

"Go to your room now," he said. "Write those letters. Write to Crispin and Sophie and tell them that you are coming home."

His face saddened a little. "I shall miss you. It will be dull without you. Karla will miss you. It has delighted her to have you here— partly because of the pleasure it has given me, but she is fond of you and the merry Tamarisk too. Go and tell them that you are going home and will be with them as soon as possible."

I put my arms about him and he held me very close to him.

"Tell Sophie that I am a blind old man," he said. "My adventuring days are over. Tell her about Casker's. Tell her it suits me to be here away from all the old haunts. Tell her I think of her every day and that she is the best friend I ever had."

I left him then. I went to my room and I wrote the letters. They would be ready when the ferry called.

. . .

WHEN I HAD written the letters, I went to Tamarisk's room, for I heard her come in as I was completing them.

I knew she had been to the mission.

"Tamarisk," I said, "I am going home."

She stared at me. "When?" she demanded.

"As soon as it can be arranged. I've just written to them to tell them."

"This is sudden, isn't it?"

"Not really. It's been in my mind for a long time."

"Why? What has happened?"

"I just don't want to stay here anymore. I want to be home. I've told my father. He understands."

She looked at me steadily. "I'm not going."

"You mean . . . ?"

"I mean I'm staying here. I'm not going back to Harper's Green with everyone looking at me and wondering whether I murdered Gaston."

"They didn't think that."

"They seemed to sometimes. I'm not going, anyway. I like it here."

"But, Tamarisk, it's just a novelty for the moment."

"It's no longer a novelty. It's interesting—the mission, these people, the feather-headed witch doctor."

"It's all so remote. It seems far from everything that is real."

"It's real to me here, and in any case I'm not going. If you go, you'll have to go alone."

"I see."

"Surely you didn't think you could decide what *you* wanted and could just say to me, come on, we're off."

"It wasn't like that."

"It seems like it to me. All right. You go. I'll stay."

"Are you sure, Tamarisk?"

"Absolutely." She paused and then went on: "It might be a little difficult. I can't stay here, can I? I'm here with you . . . as a guest. If you're not here, why should I be? There's not much room at the mission."

"I expect you could stay here."

"Until I find something."

"Find something? Where? You talk as though this is somewhere in England, where landladies let rooms!"

"Perhaps Karla would let me have a room here. You'd have to travel on your own."

"I can do that."

"It's rather unconventional."

"I think," I said, "that there are times when it is necessary to be a little unconventional."

I could see that she was adamant. She would not leave Casker's Island.

· · ·

WHEN I TOLD my father, he smiled. "That," he said, "does not surprise me."

Karla also took the news calmly. I wondered if she discussed my situation with my father. I told her that Tamarisk was wonder-

ing where she could live when I had gone,
and Karla immediately said: "She can stay
on here. Why not?"

"She had an idea that she was a guest here
because she was accompanying me and naturally would stay where I was. She thinks that
if I am no longer here she should not be and
she should find other lodgings. And where,
she was wondering, could she do that?"

"I like guests," said Karla, "and she is welcome here."

"Just think," said my father. "We shall
hear the news of the mission from the
horse's mouth, as it were. She must stay
here. I have something to tell you. I have
written to a friend in Sydney—an old friend
whom I once knew very well. She has a son
in London whom she visits from time to
time. In fact, she is always looking for an
excuse to cross the sea to him. I have suggested that she arrange to travel back with
you. She will book the passages and you can
travel together. Sibyl is amusing. You'll like
her."

"That's wonderful."

"I hope to hear from her by the next ferry.
Then we'll go into action."

. . .

THE FERRY HAD arrived. I sat with my father looking down on it as it came in.

"I can picture it down there," he said. "All the excitement of arrival. There is sure to be a letter from Sibyl. It would comfort me a great deal to know that you were sailing together. She's a very experienced traveller and I should like to think she would be with you. If she can't, well, my dear, I suppose you wouldn't be the first woman to travel to England alone. We should hear later on in the day, or perhaps tomorrow morning. They take a long time to sort out the mail."

One or two passengers came ashore. I wondered if they had come for the day and would go back with the ferry. I imagined the salesmen rubbing their hands and placating the spirits in the hope of good business.

I heard the sound of wheels coming up to the house and went out to see what was happening. A woman was sitting in the cart, surrounded by several pieces of luggage. She was incongruously dressed in a blue silk gown which appeared to be in high fashion, and on her head was perched a straw hat dominated by what must be a mythical bird —at least, I did not recognise it as belonging to any species I knew.

When she saw me she smiled warmly. "I'll guess you're Frederica. I'm Sibyl Fraser. It's nice to meet you. We're going to be travelling companions, so we'd better get to know each other."

She started to descend from the cart.

"It was simpler just to come," she said. "We can get the next ferry. It comes in three or four days. That'll give you time for last-minute preparations. I like enough time. Can't bear to be rushed."

"Come in," I said. "My father will be so pleased to see you."

Karla came out, and I said: "This is Mrs. Sibyl Fraser, who has come to take me back to England with her."

"Rather unexpected, I fear," said Mrs. Fraser. "I thought it easier to come than write. I've booked our passage on *The Star of the Seas.* It sails at the beginning of next month, so there's not a lot of time to lose."

· · ·

I WAS GRATEFUL for the presence of Sibyl Fraser. She was a light-hearted companion—the best I could have had at that time. She was, as she said, determined to look after me, because her dearest friend, Ronald Hammond, had asked her to.

"I would do anything for Ronnie," she declared. "Just anything. Not that this is an onerous task, dear. Far from it. I love to be with you, and it is nice to have an excuse for going to see my Bertie."

I had learned her history in a very short time, for she talked continuously, mainly about herself, which suited my mood.

She had been a great success during her London season. Debutante of the Year, they had called her.

"Of course, dear, I was much, much younger then. They had expected me to marry a duke, an earl perhaps, a baronet at least. But it was my Bertram Fraser I fell in love with—a rough diamond, but a 24-carat one. My dear, he was very rich indeed. It was due to gold mining in Australia. He owned several mines, and I was happy to go out there with him. A disappointment for them at home who had hoped for a coronet, but the money made up for a good deal."

"It sounds very satisfactory," I said.

"Oh my dear, it was. But then life's what you make it, I always say. I had my Bertram, and very soon young Bertie put in an appearance. What more could a woman ask for? It was wonderful for me after what I had had in the past. We were of a good family, but it was always scrape, scrape, scrape to keep up appearances and then, there I was! I only had to want something and it was mine."

"A great compensation for the loss of your coronet," I said.

"Exactly! Particularly as one of them they had in mind for me was a disagreeable old man of fifty. We were happy, Bertram and I, and then he got himself killed. It was in one of his mines. He'd gone down to see something and the thing collapsed on him. He left his fortune to Bertie and me. I was heartbroken, but I wasn't the sort to go about moping. I'd lost Bertram, but I'd got my little Bertie."

"And your fortune," I reminded her.

"That's so, dear. We had lived in Melbourne to be near the mines, but we had a place in Sydney and I moved there. It suited me better. I travelled a bit. It was on a trip to Egypt when I met your father. That was about six years after Bertram's death. We became friends . . . very good friends, and we've kept it up ever since. It was always a pleasure when we met, and we did meet through the years . . . here and there. A good friend is always a good friend. Then I got this letter. I knew he'd gone blind and that Karla was looking after him. He'd met her in Egypt. She's a good sort. Does everything for him, doesn't she? Even writes his letters for him. Well, he'll always find someone who wants to look after him. I would have done it myself."

"He is very fortunate to have such good friends."

"He's that sort. I knew he had a daughter. I used to talk to him about Bertie. Bertie went to school in England and made a lot of friends there, went round visiting, met his wife and stayed there. All very natural. He didn't want to go in for gold mining. And I didn't want him to, after what happened to his father. So he's settled there with his wife and family. Yes, I'm a grandmother, only don't tell anybody, will you? I go and see them when I can. This is a good excuse. When I've taken you to your home I shall go and stay with Bertie and his family."

"It's very kind of you to do all this for my father."

"I'd do a lot more for him. He's one of the best. We all loved him, so he must be."

"Yes, I think he must be."

"And I'm doing this for myself, too."

.   .   .

IT WAS AN emotional farewell between my father and myself. We had stayed up late on the night before the ferry which was to take us to Cato Cato came in.

My father grew very sentimental. He told

me how happy my visit had made him, how all through the years he had thought of me. Before he had left home, he had stood by my cot. "You were a most beautiful child. I could scarcely bear to leave you. Sophie . . . dear Sophie . . . she kept in touch all those years. I was so pleased when you went to her."

"I think you should have gone back to her," I told him. "She would have forgiven you for turning from her in the first place."

"No. I wasn't good enough for Sophie. It was better as it was."

"Perhaps I shall come out and see you sometime."

"With your husband. I should so enjoy that. It is my dearest wish now."

When the ferry carried us away, he stood on the shore. I knew that in his mind's eye he would have a picture of the scene. He would visualise my standing there, sad to leave him, yet eager to be going to my lover.

Karla was there beside him. I saw her hand on his, a gesture which told me she would take care of him as long as he needed her. She it was who had written those letters to Sophie, since he had been unable to, copying his handwriting because she would understand that he did not want Sophie to know of his infirmity. She had taken care of him in every possible way, and she would go on doing so.

Tamarisk was there. She was a little reproachful. She had not wanted me to go.

"Wait awhile," she had said. "We have not been here so very long."

I pointed out that we had been away from home for a very long time.

"I can't go yet, Fred," she said. "You understand that."

"I understand you, and you must understand why I have to go."

She pouted in the old familiar way, and I did wonder then how long the island would continue to be of interest to her.

There were others on the shore. The Havers were there with Luke and the boy Jaco. Indeed, most of the children on the island were there. Of course, they came to see the departure of the ferry boat, but I think the crowds were even more than usual on that day.

A sadness crept over me when the island was no longer visible. I felt that a little part of my life had gone forever, and when I looked back on that strange interlude, it seemed like a dream.

The next day we were at Cato Cato, where we spent two nights in the hotel in which I had stayed before.

Sibyl Fraser was a knowledgeable traveller, and when we arrived in Sydney she had arranged for us to stay there for a day or so while we awaited the arrival of *The Star of the Seas*.

HOMECOMING

*T*he novelty of the voyage out had been a great adventure to Tamarisk and me and therefore a source of interest; now I had seen it all before. Sibyl was a seasoned traveller, well acquainted with shipboard life which, there was no doubt, she enjoyed. She had travelled with the captain before and knew several of the officers. As she remarked to me, she knew her way around and that was always a help.

We had separate cabins, side by side. "Starboard side," Sibyl explained to me. "Port out, starboard home. Otherwise, the heat in the tropics is unbearable."

She was the best possible companion for me. She would not allow me to brood. She wanted to engage in all the shipboard activities. She played deck games, whist and danced in the evenings; she would take me off on excursions when we were in port and make sure we had attractive male escorts. She was deservedly popular, carried on a few light-hearted flirtations, chattered continuously and was always good-humoured.

When the weather was rough she kept to her cabin—and so did I. I would lie on my bed and think about arriving home. I wondered what had happened during my absence. Had anything come to light? There must have been a great deal of speculation when I left Harper's Green so suddenly after my engagement had been announced.

I would lie listening to the buffeting of the waves and the protesting creaking of the ship, as though she were moaning in agonised protest at what the sea was doing to her.

Then we would pass through the storm to calmer waters.

And so the days went by.

· · ·

WE SAILED OUT of Lisbon—our last port of call. I had been out with Sibyl and some friends. We had explored the city, visited the Jeronimos Monastery and the Carmo Church, inspected the Tower of Belém, taken coffee and watched the people passing by, returned to the ship and stood on deck while she sailed out of the bay, Mar da Palha, as we looked back on the hills on either side of the Tagus.

Home was not far away.

The next days sped by. We packed. We were in readiness. The last night had come. Tomorrow in the early hours of the morning we should sail in to Southampton.

There was, as always, a little delay before we were allowed to disembark, and the frustrating minutes seemed like hours.

Sibyl had said that we would take the boat train to London and would then go to Harper's Green. She herself would be staying in London, and I told her there would be no need for her to accompany me, but she was insistent. She had told Ronnie that she would take me to my aunt, and that was exactly what she would do.

There was no need for this, as waiting at the dock were Crispin and Aunt Sophie.

Aunt Sophie called my name with glee, and Crispin's face lit up with an indescribable joy. I rushed to them and Crispin reached me first. He lifted me up in his arms. I had never seen him look so happy before. And there was Aunt Sophie smiling at us.

"You're home, you're home, my love!"

Then she was talking incoherently and tears were on her cheeks. They were tears of joy.

I was aware of Sibyl standing there, beaming and delighted.

"This is Mrs. Fraser," I said. "She has brought me home. My father asked her to."

"We know," said Aunt Sophie. "We've just had a letter from him. We've been arranging to kill the fatted calf ever since we knew you were coming. Letters come a little quicker than people, it seems. Oh, it is wonderful to see you!"

Crispin was grasping my arm, pressing it against him. Aunt Sophie had the other.

"I am so glad," said Sibyl. "I hope I get a welcome like this from my family."

Crispin and Aunt Sophie seemed to drag themselves away from their contemplation of me and turned their attention to Sibyl.

I said: "Sibyl has been wonderful. She is such an experienced traveller. She has made everything so easy. She is coming to England to visit her son, you see."

They thanked her with sincerity and asked what she wished to do. She explained that she wanted to get to London, and from there she would go direct to her son.

·   ·   ·

IT WAS NOT until we were seated in a tearoom on the station that I heard the great news.

At Paddington we had to wait an hour for the train which would take us to Wiltshire. Sibyl had been put in a cab and had said her farewells, promising to visit us sometime, and while we were waiting for our train we sat down to talk.

I could never be on a railway station after that without recalling that day.

Crispin sat close to me. Occasionally he would stretch out a hand and touch mine, as though to reassure himself I was really there.

As soon as we sat down and had ordered tea, Aunt Sophie said: "Isn't it wonderful? Who would have thought it would have worked out like this? All the time . . ."

I said: "What is it? I know something has happened. I can see that by the way you look and . . . everything. But what? Tell me!"

"I wrote," said Crispin, "as soon as I knew. It was the first thing I did."

"You wrote? But when did you write?"

"As soon as I heard."

"You don't say," said Aunt Sophie, "that you haven't had the letter?"

"Which letter? They take a long time, you know."

"The one telling you. Crispin wrote and I wrote. And when we heard you were coming home . . . we thought that was why. Come to think of it . . . there wasn't all that time. Our letters must have crossed in the post."

"But we thought you were coming because . . ." began Crispin.

"Because what?" I cried in exasperation.

"It is like this," said Crispin. "I got one of those detective agencies working on it. She had said she was going to Australia, but I did not believe that. I had to be rid of her once and for all. I think I knew her plan was to go on making me pay."

"Of course," I said. "She would not stop the first time."

"There is no need to worry about anything anymore. I was never married to her. She was already married, and had been for three years before I met her. She only went through a form of the ceremony with me."

"Is this really true?"

"Proved without a shadow of a doubt," said Aunt Sophie triumphantly. "Crispin has proof, haven't you, Crispin? There are such things as records, you know."

"We have indeed the indisputable proof," said Crispin.

"There is no impediment," went on Aunt Sophie triumphantly. "I am so happy. I felt so guilty about seeing her and telling you. I asked myself why I had opened my mouth."

"It's over," said Crispin, taking my hand. "My dearest, it is all over. There is nothing to stop us now."

"I can't believe it," I said. "It's too . . . neat."

"Life isn't always untidy," said Aunt Sophie.

"What I don't understand," said Crispin, "is why you came home now . . ."

I looked at him steadily. "I came home because I could not stay away any longer."

"In spite of . . ."

"In spite of everything. I could not stay away from you. My father knew it too. He said I should never be happy away from you . . . so I came back."

Crispin was gripping my hand tightly.

"I shall never forget that," he said. "You came back to me before you knew."

Aunt Sophie sat there smiling at us benignly, and it suddenly occurred to me that I was living through one of the happiest moments of my life.

· · ·

WHAT A TRIUMPHANT return!

Harper's Green looked just the same as I remembered it. We took a cab to the Rowans, where Lily was waiting for us. She rushed out and embraced me. Her voice was husky as she stated the obvious: "You're back!"

"Yes, Lily, I'm back."

"About time, too."

"I missed you all."

"And don't you think we missed you! Gadding about all over the place. Come on in. Don't want to stand about on the doorstep all night."

We went into the sitting-room.

"What a wonderful homecoming!" I said.

"We'll go ahead with our plans now," said Crispin. "There's no need for us to wait. We've waited too long."

Aunt Sophie talked about weddings.

"We want it quickly," said Crispin. "We don't want to be bothered with lots of preparations."

"I reckon your mother will want to have her way," said Aunt Sophie.

"She will have to do it our way. And where shall we go for our honeymoon?"

"We'll consider it," I said. "I'm too happy to think of anything but that I am home and it's all going to be all right. And I did not know this until I was sitting in a railway teashop amid the clatter of crockery, people hurrying about and trains shunting outside!"

"What does it matter where you heard it!"

said Aunt Sophie. "You did . . . and it's the best news in the world."

· · ·

IT WAS WONDERFUL to be back. The nightmare, which had begun when Aunt Sophie came back with the news that she had seen Kate Carvel in Devizes, was over. There was nothing but happiness ahead.

When Crispin had left us with assurances that he would come next morning, Aunt Sophie wanted to hear about my father.

She was deeply shocked to learn that he was blind.

"Why didn't he tell me?" she demanded.

"He knew you would be upset, and he didn't want you worrying about him. He's like that. He's very philosophical."

"But how does he manage to look after himself? And what is he doing on that far-away island?"

I hesitated, and then told her about Karla.

"Oh," she said. "A woman. There was always a woman."

"She is half native and very kind and warm-hearted. You would love her, Aunt Sophie. She cares for him very much and does everything for him. She writes those letters to you on his dictation."

She nodded. "I knew the writing had

changed. Not much, but it wasn't quite the same."

"He didn't want you to know. Karla is very understanding. She is a sort of power in the island. She owns a plantation there."

"What adventures he has had! If he had told me . . ."

"I know. You would have tried to bring him home. He is very fond of you, and he doesn't want to *use* you. Aunt Sophie, you are his greatest friend, he said. He loves you, but he wouldn't want to prey on you now that he is helpless. I understand how he feels. I got to know him very well."

"He is a wonderful man."

"He would laugh at that. He calls himself a sinner, and I suppose a lot of people would agree with him. But I love him and you do too, and so have a great many people throughout his life."

She was subdued, but would not allow anything to cloud my happiness.

She talked about the change in Crispin. "He seems like a young boy now. Oh, Freddie, how lucky you are to be loved like that."

"I know," I said.

"And to come back without knowing . . . I'm glad you did. It shows, doesn't it? Did you see his face when he realised that?"

"I did. I had to come back, Aunt Sophie. My father understood that."

"He was never one for conventions."

"It is like a miracle that it should work out this way."

"Life has its miracles now and then. Oh, I am so happy. It is what I have always wanted. To see you happy and to keep you near me. It's everything I ever dreamed of . . . almost."

. . .

I WENT TO see Mrs. St. Aubyn. I did have a twinge of uneasiness, for I did not know how she would feel about the marriage. She would surely have wanted someone from a higher sphere of society for her son.

However, she received me warmly. She said: "How nice to see you back, my dear. Well, this will soon be your home, and you will be my daughter-in-law. I am so pleased to welcome you into the family."

She was lying on a sofa, and I wondered whether she had reverted to that invalidism from which she had retreated on the coming of Gaston Marchmont to St. Aubyn's.

"Crispin is very happy now," she said. "That is a great comfort to me. There has been such unpleasantness in the past, and that had an effect on him. I shall be so glad to see him settled with someone I know so well. It is an immense relief."

I smiled inwardly. I knew she had never been very concerned with her children's welfare.

"It will be good for the household to have a mistress," she went on, "and I am sure you will be a very good one. I, myself, have been so hampered by ill health."

I knew then that she was lapsing into the old ways. And, as Aunt Sophie would say, that was probably for the best, for I should have no interference from my mother-in-law.

"Dear Frederica," she went on, "would you pull the coverlet down over my legs? No matter how warm the room is, I feel a draught. Now tell me about my daughter. Why did she not come back with you?"

I told her about Tamarisk's interest in the mission. I gave her an account of how she had filled the bleak hall with flowers, how the children had been attracted by her golden hair and how popular she had been with them.

"How very odd!" she said. "When do you think she will be coming home?"

"I daresay fairly soon. At the moment, she is finding it all rather novel and amusing. She will be home sometime, I am sure."

"She ought to marry again." Her face changed slightly. "It was *such* a tragedy. You and I will see if we can find a suitable husband for her."

"I think she would want to make her own choice," I said.

She nodded her head sadly. "As she did before. It was such a pity. He was a very charming man."

I did not want to think of Gaston Marchmont.

.   .   .

I WENT TO Grindle's Farm, where Rachel greeted me with delight. I could see that life was good for her. Little Danielle was quite a person now; she had her own small vocabulary and was running around, taking an interest in everything.

Daniel was well, Rachel told me. There had been no more repercussions about the murder, and it seemed to be back in the past.

She wanted to hear about Tamarisk. She laughed over the flower incident and Tamarisk's unexpected interest in the mission.

"It is the last thing you would expect of her," she said.

"Well, Tamarisk was always unexpected."

"Freddie, I'm so happy for you. It is wonderful that you have come back and are going to marry Crispin." She looked at me searchingly. "When you went away like that, I couldn't understand it."

"There was a reason."

"Of course." She did not ask what it was. Rachel had always been tactful. She had realised that this was something between Crispin and me, and our affair alone.

"But now you are back and everything is all right. Oh, Freddie, you are going to be happy, I know it."

"If you know it and I am determined to be, it must be so," I said.

"Poor James Perrin!" She smiled faintly. "At one time I thought . . ."

"That I would marry him?"

"It seemed suitable. He is very self-contained, a calm, efficient sort of man. I am sure he will make a very good husband."

"He'll always be predictable—a good and faithful husband, I am sure."

"There is a rumour that he is interested in a young woman in Devizes. She is the daughter of a solicitor . . . very suitable in every way."

"I'm glad."

"They are saying that her family will help him out with the money to get a place of his own."

"Ideal," I cried.

"It is wonderful how everything is working out right, isn't it? It was all going wrong once, and then suddenly it comes right. It's like some sort of pattern. When I look back and think."

"Rachel," I said quickly, "don't look back. Look forward."

She smiled. "It is good to think you are going to be here."

. . .

I HAD A meeting with James Perrin. He looked very pleased with life. He congratulated me on my coming marriage and told me he was thinking about getting his own property. He had been perfectly frank with Mr. St. Aubyn, for he thought it only fair to give him warning so that it would be possible for a new man to have some training before he, James, departed.

His congratulations were sincere enough, yet I fancied there might have been a few regrets. But James was a practical, serious-minded young man who had his way to make in life. He had at one time thought I would be a suitable partner and, as I had made that impossible, he was now finding a replacement. He was reasonable, philosophical; he was a man who would never plunge into the

depths of despair and never reach the
heights of ecstasy, either.

I was naturally eager to call on the Lanes,
and when I did so I found it rather disturbing. But then, it had always been so.

I chose an afternoon—the time I used to
go and would find Flora sitting in the garden.

She was not there. I went round to the
front of the house and knocked on the door.
Lucy opened it.

"Oh," she said. "It's Miss Hammond.
Come in, Miss Hammond. I heard you were
back."

"I had to come and see you. How is Miss
Flora?"

She took me into the sitting-room and
bade me sit down.

"Flora is not very well," she said. "She's
resting."

"Oh, I am sorry."

"She has not been well for some time."

"Is she very ill?"

"Well, I suppose it is a sort of illness. I get
her to lie down in the afternoons. I hear you
are going to marry Mr. Crispin."

"Yes," I said.

She was holding her hands together and I
noticed that they were trembling.

"He is a good man," she said. "The best."

"I know."

"Well, I am sure you will be happy."

"I am sure we shall. Is it possible for me to see Miss Flora? I shouldn't like her to think I hadn't come to see her."

She hesitated for a moment before she stood up. She nodded, and I followed her out of the room.

"She is changed," she whispered as we mounted the stairs.

"Yes, you told me."

The door of the nursery was open. We passed it and went into Flora's room.

Flora was lying on her bed.

"Miss Hammond has come to see you, Flora," said Lucy.

Flora half-raised herself and said: "You've come back."

"Yes, and I've come to see you. How are you?"

She lay back and shook her head. I noticed then that the doll was in the toy cot near the bed.

"It's all gone," murmured Flora. "I don't know . . . Where are we?"

"We're in your room, dear," said Lucy, "and Miss Hammond has come home from foreign parts. She's looked in to see you."

Flora nodded. "He's gone now," she said.

Lucy whispered: "She's rambling a bit."

Then aloud: "It was good of Miss Hammond to come, wasn't it, Flora?"

"Good to come," repeated Flora. "He came here . . . see." She was looking at me. "He took . . ." Her face puckered.

Lucy laid a hand on my arm.

"Not one of her good days," she said quietly. "She's better left. I'll give her a pill. That'll quieten her."

I sensed that she was eager for me to go, so I had no alternative but to do so. I passed the open door of the nursery as I went and I caught a glimpse of the picture of the seven magpies.

By the front door I turned to look at Lucy. I could see that she was worried.

"She's changed," I said.

"It's one of her bad days. She wanders. She has these days now and then. Some days she's just like she used to be. Well, of course, she's been strange for a long time."

"It must give you great anxiety."

Lucy lifted her shoulders. "I know her . . . she's my sister. I know how to look after her."

"She is very fortunate to have you."

She did not answer that.

She opened the door. "Well, congratulations, I'm glad you're going to marry Mr.

Crispin. He's very fond of you. He deserves to be happy."

"Thank you."

"Yes," she said. "It's nice . . . that's what it is."

I walked away smiling, though I was faintly disturbed; but I always had been after a visit to the House of the Seven Magpies.

. . .

SIX WEEKS AFTER my return we were married. Even so, Crispin chafed against the delay. It was a quiet wedding, as we both wanted it to be. Mrs. St. Aubyn had raised objections, but they were only mild ones. In the first place, it would be celebrated from the bride's home, which was comparatively humble.

Mr. Hetherington performed the ceremony, and I think most of the neighbourhood were present.

Crispin and I were blissfully happy as everyone crowded round with their well-wishing. Rachel was there. I wished Tamarisk had been. I often thought of her. I was sure her enthusiasm for the island would, like all those in the past, not be of long duration. I saw Lucy Lane in the church, and I was pleased that Crispin spoke to her and made sure she was well looked after. I wondered how Flora was, but I am afraid I had little thoughts to spare for anything but my own marriage and the future which awaited me.

Soon after the ceremony Crispin and I left for Italy, and there followed weeks of perfect happiness.

Those were days of sheer perfection. I discovered new depths in Crispin. Never had I realised how joyous he could be. All reserve dropped from him. Now that had gone, he was completely relaxed and perfectly happy. There was enchantment everywhere.

For most people Florence is a magical city. For us it was a paradise. We bargained on the Ponte Vecchio with the jewellers and laughed over our attempts to speak the language. We visited fresco-lined churches and the galleries; we were enthralled by the Palazzo Pitti and the Boboli Gardens. We took a carriage and rode out of the city into the rolling hills of Tuscany. Each hour of those enchanted weeks was a joy. Never had I dreamed of such happiness, and to share it with the one I loved seemed the greatest benefit that could befall anyone.

It had to end, of course, but it was a time which would live with us forever.

THE SEVEN MAGPIES

And as those wonderful days sped by, I could even anticipate our return with pleasure, for I was eager to start my new life as the mistress of St. Aubyn's Park.

It seemed miraculous that our difficulties had been so easily swept away. It was not really so very long ago that there had been that unhappy barrier between us, and now we were completely happy. Crispin could not forget that I had come back to him, not because he could offer me a grand marriage, but because my love was unshakable. Mrs. St. Aubyn was welcoming to me and it seemed that, just as Fate will deal blow after blow to those she has decided to chastise, so will she shower blessings on those she favours.

Sometimes I was a little fearful of such happiness.

And then the faintest shadow appeared.

It was nothing—just a fancy. Crispin had been round the estate that morning, and in the afternoon he wanted me to go with him to the Healeys' farm. There was some trouble about one of the barns, and the visit would give Mrs. Healey the chance to congratulate me on our marriage.

"You know how these people are," he said. "Mrs. Healey says you had been to see the Whetstones and Mrs. Whetstone had given you a glass of her special cider, which you very much appreciated. So I think it would be a good idea for you to have a little chat with Mrs. Healey."

I was delighted. I liked to meet the people on the estate and to receive their congratulations, to hear what a good landlord Crispin was and how the place had prospered since he took over.

He was late returning. He said he would be in at three and we would go off immediately. At three fifteen he had not come and by three thirty I began to be alarmed.

It was soon after that when he returned. He looked rather anxious, and I asked him what was wrong.

"Oh, nothing much," he said. "I just got

caught up. Let's get going. We'll be very late otherwise."

Usually he told me what was happening. I waited for him to do so, but he didn't. I presumed that, as we had to leave at once for the Healeys', there wasn't time.

I met Mrs. Healey, drank her cider and it was all very pleasant; and I forgot about Crispin's arriving late.

The next day I was in Harper's Green when I met Rachel. She told me that she had left Danielle with the nursemaid and had come out to do a little shopping.

"I can see everything is working out wonderfully," she said. "You look radiant."

"I am so happy, Rachel. And you are too."

"How different it was! I often think back to the days when the three of us were together . . . when you and I used to go to St. Aubyn and be taught by Miss Lloyd."

"It seems a long time ago."

"Such a change." I saw the dark shadow in her face, and I wondered if she ever thought of Mr. Dorian hanging in the barn. It was a pity such thoughts had to come to spoil a cloudless morning.

Then she said: "I ran into Crispin yesterday. He looked very preoccupied."

"Oh, where was that?"

"Near the Lanes' cottage. Yesterday afternoon. He'd obviously been there. How good he is! He does look after them, doesn't he? I know he always has. I've always thought it was so kind."

We chatted a little more and it was not until later that I thought: so that was why he was so late. He had been visiting the Lanes.

Why had he not said so?

Perhaps he had thought it was not necessary.

.   .   .

MY MOTHER-IN-LAW SAID that now St. Aubyn's had a new mistress, we must have people to visit us more often.

That was how it had been in the old days, she said. "And it always was so in the past, I believe. It was only when I became so frail . . ."

And when the guests came, she did bestir herself a little.

I was busy those days. There was a great deal to learn about the management of a big house. Aunt Sophie was very helpful.

"You must show the housekeeper and the butler that you are in command. They may feel otherwise that, because you come from a comparatively humble home, they might be able to browbeat you."

I laughed. "I don't think so, Aunt Sophie."

"You're doing well. Crispin is proud of the place, remember."

"I do. After all, he has given his life to it."

"Therefore it must be of importance to you. Mistress of St. Aubyn's," mused Aunt Sophie. "I can tell you, it is beyond my wildest dreams. I wanted the best for you. I have written to your father and told him all about the wedding."

"I have also written to him."

I closed my eyes and saw it clearly. My father sitting in his chair and Karla reading the letter to him. I wondered whether they would read it to Tamarisk. She had not written, but she was apt to forget people when they were not there. I was expecting a note to say she was coming home. That was something she would have to write about.

My father would be delighted by the miraculous turn of events which had made marriage possible. I had written at length about our honeymoon in Florence. I was sure that would please him.

The days were so full that there was little time for visiting, but I did see Rachel fairly often; and one day I decided to call on Flora.

I found her in the garden. She was sitting there as she used to, with the doll in its pram beside her. I called to her; she turned her head and nodded, so I opened the gate and went in.

"Hello," I said.

I had a shock then. I had thought this would be like so many occasions in the past, but when she turned her face to me I saw the wildness in her eyes.

I sat beside her.

"How are you today, Miss Flora?" I asked.

She just shook her head.

"And the . . . the baby?"

She gave a little laugh and prodded the pram with her foot.

"Sleeping peacefully?" I ventured.

"He's sleeping forever," she said cryptically.

This was rather odd. I had expected the usual remark about his being a little terror, up to tricks, or that he had a snuffle and she hoped he wasn't sickening for something.

She turned to me, and there was an odd expression in her eyes.

"They say," she said, "you married him."

"Oh yes," I said, "I married him. We had a wonderful honeymoon in Florence."

She started to laugh, and it was not pleasant laughter.

"So you live up at St. Aubyn's now."

"Yes, I do."

"You think you're married to him, don't you?"

My heart started to beat wildly. I immediately thought of Kate Carvel. Could Flora possibly know anything about her? But it was all right. She had been married before. There was nothing to fear from that quarter.

"You didn't marry him," said Flora.

"What do you mean?" I asked cautiously.

"You think you married him," she said. Then she laughed again. "How could you have married him?"

"Yes, I am married, Miss Flora," I said.

I thought I should not be talking to her. She thinks Crispin is still a baby, of course; that is what is worrying her.

I said: "I'd better be going. Miss Lucy will be coming back soon."

She gripped my arm and said hoarsely: "You didn't marry him. How could you? He's not here."

This was getting too wild, and I was eager to get away.

I rose and said: "Well, goodbye, Miss Flora. I'll come and see you again one day."

She stood up beside me and came very close to me. She whispered: "You didn't marry Crispin. They *said* you married Crispin. It's a lie. You couldn't marry Crispin.

How could you marry Crispin? It's not Crispin you married." She started to laugh again —that dreadful wild laughter. "Crispin is not here. That's where he is."

She was pointing dramatically to the mulberry bush. She moved closer and peered into my face. "That's where he is. I know, don't I? That man, he knew. He made me tell him. You can't marry Crispin, because Crispin is there . . . there."

I thought: she is completely mad. Her eyes were so wild. She was laughing and crying together. Then suddenly she picked up the doll from the pram and threw it with all her might at the mulberry bush.

I had to get away. Lucy would have gone into Harper's Green to shop. I must find her and tell her that something was happening to Flora.

I ran out of the gate and down to the village street. It was with immense relief that I saw Lucy coming towards me with her shopping basket.

I cried: "Something has happened to Flora! She is saying the oddest things about Crispin, and she has thrown the doll at the mulberry bush."

Lucy turned pale.

"I'll see to her," she said. "You'd better

go. People upset her. Leave her to me. I'll manage."

I was only too glad to do so; the sight of Flora filled me with misgiving.

· · ·

As SOON AS he saw me, Crispin realised that I was disturbed.

"What's happened?" he asked.

"It's Flora Lane," I said. "I went to see her this afternoon."

He looked alarmed. "What did she say?"

"It was very strange. She's changed a lot. She said that she had heard that we were married and it could not be."

"What?"

"She said: 'You haven't married Crispin.' And then . . . oh, it was horrible! She pointed to the mulberry bush in the garden and said, 'You can't marry Crispin, because Crispin is there.' She looked wild and mad."

He drew a deep breath. "You shouldn't have gone there," he said.

"I've always visited her now and then. But she's changed. I think she is really going mad. Before, it was like an obsession. This is different."

"Was Lucy there?"

"Lucy was shopping. I ran out and found her."

"Lucy knows how to look after her. Heaven knows, she's been doing it for years. Poor Lucy!"

"She told me not to worry."

He nodded.

"Well, I expect she'll settle down when Lucy's there. I wouldn't go there again, darling. It upsets you."

"She used to seem as though she liked me to go."

"Well, don't worry. Lucy knows what's best for her."

I could not forget Flora, and I noticed the change in Crispin. I saw the haunted look in his eyes and the screen which came down, shutting me out. I began to feel that whatever it was which had disturbed me in the past was in some way connected with the House of the Seven Magpies.

There was constraint all through the evening. He was a little absent-minded and I knew his thoughts were far away.

I said: "What's wrong, Crispin?"

"Wrong?" He spoke almost testily. "What should be wrong?"

"I thought you seemed . . . preoccupied."

"Burrows thinks some of the fields at Greenacres should be fallow for a while. That will affect output, of course. He's asking my advice. Then there are those out-buildings at Swarles. I'm not sure whether they'd be a good thing."

But I did not think his mood had anything to do with fields lying fallow or outbuildings at Swarles Farm.

. . .

I AWOKE WITH a start. It was dark. A feeling of intense uneasiness had come to me. I put out my hand. Crispin was not beside me.

I was then fully awake. I sat up in bed. In the gloom I could make out his shape as he sat by the window, apparently staring out.

"Crispin," I said.

"It's all right. I just couldn't sleep."

"Something's wrong," I said.

"No . . . no. It's all right. Don't worry. I'll come back now. I just wanted to stretch my legs."

I got out of bed and put a dressing-gown round my shoulders; and I went to him and, kneeling beside him, put my arms round him.

"Tell me what it is, Crispin," I said.

"Nothing . . . nothing . . ."

"There is something, Crispin," I said firmly. "And it is time you told me."

"It's nothing for you to worry about—or me either for that matter."

"It is," I said. "And it is not new. It has been there for a long time."

"What do you mean?"

"Crispin, I love you very much. You and I are as one person. I am for you and you are for me, and if there is anything wrong for you it is wrong for me."

He was silent.

I went on: "I know there is something. I've always known it. It has been there between us."

He was silent for a few seconds, then he said: "There is nothing between us."

"If that were so, I should know it. You wouldn't be keeping secrets from me . . . holding something back."

"No," he said vehemently, and I looked at him appealingly.

"Crispin, tell me. Let me share."

He stroked my hair. "There is nothing . . . nothing to tell."

"I *know* there is something," I told him earnestly. "It is there between us. I can't get close to you while it is there. It's a barrier, and it has always been there. There are times when I can forget it, and then I am aware of it. You mustn't shut me out, Crispin. You must let me in."

For some seconds he said nothing, and

then: "There have been times when I have been on the point of telling you . . ."

"Please . . . please, tell me now. It is very important that we should share everything."

He did not speak, and again I entreated him. "I must know, Crispin. It is very important that I should."

He said slowly: "So much hangs on it. I cannot think what would happen."

"I shall not have a moment's peace until I know."

"I see it has gone too far. I have been debating with myself. I knew I should have to tell you some day. It goes back years . . . to the beginning of my life." Again he paused. His face was creased in anxiety. I wanted to comfort him, but I could not until I knew the cause of his trouble.

He went on: "The Lanes lived on the estate. The father, Jack, was one of the gardeners; he had two daughters, Lucy and Flora. Lucy went to London to work as a nursemaid; Flora was the younger. Jack Lane died, and his wife stayed on at the house and Flora was employed in the house. She wanted to be a nursemaid like her sister, and when a child was about to be born it was decided that she should become his nurse. In due course a son was born at St. Aubyn's."

"You," I said.

"Crispin was born," he said. "You must hear from the beginning. The parents, as you know, were not very interested in the child. They were glad to have a son, as most people are, particularly in their position, to carry on the name and inherit and all that. But they were more interested in the social life they led. They were rarely in the country. Had they been devoted parents, this might have been discovered in the beginning.

"One day, Lucy came home. She was in deep trouble. She had left her post in London some weeks before and had been living on the little money she had saved, and now that was gone. She was going to have a child. You can imagine the consternation in that cottage. The father was dead; there was the mother and Flora, who was in service at St. Aubyn's, preparing to take care of the child which was about to be born."

He stopped, and I knew that he was reluctant to go on. He seemed to steel himself.

"Lucy," he said, "was a strong woman. A good and trusting young woman. She was like many before her. She had listened to promises, been seduced and deserted. A not unusual predicament for a girl to find herself in, but no less terrifying for that. Such girls were ostracised, and when they were without means their position was desperate. Can you imagine the mother's anguish? They had been living in that little cottage among a small community for years, proud of their independence and their respectability, and now here was the daughter, of whom they had been so proud because she had had a fine post in a grand London house, come home bringing disgrace with her in which they would all share."

"She had the child then?"

"Yes. But they could not keep it a secret forever. They thought they would do so until they made some plan for the future. Mrs. Lane had practised midwifery at one time and it was easy to manage the birth. The big problem lay before them. They could not keep a child hidden forever. They thought of leaving the place and going to London, where Flora and Lucy would find work while their mother looked after the child. That was what they decided. One thing was certain. They could not remain in Harper's Green to face the scandal."

"What a terrible position for them!"

"They hesitated. There were times when Mrs. Lane thought of going to Mrs. St. Aubyn and asking for help. She fancied that she and her husband might be slightly less shocked than some of the inhabitants of

Harper's Green. And then this extraordinary thing happened."

He paused, as though he found it difficult to go on.

"Crispin was now a few weeks old. Flora was his nurse. And then suddenly there came this way out of their troubles. It was macabre in the extreme . . . but it offered a solution. And, remember, they were desperate people.

"You have seen Flora and you know the distressing state of her mind. I think she must always have been a little simple. Perhaps she should never have been given the charge of a child. But she had always been devoted to children, and many a mother in the village had allowed her to look after her children because she loved them so much. They said she was a born nurse and mother. Of course, we haven't seen her as she was then. We only know the poor deranged creature she has become. Gerry Westlake, son of one of the local farmers, began to take notice of her."

"I remember him. He came here, some little time ago. He went out to New Zealand, I believe."

"Yes, that was soon after it happened. Gerry was an energetic young man—little more than a boy. He was very interested in football and was practising throwing and kicking a ball about wherever he went. That is the story I heard. He used to do odd jobs at St. Aubyn's, and he saw Flora there. He used to whistle to her and she would come to the window to look out. He would throw the ball at her and she would throw it back to him. She would go down and stand by, watching him kick his ball. He would explain to her the importance of the manner in which he kicked it.

"It is extraordinary what happened. Remember, they were very young, both of them. Flora was flattered by Gerry's attention and was—or pretended to be—thrilled to share in the ball games with him. She would throw as he told her and catch and hope for his applause. If you think of those two—children, really—you can see how it happened.

"Then came the fateful day. He whistled to her. You can picture him—standing there looking up at her window. It was open and she looked out. She had the baby in her arms. She said: 'I'm coming down.' And she called to him, as he had so often called to her, 'Catch!' It must have seemed like a great joke to her then. Gerry must have looked up startled. She threw the child down to him."

I caught my breath in horror. "Oh no, no!" I cried.

He nodded. "Gerry realised too late what she was doing. He made an effort to catch the child, but he was too late. The child fell onto the stones of the terrace."

"Oh . . . how could she have done such a thing!"

"It's hard to imagine. She wanted to amuse Gerry. She thought he would easily catch the child—it did not occur to her that he could fail to do so—and that would make it seem like a bit of fun between them.

"Flora dashed out to the terrace and picked up the child. He was wrapped in a thick shawl and appeared to be unharmed. Flora must have been overwhelmed by relief. Poor Flora! That relief was short-lived. Gerry ran home. He would have shared Flora's relief, but I have no doubt he wanted to put himself as far away as possible from the scene. Flora took the baby up to the nursery and told no one. Imagine her shock when she realised that the child's ribs were broken. He died that night.

"Flora was dazed. She did not know what to do, so, as she did in all moments of stress, she went to her own home. Her mother and Lucy were in a state of terror. Flora had killed her charge; her sister had an illegitimate child. They could never have visualised such disasters overtaking them. This was something from which they could see no means of escape.

"Desperately they looked for a way out—and then it presented itself to them. Most young babies look alike. Crispin's parents had shown very little interest in him. You can see what they were thinking. They buried Crispin."

"Under the mulberry bush?" I said.

"And Lucy's baby went to St. Aubyn's in his place."

"You mean . . . you are that baby?"

He nodded.

"When did you know?"

"On my eighteenth birthday. Lucy . . . my mother . . . told me. She thought it only right that I should know. Before that it had never occurred to me that I was anyone but Crispin St. Aubyn and that the estate would be mine. I loved the place."

"I know. And . . . this is the secret never to be told. And the seven magpies . . . they were put into the nursery to remind Flora that she must never tell."

"Poor Flora! It turned her brain. It was soon after that when she became as we know her. Lucy looked after her always. You know Lucy took over the care of me and became my nurse. Flora came back to the cottage. She was acting very strangely by that time. It is ever on my mind."

"That this place does not really belong to you. You are afraid that someone will discover this?"

"There was a time when someone did come near to that."

"Gaston Marchmont," I whispered, a terrible fear coming to me.

"He was a rogue," said Crispin. "He deserved to die. He forced the secret from Flora. She could have gone on to the end of her life believing she was back in the past before it happened, that the child still lived. That was what she thought until he came along. You see what he has done to her . . . to Lucy? He guessed there was some secret there, some connection between me and that cottage, and he was determined to find out. He married Tamarisk for what he could get, and then he saw that he could get much more than he had even believed at first. He stole the doll and he blackmailed poor witless Flora. He had seen that silly picture. She should never have had it. But Lucy thought it would be a constant reminder to her never to tell. You must forgive Lucy. She is my mother. She wanted everything for me. Her greatest joy was to see me master of the estate."

"But it does not belong to you, Crispin."

He shook his head vigorously, as though he could thrust such a fact away.

He went on: "He made poor Flora tell him. He threatened what he would do to the doll if she did not. The shock brought reality back to her and he had the secret. And he died."

"You know who did it, Crispin?" I asked fearfully.

He turned to me and smiled gently.

"I know what is in your mind. I know how much you love me. No, sinner that I am, I did not kill Gaston Marchmont. You have to know everything. I see that now. These secrets are no help to us, and now you know so much you must know it all. Flora was in a terrible state of distress. She had betrayed the secret and at the same time this had brought home to her what had really happened all those years ago and which she had been deluding herself into thinking was just an evil dream. She had killed her precious charge in a moment of idiotic frivolity. She had done it to amuse Gerry. He had left for New Zealand soon after that. No doubt he thought the baby had lived. He, of course, knew nothing of what had happened. But the fear of those moments when the child lay on the ground may have had something to do with his decision to get away from the scene. Flora was in a state of mental disorder and Lucy thought it best to have the doll to delude her into thinking the child still lived. To Flora, when she realised that she had betrayed the secret and that the doll was simply a doll, there seemed only one way of making sure the secret was never told.

"It is amazing how she could have done this, but she did. I believe people such as she is can be very single-minded and plan with a calm precision which is remarkable. She went to St. Aubyn's. She knew the house well from the days when she had lived there. She went to the gunroom and took the gun, and then to the shrubbery to lie in wait for Gaston Marchmont. Most of the family came through the shrubbery when returning to the house. It was a short cut from the stables. He came and she was there. She shot him. Then her careful planning seemed to desert her. She left the gun on the ground and ran back to the cottage. Lucy was in deep distress. She was frantic, wondering where Flora had gone, and when she returned, drew from Flora exactly what had happened.

"Lucy's one idea was to keep the secret.

Her dream was that I should have St. Aubyn's. It would be a compensation for all they had suffered. I was her son, remember. She went back to St. Aubyn's that night. She found the gun and buried it—unfortunately, not very efficiently. It was Flora who killed Gaston Marchmont, Frederica. Please . . . please understand. This is a secret which must never be told."

I was silent for some time, bewildered by all I had heard. In spite of my horror, there was a certain relief. There were no longer secrets between us.

I was picturing it all. Flora, throwing the baby down, her agony when she realised what she had done; I could imagine those three desperate women seeking a way out of their intolerable situation; I could feel Lucy's triumph when she saw a glorious future for her son; I pictured their burying the poor broken body of the baby Crispin. I could imagine Flora's demented state; I could see the picture of the seven magpies, set up to remind her of the awful consequences if the secret were revealed. And she had told it. Gaston had forced her to tell the secret, and in her simple mind there was only one solution: to kill him before he could tell the secret which must never be told.

I said: "Crispin, this place does not belong to you."

"But for me it would be nothing now. I have made it what it is."

"Still, it is not yours. You are not the heir to this place."

"No. Lucy is my mother. My father is unknown to me."

"Lucy would know him," I said. "But the fact remains. What shall you do?"

"Do? What do you mean?"

"Crispin . . . I must call you Crispin . . ."

"I never had another name."

"It will always be there, this knowledge, even though you have told me."

He did not answer and I went on: "This place does not belong to you. That is so, isn't it?"

He did not wish to admit it . . . but it was true and he knew it.

"I think you will never be happy with what is not yours by right."

"I am happy. This place has always been mine. I could not imagine it otherwise."

"If Gaston Marchmont had lived . . ."

"He did not live."

"If he had, he would have brought this to light. And then . . ."

"Of course he would. That was his motive.

He must have had some inkling. Flora must have betrayed something. And then the fact that the doll was Crispin to her was significant. He would have claimed the place on Tamarisk's behalf—and if he had succeeded, it would have had a very short life."

"But it is Tamarisk's. She is the daughter of the house and there is no living son."

He said: "If this came out it would be disastrous. Think of the livelihoods of all the people on the estate. Everything would go. You know the secret now. No one else must. I am glad you know. You are right. We don't want secrets from each other. There must never be any more."

"I am glad you see it that way."

"There is the problem of Flora. I don't know what we can do with her. Lucy is afraid for her. You see how that man tackled her. It has upset her. She's changed."

"She must have his death on her conscience as well as that of the baby."

"She doesn't want the doll anymore. She seems to have come to the conclusion that Crispin is dead and the doll is but a doll. When she believed it was a child, her mind was at rest. She had shut out the past. But that evil man made her tell what had happened. He brought her back to reality, and that is something she cannot face."

"Crispin," I said, "there is one thing you must do or you will never know real peace of mind. Tamarisk must know that this place is hers. She must know the truth. You will never be entirely happy until you have told her."

"And when I have lost all that I have worked for through these years?"

"Tamarisk loves you. She is proud of you. She regards you as her brother. She will want you here. She understands that she would be useless to manage things without you."

"It would not be mine. I could not take orders."

"She would not give you orders."

"And what if she married? Just imagine what Gaston Marchmont would have been like if he were here!"

"He is not. I think it is right that Tamarisk should know, and I believe that you will not be truly happy until you have told her."

He said he would never tell. He had told me because we had agreed not to have secrets between us. But now that I knew, this must go no further. What good could it do to tell people that long-ago story? What good would come of accusing Flora of murder?

Poor Flora, she would have to stand up to a trial. He would not allow that. The whole story would come out. Tamarisk would not want that. All the scandal would be revived, her disastrous marriage. Poor Lucy . . . all of us. It would do no good at all to anyone.

There was nothing to be done. The murder of Gaston Marchmont would be regarded as an unsolved crime. If anyone thought of it now, they believed the murderer must have been some person from his past, which was known to have been disreputable.

No, there was nothing to be done.

We talked through the night, and in the end I made him see that there was only one thing he must do.

He wrote to Tamarisk.

.   .   .

IT WAS A long time before we heard from her, and during that time I think Crispin was happier for having told me and the course he was taking.

He did say that it was as though a great weight had been lifted from his shoulders; yet at the same time there was a deep sadness in his eyes. When he talked about the estate I would detect a certain wistfulness. I wanted to console him; and I sometimes wondered what would happen if we had to leave St. Aubyn's.

What would Tamarisk's reaction be when she learned she was the owner of a large estate? If he had lived, Gaston Marchmont would have taken charge of it. What a tragedy that would have been for so many people!

I often thought of Flora's taking the gun and killing him. The child's death had been due to her, but that was a youthful foolish gesture. To have killed Gaston was cold-blooded murder. Yet what worried her was the betrayal of the secret.

It was difficult to think of anything but those astounding revelations.

Each day we waited for news from Tamarisk. The letters which Crispin and Aunt Sophie had posted to Casker's Island had been sent back by Karla. My father wrote that he was indeed happy at the turn of events and he hoped I would bring my husband to see him on Casker's Island.

At last the long-awaited letter from Tamarisk came. It was addressed to us both and was written in the somewhat flippant style characteristic of Tamarisk.

My dear newly-weds,
    I was, as you must guess, absolutely astounded when I read your letter. What ex-

traordinary things go on in Harper's Green!

First, I will give you the most important news. Do not think you are the only ones who can marry. You'll be surprised, though perhaps the astute Frederica may have had some inkling as to the way things were going.

Yes, *I* am married. To Luke, of course. I really got caught up in that mission, didn't I? After dear old Jaco's leg, things got very exciting. We have a little school now and, believe it or not, I and dear old Muriel do the teaching! She does earnest stuff, saves their souls and all that. I am the comedy turn. They come to me and they laugh and sing and I love them all dearly. I believe they reciprocate.

Luke is getting along very well and we have a little—well—clinic, I suppose you'd call it at home. Muriel is very good at that, and John and Luke help too—and even I am called in now and then. Our success over Jaco's leg has made us famous throughout the island.

Tom Holloway is here often, and they are all very pleased with the mission.

As for what you tell me—I am just amazed. So, Crispin, you are not my brother after all. To tell the truth, I often thought it was surprising that I should have such a worthy brother, so different from myself. It doesn't make any difference. I love you and your new wife dearly.

And all that about Flora and the babies. It is like something out of the Bible or Shakespeare . . . swapping people around like that. One wouldn't have thought it would happen to real people . . . especially those in Harper's Green. Life goes on in a dreary sort of pattern for years, and suddenly drama strikes.

So St. Aubyn's is mine! What on earth am I expected to do about that? What good would I be going round seeing the tenants about crops and roofs and cowsheds?

Dear brother-that-was, please don't desert me. Don't go off to the ends of the earth with your new bride. Stay where you belong, although I must say it would be nice if you could pay a visit to Casker's Island. I know, Fred, your father would like that very much; and I should love to show you the changes we have made at the mission. We are going to put up a new building. I'm helping to pay for some of that. But dear old Saint Luke doesn't like that very much. He wouldn't want a rich wife. In fact, he thinks I am too affluent already. He isn't interested in all that. He just wants me. Very unworldly of course, but rather sweet. But then you know Saint Luke.

Now please don't let all this make any difference. The place is yours, Crispin. We all know it would be just nothing without you.

Luke says we mustn't try to be grand here. Missions are not built that way. They are built on trust, faith and understanding. You know him, Fred, so you'll understand what I mean.

I put down the letter and Crispin said: "I had not expected this. She is so flippant, as though it isn't important."

"What is important to her is her new life. She has Luke, and Luke is a wonderful person. So we shall go on as before."

"What of the future? The place is not mine."

"Crispin," I said, "it never was."

"What if she changes her mind? How long do you think she will be engrossed in this mission? You know Tamarisk. Her enthusiasms do not last very long."

That was true.

He went on: "And when she realises what this place means . . . who knows? Suppose she came back and wanted to take over?"

"You mean turn you out? How could she? She has no idea how to manage the place."

"Suppose she gets tired of this saintly husband. Suppose . . ."

"Anything is possible, of course."

"And then?"

"Crispin," I said, "we shall have each other. That is the most important thing in the world. I believe Tamarisk is learning to love as she never did before. You should have seen the change in her. She is not the same person who was deceived by Gaston Marchmont. Yes, I am sure she is learning what are the important things in life."

"As I am?" he asked.

"Yes, Crispin," I said. "As you are."

He smiled suddenly. He looked younger and contented, as I had seen him look during our honeymoon days when he believed the secret would never be discovered. But even then there had at times been the shadow of a fear. Now it was there no longer.

· · ·

IT HAPPENED DURING the night. I was awakened by strange noises, and when I looked out of the window I saw an angry glow in the sky.

I leaped out of bed. Crispin was beside me.

"Something's on fire," he said.

We put on our clothes and rushed out. Some of the servants were already downstairs.

When I saw the direction from which the smoke was coming, I thought immediately of the Lanes. We hurried to the cottage, and there before our eyes was the blazing mass of what had once been the House of the Seven Magpies.

Lucy was there. She ran to Crispin. He had his arms round her and she was crying hysterically.

It was like a nightmare—the crackling sound of burning wood, the sudden eruption of the flames as they leaped and licked the walls, followed by the crash of masonry.

Lucy was sobbing. She kept saying Flora's name, over and over again. I learned then that Flora was dead. She had leaped from the nursery window down into the garden and her crumpled body had been found beside the mulberry bush.

That night is one I shall never forget. In my mind it is a blur of images and people shouting to each other as they tried to put out the fire. For a long time it would be re-

membered as the night the Lanes' cottage
was on fire.

There was a good deal of talk about the
cause of it. Flora Lane had always been odd.
She must have left a candle burning; it could
have toppled over. Fires are easily started.
She must have jumped out of the window,
poor soul. She could have found her way
downstairs. The other sister managed it.
Poor muddled Flora!

It was easy to see how it happened, they
said.

I feel sure in my heart that Flora could
not face the truth; twice she had killed and
she could not live with that knowledge. I believed she had started the fire in the nursery
and had wanted it to be thought that she had
jumped free of the fire. She had betrayed the
secret to Gaston Marchmont and she could
not trust herself to go on living and preserv-
ing the secret which must never be told.

We took Lucy back to St. Aubyn's. She
stayed there for a while, but she wanted a
house of her own and Crispin would see that
she had it. It would be on the estate nearby,
of course. There was a cottage which was
empty. The widow of one of the estate workers had died some three months before.
Crispin was arranging for it to be redecorated and made ready for Lucy.

I talked with her. She was different towards me now, and I did not have the feeling that she was trying to get away from me. There was a new friendliness between us. She was my husband's mother. I guessed how she was feeling. She had cared for Flora over so many years. It had been a time of great anxiety and now it was lifted, but at first she could only be aware of a deep void. She explained this to me. I think she was excusing herself for the way in which she had behaved towards me in the past. I remembered her nervous comments. "That's nice," she used to say, her eyes uneasy, so that I had felt she was waiting for me to go for, of course, I may have shown my curiosity rather blatantly. But there was friendship between us now.

She said to me: "I shall be glad to be near."

"Crispin wants that," I told her.

"He has been so good to me always. Even before he knew, he was kind."

Once she said: "I can regret nothing that gave him to me."

"I understand," I told her.

"You and I must be friends," she went on. "I bore him and you have made him very happy. He is the centre of my life and he has been from the moment I saw him. It was a wicked thing to do, but it seemed the only way then, and it brought great good to him."

"I know," I said.

. . .

THERE WAS ANOTHER letter from Tamarisk. The mission was flourishing beyond their wildest dreams. She wished we would come out and see it.

Lucy visited Flora's grave every Sunday after church. We joined her sometimes, and then we would go back to her new home and spend an hour or so with her.

One day Crispin and I were out riding when we passed the remains of the old cottage. I could not look at it without a shudder. It seemed ghostly, even in the sunlight.

"It's time we built there," said Crispin practically. "Let's go and have a look at it. They could start clearing next week. The builders haven't much to do just now."

We tethered our horses to the gatepost, which still stood there, and passed through the garden where Flora used to sit with her doll, facing the mulberry bush.

"Be careful," warned Crispin as we entered what was left of the house. He took my arm and held it firmly as we went into what had been the kitchen. Most of the wall had broken away.

"It will be easy to clear this lot," said Crispin.

We went through to the stairs, which were still intact.

"They're firm," said Crispin. "It was quite a good staircase."

We mounted them. Half the roof had gone and the acrid smell still hung on the air. I gazed at the blistered wood and scorched bricks. And there on the floor, I saw it. It was lying on its face.

I picked it up. The glass had splintered and it fell away as I touched it. And there, looking at me, were the seven magpies, with smudges of grime on the picture. The paper was brownish and damp.

I took out the picture and the frame fell to the floor.

"What is it?" asked Crispin.

"It's Flora's picture—the one Lucy framed for her. The seven magpies—for a secret never to be told."

He looked at me, reading my thoughts as I tore the picture into tiny pieces. I threw them up. They were caught on the breeze which came from where once there had been a roof, and the pieces floated away.